THE
OTHER
DAUGHTER

ALSO BY LAUREN WILLIG

The Ashford Affair

That Summer

THE PINK CARNATION SERIES

The Secret History of the Pink Carnation

The Masque of the Black Tulip

The Deception of the Emerald Ring

The Seduction of the Crimson Rose

The Temptation of the Night Jasmine

The Betrayal of the Blood Lily

The Mischief of the Mistletoe

The Orchid Affair

The Garden Intrigue

The Passion of the Purple Plumeria

The Mark of the Midnight Manzanilla

The Lure of the Moonflower

THE
OTHER
DAUGHTER

LAUREN WILLIG

ST. MARTIN'S GRIFFIN
NEW YORK

THE OTHER DAUGHTER. Copyright © 2015 by Lauren Willig. All rights reserved. Printed in the United States of America. For information, address St. Martin's Press, 175 Fifth Avenue, New York, N.Y. 10010.

www.stmartins.com

Teaser excerpt copyright © 2017 by Lauren Willig

The Library of Congress has cataloged the hardcover edition as follows:

Willig, Lauren.
    The other daughter : a novel / Lauren Willig. — First edition.
        p. cm.
    ISBN 978-1-250-05628-3 (hardcover)
    ISBN 978-1-4668-6013-1 (e-book)
    1. Family secrets—Fiction.   2. Illegitimate children—Fiction.
3. London (England)—Fiction.   I. Title.
    PS3623.I575O84 2015
    813'.6—dc23

                                                    2015012460

ISBN 978-1-250-05642-9 (trade paperback)

Our books may be purchased in bulk for promotional, educational, or business use. Please contact your local bookseller or the Macmillan Corporate and Premium Sales Department at 1-800-221-7945, extension 5442, or by e-mail at MacmillanSpecialMarkets@macmillan.com.

First St. Martin's Griffin Edition: July 2016

10   9   8   7   6   5   4   3   2

To my father, Kenneth C. H. Willig,

for introducing me to history and story

THE
OTHER
DAUGHTER

ONE

C an we go look, can we go look, can we go look?" Eight-year-old
Amelie tugged at Rachel's hand, pulling her toward the stairs.

"I don't see what the point is of looking at a party you can't go to,"
said thirteen-year-old Albertine crossly.

"English, please," said Rachel automatically.

The girls were meant to speak English when they were with her; the
countess had been very clear about that. If it was a rule Rachel enforced
somewhat selectively, that, she decided, was a matter for her own conscience.

Besides, she told herself virtuously, Albertine was meant to be speaking in English. If she refused to do so, then she would just have to be
silent.

And thank heavens for that.

"The dresses are so *jolie*," said ten-year-old Anne-Marie wistfully.

"English, please," mimicked Albertine, in heavily accented English.

Anne-Marie's spectacles wobbled on the tip of her nose.

Rachel pushed them up for her. "You're right, Ammie. The dresses *are*
jolly. And I don't see the harm in looking so long as we stay out of sight."

It was the annual Easter Ball at the Château de Brillac, home of the Comtes de Brillac from time immemorial, or, at least, as long as anyone had stopped to think about it. The Brillacs generally didn't. They preferred to spend their time in Paris, where the count could concentrate on his amours and the countess on her close, personal relationship with several expensive couturiers, all of whom vied for the honor of upholstering her angular frame.

When the comte and comtesse did return to Brillac, it was on a wave of strong scent, accompanied, invariably, by a party of persons from that alien and sophisticated world. Rooms would be aired and dust sheets thrown off, and Amelie, Anne-Marie, and Albertine would creep down to their favorite viewing post, five balusters to the left at the top of the gallery.

A more superior sort of governess might have told them no, might have shooed them away back to the nursery. But Rachel had never seen the point in crushing all the joy out of her charges' lives. And if looking down upon a sea of perfectly coiffed heads made them happy, what was the harm? If they showed any signs of mischief, she would sweep them away, back to the nursery.

Rachel doubted it would be necessary. Neither Anne-Marie nor Amelie was the water-balloon-dropping sort, and Albertine's own particular brand of malice took less physical forms. After seven years of nursery governessing, Rachel counted herself something of an expert.

Anne-Marie and Amelie were pressed close together by the balusters, Albertine lurking behind, trying to pretend haughty indifference, although her eyes were as wide as the others'. Rachel joined them at the rail, spying shamelessly.

What was the point, after all, of living in the houses of one's betters if one couldn't enjoy a little vicarious glamour?

Below, the great marble stairs had been banked with flowers. The count and countess, the latter decked out *en grande tenue*, diamonds glittering everywhere diamonds could possibly glitter, stood receiving their guests. The hall where Amelie liked to go sliding in her stockings on rainy days was busy with the high chirp of voices, the clatter of beads on silk, the flash of military orders.

Somewhere, Rachel knew, beyond the gallery, there were musicians in the ballroom. There was a supper laid out in the dining room, and other rooms devoted to cards, or repairing one's gown, and heaven only knew what else. But all that lay beyond, out of view of the balusters.

"When I am grown," said Amelie complacently, "I shall go to a ball every night."

Rachel stifled a grin. "Yes, I expect you shall. But only if you remember to wash behind your ears. Clean ears are crucial for countesses."

Amelie's spine straightened a little. "But of course," she said grandly, as though she hadn't raised holy hell in the bathtub yesterday when confronted with the dreaded washcloth. "And many jewels."

"Rubies or emeralds?" queried Rachel.

Her own jewelry consisted solely of a small gold watch, pinned to her bodice, which her mother had given her as a gift when she graduated from school. Rachel didn't like to think of how many extra piano lessons her mother must have taught to purchase it, how many days without sugar in her tea. But it had proved useful for regulating lessons. There was nothing like frowning ferociously at one's watch for making restless schoolgirls settle in their seats.

"The blue ones," said Amelie firmly. "Because they match Sophie's sash."

Sophie was Amelie's favorite doll, dressed in Paris best, rather battered from being placed in situations no Paris couturier had ever imagined. Sophie led a rather rough life.

"Why not?" said Rachel.

Goodness only knew, the rich tossed away money on lesser whims, and Amelie, someday, would be expected to marry a grand hotel in Paris, a château in the country, and a suitable accumulation of porcelain and gilt-work. And, presumably, the man that came with it all, although that appeared, from what Rachel had seen over the past seven years, to be a lesser consideration.

Sometimes Rachel felt like an explorer, surveying the customs of an exotic and isolated tribe. Sometimes. Most of the time, she simply accepted her salary and concentrated on clean ears and the past perfect tense.

Rachel had always known she would have to work. She and her mother weren't poor—not in the way the Trotters down by the river were poor, with their slatternly kitchen and clutch of half-naked children—but having butter on their bread and a roof over their heads meant there wasn't a great deal for extras. Her mother eked out a living giving piano lessons to the village children, which everyone agreed was a suitably genteel occupation for a widowed lady in straitened circumstances, and one not incompatible with Friday sherry with the vicar and running the bazaar at the annual spring fete.

Had she had her own way, Rachel would have taken a typing course and sallied out into the brave new world of office work. But there were times when her mother's Victorian upbringing showed. Faced with the prospect of the typing course, she had dug in her sensible heels. Rachel to work outside the home? To expose herself to the attentions of men?

Useless to protest that everyone was doing it now, or, if not everyone, a sizable portion of the female population.

A job in a nice household, her mother insisted. That was the proper occupation for a young lady of limited means, the emphasis being on the word lady.

When Rachel pointed out that the world had moved on a bit since *Jane Eyre*, her mother had only said mildly, "It's not all Thornfield Hall. Wouldn't you like to see a bit of the world? You could travel. You could work abroad. Better, surely, than a smoky office?"

That was the problem with Rachel's mother. Just when one wanted to be usefully indignant, she would disarm by being so terribly reasonable.

It was a trick that Rachel now applied with good effect to her own charges, with some silent amusement at the thought of being on the other side of it.

Rachel might have argued, she might—as she had in other matters—have put her own not insubstantial foot down, but it had occurred to her that the real problem might not be her virtue, the protection thereof, but the cost of the typing course. It wasn't terribly dear, but it was enough to strain their slender resources.

Rachel might have sold the watch, but that would have hurt her mother terribly. She clung, Rachel's mother, to these small gestures of gentility. To have sold the watch would have been worse than a slap in the face. It would have been a reminder of everything they didn't have, couldn't afford, a reproach to her mother who had worked so hard and so long, keeping a roof over their heads all alone, ever since Rachel's father had died.

And so Rachel had swallowed her objections and gone to France. There was something, after all, to be said for France. She had gawked, that first year, as any girl fresh from the country would gawk. It had all been so new and strange, and France, even with the scars of war, was still France, glamorous and different.

She wouldn't say that seven years had entirely inured her to that glamour, but she took it, now, as a matter of course. Louis Quinze chairs and grand portraits by old masters were as much backdrop as her mother's piano and her father's battered old chess set. The reality of it all was the children, struggling through their letters, fighting their own small battles, needing to be entertained on rainy days.

Skating along marble floors was a brilliant way to beguile a rainy day. But not when the countess was in residence.

"Mees?"

Rachel rose from her perch, shaking out her plain serge skirt, as someone called her name. She might be Rachel at home, or Miss Woodley as circumstances commanded, but at the Château de Brillac, she was invariably and simply "Mees," a sign of her status betwixt and between, neither servants' hall nor front table.

"Yes?" Rachel saw Manon, the nursery maid, edging her cautious way along the gallery, a worried look on her face. "Oh, dear. Not the baths again?"

The plumbing at Brillac tended to be rather temperamental, the château having been designed in an age when baths were something that happened when one unexpectedly plunged into the river and perfume was designed to cover a multitude of odors. There was generally enough hot water for the nursery baths, but when the Paris parties descended, the backs of Amelie's ears tended to be the grimier for it.

"No, mees." Almost furtively, Manon thrust a crumpled piece of paper at Rachel. "A telegram, mees. From Paris."

"Tonight?" Rachel's fingers closed around it. Bother. If it was something important, no wonder Manon wanted to pass the responsibility on. The countess did not approve of interruptions to her festivities. "Well, let's hope it's not bad news. I'll take this straight to—"

Rachel's voice trailed off as she glanced down at the paper. Not from Paris. To Paris. And not addressed to the countess, but to her.

R. Woodley. Hotel de Brillac, Paris.

The message below was in English, not French, transcribed exactly as it had been transmitted.

Mrs. Woodley ill. Influenza. Immediate return advised. J.S.

Influenza! The dreaded word blazed out from the creased page. Influenza had come through Netherwell before, just after the war. Rachel could hear, like an echo, the tolling of the church bell, again and again and again, the endless knell of it, until the bell ringer himself was taken ill, the sudden silence worse than the constant clamor.

But that had been eight years ago. Surely, by now . . . And Jim Seddon was a good doctor, a modern doctor, a much better doctor than old Dr. Potter, whose general view on medicine appeared to be that if it had been good enough for Hippocrates, it was good enough for him.

Rachel forced the air back into her lungs. Jim Seddon was not only a good doctor but he was also the husband of Rachel's oldest friend. And her mother—her mother was made of steel, lightly covered with a lace collar. The influenza might have killed countless others, but it hadn't reckoned on Katherine Woodley.

But Jim wouldn't be asking for her unless there was reason for her to go.

A train to Calais. If she could get a car to take her to the train, she could take the train to Paris, then from Paris to Calais. A boat from Calais to Dover, then the grim process in reverse, a train from Calais to London, another from London to King's Lynn, then the change to the small local line that ran through Netherwell.

It was Monday night. With luck, and presuming the train workers didn't go on strike between here and Calais, she might be home by this time tomorrow.

Which meant . . . Rachel glanced down at the telegram, at the date on it. She looked and then looked again, sure that she must have misread the smudged numbers, that the Continental handwriting—that silly habit of crossing their sevens—must have misled her.

But there was no mistake.

The date on the telegram was Wednesday, five days before.

Rachel looked up at Manon in disbelief. "This is five days old!"

Manon's eyes dropped. "Hector brought it with him when he came up with Monsieur le Comte."

Hector was the count's man, a barrel-chested, swaggering soul whose primary qualification for his present post appeared to be having served as the count's batman during the war. He also fancied himself a ladies' man.

Rachel hadn't fancied Hector, and had made that quite plain, or as plain as a sharp heel to the instep could convey.

Which meant that if a telegram had arrived in Paris for Rachel, Hector would have taken delighted spite in making sure the message took as long as possible to reach her.

Manon twisted her hands in her apron. "He—he said he had other things to do than be a telephone exchange."

"Oh, does he?" Fantasizing about where she would like to apply a telephone wasn't doing anything to get her home to her mother. And the girls were beginning to turn; Anne-Marie already had that worried look between her eyes. Rachel lowered her voice. "Thank you, Manon. You did well to bring this to me."

Hector didn't speak English. Neither, as far as she knew, did any of the staff of the Paris house. That didn't stop her from wanting to take the back of a hairbrush to all of them. Surely, a telegram conveyed its own urgency, even if one couldn't understand the words.

Time to plot revenge later. Right now, the important thing was getting herself onto that train, with all haste. Five days' worth of haste.

With painstaking self-control, Rachel said, "Would you take Amelie,

Anne-Marie, and Albertine back to the nursery for their baths? I need to speak to madame."

"You're not meant to interrupt Maman while she's receiving," said Albertine with a sniff.

Amelie rounded on her sister. "You're not meant to be speaking in French."

"Hush, *petite*." Rachel dropped a kiss on the top of Amelie's head. "I'll be back to check your ears. Anne-Marie, you will look after Amelie for me, and make sure she gets her chocolate?"

Anne-Marie was a weather vane for any worry, quick to pick up on trouble, but she straightened her shoulders at Rachel's words and nodded, just a little.

"Good." Rachel was already moving, down the corridor, toward the back stairs, her brain already occupied with half a dozen details. "*Merci*, Manon."

She caught one of the footmen as he came out from the hall with a tray of champagne, whispered a few words in his ear. She didn't know the staff terribly well; most of them were from the Paris house, brought up for the occasion. But everyone knew who she was: the girls' English governess. She had grown accustomed to being a curiosity, like a zebra. Only rather more prosaic and with fewer stripes.

The footman went off in search of madame, his tray growing lighter along the way, and Rachel stood in the shadows, out of sight, trying not to jiggle with impatience.

Wednesday. Her mother had been ill since Wednesday, and the telegram had just sat there, crumpled at the bottom of Hector's pocket. And Jim Seddon! Why hadn't he tried again? He might have sent another telegram, or tried to telephone—

The footman returned. If Mees would follow? Madame could spare a moment in the small salon.

The name was a misnomer. The small salon was twice the size of the cottage in Netherwell, decked with gilding and mirrors designed to intimidate and overawe. No surface had been left ungilded, including madame herself, who stood by the mantelpiece, jeweled slipper tapping with impatience.

"What is it, mademoiselle, that could not wait?" she said, looking pointedly at the clock. "If one of my daughters is ill—"

She sounded more annoyed than distressed by the prospect.

"The girls are all well," said Rachel hastily. Just because madame was away for nine-tenths of the year didn't mean she didn't have maternal feelings. Theoretically. Rachel took a deep breath and pushed on. "It's my mother, madame. She is . . . very ill." Saying it somehow made it more real, more frightening. "I must return to England at once. I can—I can be back in a week. Manon will mind the nursery while I am gone."

Madame de Brillac's gray eyes, flat as uncut diamonds, swept her up and down. "No," said Madame de Brillac, and turned to go.

The word echoed oddly in Rachel's ears. Or perhaps that was her own voice, repeating, "No?"

Madame de Brillac paused. With great condescension, she explained, "It is not convenient for you to leave at this time."

And that was all.

Only it wasn't. It couldn't be. Rachel hurried after her. "My mother needs me, madame." Her mother had needed her days ago. Urgency loosened Rachel's tongue. "There are only the two of us, you see. I am the only one she has in the world. My father—"

The countess didn't care about Rachel's father. "Good night, Miss Woodley."

Good night? She wasn't paid nearly enough for this, Rachel thought furiously. The countess left her daughters for weeks at a time. She'd scarcely taken the time to interview Rachel, just a glance at her references, a look up and down, and an instruction to try to keep Anne-Marie from squinting so.

But when Rachel needed to go home—for a week! All of a week!—suddenly the countess rediscovered her maternal feelings.

The woman had the maternal feeling of a weasel.

"I am sorry, madame," Rachel heard herself saying, in cold, elegant

French. If she had been teaching, she had also been learning, and her French, by now, was as aristocratic as madame's own. "But that will not do. If you will not give me leave, I will be forced to tender my resignation. At once."

The countess paused in the doorway, her diamonds glinting coldly in the light of the great chandelier. "You may collect your wages from Gaston." As an afterthought, she added, "Leave the keys with him when you go."

Rachel gaped after her. "But——"

Surely it was less trouble to lose one's governess for a week than to hire a new one?

Apparently not. "Good-bye, Mademoiselle Woodley," said Madame de Brillac, with precisely the degree of condescension due from countess to wayward employee. Another look from those cold, flat eyes. "I trust you will not bother me for a reference."

A reference? Fury gripped Rachel. What did it matter about the reference? Anne-Marie—Amelie—How was she to tell them?

She could run after the countess; she could beg her to reconsider. And what? And stay at Brillac? Let her mother suffer alone?

The image tormented Rachel: her mother, lying helpless, too wracked with chills to move. There was no phone in the cottage; there wasn't even electricity. The cottage sat at the very end of the village, isolated from the other houses, its nearest neighbor the vicarage. It might have been days before anyone realized her mother was ill, days in which her mother, sweat-damp and miserable, battled the disease alone, too weak even to boil water.

The hall was heady with the scent of hothouse flowers and a cacophony of competing perfumes. Rachel's head swam with the horrible sweetness of it. No time to waste on ifs and might have beens; the train wouldn't wait for her.

There wasn't much to pack in her own little room, only a few skirts and shirtwaists, a handful of books, a hat that had the claim of being a "Paris hat" only by its origin, but not any pretense to style. It all fit in the one carpetbag, a hand-me-down from the vicar.

And then, good-byes.

Anne-Marie, all big brown eyes. "Why are you leaving us?" In French, but it was no time to enforce English, just time to enfold her in a quick hug.

"Because she doesn't like you." Albertine jeered very effectively, but there was something in her voice, so young beneath the scorn, that made Rachel wish she had tried harder with her, had had more time. It wasn't Albertine's fault that she was so very like her mother.

Rachel tried to put it as simply as she could. "My mother is very ill. She needs me at home."

"But we need you," said Amelie. She thought a moment. "Sophie will miss you."

Oh, Sophie. Sophie was full of pronouncements. Rachel would miss Sophie. She would miss all of them.

Perhaps, once her mother was on the road to recovery—

Rachel squelched that thought. The countess wouldn't take her back. And, even if she did, Rachel had learned, two families ago, that it didn't do to get too attached. Amelie might nestle close to her now, but in another few years, she would be ready to put up her hair and let down her skirts, and Rachel would be on her way to another family, carpetbag in hand.

She might live with them, teach them, even come to care for them, but they weren't her family.

The only family she had was her mother.

By dint of shamelessly lying to the chauffeur, telling him madame had authorized her use of the car, Rachel made it to the station in time for an eleven fifteen train to Paris. The train lurched and swayed; it was deathly cold in the car, the windows so fogged with her breath that she couldn't see out. Outside, she knew, the trees were starting to sprout their first green buds, but she could see none of that, only the ghostly reflection of her own face, her unfashionable hat drawn low around her ears to keep out the chill, her cheekbones too high, her mouth too wide, her hair dark against her pale face.

There was nothing remarkable in that face, just another nursery governess, another woman in a shabby skirt, clutching a carpetbag on her lap. Nothing remarkable except to her mother, who loved her.

On and on through the darkness the train went, the rhythm of the wheels, the puff of the engines, a steady backdrop to her anxiety. Slow, slow, so painfully, horribly slow.

Once, once upon a time, so very long ago, there had been three of them. Rachel could just remember those halcyon days. It couldn't have been summer always, but that was how she remembered it. They had lived in a little house with a garden, and if her father was frequently away, he always came back again, sweeping her up into his arms and spinning her about while Rachel squealed and clutched at his coat.

Until that last time, when he hadn't come back at all.

He had died somewhere, far, far away. He had been a botanist, her father. Something to do with rare plants, or at least that was what her mother had told her. He had fallen ill on one of his collecting trips, in a far-flung country that was just a little spot on the globe, dead of tropical fever.

Sometimes, when she was young, Rachel used to look at those specks in the vast blue of the atlas, specks with names like Martinique and St. Lucia, St. Croix and Mustique, and would wonder on which of them her father was buried. She had, as girls did, spun fancies for herself. Her father wasn't dead at all, just missing. He hadn't been a botanist, but a secret agent, off on a deadly mission. Or the heir to a lost kingdom, one of the smaller European sort, forced to go underground to evade the forces of the rebels who had taken over his homeland.

Her father was a daydream, but her mother was real. She was a cool hand on Rachel's brow when she was ill; a voice reading *Peter Rabbit*; a firm hand bundling her into her coat and off to school. More recently, she was an English postmark on a letter, a package in the post: a pair of warm gloves, a piece of the Christmas pudding for luck. Little things that made Rachel feel less far from home.

Her mother was very good about the little things.

Rachel hunched forward in her seat, urging the sleepy train to move faster. Good heavens, did they have horses towing the blasted thing? What was the point of a train at all if it didn't go any faster than that?

It was past two in the morning when the train decanted Rachel into the chill of the Gare du Nord. The ticket windows were shut, the book-stalls closed. Only a handful of stranded travelers were scattered around the echoing room, sitting on their trunks, sunk into the collars of their coats, their bundles clutched to them.

The train to Calais, according to the board, was due to depart at three.

Rachel could feel the hours stretching ahead of her. Maddening that they could zap a message across wires in a matter of minutes, but human travel was little faster than it had been a century ago. She had always enjoyed the novels of H. G. Wells. Now she found herself wishing for one of his time machines, something to whisk her back to five days ago. No, earlier, before that, twenty-three years ago, when they were all three together. She could stop her father going away, stop her mother getting sick. . . .

And what then? History did strange things when one played with it. They would never have lived at Netherwell; her entire upbringing would be different. Useless speculation to beguile the extra hour. Rachel shivered and hugged her carpetbag closer.

She didn't need to fight for a seat on the train to Calais; at that hour, it was all but empty. Only another twelve hours—how long those twelve hours seemed—and she would be back in Netherwell, back at the cottage in which she had grown up.

And her mother . . . her mother would be sitting up by now, demanding to be let out of bed, to be allowed to do something, for goodness' sake. Like all healthy people, her mother made a dreadful patient.

Apples didn't fall far from the tree, Mrs. Spicer, who "did" at the vicarage, always liked to say. If Rachel was impatient, she came by it honestly. She couldn't picture her mother sitting still; she was always moving, doing, working.

Well, she had had to, hadn't she? Just as Rachel had to work now. Botanists, it seemed, weren't too plump in the pocket. Whatever legacy her father had left, it had been enough to cover the essentials of rent and food, no more.

Even now, as a nightmare, Rachel could remember those dark days after her father died, her own childish voice, bleating, "Where is Papa? Where is Papa?" Her mother's face, still and set, her eyes red-rimmed, but her mouth firm. The hurried departure from their home, taking only those things that were most precious: her mother's piano, her father's chess set, the pawns bearing the marks of small teeth, where Rachel had used them, as a baby, to ease her aching gums. The gold brooch at her mother's breast, with its intertwined *E* and *K*.

Through it all, her mother had never broken, never wavered. She had comforted Rachel's tears, packed their few belongings, saw them settled in a new home, set about finding a way to make their meager ends meet. She'd gone on.

Dawn. The sun was rising just as the train chugged into Calais, tinting the water of the Channel rose and gold. Rachel stumbled off the train, her legs stiff, her hands cold in her leather gloves. There was something about dawn, about the right sort of dawn, that made all the frights of the night seem so much nonsense. If her mother had grown worse, Jim would have let her know, surely? There would have been more than just the one telegram.

On board the Channel packet, she lifted her face to the salt sea air, relishing the slap of the wind against her face. It was an ill wind... But this wasn't an ill wind. It smelled of England and visits to the seaside.

A change in London, and then another in King's Lynn. With each stop closer to home, Rachel felt her anxiety subside. The air still had the bite of winter to it, but the sun poured down like a blessing, and Rachel felt her feelings lift at the sight of it, despite the itch of clothes worn too long. If her mother had been that ill, Jim would have sent another telegram, found some way to find her.

The local train dawdled its way along, decanting housewives with piles of shopping and chattering girls from the school. Rachel had been one of those girls once. Swinging off the train at Netherwell station, barely a pause before the train was off again, she could imagine herself that schoolgirl again, satchel in hand, a straw boater on her head. Her boots crunched on the well-worn path, rich with the scent of mulch and loam, just a hint of coal smoke in the air.

There was a shortcut through a copse of trees, a place where the leaves twined overhead, forming a natural arch. Rather than leading into the village proper, it deposited Rachel only yards from the cottage, close enough that she could see the familiar gray stone, softened with its fall of ivy, the smoke rising from the chimney.

A sense of indescribable relief flooded Rachel at the sight of that smoke. There was light in the old, leaded windows, a warm glow that made her quicken her step, the carpetbag light in her hand.

The stones in the walk were cracked and old. With the ease of long practice, Rachel wove her way around the wobbly bits. No need to knock; the door was never locked.

"Mother?" She flung open the door. There was no hall. The front door led directly into the sitting room, that wonderfully familiar sitting room, with the hideous red plush furniture they had let with the house, and the fire that always smoked.

Someone was bent over the fire now, wielding the poker with a tentative hand.

But it wasn't Rachel's mother. Rachel's mother wouldn't have been so gingerly with the fire; she would have thwacked it smartly into submission. This woman was too short, too slight, her hair a strawberry blond instead of brown streaked with gray.

Rachel let her carpetbag drop. "Alice?"

Alice started, the poker catching on the edge of a coal. "Rachel!" Rachel's best friend thrust the poker back into its rest. "Thank heavens. I'd begun to think something had happened to you."

No time to explain now. Rachel started for the stairs. "My mother. Is she—"

Rubbing her sooty hands on her skirt, Alice scurried between Rachel and the stairs. She held up a grimed hand. "Rachel. I'm so sorry."

TWO

The pity on Alice's face awoke a host of nameless terrors.

"Where is she? Upstairs? In bed?"

Sick, wasted. Well, that didn't matter. Rachel was home now. She would take care of her. She knew a bit of nursing. They had all done their bit in the local infirmary during the war, emptying basins, rolling bandages. She could plump pillows, force broth down her mother's throat, hold her to life by sheer force of will if necessary.

Not that it would be necessary. Her mother had enough force of will of her own. Enough for three. Enough to beat anything, even influenza.

Alice lifted a hand to stop her, then let it fall. "Rachel . . . she's gone."

"Gone," repeated Rachel. What did gone mean, anyway? Gone to hospital? Gone to the vicarage?

A coal crackled on the hearth, the sound resounding like a shot in the quiet room.

"I'm so sorry," Alice said again. Her blue eyes looked bruised, ringed with dark shadows.

The stillness of the cottage pressed in on Rachel like the grave. No footsteps upstairs. No crinkle of sheets. Only the crackle of the fire and the nameless darkness of grief.

"Dead. You mean she's dead." Not at the vicarage, not in hospital, not popped out to the shops for a bit of butter.

Rachel couldn't wrap her mind around it, that the absence would be more than a temporary one, that she wouldn't hear her mother's step on the stair, her voice calling down from the landing. Her smell still lingered in the air, dried lavender and strong tea.

Alice gave a very small nod.

"When?" asked Rachel, in a voice she didn't recognize as her own.

"On Friday."

Four days ago. Four days. When had it been? Had it been while Rachel was giving Amelie her bath? When she was grilling Albertine on the kings of England? While she was doing her hair, darning her stockings, any one of a hundred inconsequential things?

Her mother had died and she hadn't been there.

Alice shifted from one foot to the other, uncomfortable with the silence. "We did wire you. Neither of us could understand why you hadn't—"

"I know." Rachel's chest was tight; she felt as though she couldn't breathe. "There was some confusion about the telegram. A delay."

If only, Rachel thought savagely, she had giggled and tittered when Hector had pinched her. If the telegram had been relayed right away . . . If she had made the very first train . . .

If, if, if. A whole legion of ifs.

Alice saw the look on Rachel's face and misinterpreted it. Defensively, she said, "Jim did try to ring the Paris house, but there was trouble with the connection."

"We weren't in Paris; we were in Normandy."

They were always in Normandy; if Alice had bothered to read her letters, she would know that. But Alice was of the opinion that France was France; such petty distinctions as city or country eluded her.

Oh, God, she was being ghastly. It wasn't Alice's fault. There was only so much that Alice and Jim could do, and she had been away, a Channel's width away.

Alice was still speaking. "Jim did everything he could, but by the time anyone realized she was sick, the disease was so advanced—"

"I know." Rachel's eyes felt gritty. She rubbed them with the back of her hand. Smoke from those trains, those endless trains. "He had other patients to tend to, I know."

She had to remind herself of that, that there were others ill, other mothers, daughters, husbands, when all she wanted to do was grab Jim by the collar and demand to know why he hadn't tried harder, why he hadn't tried again and again and again, until he might have got someone with the brains enough to ring through to Brillac, who might have told her, who might have given her a chance to make it home—

Even now, she couldn't quite comprehend it, that there was nothing she could do. How could there not be any way to go back, to fix it?

"Oh, Rachel, you can't imagine!" Alice's normally sweet-featured face was drawn; there were circles beneath her eyes and hollows under her cheeks. "There were so many sick in the village, and no nurses nearer than King's Lynn. All the Trotter boys were down with it, and Mrs. Spicer. Charles had chicken pox, and I was half frantic trying to keep Annabelle out of his room, what with Mrs. Spicer sick, too, and Polly under quarantine. By the time my father mentioned that your mother hadn't been to church—"

"You don't need to explain." Stop, stop, stop, Rachel wanted to say. She didn't want to hear it. And what did it matter, any of it? The words tore out of her, unbidden. "She was my mother. I ought to have been here."

Alice put out a hand to her, heedless of the streaks of soot. "Oh, my dear."

Rachel felt tears stinging the backs of her eyes and hastily blinked them away. "The funeral—I'll need to see to the arrangements. The undertaker—"

Alice's eyes shifted away. "The funeral was yesterday."

The floor tilted, the low ceiling rushing down at her. Rachel grabbed for the banister, feeling the room heave like the deck of the Channel ferry, the sitting room veiled by a gray haze. "What?"

"Rachel! I ought to have made you sit down first—and you're still in your coat! When was the last time you ate anything?"

Rachel breathed deeply, in and out. "Sometime around Calais, I think. No, there were biscuits just past London." The sick feeling was subsiding a bit, although she still felt clammy. She forced herself to focus. "The funeral was *yesterday?*"

Alice ducked her head guiltily, although Rachel couldn't imagine why she should feel guilty. It was Rachel, Rachel who hadn't attended her own mother's funeral. "We couldn't reach you. We tried, really, we did." She added, hesitantly, "We didn't want to leave it too long."

And wasn't that a charming image. Rachel concentrated on her breathing. No. No—she just. No.

"It was all just as your mother would have wanted," Alice hurried on, just as she had once rattled through recitations at school, faster and faster the more nervous she was. "Your cousin—the one from Oxford—he came up to see to the arrangements. It was a lovely ceremony, really, it was, and there were violets on the casket—your cousin said that your mother liked violets—and Mrs. Trotter had hysterics right in the middle of the twenty-third psalm."

"Of course she did." Despite herself, Rachel almost smiled. Mrs. Trotter's hysterics were the stuff of village legend. Rachel's mother always said—

Rachel's hands closed tight around the buttons of her coat. "It—it sounds just as it ought to have been. Thank you for seeing to everything."

There had been no funeral for her father. He had died so very far away. And now her mother . . .

Rachel thought she understood, now, why custom demanded the formality of a funeral. Without the casket, without the thump of clods on the coffin, none of it seemed real.

"We waited for you to choose the stone," Alice offered, as if that might somehow make it better.

Rachel laughed and found that she couldn't stop laughing. She put her hands to the sides of her face. "Oh, Lord. I'm sorry. Thank you. Thank you for everything."

Alice was looking at her with concern. "Please, can't I make you a cup of tea? Something? You look ready to drop on your feet."

"I've been traveling since last night. When I received the telegram." She was still in her coat.

It struck her, dimly, that these were the same clothes, the same coat, the same shoes she had scrambled into in her bedroom in the Château de Brillac a century ago. It was warm enough in the sitting room, with the fire Alice had made, but Rachel found she was loath to remove the protective shell of her coat.

Impatient with herself, Rachel shrugged out of the coat, dumping it over the banister. "I could murder a cup of tea."

Alice let out a deep breath of relief, turning hastily to the kitchen door. "I've got the kettle on. There isn't any milk, I'm afraid—"

"That's fine." Rachel followed Alice into the kitchen. She felt like a guest in her own home, out of place and off-balance. "I haven't had a proper cup of tea in months."

The kettle was already hissing gently on the hob. Alice turned her back, busying herself with the practicalities. "Did they not know how to make tea in France?"

Rachel strove for normalcy and missed by yards. "It is amazing to me that a people who do such wonderful things with coffee cannot seem to master a simple cup of tea."

"Perhaps it's because they do such wonderful things with coffee," said Alice sagely.

Water steamed into the old brown teapot with the wonky spout. The smell of tea rose like memory. Her mother's favorite tea, Irish tea, strong as sin. During the war, they'd used the leaves over and over, until the tea was little more than faintly tinted water. Rachel could remember that first cup of real tea after the war, her mother's palpable satisfaction as she poured the dark brown liquid from the pot, breathing in the scented steam.

Rachel came to herself to see Alice looking down at her, two wrinkles between her eyes. "I'm sorry, what were you saying?"

"Nothing," said Alice quickly, and set the pot of tea down on the old pine table.

They had sat like this thousands of times over the years, at this same kitchen table, this same teapot on the table between them, working on their lessons—or avoiding their lessons—as one of her mother's students plunked out tunes on the piano in the sitting room.

For a moment, Rachel thought she could hear the music from the other room. And then it was gone, nothing but the ringing in her ears. She took one of the broken biscuits Alice had set on a plate. They were stale, but Alice was right, she needed to eat something. Her mind groped after what came next. Arrangements—the arrangements had been made. She would need to see her mother's solicitor. Or had they sent a letter? Ask Alice about the mail, see Norris about the rent . . .

Anything to keep from thinking about the silence of the other room.

Tea spattered from the broken spout as Alice poured. "I imagine—I imagine you'll be going back to France?" she said hesitantly.

Rachel remembered the look on the countess's face. A hysterical laugh welled up at the back of her throat. She'd closed that road with a vengeance. "No, not back to France. Thank you." She took the cup of tea Alice handed her, wrapping her palms around the warmth. "I rather burned my bridges with the countess, you see. I don't think she'll be giving me much of a reference. Not the sort of reference one would want, at any rate."

"Where will you go?"

"I hadn't thought about it." There hadn't been time to think about anything. "Here, I suppose. Just until I find myself another position." Something in Alice's face made her say sharply, "What? What is it?"

Alice toyed with her teacup, turning it around and around on the saucer. "Mr. Norris came to the funeral. He told me that he's—reclaiming the cottage."

"Reclaiming?"

"For nonpayment of rent. He claims the rent wasn't paid to him on time last week—well, it wouldn't be, would it?—although everyone knows it's just an excuse. He thinks he can rent it out to a rich Londoner as a weekend cottage. Horrid man. That was why I was here. I wanted to make sure you had your things—your mother's piano—"

Rachel's tired brain refused to grasp what Alice was saying. "Norris is evicting me?"

"He didn't lose a minute," said Alice bitterly. "And at your own mother's funeral! It seemed unlikely he'd come to pay his respects, but I'd never imagined—" Alice scooted her chair forward. "There must be some way to fight it. The rent is all of a week overdue. If I'd realized, I'd have paid it myself, you know I would."

"I know," said Rachel numbly. This wasn't happening. It couldn't be. First her mother, and now her home, the home in which she'd grown. She glanced up at Alice. "You're not dying of some terrible disease, are you?"

Alice looked at her in confusion. "No. Why?"

"I was trying to think what the third blow might be. That's only two so far. Troubles are meant to come in threes." Her voice was too fast and too high. Rachel took a deep breath and reached for another broken biscuit. "It's an inalterable law of nature. Isn't that what Mrs. Spicer always said?"

Tentatively, Alice touched her fingers to Rachel's arm. "You know that you can stay with us for as long as you like."

"Do you need a new nursery governess?" Rachel rubbed her aching temples with her fingers. "I need to work, Alice. Now more than ever. I couldn't be beholden to your charity."

"It's not charity. We're almost sisters, remember?"

The words woke bittersweet memories. There had been a time when she and Alice had schemed to see their parents married to each other. And why not? Mr. Treadwell had been a widower since Alice was a baby, and Rachel had long since abandoned her daydreams of her father's triumphal return. At twelve, one was too old for such fancies, but not too old to fancy oneself the more matchmaking sort of Jane Austen heroine.

It would be splendid, she and Alice had agreed. They could be truly sisters, and share a room, and stay up late at night talking. With the sublime condescension of youth, they had decided it would be rather nice for the old people to have the company once Rachel and Alice were off in the world. Alice, Rachel remembered, was going to marry the Prince of Wales, while Rachel aspired to lead an expedition to the Arctic, complete with dogsleds.

It was really an ideal plan—but for the fact that neither of the adults in question had the least bit of interest in being married to the other.

Alice's father, the vicar of Netherwell, was married to the theological treatise he had been writing and rewriting, with limited success, for the past twenty years.

As for Rachel's mother, she had sat Rachel down and said firmly but kindly that she appreciated their efforts, but it just wouldn't do.

I cannot marry Mr. Treadwell, she had said. Just like that.

Why not? Rachel had protested.

You forget, said Rachel's mother gently. *I am married. And I shall be until I die.*

Those simple words had shamed Rachel into silence, the memory of her father suddenly a palpable presence between them. It made Rachel feel small and cheap for having so entirely forgotten him, for having presumed that just because the time had passed, her mother's love might be any less.

Not real sisters, then. She and Alice had admitted defeat, and had resigned themselves to being almost-sisters, sisters in everything but name.

But even almost-sisters grew apart. Rachel loved Alice; she would always love Alice. They were part of the furniture of each other's minds. But the day-to-day discussions that had been the stuff of their friendship were long since gone. They communicated now, when they could, in scattered bursts of correspondence, always months apart and, in so many ways, a world away.

Alice would always be a part of her past, but Rachel shied from the thought of intruding upon her present. If anything could make the memory of a friendship stale, it was the reality of that friend, permanently parked in one's spare room.

"I don't know what I did to deserve a friend like you." Rachel squeezed Alice's hand, then let go. "But can you imagine me living in your spare room as a carping maiden aunt?"

Alice lifted her teacup. "You don't have to carp. And who's to say that you wouldn't get married?"

Rachel looked at her askance. "The only eligible man for forty miles was Jim, and he's been quite taken for some time now. Unless you think I ought to set my cap for Mr. Norris. He is a widower, after all."

"Ugh," said Alice with disgust. She fiddled with her teacup. "Is there—"

Rachel rested her chin on her hands. "Any money? No."

She supposed she might be surprised, but she doubted it. Unless her mother had a pirate's hoard hidden beneath the bed, the sum in her post office account had never been more than fifty pounds.

Fifty pounds, a battered piano, and her gold watch. That was all Rachel had in the world.

Only it wasn't, she reminded herself fiercely. She had her own wits, such as they were. She was a hard worker. If she needed to, she could scrub floors, beat curtains. She wasn't afraid of work, any more than her mother had been.

Pushing her teacup aside, she said, "How quickly does Norris want me gone?"

Alice looked down into her cup. "As soon as possible. When I pressed him on it, he said he imagined he could give you a fortnight—at a reasonable rate."

Which meant an unreasonable rate. "How very generous of him. So nice to know that chivalry isn't dead."

There was an awkward silence. Alice pushed back her chair. "It's nearly time for Annabelle's tea. Please, come home with me." In a falsely bright tone, she added, "Annabelle has been asking after her auntie Rachel."

Rachel rose, the muscles in her legs protesting. She felt stiff and achy and strangely lightheaded. "You mean that she's hoping I've brought her a new dress for her doll."

"That, too." Alice paused, her hat in her hand. "You're dropping on your feet. Stay with us for tonight. There's a bed made up in the spare room; you can sleep as long as you like."

Rachel forced a smile. "With Jim blundering about, delivering babies?"

"He seldom delivers them in the spare room." Alice shoved her hat onto her head. "I hate to think of you here alone."

"Are you afraid Mr. Norris will try to rent me out with the cottage?"

"That's not funny." But Rachel could see the hint of a smile there all the same. Alice had always been shocked and delighted by Rachel's more outrageous comments. It was one of the many reasons they were friends. "Let me feed you supper, at least."

Making small talk with Jim? Rachel liked Alice's Jim well enough, but she didn't think she had it in her to fix a false smile to her face, to pretend nothing was wrong. All she wanted to do was sleep.

"If it's all the same, I think I'll have an early night." One of her last nights in her own bed.

Impossible to think that the room that had always been hers would soon be emptied of her possessions, like a stage set awaiting a new actress. Rachel shook her head. She shouldn't be melodramatic. What was a house? A box filled with rooms.

Resolutely, she said, "I'll go down to Oxford in the morning. I ought to thank Cousin David. For making the arrangements."

And to ask how much she owed. Nothing, he would say. But she knew that the undertaker didn't provide coffins for free, or violets, for that matter. She couldn't let Cousin David bear the whole cost of it.

How much of a dent would that make in her meager nest egg?

No point in thinking of it now. She'd sell her watch if she had to. Rachel closed her fingers around it, feeling the engraving on the underside. *To Rachel.*

"Are you sure there's nothing I can do for you?" Alice was hovering, her coat over her arm.

"You've made me tea." Rachel gestured to the anemic liquid in her cup, now cold as well as weak. When Alice still lingered, she added, "And you've reminded me that I'm not entirely an orphan. What more could I ask?"

Alice didn't need to be persuaded. Her thoughts, Rachel knew, were already shifting to Charles and Annabelle. As they should be. But it made Rachel feel more than a little lonely all the same.

Who was there to think of her?

Of all the maudlin claptrap! Rachel took a firm hand on herself and the teacups, rinsing them quickly in the cold water from the pump. There was a familiar chip on the corner of one saucer. The chip might belong to Rachel, but the cups belonged to Mr. Norris, as did the Dutch dresser into which she set them.

Tomorrow. Wearily, Rachel wiped her hands on a cloth. Tomorrow she would have to go through the cottage, make an inventory of what was theirs, and, even more important, what could be sold. There wasn't much, not really. Most of the furniture, ugly old Victorian pieces, scarred from use, had been let with the house.

Her carpetbag still sat on the floor where she had dropped it, at the base of the stairs. The sitting room was overstuffed, crammed with knickknacks—the Dresden shepherdess with a crack down one arm, the oil lamp with its crooked glass shade—but so little of it was theirs. Just their clothing, a few pictures, her father's chess set, her mother's piano.

Not the piano. She hated the idea of parting from her mother's piano. But what was she to do with it? She had never had the patience to play. And she could hardly take it with her, strapped to her back like a snail.

The money from the piano might pay for a typing course.

Rachel took a firm grip on her bag, hauling it up the stairs, treading lightly on the fourth board, which squeaked, her fingers tracing the familiar contours of the banister. The familiarity of it all closed around her. She found herself straining her ears, listening for the sound of her mother's footsteps, the fingers on the piano keys. Any moment now, the door to her mother's room would creak, and she would hear a pleasant alto voice call, "Rachel?"

The door to her mother's room was closed and still. Rachel dropped her bag just inside her own room. The glass was too low; she had to bend to see herself in it as she took the pins out of her hair, letting it fall free. She kicked her shoes off, under the bed. Maybe Mr. Norris, in all his venality, was doing her a favor. She could stay here, in her childhood room, waiting for a voice that never came, or she could go out and make her own way in the world. Pull the bandage cleanly off, that was the way.

That had been her mother's philosophy. Rachel could remember it only as a series of blurred images, their departure from their old home. It had happened so quickly. A letter one day, and, within the week, their life packed into boxes and bags, crowded onto a wagon and then a train, the old life gone, gone beyond recalling, all in the blink of an eye, as Rachel clung with one hand to her mother's skirt and with the other to her battered old stuffed rabbit, one of the few relics of their old life that came with them.

At the time, a confused four-year-old, she hadn't understood that flurried move. Now, Rachel thought she might. The ghost of her father would have been everywhere, in the garden, on the stair. Easier to start fresh than live with the memories.

Rachel had known, without being told, that she wasn't meant to ask about her father, that to do so would only bring that set look to her mother's face.

It must, she realized now, have been terribly hard. She remembered the affection between her parents: the way their hands touched as they passed, the looks that said more than words, the love and care they had lavished so freely on her. All gone, so quickly. And her mother had taken her and moved on. As she must move on.

Tentatively, Rachel crossed the hall on stocking feet, to her mother's door. It opened with the old familiar squeak. The bed had been hastily made, the counterpane pulled up crookedly over the pillows. Someone had aired the room, but there was still the lingering smell of the sickroom, camphor and stale sweat.

Oh, Mother.

Without thinking, Rachel went to her mother's bed, as she had all those years ago, after her father had died. She had been all right during the day, but late at night, when the unfamiliar dark of their new home closed around her, she had needed the assurance of her mother's body beside her, needed to touch her and smell her lavender scent, in the physical assurance that she was still there.

There was a lump in her throat, a lump twenty-three years old. The bed had seemed so high when Rachel was little. Wearily, Rachel curled into the hollow left by her mother's body, wrapping her arms around the pillow.

Something crinkled beneath her fingers.

Startled, Rachel sat up, dislodging the pillow and sending the paper, whatever it was, fluttering to the floor. It wasn't a letter. The paper was thin and glossy, the sort of paper one found in expensive magazines. It had been folded; on the side facing up, Rachel could see an advertisement for Turkish cigarettes.

Her mother didn't smoke. She would have been horrified at the very idea. Unless—perhaps it was something that Jim had accidentally dropped beneath her pillow? Yes, because doctors so frequently inserted bits of magazine beneath their patients. Leaning over, Rachel fished up the page, shaking it open.

Her father stared up at her in grainy black and white.

Rachel blinked, hard, but the picture was still there. She smoothed it out against the counterpane with hands that weren't entirely steady, wondering if she were seeing things. How long had it been since she had slept? Years, it seemed like, if one didn't count the odd doze on the train, her head jerking against her chest. Perhaps she was asleep now, asleep and imagining that she had reached beneath her mother's pillow, found this odd, odd picture of her father.

It all had the curious unreality of a dream: the picture, the image flattened by the glare of a flash; the discreet block letters at the upper right-hand corner of the page, which proclaimed the paper THE TATLER. That in itself was odd enough. The only paper her mother ever read was *The Morning Post*. *The Tatler* was for other people, people who followed society and its doings.

And the picture itself . . . the picture was her father and not her father. Tall like her father, yes, with the fair hair that Rachel hadn't inherited and the deep-set gray eyes that she had. There were the gold-rimmed spectacles, the slightly stooped posture.

There was even the slight shadow of a scar on his chin. She remembered running her fingers along that scar as a child, feeling the curious ridge of it.

But this man was older, older than her father had ever lived to be. As old, in fact, as he would have been if he had lived. And he was dressed as Rachel had never seen him, in evening clothes, a white scarf around his neck, a tall hat on his head, the ribbon of an order shimmering on his breast, and a fair-haired young woman on his arm.

The caption beneath the picture read, *Lady Olivia Standish, escorted by her father, the Earl of Ardmore.*

The date was December 1926. Only five months ago.

THREE

The paper crinkled beneath Rachel's palms.

Her father . . . and yet not her father.

For heaven's sake, what was she thinking? Rachel pushed the paper away, rubbing her knuckles against her sore eyes. Her father had died, twenty-three years ago. And she rather thought she would know if her father had been an earl. The very thought was laughable. She might as well imagine herself the daughter of the Prince of Wales.

Ardmore . . . The name was vaguely familiar. It had cropped up from time to time in her history books. There had been a d'Ardmore in the train of William the Conqueror, a Lord Ardmore switching sides at Boswell Field, an Earl of Ardmore, new-minted, whispering in William of Orange's ear in the aftermath of the Glorious Revolution. They were powerful people, important people, people so far from Rachel's touch that they might have been on the moon.

And what did she remember, at that? When was the last time she had looked at a picture of her father? She remembered him, largely, as a collection of disembodied attributes. As a cold cheek and the scratch of the collar of a greatcoat on a winter's day; as a warm lap and a pair of hands holding a book open as he read her a story; as the press of lips against the side of her forehead.

Rachel breathed in deeply through her nose, striving for common sense. When she thought about it logically, it wasn't wonderful that she should be imagining her father. It wasn't the first time, after all. When she was very young, she had imagined she saw her father everywhere.

And now—now, in losing her mother, she had lost her father all over again. They hadn't spoken of him, but he had always been there, with them, a shadowy presence just over her mother's shoulder, a whisper of a memory.

Through the sheen of tears, Rachel looked at the magazine page on the coverlet. The paper was creased, the picture blurred. She might, she thought wildly, have as easily imagined her father into an advertisement for men's hats—or, for that matter, Turkish cigarettes.

Still, just to make sure . . . There was, Rachel knew, a picture of her father in her mother's night-table drawer. It was, she had always thought, very much like her mother to keep him tucked away like that. Her mother was a great believer in keeping the personal personal.

Rachel drew out the drawer, and there it was, right on top: a faded daguerreotype in a silver frame, a tall, thinly built man, with fair hair and a pair of spectacles, not particularly handsome, not particularly remarkable, but for the love in his eyes as he gazed down at the woman next to him, Rachel's mother, eighteen and lovely, even in the high-necked, long-skirted fashion of the time.

Slowly, Rachel drew the picture from the drawer and set it down next to the page from *The Tatler*.

They might have been father and son, but for the fact that no father and son had ever resembled each other so closely, right down to the faint shadow of a scar on the chin. Her father aged before her eyes, and on his arm was another woman, his daughter.

His other daughter.

Absurd. Absolutely absurd. There had to be some explanation. Chance resemblances happened. They did.

Even down to a scar?

Even down to a scar, Rachel told herself firmly. The idea that her father might still be alive, might be, in fact, an earl—no, no, and no again. It was straight out of a twopenny novel, the sort shopgirls read on their lunch hour.

Besides, Rachel thought somberly, the Earl of Ardmore had a daughter, Lady Olivia Standish. That meant, presumably, that he had a wife. There must be—or have been—a Lady Ardmore.

People like her mother didn't have illegitimate children. In Rachel's experience, illegitimacy went with untidy houses and unwashed hair and people who dropped their aitches and didn't know who Wordsworth was. In short, the Trotters, down by the river, with their confused brood of half-clothed children.

No one was quite sure who the father of Dorcas Trotter's children was, least of all Dorcas Trotter, which, Mrs. Spicer said sagely, wasn't the least bit surprising, given that Dorcas's mother had been no better than she should be. Apples didn't fall far from the tree, especially when them apples were rotten, and no wonder.

Rachel's mother used to bring the Trotters baskets: Rachel's old clothes for the babies, soup for winter, soap and cleaning cloths and Jeyes Fluid in the summer, biscuits and oranges at Christmas.

Rachel had accompanied her mother on her errands of mercy, feeling pleasantly superior in her own neat little boater hat and tidy gloves.

Stand up, now. It's the lady from Ivy Cottage. That was what old Mrs. Trotter would say, sharply, to Dorcas, when they knocked at the half-opened door.

They called Rachel "miss" and her mother "ma'am." Rachel had accepted that, as of right.

The idea that she might be—that her mother might be—no. It was too absurd. Rachel's mother took tea at the vicarage every Friday; she played chess with Mr. Treadwell.

And usually beat him, too. Mr. Treadwell was a very sweet man, but he didn't have much of a head for chess.

No, thought Rachel. They were positively mired, steeped, in respectability. It was a chance resemblance, nothing more. That, in all likelihood, was why her mother had kept the clipping. She must have been struck by it, too. Rachel had never known her mother to read *The Tatler*, but perhaps Alice had brought it. And with flu-dimmed eyes, her mother had seen the picture and imagined her husband alive again.

Her husband, Edward Woodley, botanist. Just repeating her father's name was reassuring. Edward Woodley. Not Edward Standish, Earl of Ardmore. The fact that they were both Edwards meant nothing. England was peopled with Edwards. One might as well suspect the late King Edward or the Prince of Wales of being her father.

All the same, Rachel tucked the *Tatler* page into her purse before she left for Oxford the next morning. As a curiosity, she told herself.

Cousin David was the one person who had known them before Netherwell. He'd held Rachel as she'd been baptized, had guided her straggling baby steps across the garden in that half-remembered home of her infancy, and, once she was old enough to crave penny candy from the village shop, slipped her shillings beneath the seals of his letters, just as, he said, his godfather used to do for him when he was a boy at school.

Perhaps the Earl of Ardmore was a distant relation. Cousin David would know. He was a historian, after all.

And it was easier, Rachel thought wryly, as she stepped out of the train at Oxford station, to fret over fairy tales than to think of any of the many troublesome realities awaiting her, such as how she was to make her living.

Rachel pulled her coat more closely around her. Spring was clinging stubbornly to the memory of winter; there was frost in the air and the sky was dark as slate, threatening rain. The stones of Oxford, which glowed golden in summer, were a flat, unrelieved gray in the gloom.

Undergraduates might come and go, but the porter's lodge at Merton looked just the same, with its litter of bicycles, the baskets piled high with books and bunched-up gowns and what looked like someone's lost top hat.

The porter's face was forbidding beneath his bowler hat, but it lightened as soon as he recognized Rachel. "I hardly knew you, miss, you look so grown up! I thought you were one of them women students."

The way he pronounced it made it sound just a step away from scarlet woman. Suggs was a purist when it came to his university.

Rachel held out a hand. "How do you do, Suggs?"

When she was a little girl in a sailor hat and her best dress, Suggs used to conjure boiled candies from his bowler hat. They were always lightly fuzzed with lint, but Rachel had eaten them all, every one. It wouldn't do, her mother had said, to hurt Suggs's feelings.

Rachel could picture her mother standing there, in her good wool coat, her gloves pristine, her hair coiled beneath her hat, holding tight to Rachel's hand as she urged her to say thank you to Mr. Suggs.

"I've seen better days," said Suggs darkly. "But there you are. And you're a sight to cheer a dark day, miss. It's nice to see a woman what looks like a woman."

With that, he cast an ominous look down the street, where a lady scholar, gown flapping over her frock, was bicycling toward the High Street.

"I'm just back from France," said Rachel briskly, avoiding both the compliment and the complaint. "It is nice to be back."

Suggs nodded knowingly. "You'll be wanting to see your cousin."

"Is he in?" Rachel didn't know what she would do if he wasn't. Build a willow cabin at his gate?

Suggs inclined his bald head. "For you, miss, he's always in."

"Please give my regards to Mrs. Suggs," said Rachel politely, and went up the familiar stair, to Cousin David's rooms on the second floor.

The oak was, mercifully, unsported. Rachel knocked, for form's sake, on the inner door, before letting herself in. They had only visited two, perhaps three times a year, but she had had the run of these rooms for as long as she could remember.

The familiarity of it all enfolded her like a comfortable old coat, the old-book smell of Cousin David's rooms, mingled with tobacco, last night's Stilton, and just a hint of Jeyes Fluid. There was the chair where she had kicked her heels as a small girl, and the window with its cracked and bubbled old glass. She used to look for patterns in the bits of lead that held together the fragments of old glass, finding letters and shapes.

Cousin David was in his favorite chair by the bookcases, a long-necked lamp behind him, a hassock at his feet piled high with books. The books might have changed over the years, but the chair and hassock hadn't.

At Rachel's entrance, he jumped to his feet. "Rachel!"

"Cousin David," she said, and lifted her cheek to be kissed, as she used to when she was a little girl. They didn't embrace—her godfather wasn't an embracing sort of man—but Rachel felt her shoulders begin to relax at the warmth and nearness of him. "Thank you for seeing to the arrangements."

"I can't say how sorry I am." Cousin David looked nearly as weary as she felt. "We tried to find you, but—"

"I know." Unreasonable to ask him why he hadn't tried harder, why he hadn't waited longer. Rachel spoke as lightly as she could. "I could murder the count's valet—he didn't bother to pass the messages on. I didn't even know she was . . . ill until Monday."

Cousin David awkwardly patted her arm. "You mustn't blame yourself."

Rachel's lips twisted. "Wouldn't you?"

"Er," said Cousin David eloquently. Rustling himself into action, he waved a hand in the general direction of the tea table, an octagon of dark walnut, heavily carved in an exaggerated example of Victorian gothic. "You'll be wanting coffee, I imagine? You mustn't worry that it's the swill they serve in Hall. Spence makes coffee that is coffee. Hi, Spence!"

Feebly, Rachel protested. "Really, it's quite all right. I've had so much tea I'm sloshing with it. I don't need—"

"No, no, you mustn't worry. It's no trouble at all. Two coffees, Spence," said Cousin David, thrusting the coffee things at his scout, who received the tray impassively. "And I should have some brandy about somewhere. . . ."

He began poking through a forest of bottles incongruously stashed in a cupboard below the bookshelves.

"Please, Cousin David, if I have any brandy, I'll be asleep before Spence brings the coffee." Rachel touched a gloved hand lightly to his shoulder. "You needn't fuss, really."

Cousin David rose slowly, brushing his hands off against his trousers. "I just wish—"

"I know." She didn't, really, but she couldn't bear the thought of sympathy just now, even from Cousin David. Especially from Cousin David. Better to be brisk and businesslike, to focus on the necessities. "I understand you took charge of my mother's affairs?"

"Yes, yes. Just let me find the papers. . . ." He began rustling in a pile on one of the tables. The appearance of disorder was deceptive. Cousin David could locate a specific source from underneath a chair. In this case, it only took him a moment to extract a thin sheaf of papers and hand them to Rachel. "You should find it all present and accounted for."

"All" consisted of her mother's will, a short and simple document, written in her mother's own hand and witnessed by Jim and the vicar. The writing was sloping and uneven, very different from her mother's usual tidy script. It would, Rachel realized, never have occurred to her to make a will. Before.

Biting her lip, she went on to the next item in the pile, her mother's bankbook, with a balance of one hundred and thirty-eight pounds.

Rachel drew a deep breath, struggling for equanimity. "I'm better off than I expected. If I'd known, I might have splurged on a second-class ticket."

There were worried lines between Cousin David's eyes. "It's precious little to be going on with. Will you be returning to France?"

"Everyone seems very eager to send me back to France. Thank you." Rachel took the chair he pulled out for her, tucking the will and bankbook into her bag. "If I can scrape the funds together, I'll take a typing course and hire myself out as a secretary."

Cousin David moved a pile of books out of the way and sat down across from her. "If training is what you want," he said hesitantly, "I can find you a course here. And then . . . the dean of Somerville might be in need of a new secretary."

"You mean that you'll ask the dean of Somerville if she could possibly be in need of a new secretary?" Rachel couldn't hide the affection in her voice. "There's no need to contrive for me. I'm quite looking forward to the challenge of it, striking out on my own."

He couldn't quite hide his relief. Cousin David might love her as a niece, but he had no desire for a daughter. "If you ever need anything...Ah, thank you, Spence."

The cups were set out before them, the fragrant brew poured. Rachel waited until Cousin David had put sugar in his coffee before asking diffidently, "Did you see my mother, before—?"

"Yes." Cousin David stirred his coffee, around and around and around. "I arrived in Netherwell on Friday morning."

"Did she—" Rachel concentrated on her coffee. "Did she say anything?"

A shadow crossed Cousin David's face. "She was rambling," he said at last. "Delirious with fever. But she did give me this to give to you."

Cousin David fished in his waistcoat pocket, drawing out a thick golden oval, a thin chain threaded through the hasp. His fingers closed around it for a moment in a quick, convulsive grasp, before he held it out to Rachel.

"Here. It's only right that you have it."

The gold was heavy on Rachel's palm. It was a brooch, ornate, old-fashioned, dominated by two intertwined filigree letters: *E* and *K*. Edward and Katherine. Her mother had once had other pieces of jewelry. A pearl ring that Rachel remembered from when she was little. A little brooch of seed pearls. A heavily engraved gold bracelet that had belonged to Rachel's grandmother. All those had disappeared, piece by piece, to pay the butcher and the baker, and, later, Rachel's school fees.

But the brooch had never left her breast.

"Thank you." Rachel's throat was tight. Her fingers closed around the brooch. "I can't remember her without it."

"No," Cousin David agreed. "It was one of the few things she had left of your father."

"Speaking of my father..." Rachel looked down at the elaborate *E* and *K*, woven together for all eternity. Easier to think about oddities than about the brooch and what it meant that it was now in her possession. "It sounds silly even to ask, but—is the Earl of Ardmore a relation of my father?"

Cousin David's hand jerked on his coffee cup, spilling brown liquid. "Clumsy, clumsy," he murmured, mopping at the liquid with a napkin. "Why do you ask?"

Rachel reached into her bag, drawing out the page from *The Tatler*, folded neatly into fourths. "I found this in my mother's room last night. Under her pillow, of all strange places."

Cousin David's fingers touched the edge of the paper. He drew it slowly closer to him.

"It is curious, isn't it?" She ought to have been prepared for it this time, but the sight of her father's face, beneath another man's top hat, was deeply disconcerting, like passing a mirror and seeing someone else's face reflected.

"Hmm. Yes. Curious." Cousin David's face was set and still, his eyes fixed on the little cutting. Clearing his throat, he said, "I didn't think Katherine read *The Tatler*."

"She didn't. Not that I know of. I imagine Alice must have brought it. Or a nurse. But that's not really the point, is it? When I saw it—when I saw it, I had thought it might be my father. Of course, then I realized how foolish that was," she added hastily. "But it does look very like, doesn't it?"

"Very like."

There was something about his stillness, about the short nature of his response, that was making Rachel edgy. She scooted forward in her chair, crossing her legs at the ankle. "That's why I wondered, you see. Whether they might be related. The resemblance is rather remarkable," she prompted.

Now was David's chance to say, yes, the earl was a fifteenth cousin twice removed, but he simply nodded his head, jerkily, like a puppet. "Yes. Quite remarkable."

Even down to the scar on his chin. "You'll think I'm mad." Rachel's voice seemed to echo in the stillness, too loud, too high. "I was imagining the most absurd things. He looks so like my father. But—my father is dead."

Silence.

Rachel looked across the table at Cousin David. "He *is* dead."

"I told your mother that it would come out eventually." Cousin David's voice was so low that she could hardly hear him. "I wanted to tell you. Years ago."

"Tell me." The edge of the chair bit into the backs of Rachel's legs. "Tell me what, exactly?"

"It isn't a chance resemblance." Cousin David sat a little straighter in his chair, his voice quiet, but clear. "The Earl of Ardmore looks like your father because he is your father."

FOUR

"That isn't funny," said Rachel sharply.

"I'm not trying to be funny. Please—" Cousin David half rose. "Sit down? And I'll try to tell you what I can."

Rachel hadn't realized she was standing. "My father was a botanist. He died when I was four years old."

"It seemed best at the time—" Cousin David started, and then shook his head. "I shouldn't be the one telling you this. Your mother—"

Her mother wasn't here. She wouldn't be telling anyone anything again.

There had been some small consolation in the thought that her parents, at last, were together.

They had to be. This nonsense about her father being alive—it was just that, nonsense. And cruel. So cruel. She hadn't thought David could be cruel.

"This isn't true." Rachel blundered back, the legs of her chair scraping against the worn floorboards. "My father is dead."

There was discomfort on David's face, discomfort and guilt and, worst of all, pity.

Rachel could feel panic rising in her chest. "He was a botanist. He died on a collecting trip. You know that. You were there. You helped us—you helped us move."

That haphazard departure, clothes flung into trunks, her mother's head down, shoulders stiff with determination, Rachel clinging to her skirts, whining to be picked up. In her memory, it was always darkness, lit by the light of a few candles, as her mother moved from wardrobe to trunk, trunk to wardrobe.

"Your mother thought that it would be easier for you if you believed that your father had died." She could see the spots of sweat on David's forehead, although the room was cool and damp. "Metaphorically, you might say in a way that he did."

"Metaphorically," echoed Rachel. "Meta*phor*ically? One doesn't die metaphorically. One is either alive or one isn't."

Her father couldn't be alive. Her father couldn't be alive, because if he was, it meant that he had abandoned them. He had crumpled them up and thrown them away like the newspaper from a twist of chips.

"It wasn't my choice," said Cousin David quickly. "Your mother thought it was better that way. She didn't want you to be . . . confused."

Confused? That didn't begin to approach it. The clipping lay on the table still, where Cousin David had discarded it.

Lady Olivia Standish, escorted by her father, Edward, Earl of Ardmore.

Her father.

Rachel's father.

"More confusing this way, don't you think?" said Rachel, clinging to her composure by keeping her voice hard and her face harder. "You told me my father was dead. Forgive me if I find his sudden resurrection disconcerting."

"My dear." David took a step toward her, stopped. "I'm so sorry. If you could pretend—"

"Pretend that I never saw *that?*" Rachel gestured sharply toward the clipping. She was pacing now, in short sharp bursts, her skirt tangling around her legs. Why? Why couldn't David have lied? He could have lied, said it was a chance resemblance. He could have let her keep her father, the father she remembered, the father she believed had loved her.

She could feel grief rising within her, swamping her, grief for that father she remembered so dimly, the botanist who had died on a faraway island. She remembered the feel of his hair beneath her hands, barley fair; the glint of his spectacles in the lamplight; the joy of being hoisted aloft on his shoulders.

Rachel could feel him receding from her, slipping away, the father she thought she had known.

Rachel came to a hard stop against the back of the chair. "He was alive. All this time. He abandoned us."

"It wasn't like that."

The heavily carved walnut bit into her palms. "What was it like, then?" Rachel demanded. "Was he kidnapped by gypsies? Did he lose his memory? Or did he simply forget the way to our door?"

"He didn't—he didn't know where you were. It was your mother's wish that there should be a clean break."

Anger flamed through Rachel. "My mother *loved* my father."

"Your father loved your mother," countered Cousin David. "Truly, he did."

"Not enough to marry her."

It was a shot in the dark, but it hit its mark. Cousin David made a helpless gesture with one hand. "There were circumstances. . . ."

"Circumstances," Rachel echoed.

There had been no little church in the countryside, no marriage lines. The ring on her mother's finger, the widow's weeds she had worn for a year after they had moved to Netherwell—lies. All lies. The respectability that had guarded and cloaked Rachel all her life was nothing more than a flimsy sham, a thing of paste and cardboard.

Cousin David reached for a decanter and set it down heavily on the table. "Your father wasn't meant to be earl. When his older brother died—the world changed." He looked helplessly at Rachel, the crystal stopper in one hand. "I wish I could make you understand the obligations—the expectations. He was forced to give up his old desires and ambitions."

"His old daughter?" Rachel shot back.

Cousin David's eyes flicked down, to the clipping on the table. "Would you—would you like some sherry? It's really quite drinkable."

"No, thank you." She was all full up with wormwood and gall. Rachel braced her hands against the table. "Was everything a lie, then? Are you even my cousin?"

Uncle David managed a crooked smile. "For my sins, yes." He paused for a moment before adding quietly, "On your father's side. His mother and my mother were sisters."

Another betrayal. Such a small lie, on top of all the others, but Rachel felt as though she had been slapped. She straightened, so abruptly that her hip knocked against the chair. "No wonder you take his part."

Cousin David cleared his throat painfully. "Your father wouldn't see it that way. I haven't spoken to him since—It's been a long time."

"Twenty-three years?"

"I—" Cousin David poured himself a sherry and drank it like whisky, stiff-wristed, in one shot. He said thickly, "The three of us, we were raised together. I loved your mother like a sister."

It was the same Cousin David, the same well-worn suit, the same thinning hair, but Rachel felt as though she were seeing him for the first time. "Brothers don't usually sell their sisters. There's a word for that, isn't there? Pandering."

And there was a word for what her mother had been: a mistress. A kept woman, hidden away in a little cottage in the country.

No wonder there was no other family. No wonder they had never had any guests other than Cousin David. No wonder they had moved so far away, all the way to Netherwell, to a quiet village where no one knew them, where no one would ever guess that that quiet, nice Mrs. Woodley was no better than she should be and her daughter the fruit of shame.

"Rachel—" Cousin David reached for her.

Rachel dodged out of the way. Laughter bubbled out of her throat, corrosive as lye. "And all these years, I'd thought my father was a botanist." It seemed ridiculously funny now. "A botanist."

"He would have been a botanist," said Cousin David, seizing on that small thing. "If his older brother hadn't died. That was the tragedy of it."

"*That* was the tragedy of it? That he couldn't be a botanist?"

"No! That wasn't what I meant. You have to understand—your father—" David checked slightly at the look Rachel gave him, then blundered valiantly on. "Your father never wanted to be earl. He might have been a botanist. He might"—he took a deep breath—"he might have married your mother. But then his brother died."

"My heart bleeds for him," said Rachel acidly. "He ought to have considered that before he anticipated his wedding night."

Helplessly, Cousin David said, "Your father loved you. You and your mother."

"The Earl of Ardmore," said Rachel, in a voice that was too loud and too hard, "is not my father. My father is dead. He died when I was four years old."

Her hands were clenched into fists at her sides; her chest rose and fell as rapidly as if she had been running.

They might have stood like that indefinitely, but for the light rap of fingers against the doorframe.

A clipped, aristocratic male voice, rich with humor, drawled, "I hate to intrude. . . ."

There was a man. A man lounging just inside the doorframe. He leaned bonelessly back against the old oak, his pale gray suit molding itself to his long form, a miracle of expert tailoring.

The man looked just as expensively constructed as his suit, along the same long, elegant lines. Beneath close-cropped, curly black hair, a pair of high cheekbones slanted down across his face. His lips were red and sensual, lips for eating strawberries with, but his black eyes were alert and all too keen.

Right now, they were focused on Rachel.

Rachel's cheeks turned crimson. "I was just leaving," she said, with as much dignity as she could muster. To Cousin David, she said, "You needn't bother to see me out. I know the way."

"Rachel—"

The man in the doorway straightened, brushing a speck of invisible dust from his trousers. "Don't let me interrupt. I merely came to return this."

This was a leather-bound book, suitably musty about the edges.

Cousin David looked from the intruder to Rachel and back again, three little furrows between his eyes. He murmured, "Simon Montfort, my cousin—Rachel Woodley."

Cousin David hesitated slightly over her name.

It took only a moment for Rachel to realize why. Her name—oh, Lord, what was her name? Woodley was the name of her fictitious father, the botanist who never was. A feeling of panic welled in her breast. Even her name wasn't her own.

It was an uncomfortable, shivery sort of feeling, like going out fully clothed only to discover that all the seams had gone, and she was standing in the middle of the street, naked.

Pulling herself together, Rachel nodded stiffly. "Mr. Montfort. Cousin David."

Cousin David looked at her pleadingly. "If you'll just stay a moment . . ."

For what? For now, all she wanted was a dark and lonely burrow. "I must be going. Good day, Mr. Montfort."

Rachel didn't look back as she left the room. She felt like an old glass window, cracked and leaded back together, ready to shatter at a sound.

Behind her, she could hear Cousin David saying, in a low voice, "How much did you hear?"

"I hear no evil and I see no evil. I am deaf and dumb."

"It isn't funny, Simon." Cousin David was speaking low and earnestly; Rachel only caught bits and pieces. "Not fodder . . . essential that this not get out . . . the embarrassment . . . unfortunate. . . ."

Embarrassment? Rachel paused, with her hand on the staircase rail. Of course. She was the embarrassment. The unwanted, unknown child of the Earl of Ardmore.

All of these years, swaddled in respectability, she hadn't realized there was a scarlet brand lurking just below the surface. The world swayed and dipped; everything turned upside down.

"Hullo." Mr. Montfort clambered down the stairs. "Miss . . . Woodley, is it?"

Rachel resolutely resumed her progress. "Mr. Montfort."

She didn't look at him, but Mr. Montfort was looking at her, cataloging her features with a thoroughness that amounted to rudeness. "So you're Ardmore's daughter."

Her father had another daughter, an official daughter, a daughter with fashionably marcelled blond hair and gowns that shimmered in the flash of the camera.

No, not her father. The man who had fathered her. Her real father, the man who had held her, had played with her, had soothed her childish fears, was dead, dead twenty-three years ago.

"No," said Rachel woodenly. "Lady Olivia Standish is the Earl of Ardmore's daughter."

"His other daughter, then." Mr. Montfort reached the door to the quad ahead of her, holding it open with a flourish. "His unacknowledged daughter."

"Why sugarcoat it?" retorted Rachel, stung into response. "Why not just say illegitimate and have done?"

"Because I'm not done." Sauntering beside her, his hands in his pockets, Mr. Montfort subjected her to a long, thorough scrutiny. "You don't look like him—"

"Thank you!" said Rachel furiously.

"Except about the eyes. Those are Standish eyes. You'd best not go gazing into anyone's or they'll spot you right off. Unless, of course," he added casually, "that's what you want."

Rachel's shoulders were painfully stiff beneath her good wool jacket. The mist was rapidly turning to mizzle, stinging her eyes and damping the shoulders of her suit. "What makes you think I want anything to do with him?"

Mr. Montfort regarded her with something like pity. "You are bursting for revenge. The most casual observer could see it."

The worst of it was that it was true. "I didn't invite you to observe."

"Of course not," said Mr. Montfort imperturbably. "If I waited to be invited, I would never go anywhere at all. I've been asked to give you a cup of tea."

"Consider your duty discharged." Rachel raised a hand to Suggs, who was enjoying his afternoon smoke by the door of the lodge and eyeing a party of undergraduates in commoner's gowns in a rather forbidding fashion. "Good day, Mr. Suggs."

"Miss Rachel." The porter nodded respectfully to Mr. Montfort, saying, "Good to see your face back here, sir."

"Likewise, Suggs, likewise." Montfort adjusted his stride to Rachel's, hands in his pockets, shoulders back, face lifted to the slate-gray sky. "Let me guess. You intend to go storming off to Ardles and challenge the earl with the fact of your existence. There will be a tearful scene—his, not yours—after which he will repent and declare you his joy, his treasure, and his sole heiress."

Rachel turned her heel on an uneven piece of paving. "That's nonsense."

"Yes, it is. Arrant nonsense. More likely, the butler won't let you past the door."

"There's no need to be cruel." Resolutely, Rachel turned up the collar of her jacket, wishing she had had the forethought to wear a mackintosh.

The mizzle had made up its mind to be rain, turning to a hard drizzle that dripped down her cheeks like tears and made her hair stick in wet half curls against her ears. She had, she realized, left her umbrella in Cousin David's rooms, but nothing could induce her to go back and retrieve it, even without Mr. Montfort hovering over her like an ill wish.

"It's not cruel, it's honest." Mr. Montfort produced his umbrella. "You appear to be in want of one of these."

"Such gallantry," said Rachel sarcastically. "There's a puddle. Would you like to drape yourself over it?"

Mr. Montfort obligingly held the umbrella closer, stepping next to her so that they were both sheltered beneath its brim. "Not even for your dainty foot. I rather like this suit. And this isn't pure chivalry. I owe your cousin a debt."

Both Mr. Montfort and Cousin David could go directly to a hot place populated with pitchforks. "Find some other way to discharge it. There must be dragon to be slain somewhere."

"I'm fresh out of dragons and phoenix feathers." Mr. Montfort placed a hand beneath her elbow. "I refuse to argue with you in the middle of St. Giles. Come have a cup of tea."

"Then don't argue with me at all." Rachel shook off his hand, speeding her step on the rain-slick flagstones. "I don't want tea."

"Would you rather have gin?"

"No!"

"Tea it is, then," said Mr. Montfort conversationally, "and here is a Fuller's conveniently to hand. They will, as I understand, purvey brown liquid in a pot."

Rachel swung to face him. "You mean you're to keep me from storming off to bother—" She'd nearly said *my father*. "The Earl of Ardmore."

Mr. Montfort's eyes met hers. His were black, true black, so dark that there was no distinction between pupil and iris. "I don't give a damn about the comfort and convenience of the Earl of Ardmore. But I did promise your cousin I'd make sure you didn't walk in front of a train."

The rain was seeping down through Rachel's collar. Inside, the Fuller's looked bright and inviting, the windows steaming with warmth.

And even the company of Mr. Montfort was preferable to being left alone with her own thoughts.

"Oh, all right," Rachel said disagreeably. "It's too much bother to fight with you."

"Many people have said the same." With a mocking half bow, Mr. Montfort gestured for her to precede him through the door of Fuller's.

Rachel submitted to being ushered to a table, where Mr. Montfort installed her in her chair with the exaggerated reverence due a duchess.

She placed her bag firmly on her lap, determined not to let Mr. Montfort get the first word.

"Do you know"—Rachel couldn't bring herself to say *my father*—"the Earl of Ardmore?"

Mr. Montfort seated himself in his own chair, spreading out his long frame, so that he seemed to command far more than his allotted space. Slowly, deliberately, he removed a cigarette case from his breast pocket. "I spent some time at Caffers after the war." At Rachel's blank look, Mr. Montfort translated, "Carrisford. Carrisford Court. Home of the Standish family since time immemorial—or at least since the third earl pulled the whole bally thing down and built it up again."

It all felt impossibly remote. "I know nothing about the family."

"Don't you mean your family?"

"Hardly." Why would she lay claim to anyone who didn't want to claim her? Rachel had done very well without the Standishes for these twenty-odd years and she would do very well for twenty-odd more. "I'd scarcely heard of them until today."

"Were you hoping to touch Ardmore for money?" Mr. Montfort regarded her with dispassionate inquiry, as if she were a specimen on a naturalist's table. "If so, you're doomed to disappointment. Everything he has is his wife's. Her father did a brilliant job of tying it all up in settlements."

Rachel stared at him, the blood roaring in her ears. "Oh, I see. Because I'm a by-blow, I must be venal?" Her fingers closed tightly around her slim purse. "I manage very well on my own, thank you very much."

Mr. Montfort signaled to the waitress. "We'll have a pot of the Lapsang." To Rachel, he said, "You would be surprised what one might do under the influence of an empty stomach."

Rachel lifted her head proudly. "Mine is hardly empty."

It would have been more convincing if her stomach hadn't chosen that moment to rumble.

"And a slice of walnut cake," said Mr. Montfort to the waitress.

"I detest walnut cake." Rachel shook out her napkin. "I have a little money. Not what you would call money"—or her father—"but enough to keep me until I find another position."

Mr. Montfort tapped an unlit cigarette against the table. "Oh? And what do you do?"

"I am a nursery governess," said Rachel defiantly. "You needn't look like that. I can't imagine you have ever spent a day trying to make three ill-mannered children mind you."

"No," admitted Mr. Montfort, making no effort to hide his amusement. "I cannot say that I have." Leaning back in his chair, he extracted a lighter from his pocket. "Gasper?"

Wordlessly, Rachel shook her head, overwhelmed by the oddity of it all, sitting across from this man she hadn't known from Adam an hour before, the most intimate details of her family history laid out like so much dirty laundry.

She hated feeling so naked, so exposed; everything she'd thought she was turned inside out and upside down, for the delectation of this inscrutable stranger.

"There's no need to study me so intently," said Mr. Montfort lazily. "If I had designs on your person, I would hardly be plying you with tea."

Despite herself, Rachel smiled. In her dilapidated hat and boxy suit, she was hardly the stuff of men's wanton fancies. "Don't forget the walnut cake."

"Food of the gods. The more vengeful sort. Ah, thank you." That last was to the waitress, who set down the tea and the despised walnut cake. "Shall you be mother or shall I?"

Rachel appropriated the teapot. "I'll pour."

"To prevent me putting mysterious powders into your tea?"

"I can't imagine what you read, Mr. Montfort," Rachel said coolly. "Sugar?"

"Only on alternate Tuesdays." Mr. Montfort nodded to the plate. "Eat your cake. You'll feel better."

Rachel dug her fork into the cake; refusing to eat merely because Mr. Montfort was being provoking would be foolish. And, whatever she might have said to Mr. Montfort, Fuller's walnut had always been a favorite.

Across from her, Mr. Montfort sat calmly smoking his cigarette. In half an hour, they would go their separate ways; Rachel to her train, Mr. Montfort to wherever it was that he belonged. It was unlikely their paths would cross again.

And he knew her father. Not well, perhaps, but he knew him.

Quickly, before she could think better of it, Rachel set down her fork. "What can you tell me about my father?"

Mr. Montfort raised a brow.

"You say you know him. I'm unlikely to meet anyone else who does."
It was a disconcerting thought, but true. But for that clipping, she might
have gone her whole life never knowing, never guessing. "You have to admit,
anyone would be curious. In my circumstances."

"In your circumstances." Mr. Montfort stretched out his long legs,
those midnight eyes on Rachel's face, taking in her dowdy hat and tousled
hair. "Yes, I imagine one would be."

Rachel could feel the color rising in her cheeks. "I'm not after his money.
I just want——" What? To know who he was? Why he'd done what he'd
done? She reached for her bag. "Oh, never mind. It doesn't matter. And
I've a train to catch. How much do I owe you for the tea?"

"I'll send the bill to your cousin." Mr. Montfort's hand, on hers,
sent a momentary jolt of electricity through her. "As for your father . . .
Ardmore is held up as the perfect example of an English gentleman. A
lord to a lord and a man to a man."

There was an edge to his voice. Rachel paused in fussing with her purse,
looking sharply at him. "Do you not share that view?"

"You're here, aren't you?" The insult was delivered so casually that
it took Rachel a moment to feel the sting of it. "You wouldn't be quite
so shocking if Ardmore didn't have such a reputation as a pillar of
virtue."

"I could be an imposter."

Mr. Montfort assumed a meditative pose. "*I should think this a gull but that
the white-bearded fellow speaks it. Much Ado About Nothing.*"

"Yes, I know." Her father had read Shakespeare to her on winter
evenings. Back in the days when she had believed they were a family.

"In plain words," said Mr. Montfort, lounging back in his chair,
"David says it, ergo it must be true. He wouldn't lie."

The cake tasted like ash on Rachel's tongue. "Oh, wouldn't he?"

Mr. Montfort flicked ash from his cigarette. "We are most likely
cousins—in the twentieth degree or thereabouts. Your family and mine
came over with the Conqueror together and haven't stopped reminding
anyone since."

"In other words," said Rachel smartly, "hangers-on in the train of an opportunist."

"Baseborn, no less," said Mr. Montfort, and Rachel realized that she had, somehow, walked herself right into that. "But no one cares about a few marriage lines more or less once one has a crown on one's head."

Rachel poked violently at a walnut. "If I had wanted a history lesson, I would have applied to Cousin David. This is all very entertaining, but—"

"Your cousin David was my tutor," said Mr. Montfort, taking a leisurely sip of tea. "He's very sound on the twelfth century but somewhat wobbly when it comes to the Conquest."

"Oh?" said Rachel. The sudden shift to the neutral was a bit dizzying. "And are you also a don?"

Silly that there was something reassuring about that. Dons were just as prone to poor behavior as other mortals, but one tended to think of them as something akin to monks, closed into their cloisters, their minds on higher things. When they weren't swilling port in hall, that was.

Mr. Montfort leaned back in his chair. "The *hortus conclusus* of academe has been closed to me. These are degenerate times. Where once learning flourished, now *plus valet pecunia*."

"English, please," said Rachel. "I'm a nursery governess, not a scholar."

"I was once one of your cousin David's students. Now, for my sins, I have to get my own living. I write tittle tattle. For the *Daily Yell*." He brushed an invisible speck off his immaculate cuffs. "You'd be amazed at how lucrative a bit of libel can be."

A gossip columnist. That was what it translated to, in plain English. And Rachel had trotted meekly along like a lamb to slaughter.

Her hands tightened around her purse.

"No wonder you offered to take me to tea." Rachel did her best to keep her voice calm. Flinging a cup of tea in Mr. Montfort's face would only provide him more copy. "Lost daughter of earl confides in our columnist. . . . Full feature on page six?"

FIVE

How could she have been so gullible? He must have seen her coming, Rachel thought wrathfully.

She leaned forward, across the table. "Did Cousin David even ask you to give me a cup of tea? Or was this an investment in pursuit of a story?"

"I haven't sunk that low." Mr. Montfort took a quick pull on his cigarette, his dark brows drawing together. "I said I'd be deaf and dumb, didn't I? Your guilty secret is safe with me."

"My father's guilty secret, you mean." She had needled him; there was some comfort in that. "What reason do I have to trust you?"

"None," Mr. Montfort said equably. "I won't do you the injustice of asking you to take my word. Words are cheap. Let's just say that in this your interest and mine align."

"I don't see how." Rachel poked viciously at her cake. "You need a story. I am one."

"I'd sooner fish for carp in the corporation garbage dump," said Mr. Montfort bluntly. "It would create less stink."

"Stink for me. Not for you."

Nursery governess one day, scandal the next. What would this do to her hopes of employment? Rachel couldn't imagine most businesses would want to hire an earl's by-blow—made notorious in the popular press—to type their letters and file their invoices. They certainly wouldn't want one living in their homes and educating their children.

"My dear girl." Mr. Montfort leaned his well-tailored elbows against the table. "My job depends on my victims being willing. They like seeing themselves spread across the pages of the *Daily Yell*—provided the spread is largely favorable. I write about who wore what, who went where, and who might possibly be engaged to whom." He paused, lifting his teacup to his lips. "Groundbreaking stuff, I know."

"Your point being?"

Mr. Montfort sighed. "If it gets around that I'm exposing old scandals, no one will invite me anywhere. And if I'm not invited, I have no copy. It's as simple as that. Your cousin asked me to see you safely to the train. That's all."

Rachel looked at him through narrowed eyes. "I thought he asked you to give me a cup of tea."

"That as well," said Mr. Montfort easily.

She wasn't entirely sure she believed him. But if she didn't? There was little she could do about it. Mr. Montfort looked like a man who did what he pleased and bothered about the consequences later.

Part of her was tempted to tell him to publish and be damned. A lord to a lord, Mr. Montfort had called her father. The perfect example of an English gentleman. What would the world say if they knew he had a daughter tucked away in Norfolk?

For a moment, Rachel wallowed in the vengeful fantasy of newspaper headlines, black and screaming. *Earl's Abandoned Daughter Seeks Justice!*

But who would it hurt in the end? Not her father. Reality stared Rachel in the face, grim and uncompromising. Even if there was a scandal, he had his estates to retire to. He could wrap himself up in his wife's money. Oh, perhaps there would be an obligatory exile, a villa in Venice or an apartment in Paris, just until the scandal died down, but it wouldn't touch him, not really. An earl was an earl was an earl.

Mr. Montfort glanced casually at his watch. "I don't want to chivy you, but I'd best be getting on. I'm due at a house party this evening. Can I give you a lift anywhere? My motor is in the Clarendon Yard."

She might at least get a ride out of it. "If you could drop me at the station . . ."

Mr. Montfort scattered a few coins on the table. "I can do better than that. Where are you bound?"

"Norfolk." She had promised Alice she would join them for supper. What was she to tell Alice? "But you needn't bother."

Mr. Montfort ignored her. "I can't take you as far as that, but I can save you a change, at least. I can drop you at"—a moment of quick calculation—"Loughborough. That should take you direct to King's Lynn."

"That's very kind of you," Rachel said warily.

Mr. Montfort shrugged. "It's on my way."

The rain had lifted to a light mizzle, but the clouds were still heavy in the sky, creating an early dusk. Rachel followed Mr. Montfort blindly through the twisting byways of Oxford, so beautiful from a distance, so dark and narrow when one was in the middle.

If Alice were to find out— Something tightened in Rachel's chest. Alice was the doctor's wife, the vicar's daughter, respectability personified. How would Alice feel knowing that her daughter's godmother was nothing more than an earl's by-blow?

Alice would hug her and tell her it didn't matter, because Alice was like that. But it would matter. It was a small enough village. There would be whispers and mutterings, and all the people Rachel loved would be tainted by her shame.

Her shame. The phrase caught in Rachel's throat. As if she had done something shameful, when all she had done was be born to the wrong father. All these years, going to church on Sundays, working for good marks in school, working and working to send money home—all of that, now, gone for nothing.

While her father merrily draped his other daughter in diamonds.

"This is my bus." Rachel was so lost in her own thoughts, she nearly walked right into the door that Mr. Montfort held open for her. The car was black, with a bonnet that seemed to go on forever and bulbous lamps on either side.

Old habits died hard. Rachel found herself hesitating at the door, knowing what her mother would say about accepting a ride with a strange man. It didn't matter that he was Cousin David's friend; there was something unsettling about Mr. Montfort, an animal energy tamped down beneath a deceptively languid exterior.

But what did it matter, now? Rebelliously, Rachel clambered into the car, sinking down into the leather seat. If she was already damaged goods, she might at least get a comfortable ride out of it.

"There's a rug on the floor," said Mr. Montfort.

"I'm all right." She had her rage to keep her warm. "Where is it you say my father lives?"

Mr. Montfort slipped into the driver's seat. "Mostly in the country, at Carrisford." He pronounced it "Cafford." He closed the door and turned to face Rachel. "You're not thinking of trying to storm the castle, are you?"

"Why shouldn't I?" Had her father thought of them at all these past twenty-three years? Wondered about them? Or had he merely married his heiress and waltzed off on his merry way? "I don't see what I have to lose."

"A little more of your pride?" Mr. Montfort's voice was surprisingly gentle. More practically, he added, "You haven't much chance of admission. Unless you were to go as someone else. If my cousin, a Miss . . ." Mr. Montfort glanced out the window and suddenly grinned, a pirate's grin, all white teeth and red lips. "A Miss Merton were to appear in town . . . well, that would be another story."

Rachel had to raise her voice to be heard over the roar of the motor. "Wouldn't anyone know?"

Mr. Montfort considered the question, his elegant face in profile. "I have a great many cousins, most of them damnably dull. Add in a few removes, and why would anyone bother to untangle the family tree?" His fingers drummed against the steering wheel. "It's quite an amusing idea, really. If I were to pass a nobody off into society . . . it would be the stunt of all stunts. The elusive and sought-after Miss Merton—Miss Vera Merton. You have the cheekbones to be a Vera."

Absurd to feel flattered by that, but she did, just a little. Rachel could picture Vera Merton, with her long red nails, her bobbed hair, her general air of devil-may-care. Vera Merton wouldn't stay on the wrong side of the green baize door; she would breeze merrily past the butler, greeting everyone with a breathy "Darling!"

Vera Merton would quaff cocktails with Rachel's cousins; she would know them all by name, whisper intimately in their ears.

What would it be like to be that woman? Not earnest, hardworking Rachel Woodley—the Rachel Woodley who didn't really exist—but someone entirely different. Someone sophisticated. Someone hard-edged.

Someone who could approach her father on his own terms.

Mr. Montfort waved a dismissive hand. "The clothes and the hair are all wrong, of course—"

"What's wrong with my hair?" Rachel had always been rather vain about her hair, thick, dark, and so long she could nearly sit on it.

"Nursery governess hair," said Mr. Montfort succinctly.

Hair could be cut. "If I had the right hair and clothes . . ."

The force of her own longing was staggering, all the more so for being so unexpected. Like a newsreel, the same frayed images played over and over—a garden, in that house she so barely remembered. Her father, flinging her up into the air. Her own squeals of delight. The sunlight glinting off the rims of his glasses.

How many times had she imagined that scene? How many times had she dreamed of her father coming home?

"Why couldn't it work?" Rachel twisted on the seat, lifting a hand to screen her eyes from the glare of the lamps. "You said it yourself. It would be the stunt of all stunts."

"I wasn't serious." The car slowed as they approached a light. "It's only a stunt if someone knows I've done it."

"You would know you'd done it." She wanted this, more than she'd ever wanted anything. Urgency made Rachel reckless. "Think of the power of it, fooling everyone like that."

Mr. Montfort frowned at her. "You would need a place to stay."

"A bedsit—"

"In the wrong part of town? No." Before Rachel could respond, he said slowly, half to himself, "There is my mother's flat. She's always having cousins to stay."

"Wouldn't she mind?"

"She's in America at the moment. In New York." Mr. Montfort kept his eyes on the road, one hand relaxed on the wheel. "I could have the whole of the Ballets Russes to stay and she wouldn't raise a brow—she might rather like that, actually."

"I wouldn't want to put you out."

"We wouldn't be sharing a washbasin. I have my own bachelor quarters in Piccadilly. It's perfectly respectable." His gaze flicked sideways, toward Rachel. "You would need a good story as to why no one had heard of you before."

"I've been in France . . . with an invalid mother." In the car, in the gathering dusk, Rachel could almost believe that this might be possible, brick by brick, lie by lie. She could feel her excitement rising with the roar of the engine, the thrum of the wheels against the road. "At an obscure watering place."

"That would," said Mr. Montfort, moving smoothly around a dawdling Morris, "explain your lack of worldliness."

"I'm not unworldly," Rachel protested.

She'd seen the world. Admittedly, she'd seen it in snippets, from odd angles: when she brought the children down to curtsy to their parents, through the gossip in the servants' hall, from the top of the stairs as guests swirled in below, jewels sparkling, hair coiffed. Peering through the banisters with the children had provided an excellent view of the top of a great many heads.

"There are worlds," said Mr. Montfort, "and there are worlds. This particular world is a very small one. It has its own rules, its own language."

"Are you afraid I would embarrass you? I know which fork to use."

"You haven't the slightest idea, have you?" He was not referring to forks. He swung the car smoothly to one side, down a lane where the hedgerows crowded thickly on either side of the car. "No. As much as I enjoy putting the cat among the pigeons, I do draw the line at cruelty to kittens."

"Don't be ridiculous." Unlike her sister, the lovely Lady Olivia, Rachel was no pampered debutante. She'd been making her own way since she came of age. And, at the moment, she was feeling particularly fierce. "I'm twenty-seven—nearly twenty-eight. I cut my claws years ago."

The lane had broadened ahead of them. Mr. Montfort pressed down on the accelerator, making the great car swoop forward.

Rachel grabbed for the edge of the seat.

Mr. Montfort pitched his cigarette neatly out the window. "Not among this set, you haven't . . . Vera."

"That was a cheap trick."

"Life is a cheap trick. Hadn't you realized?"

"Not until today." She had always believed that if one worked hard, if one did unto others and put money in the collection plate, the universe would respond accordingly. That was what her mother had taught her, and Rachel had never seen any reason to doubt her. If they didn't have much, they still had more than many. And they had each other.

Rachel felt rebelliousness boil up within her, raging like the workings of the car's engine. Her mother had lied; Cousin David had lied; it wasn't fair, any of it.

"If you won't help me, will you at least promise not to expose me?"

Something in her voice, an edge of desperation, perhaps, caught her companion's attention. The great car slowed, then stopped. Mr. Montfort turned in his seat, his eyes on her face. "You're determined, aren't you?"

Rachel nodded, wordlessly. She didn't trust herself to speak.

For a long moment, they sat frozen in tableau, Mr. Montfort's eyes, dark and inscrutable, studying her, so intently that Rachel found she was holding her breath, her chest tight with the effort. Around them, the world was dark and still, the only sounds a lamb bleating in the darkness, a bird trilling in a tree.

With an abrupt nod, Mr. Montfort put the car into gear. "All right. I'll help you. But for my own reasons. Not yours."

His eyes were focused on the road; all Rachel could see was his profile, the long line of his jaw, the tense set of his shoulders. Instantly suspicious, she asked, "What reasons?"

He gave a brief, humorless laugh. "Nothing like that."

Rachel sat up a little straighter. "I didn't think—"

"Didn't you? You ought." Mr. Montfort cast her a quick sideways look that made the color rise in Rachel's cheeks. Before Rachel could think of anything to say, he added, more prosaically, "My column grows dull. The same old names, week after week. You'll make a change. The lovely and elusive Miss Vera Merton—"

"Not too elusive," said Rachel smartly. "I need that invitation to—"

"Caffers," said Mr. Montfort. "Short for Carrisford Court. Ancient seat of the Earls of Ardmore. The house in Eaton Square is Ardmore House. Ardles for short."

The names rolled off his tongue like an incantation. Uneasily, Rachel glanced at the man sitting beside her in the car. She knew nothing of him, not really. Only that he had once been Cousin David's student. Or so he said.

But one thing was clear: he knew her father's world. He spoke its language.

"I'll square it about the flat," said Mr. Montfort, as casually as though he were ordering tea. "And see about your wardrobe."

Rachel turned in her seat to look at him, the lights playing off the planes of his face. "You're going to a great deal of trouble."

"If it were trouble, I wouldn't do it." His voice was clipped, brisk, a warning not to inquire further. With a deliberate effort at urbanity, he said, "Isn't there an expression about gift horses?"

Yes, but when one was advised not to look them in the mouth, it was generally because something was wrong with them.

Rachel glanced sideways at Mr. Montfort. His long, lean form was sprawled comfortably in his seat, his mobile mouth relaxed, but his hands, tense on the steering wheel, told a different story. *My reasons*, he had said. *Not yours.*

Rain silvered the windows, making the landscape beyond shiver and shimmer, curiously insubstantial, the world seen through a soap bubble.

How dreadful could it be? He was hardly going to sell her into white slavery, Rachel mocked herself. That was straight out of the world of penny dreadfuls. Mr. Montfort was offering her a place to stay, a wardrobe, an entrée into her father's world. She would be mad to refuse.

Whatever his reasons.

Rachel straightened her shoulders. "What do I need to do first?"

SIX

The salon at which Mr. Montfort made Rachel an appointment was in King's Lynn, on a side street. The windows were dingy, the brave gold paint of the lettering flaking off in large chunks. The bright spring sunshine was merciless, ruthlessly revealing every inch of peeling paint, every streak of soap scum on the windows.

The place had a downtrodden air about it, the sort of establishment patronized by shopgirls hoping to look like what's-'er-name from the talkies.

That was part of the plan, wasn't it? Rachel reminded herself. She wasn't meant to be seen anywhere she might be recognized until she'd made her transformation. No one in this sad little shop would think to connect Miss Woodley, in her worn hat, with the glamorous Miss Vera Merton, darling of the London gossip sheets.

Presuming that Simon Montfort made good on his promises. It had been nearly ten days since that wet afternoon in Oxford. What had seemed entirely reasonable in Mr. Montfort's motor, with the engine a soft thrum in the background and the lamps glittering on the raindrops, seemed distinctly less plausible on a bright May morning.

Rachel couldn't let herself think about that. Forge forward, that was the order of the day. She'd begun the grim task of sorting her mother's clothes into boxes and bundles, searching for a clue, any clue, anywhere, as to her mother's secret past. It didn't exist. Aside from that one telling *Tatler* clipping, her mother's belongings were exactly what they should be, the workaday attire of a genteel widow fallen on hard times.

She hadn't told Alice what she'd meant to do. Instead, Rachel had told her she'd scrounged up the money for that typing course, in London. Alice, run off her feet with Annabelle and Charles and the various demands of Jim's patients, hadn't inquired too closely, for which, Rachel told herself, she was grateful. She was.

"Miss Woodley." A long gray shadow unfolded itself from the wall beside the window. "Prompt on your hour, I see."

"Mr. Montfort." Sun-blinded, she hadn't seen him there. Rachel frowned into the brightness, which created a nimbus around his dark head, casting his features into shadow. "I didn't expect to see you here."

That wasn't part of the plan. They weren't to have any contact until Miss Vera Merton came breezing into London. It was safer that way. They'd agreed.

Mr. Montfort proffered a large square package. "I'd thought you might rather this not show up at your humble cottage. And you can hardly appear in Mayfair wearing that."

He gestured languidly toward Rachel's good suit, the same suit she'd worn to Oxford, far too warm for a May day that had delusions of being summer.

Rachel's hands were busy with the strings on the box. Inside was a silk crepe dress, an impractical white with navy blue accents, with a handkerchief collar and box pleats on the skirt. The fabric felt slippery and rich beneath her gloved fingers. Beneath it, pristinely wrapped in tissue paper, were matching gloves, bag, and a narrow, close-fitting hat, with a jaunty bow on one side.

It was an ensemble straight out of the fashion papers, the sort of thing the guests at the homes where she had worked might have worn.

While Rachel stared, Mr. Montfort added off-handedly, "The rest of your wardrobe is waiting at the flat."

The rest of her wardrobe? He'd said something about seeing to her wardrobe, but she'd never imagined anything like this. There was something surprisingly intimate about it, the fabric that would drape her body, the hat designed to nestle close around her head. Intimate and a little disquieting.

Rachel bundled the clothes back into the box. "You are a very thorough Pygmalion, aren't you?"

Mr. Montfort grimaced. "I have always thought there must be something rather lacking about a man who finds it necessary to chisel his mate from marble. I'm not in the market for a Galatea. This is a business arrangement, nothing more."

Rachel juggled the heavy box. "And if our venture goes belly-up?"

Mr. Montfort plucked the box from her, tucking it effortlessly beneath his arm. "Vera Merton will disappear back into the woodwork and poor, honest Rachel Woodley will return—with a decent haircut and some proper clothes."

Which reminded Rachel. "About those clothes. You must let me know how much—"

"They're hand-me-downs," said Mr. Montfort. When she started to protest, he added, "And quite above your touch."

Well, that put her in her place. "From your mistress, I suppose," Rachel said tartly.

"My sister."

Caught unawares, Rachel gaped.

Mr. Montfort laughed. The expression made his entire face lighten. "What? Did you think I leapt from Minerva's head full blown? My sister is the child of my mother's"—he paused to count on his fingers—"fourth marriage. Her father is an American copper baron. Filthy rich. She won't miss the frocks."

"Won't she notice?" Rachel was reminded of Goldilocks, creeping into the bears' home, eating their porridge, sleeping on their beds. Or, in this case, wearing their frocks.

"That, my dear, is one of the first things we need to work on. You must learn to stifle these virtuous, bourgeois impulses. What's a frock more or less?"

"Or three dozen," interpolated Rachel.

"Or three dozen," said Mr. Montfort equitably. "You, until now, have belonged to the class of people who only buy what they can pay for. I imagine, for example, you wouldn't take a taxi if you didn't have the fare."

"Of course not."

"If this illusion is to be convincing, we need to train you out of your middle-class habits." Mr. Montfort swept one arm in the direction of the hairdresser. "Chop off your locks and your inhibitions."

Rachel cast him a withering look. "I don't think the one necessarily leads to the other."

"Crushed," drawled Mr. Montfort. "Let's try it and see, shall we?"

He held open the door of the salon with a flourish.

There was something terribly lulling about Mr. Montfort's calculated rudeness, about the mockery he made of the normal rules of behavior. Like a court jester, constantly mumming. But she'd be a fool, Rachel thought soberly, to let herself be taken in by that. Beneath the banter lay something else entirely, something dark and dangerous and disconcertingly serious.

And she was, by her own choosing, placing herself in his power.

"Of course," said Mr. Montfort blandly, "if you would rather just go home . . ."

Home. Home to Netherwell, where her belongings were sorted into stacks. After that, the alluring prospect of a cold-water flat, with a meter for electricity and a loo down the hall, shared with a half dozen other industrious souls, bickering over who had used whose cake of soap. Cabbage smells from the kitchen and stale biscuits for tea.

"Don't get your hopes up," said Rachel, and swept past him into the salon. "I mean to see this through."

The hairdresser was swift. Hanks of hair fell around her. Rapunzel hair, long ropes of it. The hairdresser lifted the cloth from her shoulders, using a soft-bristled brush to sweep the last strands of hair from her back.

Rachel's head felt strange, the back of her neck naked. She couldn't help glancing at the hair on the floor, years and years of it, gone in an instant.

Dropping his paper on the bench, Mr. Montfort strolled over to her. She'd half expected him to leave, his box and message delivered, but he'd stayed, one shoulder propped against the wall, keeping up a running patter of sardonic commentary on the day's headlines as the hairdresser did arcane things to the back of Rachel's head.

"Cheer up," came Mr. Montfort's voice from behind her. "You've hardly sold away your soul."

"No, just my hair." The hairdresser swirled the chair around, holding up a mirror so that Rachel could see.

Mr. Montfort was right; the short cut did highlight her cheekbones. *You have the cheekbones to be a Vera.*

Rachel didn't know who the woman in the mirror was, but she rather liked her.

She looked up at Mr. Montfort, who stood, frowning down at her.

"Well? What do you think?" Rachel demanded cheekily.

"You'll do," he said curtly.

Rachel gave her head an experimental shake, enjoying the way her hair swished across her jawline, the lightness, the freedom of it. "Keep paying me compliments like that and my head will be too big for my hat."

Mr. Montfort didn't take the bait. He bundled his paper up under his arm. "How soon can you come up to town?"

Rachel scrambled down out of the chair. A business relationship, he had said. He was certainly all business now. She hurried after him, toward the door. "I need another week to get my affairs in order." A week to transfer her old life into boxes and bags. "You seem very keen all of a sudden."

Keen wasn't quite the right word. More like a man hurrying to the dentist for a tooth extraction. It was hardly, thought Rachel wryly, a flattering comparison.

But, then, she couldn't blame him, could she? It was his reputation as well as hers on the line. If it came out that he'd tried to pass off a nobody and failed . . . he'd have to endure a great deal of ribbing, at the very least.

Could he lose his job at the paper over it? Rachel wasn't sure.

Mr. Montfort shrugged. "I don't like letting I dare not wait upon I would. Unless . . . you're getting cold feet?"

"Only from standing here." Resolutely, Rachel took the large box from him, squinting into the sunlight. If it were done, it was best done quickly. "Shall we say a week Thursday?"

❧

"This the place, love?" The taxi driver pulled up by a modern block of flats on South Audley Street.

"Yes, thank you."

Rachel dropped the right number of coins into the cabbie's waiting hand and emerged from the taxi, her French heels clicking against the pavement, her pleated skirt swishing just so against her knees. In the sunlight, she could see herself reflected in the window of the florist's shop opposite, a walking fashion plate from her blue hat down to the matching heels. Her silk stockings—real silk, not rayon—were decadently slippery against her legs.

There was a porter encased in a glass box. Rachel started in his direction—she had her speech memorized—but before she could reach him, Mr. Montfort emerged from the vestibule.

"Cousin Vera!" He pecked Rachel on both cheeks with the awkward earnestness of a long-lost cousin. "I trust you had a safe journey?" In an undertone, for her ears only, he added, "If you gawk like that, they'll know you for a fraud before you open your mouth."

"*Dearest* Cousin Simon." Rachel rose on her toes and pressed her crimson lips to his cheek, leaving a defiant smear of red. The lipstick hadn't been a part of Mr. Montfort's package. That she'd added herself, courtesy of Woolworth. "You *are* a pet to meet little me."

Mr. Montfort squeezed her waist. "When the mater demands . . . Hullo, Simms. Do you think you might give us a bit of a hand with the trunks?"

"I'll have them sent right up, sir."

Pausing, Mr. Montfort turned back, waving a hand at Rachel. "Oh, and this is my cousin, Miss Merton. She'll be staying at the flat." To Rachel, he added, "You don't want to get on the wrong side of Simms, my dear. He knows where all the bodies are buried."

Simms smiled indulgently. "Don't mind Mr. Montfort, miss. He will have his little joke." He touched a hand to his cap. "I trust you will have a pleasant stay."

"Yes, thank you, Simms. I am sure I shall." She sounded like a schoolgirl, too prim and polite.

Rachel avoided Simon's eyes, concentrating on not tripping in her unaccustomed heels. A dress rehearsal, she told herself. A bad dress meant a good first performance.

"If you will allow me?" Mr. Montfort possessed himself of Rachel's arm, steadying her.

"Thank you," Rachel murmured as he led her to the lift. This had seemed much easier in theory than in practice. In the taxi, in her fashionable frock, she'd felt so sure of herself. But it was one thing to look the part, and another to be it. It was a self-operated lift. The doors closed behind them, leaving them entirely alone.

The bread and cheese she'd gobbled down on the train turned over in Rachel's stomach; her hands felt slick inside her expensive gloves. She missed the weight of her hair, the solid bulk of it at the back of her head, anchoring her.

Leaning over, Mr. Montfort murmured, "There's no need to look quite so Sabine, darling. I'm hardly going to ravish you in the lift."

Rachel snatched back her arm, managing an uneven laugh. "I'm merely reeling from your cologne."

"Guaranteed to make the ladies swoon," said Mr. Montfort smoothly, "or so the advert would have us believe. Would you like to provide a testimonial? *It made me go all weak at the knees,* says society beauty Miss Vera Merton. . . ."

"Yes, like the Thames on a hot day." The bread and cheese settled back into Rachel's stomach; the sense of blind panic lifted. There was something oddly steadying about Mr. Montfort's nonsense.

"They've done wonderful work cleaning up the Thames." The lift doors opened, depositing them on a landing with four doors. Mr. Montfort gestured Rachel to the door on the far right.

"I still wouldn't want to swim in it," retorted Rachel.

There were two locks on the door, shining and new.

Mr. Montfort slid a key into the first lock. "Better not," he agreed blandly. "Those are deep waters. With swiftly moving currents. Unless you're a stronger swimmer than you look?"

The second lock shot free and the door swung open.

"I can keep my head above water," said Rachel, and strode across the threshold. She was so busy making a point—and trying to balance on her heels—that she was several yards in before she looked, really looked, at the flat that was to be her home for the next month. "Good heavens."

"Like it?" Mr. Montfort leaned comfortably in his favorite pose, propped against the wall, pleased by her reaction.

"I'm blinded." Sun slanted through the long windows, glittering off a glass-topped chrome-legged table. A sofa of dazzling whiteness sprawled beneath a Venetian glass mirror that looked as though it had been squeezed into shape by a crazed geometer, all unexpected angles.

Rachel had thought she was accustomed to the whimsy of the wealthy. The Brillac town house in Paris had dazzled with gilded walls and ormolu embellishments and enough mirrors to put Louis XIV to shame.

But this—this was something different.

Nothing in the room, Rachel realized, was quite what it seemed. The wall began in shades of navy blue at the base, but lightened nearly to white by the time it touched the ceiling, all shading so seamlessly together that it took one a moment to realize that the color changed every time one looked at it. The effect made Rachel's eyes ache. And that was only the start of it. The doors of a respectable-looking eighteenth-century chinoiserie cabinet were propped open to reveal a hidden bar, boasting a daunting array of cocktail implements, sleek in silver. A gramophone horn peeped coyly out of a Louis XIV commode, while Chinese vases of impossible antiquity shared space with elongated figures cast in porcelain.

It was all designed to make one look and look again, a vast visual tease.

Cautiously, Rachel ventured onto the white carpet. "Will it crack if I set my bag down?" she said, indicating the glass-topped table.

"Don't be provincial," said Mr. Montfort, and tossed it down for her.

"I don't want to risk seven years' bad luck."

"That's only mirrors, not tables." He made his way unerringly to the chinoiserie cabinet that housed the impromptu bar. "What will you have?"

She'd had the odd bit of sherry over the years, but cocktails were a mystery. "You choose."

"How very trusting of you."

"Hardly. If you'd meant to ravish me you would have done so already." The words were out of her mouth before Rachel could reconsider them. Frankness had always been her besetting sin. One of them, at any rate.

Gin bottle in hand, Mr. Montfort raised a brow. "Perhaps I was merely waiting until I had you in my lair."

"And muss the white carpet?"

"That's what the maid is for. She scrubs up after all my orgies. Lovely woman." Mr. Montfort was busily pouring potions from glass bottles into a silver shaker. "A little Jeyes Fluid, and, voilà! Virtue restored."

"So long as there's no Jeyes Fluid in my drink." Whatever he was pouring certainly smelled astringent enough.

"We haven't quite been reduced to that. Unlike the States, where they'll quaff rubbing alcohol if you pour it into the right sort of glass and mix it with bitters." Glass and silver tinkled. "I believe you'll find this reasonably potent."

His smile as he held out the drink was so natural, so friendly, that Rachel found herself, for a moment, wobbly on her unaccustomed heels, the world out of balance.

Rachel's fingers closed around the cold glass, the outside already slick with condensation, and Mr. Montfort turned away again, back to the bar, and the world settled back into place. It was the slanting shape of the mirrors, the shifting colors of the wall, Rachel told herself; they were enough to make anyone dizzy. There was no point in letting herself be so undone by a momentary show of—what? Ordinary kindness?

Mr. Montfort was many things, but she doubted he was kind. She'd do best to remember that.

They were business partners, that was all.

If he'd noticed her momentary confusion, Mr. Montfort made no sign. He was busy mixing another drink, dashing in a bit of this and a bit of that with a practiced hand. All the same, clasping her hands behind her back, Rachel made a show of examining the paintings on the walls, striving for a sophistication she was far from feeling.

Most of the paintings were modern, abstract to the point of incoherence. All except for the portrait dominating one wall. It featured a woman in the costume of the turn of the century, her hair piled high on her head, her neck impossibly long. Her arms curved around a child in a white lace smock, his head an angelic mass of curls.

On the face, it was a sweet domestic portrait. But when one looked closer, Rachel thought she could see a familiar glint of mischief in the moppet's dark eyes. Black eyes, eyes so dark one couldn't detect the difference between iris and pupil.

"How too precious." Rachel masked her nervousness with mockery. "Was that you?"

"Was and is." Mr. Montfort poured out his drink with a professional twist of the wrist. "Minus the curls, of course."

"And that is your mother?" The picture was too stylized to provide a good sense of likeness, but there was something very like Mr. Montfort about the cheeks and chin. It was a striking face, but not necessarily a restful one.

"Brilliantly spotted," drawled Mr. Montfort. He dropped a cherry into Rachel's drink. "Most beautiful debutante of her generation and international scandal."

Rachel lifted her drink, sniffing it warily. "We have that in common, then. Scandalous mothers."

"Mine married them. One after the other." Before Rachel could decide whether or not to take offense, Mr. Montfort nodded to her drink. "Are you going to drink it or merely admire it?"

Rachel looked doubtfully at the murky liquid, the cherry bobbing in the midst. "What is it?"

Mr. Montfort raised his brows, his expression a dare. "A Montfort Original, of course."

Was this a test? The glass was slippery in Rachel's hands. Or maybe it was her hands that were slippery. She played for time. "Original sin?"

Mr. Montfort downed half his drink, his expression abstracted. "No sin is original, no matter what the Bright Young Things may hope. We're all merely playing to a theme."

Rachel narrowed her eyes at him. "How unambitious of you."

His attention recalled to her, Mr. Montfort's lips lifted in an unexpected smile. He saluted her with his cocktail glass. "You have put me in my place."

Rachel sat gingerly on the white sofa. "It's my training as a nursery governess. You are nothing compared to Albertine, Amelie, and Anne-Marie."

"I am reduced to my proper place, among the infantry." The cushions creaked as Mr. Montfort joined her, his long legs seeming to take up half the space in the room. "It's not a bad analogy, though. You won't go wrong if you think of the set to which I am about to introduce you as members of a nursery party. They enjoy making mud pies and can generally be soothed by sucking on a bottle. They are also," he added, "impossibly young. You'll be on the geriatric side, but I imagine we can smooth that over."

"I shall endeavor to keep my old bones from creaking too audibly," said Rachel.

"You seem to keep the gray at bay." Mr. Montfort leaned forward, curling a stray lock of hair behind her ear.

The gesture was entirely natural, unstudied, but Rachel froze all the same.

Mr. Montfort looked down at her, close to her, but not touching. "We're cousins, remember?"

She could feel the deep murmur of his voice straight through to her bones.

Nervously, Rachel moved back, tucking the same strand of hair back behind her ear. "I'd thought we were distant cousins."

"As in opposite ends of the couch?" The mocking note was back. Mr. Montfort leaned back, against the far cushion. "Is that distant enough to suit you?"

Rachel felt, obscurely, annoyed at both herself and him. At herself, for the loss of a closeness she knew was only illusory, and at him for putting her in this position in the first place.

"Yes, thank you," she said primly.

In his most obnoxious society drawl, Mr. Montfort said, "You have been in France all this time, after all. The last time I saw you . . . you were a mere ankle biter with skinny legs and big bows on your braids. Just think of my astonishment at seeing you all grown up!"

"And think of my astonishment," retorted Rachel, "at seeing you so sadly reduced to writing sensational pieces for the papers!"

Mr. Montfort grinned at her. "Now, now, play nicely. You ought to be grateful for my miserable column; it's the reason you're here."

Rachel crossed her legs at the ankle. "A business venture."

"Precisely." He watched her from beneath lowered lids. "If we're to pull this off, you ought to call me Simon. If you can do so without doing violence to your principles."

"I believe I can manage." What a fool she was. It was all playacting. That touch on her cheek had been nothing more, just part of the game. Cousinly closeness. "I'm hardly so Victorian as that."

Mr. Montfort—Simon—retrieved a torn piece of newspaper from beneath his jacket and set it down in front of Rachel. He had folded it so that the caption was hidden. "Do you recognize him?"

The man in the picture wore riding kit, his face blurry beneath the overhang of his helmet, the features rendered even more anonymous by the strap under his chin. There was a champagne bottle in one hand; the other held the bridle of a horse. A woman, a fashionable one, with a fur wrap so large it appeared to be eating her chin, simpered from the side of the picture.

Rachel shook her head. "No. Should I?"

Simon cast her a look of mingled amusement and reproach. "You ought. This is your brother, Viscount Summerton. Better known as Jicksy."

She had a brother? It shouldn't have come as such a shock, but it did. She'd known her father had another daughter, a daughter in silk and pearls, a daughter with an honorific before her name. But she'd never stopped to think that there might be others.

Rachel's hand tightened in her lap, to stop herself from grabbing for the paper. "Half-brother."

"As you will." Mr. Montfort—Simon—shook out the paper, so that she could see the full picture, with the caption beneath. "He's currently up at Oxford. In theory, at any event. He spends more time in London than at Christ Church. He makes excellent copy. He can usually be found smashing motor cars against telegraph poles and pinching policemen's helmets. Often at the same time."

This was what her father had left them for. "He sounds a paragon."

"He's a cliché," said Simon dismissively. "His exploits wouldn't raise nearly as many eyebrows if Ardmore didn't have such a reputation as a pillar of virtue."

The irony of that wasn't lost on Rachel. She cleared her throat, saying, with difficulty, "Why Jicksy? That can't possibly be his real name."

"Something dating back to the nursery, no doubt. You'll have to get used to it. It's all part of the argot. Someone," said Simon lazily, "ought to compile a dictionary. Mayfair to English, Commoners, for the Instruction Of."

Was the change of subject for Rachel's benefit, to give her time to compose herself? Before she could stop herself, she asked, "Does my sister have a nickname, too?"

"No." Simon tossed the paper to one side.

Rachel might have let it go at that, but the image of the *Tatler* clipping haunted her still, her father's other daughter, poised and groomed on his arm. "What ought I know about Lady Olivia?"

Simon took a long swig of his drink. "Lady Olivia recently announced her engagement to a rising young Tory MP. He's only a baronet's son, but they say he'll go far. Everyone agrees that it will be the wedding of the year—if they ever set a date."

"How lovely for them." Happily ever afters all around. It shouldn't have hurt, but it did. Rachel asked fiercely, "Are there others? Other children?"

"Only one. That I know of."

It took Rachel a moment for the penny to drop. "Me?"

Simon raised his glass to her. "Who else?"

Who else, indeed? Rachel took a tentative sip of her own drink, sweet on the surface, but with a burn beneath. For all she knew, her father might have a dozen bastards tucked away in the countryside, littered around little hamlets like Netherwell. What made her think she was unique? Just her own muddled memories of warm arms around her, tucking her battered stuffed rabbit in next to her in bed, lips brushing her hair.

She blinked away sudden, unexpected tears. "I'm sorry, you were saying something?"

"Just sound and fury, signifying nothing." Simon gave her a long assessing look. "We don't have to go through with this, you know."

"And waste all this?" Rachel gave her pleated skirt a shake. "No. I'm ready. Really, I am." She was painfully aware of just how unconvincing she sounded. "Well? Do we have a plan?"

"We?" Simon didn't stint on the sarcasm, but he didn't, as Rachel half expected, try to argue her out of it. "Assuming that Jicksy doesn't drink himself into an early grave before the third of August, the earl and countess will be rolling out the red carpet, laying in the champagne, and hauling half of London out to Caffers for the official celebration of Jicksy's twenty-first. An heir," he added, "is an heir, is an heir, no matter how much of a wastrel he might be. And the countess does like putting on a good show for the tenantry."

Rachel shifted on the couch, the cushions too soft, too deep. "What has that to do with me?"

Simon's eyes were very black and very blank. "If we're to pull this off, we need to secure you an invitation to Jicksy's twenty-first."

"The third of August is two months away," Rachel protested. "Don't tell me you want to be lumbered with me for that long."

"Little enough time to establish your bona fides." Simon twisted his glass, studying the effect of the light on the liquid. "It is a large enough event that a Miss Vera Merton might slip by. Provided you make the right friends between now and then."

Rachel smelled a rat, although she wasn't sure why. Maybe it was something in the fixed way Simon was regarding his glass.

Or maybe it was just that every fiber of her being revolted against the idea of joining in the celebrations for her father's son by another woman. All hail the legitimate heir!

Rachel set her own glass down on the table with a decided clink. "But—"

Simon kept going as though she'd never spoken, raising his voice to be heard over her. "There is every chance we'll stumble across your brother, sooner rather than later—he runs with the fast and the fashionable. Although it might be more apt to say that he staggers along with the fast and the fashionable."

Rachel's stomach was twisting itself into knots. She didn't give a damn about her brother, except as a means to an end. "Is that the plan, then? Do I make friends with—with Jicksy, in the hopes of an invitation to his twenty-first?"

"Make friends. How sweetly you put it. No. Leaving aside the slight matter of incest—" Simon raised his voice to be heard over her exclamation of disgust. "—as I was saying, leaving aside the matter of incest, your brother doesn't consort with nice women, and the sort of women with whom he does consort would never be invited home."

"The fast and the fashionable?"

"There's fast and there's fast. We need to establish you as one of the latter. Fast enough to be interesting, respectable enough to be received. It isn't your brother's affections you need to win." Simon took a long swig of his own drink, draining the glass as though it were water, not gin and goodness only knew what. "It's your sister's. Jicksy's friends aren't received at Caffers. Lady Olivia's are."

Of course. Lady Olivia. The favored child. Rachel could see her, demure in smudged newsprint, as dainty as a Dresden shepherdess on her father's arm.

Rachel took a quick shot of her drink, just managing not to choke on it. "Is Lady Olivia one of the fast and fashionable, then?"

"No," said Simon succinctly. "Lady Olivia is all that is good and pure, *sans peur et sans reproche*."

Rachel felt a wave of irrational dislike. "In that case, how—"

"*But*," said Simon, raising his voice over Rachel's, "she does have a cousin who is. Fast and fashionable, that is. Cecelia Heatherington-Vaughn. Cece is the brightest of the Bright Young Things. No party is complete without her, no bacchanal sufficiently bacchanalian. We can't get you to Olivia, but we can get you to Cece."

This was all beginning to seem increasingly tenuous. "If Cece is so wild, why would the virtuous Olivia pay her any mind?"

"For all her many sins—and they are impressive in scope—Cece is still received. Her mother, Lady Fanny, is one of those awe-inspiring society matrons whom no one likes to cross. Cece will provide the introduction to Lady Olivia. Befriend Lady Olivia . . . and the doors of Carrisford Court will be open to you."

"That easy?" said Rachel sarcastically.

"If it seems easy, you've already had too much of this." Simon rose gracefully from the sofa, taking his own empty glass with him. "You'll need a stunt."

"A what?"

"A stunt," said Simon, with painful patience. "Something to catch Cece's attention. And the attention of my readers."

She'd nearly forgotten about his column. Rachel set her drink down on the glass table. "Stunts weren't part of the agreement."

"This entire masquerade is a stunt," Simon said bluntly. He emptied the dregs in the shaker into his glass. "But not one we can use to catch the attention of Cece and her jaded little friends. You might try dancing top-less on a table—"

"Really, Simon—"

"How naturally you squawk my name!" Simon held up a hand. "Smooth your ruffled feathers, darling. It's already been done. No one would look twice."

Rachel wasn't sure whether she was meant to be reassured or insulted. "Would you like me to learn to juggle?" she asked tartly.

"Too crude." Simon discarded both glass and shaker at the bar. "You don't by any chance play the ukulele?"

"My education has been sadly lacking." Rachel half rose, but Simon gestured her back into her seat.

"Don't worry. We'll remedy that." Neatly, Simon scooped his hat off the table by the door, setting it jauntily on his head. "Think on it. I'll call for you at nine."

Rachel blinked, trying to regain control of the conversation. "Tomorrow?"

"Tonight." Her evil genius didn't wait for her to rise. He let himself out, pausing only to issue one last instruction. "Wear something decadent."

SEVEN

It was nearer ten than nine when Simon rang the bell of the flat.
Rachel grabbed up the beaded bag that went with her gown and
stalked to the door, ready with a series of choice comments about punctuality, the virtues thereof.

But the Simon in the doorway was a different Simon from the one who
had sprawled on the white couch four hours ago. He wore his evening dress
as one born to it. Nothing off the peg for Simon Montfort. His wardrobe
bore the indefinable hallmark of a West End tailor, the pants and jacket
perfectly tailored to his long frame. His cuff links were mother-of-pearl,
as glittering and enigmatic as his eyes.

For a moment, Rachel felt as that long ago beggar maid must, when
King Cophetua came along and swept her up willy-nilly: oppressed by the
vast gulf between them and painfully aware of her own inadequacies.

Oh, for heaven's sake. However well tailored, it was just a suit. She might
be a by-blow, but he was a gossip columnist, singing other people's secrets
for his supper. King Cophetua didn't come into it.

"You're late," said Rachel, but it lacked the bite she'd intended.

Simon looked Rachel up and down from her French heels to the gold filigree band that spanned her forehead.

"You took me at my word," he said.

"About—oh, right." *Something decadent.* Flustered, Rachel snatched up the matching wrap, an illusory nod to modesty; the fabric was as sheer as the dress. "You supplied the wardrobe."

And quite a wardrobe it was. It must be nice to have a copper baron for a father. The clothes in the great white wardrobe in Simon's sister's bedroom might be a season old, but there wasn't a one that didn't shout Paris-made. Rachel had hesitated at first. All the money in her bankbook wouldn't cover the cost of a torn flounce on one of those dresses.

But Simon had said to make herself free of them, hadn't he? So, in the end, she'd succumbed to sheer lust and chosen a dress of flame-colored chiffon, glittering with a subtle pattern of beads on the bodice, the skirt falling in uneven layers around her legs.

Wearing it, she felt like a Vera, like a woman of the world, the sort of woman who went out at ten at night, who drank and danced, without another care in the world.

And from the look in Simon's eyes, he clearly agreed.

"Credit given where due?" Simon put a hand on her back to lead her into the lift, the conventional gesture rendered fraught by the unusual sensation of skin on skin. The dress plunged in a deep V, baring Rachel's back nearly to the waist. "One can only work with the material one is given."

Simon's breath ruffled the short hair by her ear. Rachel could smell spirits on his breath. Brandy, perhaps? She didn't know enough to tell.

Rachel chose her steps carefully. The matching heels were higher than she was accustomed to and at least half a size too large. She had tried to cinch them in by tightening the straps, but it was a precarious arrangement at best. "I thought you had no interest in playing Pygmalion."

"Not in molding marble." Simon's fingers stroked her bare back in a barely perceptible caress. And then poked. Hard.

Rachel jerked back. "Ouch! What was that in aid of?"

"Your posture. It's far too good. Slouch a little. You look as though you're about to have tea at the vicarage."

"Not in this dress."

"That depends on the vicar. Ah, Simms!" Simon raised a lazy hand to the porter, effectively cutting off any rejoinder. "My taxi is outside?"

"Right where you left it, sir."

With a long sidelong glance, Rachel followed Simon out into the June night. The breeze fluttered her chiffon draperies, the chill cutting through the thin fabric. The florist shop and chemist's across the street were both closed, the shutters drawn.

The taxi was, indeed, where Simon had left it, out front, the headlamps casting long shadows through the gloom.

The taxi driver had settled in for a smoke, and not his first judging by the butts in the street. Rachel mentally calculated the cost, all those cigarette butts translated to minutes, the minutes to pence and shillings. For a man who claimed to have to earn his living, Simon was remarkably free with his funds.

Bourgeois, Simon would call her. But she was bourgeois. Or, at least, she had been.

This was madness, wasn't it? Put the girl from Netherwell in a daring frock and she was still the girl from Netherwell. One word out of her mouth and they'd be sure to know, all of them, Sylvia and—

Only it wasn't Sylvia, was it? It was something else. Cecily—no, Cece. Oh, Lord. She'd failed and she hadn't even begun.

Rachel stumbled on her too-high shoes, and would have tripped, but for Simon's hand beneath her elbow.

As they climbed into the backseat, the taxi driver chucked his cigarette out the window, saying cheerfully, "Where next, sir?"

"Dean Street," said Simon briefly.

"Right-o," said the driver, and pulled away with a screech of wheels, past the shuttered shops and dark windows. The streetlights illuminated the odd person here and there, walking briskly, emerging from a cab, but for the most part the streets were quiet, the virtuous long since in bed.

"What's on Dean Street?" asked Rachel, pulling her wrap closer around her shoulders. The inside of the taxi felt stuffy and close, redolent of stale cigarettes. Or maybe that was Simon's jacket.

"The Gargoyle Club."

Simon slid a hand into his waistcoat. Paper crackled, but he passed over whatever it was in favor of a slim silver cigarette case. He tapped it against his hand, absently, before drawing out one of his Turkish cigarettes.

His face was turned away from Rachel, his profile illuminated by the shimmer of the streetlights through the window.

"Is that its name, or merely your opinion of the occupants?" Rachel pleated the edge of one of her chiffon flounces beneath her fingers.

The cousin's name was Cece. She was Vera. She'd been living in France. She wasn't to mention things like the cost of taxi fares.

"Its name," said Simon. There was a click, and a small flame flared to life between them, lighting the strong lines of his jaw. Relenting, he said, "It's a club in Soho, frequented by the artistic set. David Tennant founded it so he would have a place to dance with Hermione Baddeley."

Rachel seized on the bit of that she understood. "Is Miss Heatherington-Vaughn artistic?"

If she was, Rachel was in trouble. She didn't know the first thing about art, other than flower sketches and the sort of muddy watercolor de rigueur for young ladies.

Simon seemed to bring himself back from a great distance. "Not a whit. But it's fashionable to dabble around the fringes of bohemia. Everyone's painting a picture or writing a novel or sculpting little figurines."

"Let me guess," said Rachel, a little too loudly. "You're writing a novel."

Simon glanced down at her. "And stain these precious fingers with ink? I don't like getting my hands dirty."

"Fine words from a gossip columnist," Rachel taunted.

"Ah, but there's the difference. I expose the weaknesses of others. Not my own." For a moment, Rachel thought she saw something on his face, something raw and honest. But then he shrugged, saying glibly, "One can't write a novel without stripping one's soul. Really, when you think of it, the entire endeavor is quite indecent."

Rachel grabbed at her bag as the taxi rocked around a sharp corner. The lights were brighter here, the streets more populous. "That would depend on the soul in question, wouldn't it?"

"Pious screeds went out with the nineteenth century. Judging by the latest crop of romans à clef, most of today's souls are filthier than the window of your average taxi."

"Which you," pointed out Rachel, "are fouling with smoke."

"Oh, we're all complicit." Simon breathed out another trail of smoke. "The whole rotten lot of us. But if Rome is burning, why not light a cigarette in the flames?"

"I don't think the Romans had cigarettes," said Rachel perversely. "Isn't tobacco a product of the New World?"

"True, but immaterial. If they'd had them, they would have smoked them."

Rachel started to say something, stopped, and shook her head. She'd give Simon one thing: he'd cured her nerves. She couldn't be sure whether that was intentional or just Simon being Simon.

With Simon, Rachel was beginning to suspect, one couldn't ever be sure of anything.

"Talking to you," said Rachel ruefully, "is like tumbling through the looking glass. I always seem to lose my bearings."

"True north," said Simon. "If you count me mad north by northwest."

"No one," said Rachel sternly, "could make such a pretense of lunacy without being entirely sane."

"I shouldn't place too many wagers on that, but I'll grant you the general point. I'm no madder than anyone else I know, which isn't saying terribly much."

"We're all mad here?"

"You begin to understand." Pinching the cigarette neatly between his fingers, Simon tossed the butt out the window. "Ah. Here we are." Leaning forward, he tapped the cabbie on the shoulder.

"Here?" Rachel looked dubiously out the window. There was a cluster of women before the door with peroxide blond hair, crimson lips, and frocks that made Rachel's flame colored chiffon appear modest and retiring. The accents that wafted through the window of the cab were reminiscent of Shaw's Miss Doolittle. "Are those . . ."

"*Filles de joie?*" Abstracting himself from the cab, Simon held out a hand to Rachel. "Yes, although it's rather hard to tell the difference these days."

Rachel took his hand, let him help her out of the cab. His attitude might be languid, but his grip was strong. "Now who's being old-fashioned?"

Simon raised a brow. "Did I say I was complaining?"

Rachel glanced uncertainly back over her shoulder at the gaggle of women in the doorway, peacocking in their tawdry finery. She felt suddenly very aware of her own bare arms, legs, back. Wearing a dress she hadn't paid for.

She didn't feel fast and fashionable; she just felt cheap. In inverse proportion to the cost of her dress.

As they made their way through the gaggle of prostitutes up a long flight of stairs, she said quietly, "You wouldn't take my sister here. Would you?"

The steps seemed to go up and up and up. "I'm not in the habit of taking your sister anywhere at all."

The sounds hit Rachel first, with the force of an oncoming locomotive, a wave of sound so strong, she could practically feel her hair blow back with the force of it. The wail of the saxophone competed with the clatter of glasses, the staccato tap of heels, and, above it all, an overwhelming wave of high, shrill chatter, voices upon voices, all talking at once.

The man at the door knew Simon. In the din, Rachel caught only, ". . . cousin . . ." and "list." A few coins changed hands and they were waved through into a room that glittered with glass, set into the floors, the walls, arranged in complex mosaics whose patterns taunted the eye; a million tiny bits of mirror reflecting jagged bits and pieces.

It was like walking into a kaleidoscope, the same dizzying feeling of everything being broken and reassembled, whirling around and around and around.

Rachel wasn't entirely sure she liked the effect. She preferred to be left in one piece, thank you very much.

"Vera. *Vera.*" Simon poked her again.

Rachel jerked away. She wasn't going to do very well at this if she couldn't even remember her own name. "Isn't my posture bad enough?"

"No, but that's beside the point." He ran a finger down the side of her cheek, tucking a strand of dark hair back into her golden fillet. "Flirt with me."

"I beg your pardon?"

Simon's lips were smiling, but his eyes rolled back in a discreet gesture of impatience. "Stop looking so censorious. People are here to drink and dance and forget their woes. And, incidentally, to flirt."

"Is that my stunt?" asked Rachel.

"No. It's just normal human behavior. Take this." He pressed an ebony cigarette holder into her hand. "If you won't flirt, you can pose wreathed in smoke and ennui. You'll be surrounded with eager admirers in no time."

Rachel turned the cigarette holder over in her hands. It was an objet d'art in its own right, chased with gold bands that echoed the bangles clasped above her elbows. "I don't smoke."

Simon slipped a cigarette case into her bag. "Consider it a prop."

Rachel clipped the bag closed, moving it to her other hand. "And here I thought I had you for that."

"Surely you know better than to rely on me." The room shimmered with cigarette smoke, filming the mirrors with a haze like mist. "One foot on sea and one on shore, to one thing constant never."

"That's just pure self-indulgence," retorted Rachel. "Excusing yourself in advance doesn't make it right."

Simon smiled charmingly. "But it does constitute fair warning, don't you think?"

"Some would take it as a challenge."

"Don't." Before she could respond, Simon raised a hand in the air, trilling in a saccharine falsetto, "Cece, my sweet! How too thrill-making to find you here."

A woman in an ice-blue frock was standing in the middle of a chattering group, a cigarette dangling dangerously from one hand, a cocktail spilling sideways from the other.

At the sound of Simon's voice, she lurched forward, wrapping a pair of slender arms around his neck, her drink dribbling down the dark wool of his jacket. "Simon, darling! Have you come to rescue me from boredom?"

With her retroussé nose and puckered lips, Cecelia Heatherington-Vaughn looked like the more pampered sort of pug dog. If pug dogs wore slips of ice-blue satin embroidered with strings of tiny crystals. Her hair was faded fair, an indeterminate ash blond, her cheeks sallow beneath a dusting of powder.

"My dear, I never undertake charity work." Simon detached her arms from about his neck, looping an arm about her waist instead, presumably to keep her from tipping headfirst into the champagne cooler. "Cece, my cousin, Vera Merton. Vera, this is the woman I've been telling you about, the inimitable Cecelia Heatherington-Vaughn."

"How do you do?" said Rachel politely.

She might not have spoken. Cece pushed unsteadily out of Simon's embrace. "You can be such a beast, Simon."

Simon snagged Cece by the arm before she could fall, turning her neatly toward Rachel. "You see? You have that in common. You can unite in reviling me."

"Don't be an ass." Cece peered muzzily at Rachel. Her eyes were a pale blue, watery, and vaguely protuberant. The effect ought to have been unattractive, but it wasn't. It gave her a slightly helpless air, the perpetual damsel in distress. Her lashes had been blackened, making her eyes seem even larger and paler. "Merton . . . I haven't met you."

"How could you?" said Simon. "She's just come from France."

Cece shrugged pettishly. "I can't be expected to keep track of all your cousins." She tugged on Simon's arm, as though Rachel weren't there. "If you're going to be horrid, you might at least dance with me."

"On that swamp of a dance floor? It would take a braver man than I. Besides . . . don't you have one of your trained monkeys for that?"

"Jealous?"

"Invariably. Which one is it tonight?"

"Goff." It sounded like a cough. Rachel belatedly realized it was meant to be a name. "Too sleep-inducing."

"You mean he's been slow filling your glass." Simon expertly hefted the champagne bottle in the cooler and tipped the remains into Cece's glass. "Drink this and you'll feel better, there's a good girl." He kicked a chair out from under the table and sat on it, drawing Cece down beside him. "Now. Tell us what we've missed."

"Why? So you'll have something to put in your column?" Without waiting for him to respond, Cece went on, "It's been a deadly evening. The two Evelyns have been cooing together in the corner. Elizabeth Ponsonby tripped over a chair and ripped her frock and went home. Brenda—"

No one pulled out a chair for Rachel, so Rachel extracted one for herself. Apparently, regular rules of conduct didn't apply in nightclubs. Or maybe it was just that they didn't apply with Simon.

Wasn't she meant to be catching Cece's attention?

Simon angled his dark head toward Cece's fair one, listening with flattering attention as the endless catalog of names went on. Or, at least, giving a fairly good pretense. His eye caught Rachel's, and he made a slight gesture with his head.

Sit? Stay? Roll over?

Rachel arranged her chiffon panels carefully around her legs, trying not to fidget. What would Vera Merton do?

Dance topless on the table, no doubt.

"—and Brian is flirting shamefully with one of the waiters—"

There was a bottle of champagne in the cooler on the table, but the only glass was Cece's. Rachel took the ebony cigarette holder from the bag and fitted a cigarette carefully into place.

"You appear to be in need of a light." Simon's hand suddenly appeared beneath her nose. "Cece, gasper?"

"Thanks awfully, darling." Cece helped herself to Rachel's cigarettes without so much as a nod. Turning back to Simon, she said all in one breath, "It's all frightfully dull and I don't even know why I bother."

Cece dragged in deeply on her cigarette, trailing ash and ennui. Rachel felt like a nursery governess again, relegated to the quiet seat in the back of the room, seen and not heard.

So much for the effects of a flame-colored dress.

"Tomorrow and tomorrow and tomorrow," Simon agreed solemnly. "Too sick-making. What is one to do with oneself?"

"Have you tried nursery governessing?" murmured Rachel. That would cure her ennui.

Simon shot her a warning look.

More loudly, Rachel said, "In France, when we were bored, we used to pass the time at the castle telling fortunes."

She hadn't expected Cece to pay any attention, but she did. Her cigarette tilted in Rachel's direction, and her watery eyes focused on her for the first time, instead of just shifting past her. "Oh?"

Simon raised a brow. "O my prophetic soul?"

He still hadn't introduced her, not properly. Well, if he could carry on as though that didn't matter, so could she. Rachel flicked ash off her untouched cigarette. "You're mixing your plays. That's *Hamlet.*"

There was amusement in the depths of Simon's dark eyes. "I am nothing but a howling void of unrelated information."

Rachel looked pointedly at him. "All sound and fury signifying nothing."

"A tale told by an idiot," Simon agreed. "Flies to wanton boys, and all that." Turning to Cece, he said blandly, "There's your antidote to boredom, darling. Hold out your hand, and all shall be known. Coins in the box in the front, mockers and doubters to the back of the line. Meet my cousin Vera, mistress of the mystic arts."

He'd dropped her in it now, hadn't he?

But it had its results. Cece leaned her elbows on the table. A diamond-encrusted bangle glittered on her wrist. "Can you really tell the future?"

EIGHT

"Well..." An evil imp took hold of Rachel. Simon had said she
needed a stunt, hadn't he? "I didn't believe it myself, at first. Fortunes! Too terribly superstitious and silly. But, then, there was that affair
with Jean-Luc...."

"Jean-Luc?"

Rachel shook back her dark hair, leaning forward in an imitation of
the other woman's fashionable slouch. "We laughed when we saw the
cards ... but, then, when his horse came back to the stable without
him..."

"Shocking," said Simon drily.

Cece's eyes were as glassy as the mirrored tiles on the wall. "Was he
dead?"

Rachel thought fast. "Fortunately, his groom had heard about the
cards—you know how servants gossip—and found him before it was too
late. *He* believed. And, then," she added, "there was Leonie. The cards
warned her to avoid dark men. But did she listen?"

"Ah, yes," said Simon seriously. "Poor Leonie. A shocking affair. Too
tragic."

Rachel sent him a warning look, but she needn't have worried; Cece was lapping it up. "Can you tell my fortune?"

"Perhaps." Rachel leaned back against the chair, crossing her silken legs at the knee as Cece had. Her bangles jingled on her wrists. "You needn't cross my palm with silver, but I wouldn't say no to bubbly."

"That can be arranged." Simon signaled to a passing waiter. Holding his hands in the air, he intoned, "The spirits are telling me . . . you'll have a terrible head in the morning."

"Be quiet, Simon. Well?" Cece imperiously thrust one hand at Rachel, palm up.

Despite herself, Rachel felt a sudden twinge of sympathy. Cece's voice and dress were all sophistication, but her hand was as small as a child's, the large rings on her fingers a child's trumpery trinkets.

Except that they weren't. And Cece Heatherington-Vaughn was no child. At her age, Rachel had already been earning her own living.

"Darling!" Rachel imitated the other woman's twittering tones. Time to think quickly. "Only little old gypsy women can tell your fortune by peering at your palm. I'm hopeless without my cards."

"Do you have them with you?"

"Yes, coz," echoed Simon. He was watching her as a man might a bear who blundered into a jig, impressed and amused, slightly disbelieving. "Do you?"

Rachel gestured at her tiny beaded evening bag. "They're at the flat."

She half expected Cece to demand they hop in a taxi right away. "Thursday, then," said Cece decidedly. "My mother is having a deadly little person come to lecture. You can bring her, Simon."

"One of your mother's lectures?" Simon made a show of stifling a yawn. "Darling, we'd have to be mad."

Rachel tried desperately to catch his eyes. An invitation to Cece's home? It couldn't be better.

And she hadn't even had to dance topless.

"No, really. You must come. We'll slip away to the study." With that decided, Cece raised a jeweled arm in the air, waving it languidly in the direction of the group of men standing behind them. "Brian! Darling! Look who I've found!"

"M-M-Montfort." Rachel swallowed her annoyance at the interruption as a dark-haired man sauntered over, looking, Rachel thought, like a particularly well-fed cat. "Are you sniffing out sc-scandal for your de-de-delightful little column?"

"Always." Simon slanted one last thoughtful look at Rachel before turning to the newcomer. "Anything to share, old bean? Or is it merely more of the same?"

"D-d-don't look to m-m-me, my dear! I reek of virtue, p-p-positively I do." The man's heavy lidded eyes roved toward Rachel. "And who is this r-r-ravishing creature?"

Cece leaned bonelessly back in her chair, dangling one high-heeled slipper from her silken toes. "This is Simon's cousin, Sarah—"

"Vera," Rachel corrected, smiling determinedly at Cece, feeling edgy and alert, a soldier in the thick of battle.

"—who is going to tell my fortune."

"How d-d-droll." The man called Brian took a delicate sip of his drink, a frothy concoction of cream and something else, smelling strongly of nutmeg. "Shall I c-c-call you sylph or s-s-sibyl?"

The man's pose was languid, but those heavily lidded eyes were assessing. Sniffing for a whiff of scandal? Well, she was meant to be a scandal, wasn't she? The right sort of one.

Rachel struck a pose with her ebony lighter, saying, "You can call me either—but I answer to Vera."

"Vera . . . veritas . . ." Brian turned the name over on his tongue, rolling it, playing with it. "Come to t-t-tell truth?"

"Come to drink bubbly," said Simon, as the waiter set a fresh bottle into the cooler, doling out glasses all around. "Vera?"

"I never say no," said Rachel provocatively, and stretched her arm out for the glass, setting her gold bangles glittering.

Her hand brushed Simon's. For a moment, as he handed her the glass, they were shielded from the others, his lips close to her ear. "Not bad for someone so long in France," he murmured.

Rachel could feel energy fizz through her like champagne. "I've always been a quick study . . . Cousin."

Now was clearly not the time to tell him about the vicar's annual amateur theatrical.

Brian seated himself beside her, brushing back his tails. "Now. You m-must tell me. Where has darling S-Simon been hiding you?"

Rachel opened her mouth to parrot the planned story about being abroad, with suitable embellishments, but Simon got there first.

With a lazy smile, he said, "That would be telling."

Brian clasped both hands over his heart and feigned a stagger. "My d-d-dear. You whet my c-c-c-curiosity, you positively do."

"Good," said Simon. Taking Rachel by the hand, he drew her up from her chair. "If you'll excuse us? Vera made me promise to show her the Matisse on the stairs."

"You are a d-d-disciple of the m-m-muse?"

"Purely an admiring amateur," Rachel said hastily. She was vaguely aware that there was art labeled as modern, but what it was, and what one was meant to see in it, she hadn't any idea. It all looked like so much mush to her. "I can't draw a straight line."

"My dear! How refreshing." In Brian's plummy accent, the *r*'s came out as *w*'s. "Now tell me you aren't writing a novel, and we shall be friends for l-l-life."

"Why should one chronicle life when one can live it?"

"My dear boy"—Brian blew a smoke ring at Simon—"how, but how, did you find this treasure?"

"An accident of birth," said Simon blandly. "Come, *Vera*. You mustn't miss the Matisse."

Rachel waggled her fingers over her shoulder at Cece and Brian. "He will insist on trying to educate me," she said gaily. To Simon, she murmured, "You'd promised I didn't have to be artistic."

"That was before I knew the full extent of your talents." Simon lowered his head intimately to hers. "*Do* you know how to read the cards?"

"I will by tomorrow evening."

There had to be books on that sort of thing. If the cook at Brillac could do it, so could she. At worst, she could make it up as she went along. Cece, steeped in champagne and gin, would hardly know the difference.

Simon raised his brows. "You have a talent for deception."

Rachel's smile turned sour around the edges. "I come by it naturally."

Together, they wove their way around the crowded dance floor, Simon's hand beneath her elbow. "A useful legacy."

Some of Rachel's elation at her successful first foray ebbed away, leaving her feeling cold and tired. "Under the circumstances."

"Under any circumstances. We're all liars, my sweet. Some of us are simply better at it than others."

To argue would be to fall through the looking glass again, talking in circles until she'd forgotten her original purpose. Simon had a talent for that. Rachel kept herself sternly to the point. "Who was that? With Cece?"

"You mean Brian? Brian Howard. Self-proclaimed man of letters and man about town. His opinion matters with this lot." Glancing down at her, Simon added, "You handled him well."

A little praise shouldn't please her so.

Rachel shrugged, saying brusquely, "That wasn't me, it was Vera."

"Pass my compliments to Vera, then." With a light touch on her bare arm, Simon stopped halfway up the stairs. "Here is the infamous Matisse. I need to see a man about a dog. Can you look after yourself for a bit?"

"But—" Rachel bit down on her lip, swallowing her instinctive protest.

Simon paused, looking at her searchingly.

"That invitation," Rachel said hastily. "Was it good?"

If Simon knew that wasn't what she'd intended to say, he gave no sign. "Do you mean will Cece be sober enough to remember in the morning? Yes. And if she's not, I'll remind her by ringing up. Protesting volubly all the while. I think you might have another engagement . . . but can be persuaded into doing her the favor of stopping by."

"Be careful." She wasn't sure she had it in her to come up with a second stunt.

"I know what I'm doing." Simon moved aside as a cluster of women came down the stairs, chattering together. "Trust me."

"That's the last thing I would do," Rachel shot back.

Simon laughed, a genuine laugh. It made him look much younger. "Wise girl. You'll be all right?"

If she said no, would he stay with her? Rachel grimaced at herself. Perish the thought. Simon wasn't the sort to play nursemaid. And she wasn't the sort to cling to a man's coattails. However tempting it might be.

Rachel took a long, deep draft of her champagne. It was warm and beginning to go flat. "You needn't worry yourself. You've performed your part of the bargain."

"My dear, we're only just beginning." Simon paused three steps up, and nodded toward her glass. "Go easy on that."

"Sauce for the goose," said Rachel defiantly, and had the dubious pleasure of seeing Simon's fleeting grin.

And then he was gone, lost to view through a door at the top of the stairs, leaving Rachel alone with a half-empty glass of champagne in one hand, staring at a painting that looked as though it had been composed by a prurient ten-year-old boy.

Not entirely alone, Rachel reminded herself. She could go back, find Cece Heatherington-Vaughn, or that Brian person. She could pretend she'd just been to the powder room and lost Simon on her way back. But she wasn't sure that would be wise. She wanted to keep her air of mystery, to keep Cece guessing. She might have impressed Simon, oh so briefly, with her veneer of Vera, but she wasn't sure it would maintain prolonged scrutiny. Particularly after half a glass of champagne.

Rachel glanced uncertainly up the stairs, the way Simon had gone. No knowing what was up there, or just how long this man with a dog was going to take, whatever that dog might be.

Could she just go home? Go down the stairs, get herself into a taxi? It was a tempting thought. It had to be past midnight already, and her ankles ached in her ill-fitting shoes. But she oughtn't go without telling Simon.

A bit, he had said. How long was a bit?

Rachel shifted uncomfortably from one foot to the other, feeling gauche and out of place. Serve Simon right if he came back and found her gone. She ought to have suggested it herself before he left.

But for the fact that she never seemed to be able to quite get her thoughts in order where Simon was concerned.

It was, she decided, his elliptical style of conversation, which was quite as muddled and muddling as the poor excuse for a painting on the wall in front of her.

"It's hardly that bad." The voice came from behind her, a pleasant tenor, lighter than Simon's, without the supercilious drawl. Rachel looked down to find a man standing two steps below, his hand on the banister. With a friendly smile, he nodded to the wall in front of her. "The picture."

Rachel spoke without thinking. "It looks as though it was drawn by a ten-year-old boy with a poor sense of perspective."

"Shh," said the man, "they'll toss you out if they hear you. Even if I do happen to agree with you. John——" His last name was lost in the blare of a saxophone.

Rachel nodded distantly, glancing up the staircase. No sign of Simon. "Vera Merton."

John whatever-his-name-might-be stayed a respectful two steps down. Rachel judged him to be about medium height. His hair was a sandy light brown. Altogether, an entirely unthreatening character. "Have you lost your party?"

"Misplaced them on the dance floor," Rachel lied. She borrowed Simon's excuse. "I'd thought of venturing out there, but it's a sort of swamp, don't you think?"

"Frightfully murky." A ghost of a dimple appeared in his right cheek. "I've lost my people there as well."

Despite herself, Rachel began to relax. No one with a dimple could be all bad. "Do you think we ought to send out a search party?"

"Too perilous," John said solemnly. "They'd be trapped themselves, and then where would we be?"

Rachel hefted her glass. "Left finishing all the bubbly on our own?"

"I'll leave that to harder heads than my own." He was holding a glass filled with a pale amber liquid, but it looked scarcely touched. His voice was as clear as his eyes. "Is this your first visit to the Gargoyle?"

So much for being wicked and worldly. "Does it show?"

"Well . . ." There was that self-deprecating smile again, lending his otherwise unremarkable features a potent charm. Green and gold flecks danced in his brown eyes. "Let's just say you don't have the requisite bags beneath your eyes."

"Neither do you. You look far too well rested to be out this late."

"I'm not usually," her companion confessed. Holding his glass in both hands, he confided, "I'm only here as a favor."

Rachel struck a pose, cigarette holder in one hand, champagne glass in the other. "I've heard that before."

"In this case, it's true. I'm only here to make sure my friend is delivered safely home at the end of the night. Last time he was left to himself, he stole a policeman's helmet and tried to park it on the top of Nelson's Column."

Rachel choked on a laugh. "I thought Nelson already had a hat. A rather wide one."

"Yes, not to mention that he's rather a ways off the ground. It was pure luck that he didn't break his fool neck." When Rachel looked at him quizzically, he said, with a quick grin, "Fortunately for him, he managed to land on the policeman."

"I shouldn't laugh, but . . . poor man!"

"Which one?"

"The policeman, of course."

"Sympathies here would tend to run in the opposite direction. Pinching policemen's helmets is the urban equivalent of chasing foxes." John's amiable face turned serious. "It's a damnable waste, all of it."

"A few hats?"

"It's more than the hats. It's the waste of time and talent. Where are all the men who ought to be our natural leaders? They're frittering away their time in schoolboy pranks. If even half of them would own up to their responsibilities and just *do* something with their time—How are we to expect the lower orders to do their bit if we don't do ours?"

Rachel Woodley agreed. Vera Merton wasn't supposed to. "Isn't being decorative rather a lot of work? They also serve who only powder their noses."

"I'm sure Marie Antoinette thought the same thing," said John grimly.

"Are we to be faced with a trip in the tumbrels, then?" Rachel kept her voice deliberately light.

"It was less than a year ago that we were under martial law," said John seriously. "We're only fortunate the general strike ended when it did. As peaceably as it did. Prices are high, wages are low, the Bolshies are stirring the pot from abroad—"

"And here we are," Rachel finished for him, "fiddling while Rome burns."

Simon would have made a comment about it being a pleasant enough tune. John looked grim. "Just about, I'm afraid. If we have a summer like the last one—"

"I wasn't here for the last one," offered Rachel. "I've been abroad. In France."

"And I'm spoiling your homecoming with gloom and doom." There was a moment's pause, and then John said tentatively, "Might I make it up to you with a drink?"

Looking into his warm brown eyes, Rachel felt a little fizz of pleasure. There was something terribly gratifying about being offered a drink by a handsome man.

Rachel quashed it. She wasn't meant to be flirting; she was here to make the acquaintance of Cece Heatherington-Vaughn. And she had. Once Rachel had secured that all-important meeting with her father, Vera Merton would vanish from London society as though she had never been.

Hoisting her glass, Rachel said, "I still have most of this one. And there are no apologies needed, really. I found it—refreshing."

There were smile lines at the corners of his lips. "As long as I haven't put a damper on your evening."

"Quite the contrary. I enjoyed it tremendously. Not the prospect of the tumbrel," Rachel added, with mock seriousness. "But the rest. It made a nice change from shouting nonsense over the sound of the band."

John rested a palm on the banister. "If you don't like nonsense . . . what brings you here tonight?"

Rachel opted for a version of the truth. "It was my cousin's idea. . . ." She glanced up, and, as if summoned, there was Simon at the top of the stairs. Rachel raised a hand. "There he is now."

She could tell the moment Simon spotted John. He checked slightly, so slightly that Rachel almost missed it. When he resumed his downward progress, it was with an exaggerated grace that was all the more aggressive for being so controlled.

"Trevannion." Simon's voice was smooth as cream; he practically purred. "I see you've met my cousin."

"Montfort." Mr. Trevannion wasn't purring. His back was very straight. Turning to Rachel, he bowed stiffly, from the neck. "Miss Merton. It was a pleasure to make your acquaintance."

"And yours," said Rachel, but she spoke to his retreating back.

Simon glanced down at Rachel. His lips were smiling, but his eyes were cold. "Well, well," he said softly. "Still waters."

Rachel pulled her chiffon wrap around her shoulders. "Did you see your man about a dog?"

"Yes, a great barking mastiff. But you seem to have found even larger quarry."

"I don't understand."

"Don't you? That, my dear, was John Trevannion."

The name meant nothing to her. "Yes?"

"You really don't know, do you?" Simon's lips twisted in a crooked smile. "Angels waltz . . ."

"Angels," said Rachel sharply, "aren't doing anything of the kind. Not here. What on earth are you on about?"

"No," agreed Simon. "Here they do the Charleston. They shuffle and shimmy and soil their little wings."

His eyes rested thoughtfully on Mr. Trevannion. At least, Rachel thought it was he. It was hard to distinguish one dark-coated man from another in the swiftly moving crowd.

"Is there something I'm meant to know about Mr. Trevannion? In plain English this time."

"In plain English." Simon raised his glass in a silent toast. "John Trevannion is your sister's fiancé."

NINE

There was no reason to feel quite so defensive, but Rachel did, as though she'd been caught out in something illicit and more than a little sordid.

Her sister's fiancé?

It wasn't as though she'd known. And if she had . . .

Rachel's mind groped after that thought and failed. If she'd known, she'd most likely never have spoken to him. He wasn't at all what she would have imagined for the polished, marcelled girl in the picture in *The Tatler*. He had been . . . pleasant. That was all. Pleasant.

And there had been nothing at all sordid about it.

Rachel took refuge in flippancy. "Can he get me into Carrisford Court, then? It will save me the bother of fortune-telling for Cece."

"Save your seductive wiles," said Simon sardonically. "Only the countess issues invitations to Caffers."

Rachel bristled. She'd just been speaking politely to the man; she'd hardly tried to vamp him. "And yet she invited you."

"My situation was somewhat unique." Before Rachel could press him, he raised his voice to call out over her shoulder, "Waugh! I've fodder for your column. Vera, this is my competition at the *Daily Express*."

Rachel forced a social smile onto her lips as a slender man dressed with dandyish attention to detail paused on his way down the stairs.

"Not anymore," he said. "They've given me the sack."

"In that case," said Simon drily, "I won't spell my cousin's name for you."

"No, but be sure you get mine right." Waugh started down the stairs and paused. "I say, since I can't use it . . . Did you hear what happened to Sybil and Mamie?"

"Other than the usual debauchery?" Simon spoke as though they had all the time in the world.

Rachel glanced longingly toward the base of the stairs.

Waugh leaned an elbow on the banister, settling in for a good story. "They left their latchkey at home—and they haven't a night porter, you know. So they knocked up a neighbor from home." There was an impish glint in his eye. "His London residence just happens to be . . . number ten Downing Street."

"The prime minister?" said Rachel incredulously.

"None other." Waugh appeared well pleased with her reaction. "Can you imagine the horror on the part of the provincial conservative women's caucuses? Society beauties at the door at midnight! Orgies at number ten! The Leader of the Opposition up in arms, miners protesting . . . Let's hope it doesn't bring the government down."

"You'd best save it for your book," said Simon lazily. "It's too hot for my column."

"Oh, I shall, I shall." Wafting a hand in their general direction, the other man continued none too steadily down the stairs. "Don't worry; I'll find a place for you in there, too, Montfort."

"Oh, joy, oh, rapture," murmured Simon. "Like everyone else, Waugh is working on a novel."

"Yes, that's all very well." Rachel couldn't be less interested in a stranger's scribblings. "You say your situation was unique. How did you procure your invitation to—to Caffers?"

"Very nice," said Simon approvingly. "You almost said the name as though you meant it. Try it again, this time without the pause."

Rachel handed Simon her empty champagne glass. "You're avoiding the question."

"Am I?" Setting the glass down on a tray, Simon led her down the stairs, saying conversationally, "Have you had enough for one evening, or would you like to join Cece on the rounds of the nightclubs?"

Rachel could feel the kohl around her eyes melting with the heat. Her chiffon flounces felt limp, and there was a blister forming on one heel. "There's more?"

"All right, Cinderella." Solicitously, Simon placed a hand on the small of her back, ushering her inexorably down the stairs. "You've done very well for your first time out. I'll see you into a cab."

They paused on the doorstep, the cool night air against Rachel's damp skin making her shiver. "What about you?"

There was a group of revelers piling out of a cab, somewhat clumsily, talking and laughing and stumbling into one another. A woman stepped on her own hem, tearing it with a loud rending sound. They all seemed to find this hysterically funny.

Simon raised a hand to attract the driver's attention. "Did you, in your time in France, encounter that charming French idiom about cats and whipping? In simple terms, *j'ai d'autres chats à fouetter.*"

Rachel did know the phrase. It was colloquial and brusque and, in any language, a neat brush-off. "I thought it was a dog you had to see a man about."

"My interests are many and varied." Simon handed her into the taxi and gave the driver his mother's address. Looking Rachel up and down, he said, "Get some sleep. You've Lady Fanny to impress tomorrow."

Rachel huddled into the backseat, feeling suddenly cold as the taxi trundled away through the midnight streets. They had accomplished what they set out to do for the evening.

Why, then, did she feel so unsettled?

❧

Rachel dreamed she was on a ship. The captain was ringing the alarm, calling everyone to the boats. People were running, banging into one another, and, above it all, the bell was ringing and ringing, harsh and implacable. John Trevannion was holding out a hand to her, trying to help her into one of the boats, but her mother was still below, asleep in their cabin, and Rachel wouldn't go without her.

She just needed to get to the stairs. Simon Montfort was standing with Cece Heatherington-Vaughn, champagne glasses in their hands. To get to the hatch, Rachel would need to get around them, but, unlike everyone else, they seemed in no hurry to move.

"Drowning—*such* a bore," Cece was saying.

Rachel tried to cut around them, but Simon was in her way. He dangled a life preserver before her. "Aren't you forgetting this?"

Rachel shouldered him aside. The ship was listing and the bell was ringing, ringing, ringing. . . .

There was a shout. The last of the boats had cast off. Staring down into the choppy waters, Rachel caught a glimpse of her father's face—and then she was awake, and the ringing resolved itself into the insistent shrill of the telephone on the nightstand.

Rachel blinked at it, still shivering, still cold, despite the mess of sheets and blankets lying crumpled around her. A dream. Only a dream. With the realization came both relief and a terrible sense of loss. Her mother wasn't in a cabin below; her mother wasn't anywhere.

The telephone bell jangled one last time and went still. Rachel pressed her face into the pillow, taking a deep, shaky breath.

The pillowcase was soft against her cheek, faintly scented with an unfamiliar perfume. Rachel raised her head, taking stock of her surroundings. There was something rather disconcerting to waking up in a strange bed, even when the bed was the most luxurious she had known.

Perhaps because the bed was the most luxurious she had known.

The sheets on which she was lying were nothing like the coarse stuff that the Comtesse de Brillac had considered sufficient for the nursery governess or the much-mended sheets provided by Mr. Norris with their cottage, washed again and again to time-softened thinness. There were pillows of goose down beneath her head, and, half off the bed, a pale-green satin counterpane that matched the color of the drapes and the accents on the woodwork.

The scarlet dress she had worn the night before was draped languidly over the back of a chair, the matching shoes sprawled below.

The telephone, which had gone silent, began to ring again.

Rachel groped for the receiver, saying hoarsely, "Hullo?"

"Good morning, my sweet." There was no mistaking that voice, in its most saccharine tones. "I trust you were up with the lark?"

"There are no larks in London." Rachel's throat felt abominably dry. She felt at a distinct disadvantage, telephoning in bed. "What time is it?"

"Past ten," said Simon smugly, sounding far too awake for a man who had been off doing only heaven knew what for most of the night.

"Past *ten*?" Rachel struggled to a sitting position. She never slept this late. She was up before six, most days. Seven, if she were being truly decadent.

But, then, her bed wasn't usually nearly this comfortable.

The voice on the other end of the line went on. "I've spoken to Cece. You're to present yourself at the family manse at half past three."

"And where might that be?" The strap of her borrowed nightdress slid off her shoulder. Rachel hitched it hastily up again.

"Park Lane," came the voice from the other end of the line. "The taxi driver will know it. Wear the navy-and-white foulard."

Rachel held the receiver away from her ear. "Would you like to choose my shoes and bag, as well?"

But Simon had already rung off.

Rachel wore the navy foulard. She didn't take a taxi. It was a small defiance, but it made Rachel feel more herself to walk. She felt, without being able to say quite why, that it was important to cling to these small bits of Rachel.

It was a beautiful day, the sort of day that justified the weather the rest of the year round. Sunshine glinted off black railings and the smooth tops of taxis, dusted tree leaves with gold, and made the nannies wheeling their charges toward the park cluck and fuss and draw the canopy up just a little bit higher on the pram.

She ought to have enjoyed the walk, but she found herself fussing with the buttons on her gloves, peering at passing faces, as though her father might suddenly pop out from behind a hedge. No use to tell herself that Simon claimed he was generally in the country; she was in his territory, deep in the heart of Mayfair, and Rachel's imagination conjured him everywhere.

Was this, she wondered belatedly, why her mother had insisted she go to France, rather than London, for her foray into nursery governessing? Not foreign polish, then, as her mother had claimed, but the fear that she might see her father through the railings at a ball, catch a glimpse of him from her place at the back of a drawing room, wondering if she were seeing ghosts, thrust suddenly into the nightmare of an unexpected resurrection.

Would her father be at the lecture? The thought struck Rachel like an electric jolt. She knew, reasonably, that he wasn't likely to be there, but she couldn't help imagining it all the same, the look on his face as he saw her, confusion turning to recognition, recognition to shock. Would he bluster? Make excuses?

Or would he pretend not to know her at all?

Heatherington House was a vast Italianate pile, designed to awe. Rachel had no doubt one could fit all of Netherwell into a single wing. Other guests were drifting up the front stairs, but there was no sign of Simon's distinctive dark head.

Rachel hung back, pretending to hunt for something in her bag. Three thirty, Simon had said. It was past that now. Would he have gone in without her? Technically, she had been invited. But Cece had been in no position to remember much of anything, much less Rachel.

There was a line of chauffeured cars decanting their passengers. A taxi drew up behind them, and a man climbed out, the sun gilding his light brown hair.

With relief, Rachel moved forward, trying not to seem as though she were hurrying. "Mr. Trevannion!" she said warmly. "Have you come for the lecture?"

"Miss Merton." Mr. Trevannion's greeting was reserved, in sharp contrast to his demeanor of the night before. "Yes. It is a topic in which I take an interest."

It might, Rachel realized, have behooved her to determine the topic before attending. Too late now.

"Yes, I can see why," said Rachel vaguely. She fell into step beside him as they trailed behind the others up the stairs. "Did your friend make it safely home last night?"

Mr. Trevannion's voice warmed slightly. "He's most likely still sleeping it off, but at least he's sleeping it off in his own bed. It's kind of you to ask."

Rachel's lips curved. "I couldn't help thinking of poor Lord Nelson."

"Lord Nelson passed the night unmolested," Mr. Trevannion assured her. They were nearly to the top of the stairs, where a very important-looking personage held the door open for the arrivals. "Your cousin isn't with you?"

"Oh, I'm sure he'll be along eventually," said Rachel, glancing behind them. Middle-aged ladies in pearls and droopy frocks, an elderly man stomping along with the help of his cane.

Blast it all, where was Simon? A nightclub had been one thing; any-one could go to a nightclub, provided they paid the fee. This was differ-ent. The people, the accents, the massive portraits at the bend of the staircase, the smell of beeswax and lemon oil and expensive perfumes, all proclaimed this as a world apart, one of the inner sanctums of Mayfair to which only the elite were admitted.

With a lightness she was far from feeling, Rachel said, "I hope Lady Frances won't think I'm gate-crashing. Simon was meant to introduce me."

"Was he?" Mr. Trevannion's mouth set in grim lines. Glancing at Rachel, he started to say something, looked away, and then said, abruptly, "You've been abroad, you said?"

"Yes," said Rachel warily. Just so long as he didn't ask where or with whom. She parroted the story she and Simon had concocted. "I've been away for some time. My mother wasn't well, you see."

Mr. Trevannion looked at her with troubled eyes. "Then you wouldn't know."

They had slowed nearly to a stop. The others eddied around them. Rachel looked up at him from beneath the brim of her hat. "Know what?"

Mr. Trevannion mustered an unconvincing smile. "Lady Frances, of course."

It was, Rachel was quite sure, not what he had originally intended to say.

Before she could press him, Mr. Trevannion placed a hand beneath her elbow. "Allow me to perform your cousin's office."

It was one thing to bilk Cece, but Rachel felt a bit guilty about Mr. Trevannion. In introducing her, he made himself responsible for her. And if she were caught . . .

"You are very good," she said soberly.

He gave a short laugh. "Not as good as I ought to be. But I can make you known to our hostess."

Mr. Trevannion led her past the butler, into a front hall dominated by a massive marble staircase, which branched out in either direction, adorned by a vaguely Moorish-looking colonnade. Their hostess stood at the foot of the stairs, sending people up the staircase in ones and twos.

The line filed slowly forward, the people in front of them blocking Rachel's view of her hostess. Rachel took a deep breath, resisting the urge to fiddle with the paste pearls in her ears. She looked the part, there was that at least. Simon hadn't led her wrong with the white-and-navy foulard. But there was more to it than wearing the right frock. Her diction was impeccable, her mother had seen to that, but she didn't know their idioms, their slang, their private jokes.

If Lady Frances pegged her as an imposter . . .

Too late. The line had filed forward, and Mr. Trevannion was saying, in his pleasant tenor voice, "Lady Frances, may I present Miss Vera Merton?"

That was Lady Frances? From Simon's description, Rachel had imagined a dowager with a bosom like a pouter pigeon, her neck encased in a boned collar à la Queen Mary.

Instead, Lady Frances was a slight woman, half a head shorter than Rachel, her brows tweezed, her hair elegantly waved, her expensive skirt just skimming a very well-preserved pair of knees. Next to her, Rachel felt distinctly gawky.

"How do you do?" Lady Frances's eyes were the same pale blue as her daughter's, but far sharper. Sapphires glittered in her ears. "You must be one of my daughter's friends."

Rachel's throat felt dry. She summoned up her best tea-at-the-vicarage manner. "My cousin, Mr. Montfort, was kind enough to introduce us. I've only just returned from abroad—"

"Montfort . . ." Lady Frances nodded to herself. Rachel had the disconcerting impression of entries being filed in a mental ledger. "Are you one of Callista's girls? Or one of Penelope's?"

Behind Rachel, the line of invitees was beginning to pile up; she could hear their voices behind her. If she was ejected from Heatherington House, the humiliation would be public and final.

"It's a more distant connection than that, I'm afraid," Rachel began, when a voice came from behind her.

"Hullo, Vera." Skirting the waiting guests, Simon loped over to Lady Frances's side. Possessing himself of Lady Frances's jeweled hand, he made a show of lifting it to his lips for a resounding kiss. "Dearest and most generous Cousin Fanny. Forgive my tardiness?"

"If I do, it will only encourage you to do it again," said Lady Frances, but the sharp words were contradicted by the squeeze she gave his arm. "How is the general?"

"The pater is as ill-tempered as ever. He threw a boot at me last week."

"I'm sure you deserved it. And Hypatia?"

"Still gallivanting about the colonies with my esteemed stepfather."

"Tell her I demand her return immediately. London is too dull without her." Turning back to Rachel, she said impersonally, "I do hope you enjoy the little talk, Miss Merton. Such an important topic, don't you agree? Ah, Helen! How darling of you to join us."

Rachel let out the breath she hadn't realized she'd been holding.

"Move, wigeon," breathed Simon in her ear, and Rachel automatically moved along with him, up the staircase to the first-floor landing.

Rachel smiled sweetly up at her so-called cousin. "Half past three?"

Simon bared his teeth right back. "Punctuality is so confining." As they drew to a stop on the first-floor landing, he nodded to someone behind her. "I see you've entertained yourself in my absence. Hullo, Trevannion."

Rachel hadn't realized, until then, that Mr. Trevannion was right behind them.

Detaching herself from Simon, she moved to Mr. Trevannion's side. "Mr. Trevannion was kind enough to make me known to my hostess in your absence."

"It was the least I could do," Mr. Trevannion assured her, looking pointedly at Simon.

"Well, well," drawled Simon. He leaned against the marble balustrade in an attitude of exaggerated repose. "How very chivalrous of you, Trevannion. Of course, I would have expected nothing less."

"Should we secure seats?" Rachel said swiftly. She could feel the tension between the two men like a gathering storm. "I shouldn't wish to miss the lecture."

"Oh yes, you would," said Simon, without bothering to lower his voice. "It's bound to be pure drivel. The man thinks he can cure criminal behavior by injecting pigs' glands into the livers of potential felons."

"You're joking." Looking from Simon to Mr. Trevannion, Rachel realized he wasn't. Quickly she said, "I hadn't realized that pigs were such miracles of good temper."

"Provided they have a bit of mud in which to wallow," said Simon caustically.

There were pots and there were kettles. Rachel wasn't letting him get away with that. "Brought to them courtesy of the gossip column of the *Daily Yell*?"

Simon lowered his chin in acknowledgment. "A hit, a palpable hit. The principle is largely the same." He gestured over the parapet, toward the people milling about in the hall below. "Bread and circuses make for a happy mob. Or, in this case, slime and slander."

"It doesn't actually turn people into pigs," said John patiently. "I can't claim to understand the science of it—"

"Dr. Radlett's theories are about as scientific as bleeding to balance the humors." Simon struck a pose. "Does your neighbor have too much bile? Are you detecting signs of choler in your spouse? Suffer in silence no more. Pig spleen will soon set them right."

"A vast simplification." Mr. Trevannion spoke only to Rachel. "The tests—"

"Simples for the simple."

Mr. Trevannion's smile was ragged around the edges. "Even you, Montfort, must allow that the potential uses are inspiring."

"Must I?" Simon extracted his cigarette case from his jacket pocket. "I, personally, would prefer to not be shot full of extract d'oink."

Mr. Trevannion pointedly turned his back on Simon. He turned to Rachel, his eyes bright with enthusiasm. "For centuries, we have grappled with the baser parts of our natures."

"Maybe you do," murmured Simon. "I like to cosset mine and take it out for tea."

Rachel had to disguise her laugh as a cough, hiding her smile behind her hand. She doubted that Mr. Trevannion shared her amusement.

Speaking only to Rachel, Mr. Trevannion said, "Right now, the best we can do is punish the wrongdoer. Our prisons overflow with men who were a prey to their worst instincts. But if we could find a way to negate the impulses that cause such behavior . . ." One lock of hair tumbled across his eyes. He pushed it aside, his face glowing. "Just think of the advances we might make! Imagine a world without crime—without war."

Simon snorted. "Not until man is made out of some other metal than earth. In the meantime, the best defense is to hit as hard and as fast as one can, before the other chap can get his fist in."

"That's rather biblical, isn't it?" protested Rachel. "An eye for an eye?"

Simon breathed out a plume of smoke. "Not if you blind them first."

Mr. Trevannion looked disapprovingly at Simon's cigarette. "That's the old way of thinking. It didn't do very well for us last time, did it?"

"Last time," said Simon grimly, "we tried to play by Queensberry rules. War is a gutter game, not a gentleman's sport. Once the cabinet gets that into their heads, we'll be a damned sight better off."

"The point," said John patiently, "is that there needn't be any war at all. What happened last time was regrettable—"

"Regrettable?" Simon choked on a mouthful of smoke. "Do tell me more, dear boy."

"—but if violence is a disease, then it can be cured."

He seemed to be waiting for Rachel to respond. "It's certainly an attractive notion, but . . . what of all the diseases we haven't cured?" She could still see the gray churchyard, the bells tolling. "If we can't stop the influenza, how do we change the fundamental nature of man?"

"We don't," said Simon bluntly. "Men do vile things because men are fundamentally vile."

Mr. Trevannion's lips thinned. "If you're so set against it, Montfort, why are you here?"

Simon flicked his cuffs. "Why do people visit circus sideshows? It's always edifying to see the freaks being put through their paces."

The sheer viciousness of the comment took Rachel aback. She looked at Simon in surprise. "Surely—"

Neither man took any notice of her.

"At least," said Mr. Trevannion, with visible restraint, "some of us attempt to do something to improve the lot of man."

"Such touching concern for the masses"—Simon leaned back against the balustrade, the point of his cigarette glowing red as he took a long drag—"from a man about to marry an earl's daughter."

The words dropped like a stone between them.

In the resulting silence, Rachel heard the patter of heels on the stairs and a breathless voice, saying, "John?"

Turning, she saw what Simon had already seen.

There was a woman making her way up the stairs, her face flushed with the exertion, her hair escaping in wisps beneath her hat. She hadn't seen

Simon, leaning back in the shadows against the balustrade, and, if she had seen Rachel, her presence didn't register. The woman's attention was entirely for Mr. Trevannion.

"I'm so terribly sorry to be late," she was saying, and Rachel didn't need the little smile playing around Simon's mouth to tell her who the other woman was.

Lady Olivia Standish.

Her sister.

TEN

Half-sister.

Lady Olivia held out her hands to John Trevannion. Such small hands, dainty in their pale-blue leather gloves. "Aunt Fanny told me you had gone up."

She was smaller than Rachel had expected. In the papers she had looked taller, a trick of perspective and newsprint. In person, she was petite, a good head shorter than Rachel. Everything about her was muted, from the pale blue of her frock to the soft contours of her face. It was, thought Rachel, as though she had been painted in watercolors rather than oils. Her hair wasn't golden; it was ash blond, too soft for shine.

Like their father's.

There was a sick feeling at the base of Rachel's stomach. Part of her, perhaps, had still hoped it wasn't true, any of it. That this was all a bizarre sort of game. But she could remember, in one of those rare, sunbathed memories of childhood, her father, bareheaded, in their garden. He must have been holding her, because her small hands were fisted in his hair. She could remember, in the tips of her fingers, in the palms of her hands, the texture of it, so different from her mother's or her own.

This interloper, this Lady Olivia, had the gall to have their father's hair.

"Olivia," began Mr. Trevannion, his eyes shifting toward Simon and Rachel.

Lady Olivia didn't notice. In a rush, she said, "You were so kind to take care of Jicksy last night. I can't think what might have happened otherwise."

Through the humming in her head, the words only just vaguely registered. The friend—the one with designs on Lord Nelson's hat—that was who it had been? Lady Olivia's brother?

Her brother.

Rachel's head was beginning to ache; she felt as she had years ago when she'd stayed too long on the pond with Alice on a hot July day and been sent to bed by her mother in a room with drawn curtains and a cold compress on her brow. Everything ached, and little lights shifted in front of her eyes.

"Nothing too terrible, I'm sure," said Mr. Trevannion with false heartiness.

Lady Olivia shook her head. "If there were another scandal . . . I don't think Father could have borne it."

The heightened color in her cheeks brought out the unusual shade of her eyes, a pale gray. The same eyes that Rachel saw in her mirror every morning, a paler-lashed version to be sure, but otherwise the same, her own eyes in a stranger's face, a stranger with the right to everything she lacked.

Rachel found herself, suddenly, prey to a wave of pure loathing, loathing for Lady Olivia, in her frumpy frock, with her undistinguished features and her baby-round face, Lady Olivia, who didn't have to try to be anything but what she was.

Her father's daughter.

Awkwardly, Mr. Trevannion said, "*Olivia*. I don't believe you've made the acquaintance of Mr. Montfort's cousin. Miss . . . Merton?"

That slight, studied hesitation felt like a slap. Taking a deep breath, Rachel pasted a bright social smile on her face like crimson lipstick. "Yes. Lady . . . Olivia?"

After the first startled look, Lady Olivia's features seemed to flatten, as if she were a children's book illustration or a picture in a fashion paper, a two-dimensional image. "Forgive me," she murmured. "I hadn't . . . How do you do, Miss Merton? Mr. Montfort. I had thought you were . . . away."

Her voice was soft, and just a little husky, with a certain hesitancy about it which made her sound, thought Rachel, even more removed from the world, a product of marble halls and nurseries ruled by white-aproned nannies.

"I was away," said Simon blandly. "I came back."

"Like a bad penny," contributed Rachel brightly. She had to keep bantering or she might simply fold in upon herself, like a cheap paper doll. "One simply can't get rid of Simon."

"No matter how you chuck me in the gutter," said Simon, sliding a cousinly arm around Rachel's shoulders. "I always manage to crawl out again."

His tone was all that was genial, but something in the words made Lady Olivia color faintly and look away.

"Have you been to Heatherington House before, Miss Merton?" Lady Olivia asked in a restrained, polite voice.

"This is my first visit." Rachel detested having to make the admission, particularly to Lady Olivia, who clearly had had the run of the house from birth. "Before you arrived, we were just discussing Dr. Radlett. What do you think of his theories?"

"I am afraid I am not very well informed—" Lady Olivia was the picture of aristocratic reserve.

"Admit it," broke in Simon. "You think it's rot."

"The Inquisition thought the same about Galileo." Mr. Trevannion moved to stand closer to Lady Olivia.

"My heart bleeds for Galileo," said Simon drily. "The poor man is exhumed in the interest of every charlatan with an implausible theory. Lady Olivia? We know what Mr. Trevannion thinks. What about you?"

Lady Olivia fiddled with the pearl buttons on her gloves. "I think," she said primly, "that Galileo must be an inspiration to anyone with an interest in the natural sciences."

Simon essayed a mocking half bow. "Spoken like a true politician's wife."

It might have been a compliment. It didn't sound like one.

Apologetically, Lady Olivia said, "I shouldn't like to judge without knowing more."

"Of course," agreed Simon smoothly. "An opinion is a dangerous thing to have."

Lady Olivia lifted her large gray eyes to Simon's, and, like a shock, Rachel could feel the connection that ran between them, a silent communication that said far more than their words. This was, she realized, no casual acquaintance. There was something there, something that ran deep.

"Wouldn't that depend on the opinion?" said Lady Olivia softly.

"I try never to have opinions before cocktails," announced Rachel loudly. Her voice sounded too loud, too brash; it echoed off the marble columns. She turned to her sister's fiancé. "What about you, Mr. Trevannion?"

"I am afraid," said Mr. Trevannion, with a rueful smile that brought out the green and gold flecks in his eyes, "that opinions are part of my stock in trade. Although I prefer to call it having the courage of one's convictions."

There was something terribly humbling about the way he said it. It made Rachel feel cheap and small, as though she ought to be something better than what she was.

"Well, if one were to truly believe in something—" she began, and then caught herself. Because what was she but a fraud?

"What do you believe in, darling Vera?" inquired Simon. His voice was smooth as velvet, but there was a warning in his eyes. "Other than a well-mixed cocktail."

When he had agreed to her mad scheme, it had seemed too good to be true. And perhaps it was. Rachel felt suddenly sick of herself, of their deception, of everything.

"Justice," she said defiantly. "I believe in justice."

She was spared Simon's answer by a brassy clanging that reverberated through the hall, once, twice, and then again.

"That's the gong," said Lady Olivia, placing one hand lightly on Mr. Trevannion's arm. "We really must—"

She was forestalled by Cece, who whirled along the gallery in a confusion of pleats and powder. "Darlings! What a mercy. I've been aching, positively *aching* with boredom."

Rachel managed not to flinch as Cece flung herself first at Simon, then at Rachel, pressing her powdered cheek against hers.

"And darling Olivia! What a . . . dear frock. John, my poodle-pie. I shan't keep you from Mummy. She's mustering the faithful in the Red Salon." Having dismissed those inessential to her amusement, Cece turned back to Rachel. "You've brought your cards?"

"Cards?" Mr. Trevannion looked quizzically at Rachel. "You're short one for bridge."

Cece twined an arm through Rachel's. "Simon's lovely cousin has promised to tell my fortune."

Lady Olivia was making movements in the direction of what Rachel assumed must be the Red Salon, but Mr. Trevannion hung back. "Surely you don't believe in any of that."

"Why not?" asked Simon lazily. "Weren't you the one touting the courage of one's convictions?"

"Yes . . ." admitted Mr. Trevannion. "But there are convictions and there are superstitions."

"One man's superstition," said Simon, "is another man's science. Or how else can we explain Dr. Radlett?"

Cece rolled her eyes toward the ceiling. "Not that tedious man again."

"I had thought you didn't hold with Dr. Radlett," put in Rachel.

"I don't," said Simon. "But if one is willing to condone one sort of superstitious claptrap, it seems poor form to sneer at the others. Hypocrisy is never attractive."

Mr. Trevannion's eyes narrowed. "You'd argue with the devil, wouldn't you, Montfort?"

The response came from an unlikely source. "Better to argue with the devil than the opposite, I should think." Lady Olivia's voice was soft as ever, with that curious hesitancy, but it arrested the attention of her hearers. "Look at poor Faust."

Simon's teeth flashed in a grin. "Oh, he argued. Just not very well."

Mr. Trevannion did not seem best pleased to have his fiancée coming to Simon's defense. "I assume you imagine you would do better?"

"Oh, I leave the politicians to make the devil's bargains." Simon smiled sweetly at Mr. Trevannion. "I'm content to go to the devil in my own way."

"Well, hurry, then," said Cece, with an impatient tug on his arm, "before Mummy catches us and makes us sit through that deadly lecture. Quick, before she sees us."

"Speaking of the devil . . ." said Simon.

"Hush. It's hardly nice to speak of Mummy that way."

"I didn't mean your esteemed parent. I meant my lovely cousin's fortune-telling."

Rachel was very aware of Mr. Trevannion's eyes on her. "There's nothing devilish about the cards. It's hardly black magic, just a . . . knack." And three hours spent with a book about the basic forms of tarot reading. She would hardly pass muster among the cognoscenti in the kitchens of the Château de Brillac, but she had faith that she could put on enough of a show for Cece. With a false show of goodwill, she looked first to Lady Olivia, then to Mr. Trevannion. "Come with us. I'll show you."

Lady Olivia answered for both of them. "Some other time, perhaps."

The words were a mere social nicety. There wouldn't be another time. Once she walked away, that was all. The end of the acquaintance. Rachel felt as though she were scrabbling for a handhold on the side of a cliff, seeking desperately for purchase before she found herself sliding down, down, down to crash on the rocks below.

"Next Thursday night, then," said Rachel quickly, before her sister could walk away. "I'm giving a small party in my flat."

"Oh?" Simon raised his brows.

Rachel ignored him, barreling on. "It was only meant to be cocktails, but . . . why not make it a Prognostication Party? We can tell the cards, and, oh, crystal balls, and all that."

"A Ball and Bottle party! It's too perfect," said Cece with relish. "We can tell everyone to dress up as gypsies. Can't you just see Brian with a dear little kerchief over his head and gold hoops in his ears? How too brilliant!"

"Brilliant," echoed Simon, his eyes on Rachel. Rachel couldn't tell whether he was intrigued or annoyed. "Darling Vera is a font of surprises."

Cece was off and running. "We'll hardly fit into your flat. The upper room at the Golden Calf might do. . . . What shall we call it? A Crystal Ball and Bottle party? Or Cards and Cocktails?"

"What about Mystics Run Amok?" suggested Simon lazily.

Rachel kept the force of her focus on Lady Olivia. "Will you come and have your fortune told? Do say yes. We shall have *such* fun."

Simon raised a brow at Mr. Trevannion. "Or are you too scared of what the future might hold?"

Mr. Trevannion mustered a reluctant smile. "I can't have Montfort calling me a coward." He took Lady Olivia's small hand in his. "What do you say, my dear?"

Lady Olivia looked flustered. "I had promised Mother we would be part of her party for the Massingham dance. . . ."

"Afterward, then," said Rachel gaily. "You can come in all your finery and put the rest of us to shame."

"Why not?" said Mr. Trevannion.

"Perhaps the cards will tell you whether you'll win your next by-election," commented Simon.

Lady Olivia glanced up at Mr. Trevannion. Dutifully, she said, "We don't need a crystal ball to tell us that."

"No, just a safe seat," said Simon. With a flourishing gesture, he said, "But where are my manners? I mustn't keep you from Dr. Radlett's deathless words of wisdom. I shall be lined up and waiting for my injection following the program, after which I shall take my place as a model member of society."

"Montfort," said Mr. Trevannion, taking his fiancée's arm. "Miss Merton."

Lady Olivia inclined her head a scant fraction of an inch. Together, she and Mr. Trevannion passed through the arch into the gallery, leaving Rachel feeling snubbed, frustrated, and deeply unsettled.

So much for blood being thicker than water. If it weren't for Mr. Trevannion, Rachel doubted she would have received even a nod.

Despite herself, Rachel couldn't help wondering what he saw in Lady Olivia. Did she have hidden depths?

Or was it only that she was an earl's daughter?

Rachel quashed the ugly thought.

"Don't forget," she called gaily. "Next Thursday!"

Lady Olivia glanced back quickly over her shoulder, but it wasn't at Rachel that she was looking. Her large gray eyes settled on Simon, and then, just as quickly, looked away again.

And then they were gone, through the arch and down the gallery, leaving a curious sensation of emptiness in their wake.

What had she expected? That Lady Olivia would open her arms, recognizing her as the long-lost sister of her heart? They'd nothing in common.

Except, it seemed, Mr. Simon Montfort.

"That will never do," said Cece. It took Rachel a moment to remember what she was talking about. "We can't possibly be prepared by Thursday. Perhaps a month Thursday—oh, what *is* it, Daisy?"

"Telephone for you, Miss Cecelia."

"Really, Diana can't go ten minutes . . . I'll just be a moment. Wait for me in the study. You won't abandon me?"

"I make no promises," said Simon.

"You never do." Cece rolled her eyes at him and whirled out in a wave of scent.

Following Cece's instructions, Simon ushered Rachel into a narrow room, shutting the door carefully behind them. "A prognostication party. Very original."

"I'm amazed you didn't foresee it." Rachel fidgeted with the clasp of her bag, pacing restlessly from the fireplace to the window. The small, dark paneled room made her feel claustrophobic. Or perhaps it was just the feeling that she was hemmed in by everyone else's plans and schemes, by currents she didn't entirely understand. "Do you mind my hosting a party in your mother's flat? I know I ought to have asked first, but the opportunity arose, and——"

"You can do what you like with the flat. Just don't pawn the silver." Simon paced abruptly toward the window, leaving Rachel speaking to his back.

Rachel's temper flared. "You didn't mention that you were so well acquainted with Lady Olivia."

"I'm acquainted with everyone." Simon lifted a silver-framed photograph, held it up to the light, and set it down again. "I happen to be damnably well connected. I can't enter a drawing room without bumping into about sixteen sixth cousins—fortunately for you."

"Lady Olivia isn't a sixth cousin," said Rachel, doggedly following Simon.

The table by which Simon stood was littered with portraits. There was Cece, looking ethereal in her presentation dress; a young man in uniform; children on a croquet lawn; a man with a short beard, like Edward VII, and dissipated eyes. All the effluvia of family life.

Simon strolled toward the heavily draped windows. "No. She's more on the order of a twentieth cousin fifteen times removed. You can consult the good people at *Debrett's* if you are desirous of the details."

That wasn't at all what she had meant. Rachel was tired of innuendo. "What is your interest in Lady Olivia?" she asked bluntly.

Simon didn't meet her eyes. "Why, yours, of course. Wasn't that the object of this exercise? You'll never secure an invitation to Caffers without Lady Olivia's . . . support."

Rachel regarded his well-tailored back. "Or so you say."

Simon fingered a silk tassel, his voice carefully expressionless. "Do you have a better plan?"

"No," said Rachel reluctantly.

"Your prognostication party is a brilliant idea in its way. It will make excellent copy for my column." Simon flicked imaginary dust off the drapes. "You have an instinct for the stunt. If one didn't know better, one might even think that you were what you claim to be."

"Thank you. I think." Rachel steeled herself not to rise to the bait, not to snap back, into what would surely be another of those pointless, circular arguments.

"*But,*" Simon continued, in that same maddening, patronizing tone, "it won't serve your purpose at all."

Her purpose? Or his? "I thought the point was to further my acquaintance with Lady Olivia."

Simon sighed. "And just how, my dear Lady Machiavelli, do you propose to do that at a party? At a party at which you are hostess? You'll be far too busy filling glasses and soothing wounded little feelings to worm your way into Lady Olivia's confidence. *If* she appears at all."

Rachel's lips snapped shut on her immediate denial. The infuriating thing was that he was right. Not that she would ever admit it.

"All right, then. What do you propose?"

Simon prowled restlessly around the room. "I spoke to Lady Ardmore's secretary this morning. Darling woman. She tells me Lady Olivia will be picking up a pair of gloves at Debenhams tomorrow. She will let me know the precise time as soon as Lady Ardmore orders the car."

"Debenhams," repeated Rachel flatly.

"An emporium of sorts," said Simon helpfully. "Located on Oxford Street."

Rachel set her hands on her hips. "I am aware of the location of Debenhams." She wasn't, really, but she might have been. "If you had that in mind all along, why are we here?"

"Here," said Simon, "is a very broad term. Heatherington House? Mayfair? Your dear aunt Fanny's study?"

For a moment, Rachel assumed he had misspoken. Lady Frances wasn't her aunt Fanny. Her cousin Fanny, perhaps, if they were meant to be keeping up the pretense that she was Simon's cousin. Or—

Rachel's eyes snapped up to Simon's as his meaning hit her.

"Before her marriage," Simon said softly, "Lady Frances was Lady Frances Standish. Your father's sister."

Her aunt. Which meant that Cece was her first cousin. She couldn't quite make sense of it; it wouldn't seem to go together in her head.

Rachel felt as though all the breath had been squeezed from her chest. "You might have told me before."

"You might have opened any copy of *Debrett's*." Simon was watching her closely. "Why didn't you?"

Because she didn't want to think of her father's other connections, his other life. She wanted him back, as he had been, all those years ago, when he had belonged to her and her mother in that little cottage in a village whose name she had long ago forgotten.

Breathe, she told herself. Breathe. It was all distraction, that was what it was, just Simon being Simon, playing his games.

Rachel managed a shrug. "My sort of people don't own copies of *Debrett's*. It would never have occurred to me."

Those silver-framed pictures on the table. Cousins. She had cousins. An aunt. She'd never thought of such things, any more than she had thought of siblings; they'd grown so used to being alone in the world, Rachel and her mother.

Rachel forced herself to stop. It didn't matter. As far as they were concerned, she didn't exist. Only Vera Merton, the cousin of Simon Montfort.

"If you wanted me to ambush Lady Olivia at her shopping, why go through Cece?"

"Ah, but you know her now," pointed out Simon with impeccable logic. "You could hardly have attacked a total stranger over the gloves counter, could you?"

"I've met her," Rachel countered. "I don't know her at all." And she didn't want to.

Simon leaned over her, one hand on the paneled wall behind her head. "You know her enough to speak to. You've been introduced."

"If one can call it that." Rachel glowered up at him, too angry to be intimidated. "I didn't get the impression she was anxious to further the acquaintance."

"That," said Simon, "is what tomorrow is for. You need to win her confidence."

"Over the glove counter?"

"Was ever woman in this humor wooed? If Richard the Third managed to win Queen Anne over her dead husband's body, surely you can engage the affections of Lady Olivia over the glove counter." He paused for a moment, then added, with seeming casualness, "She likes poetry. Tennyson. You might want to mention 'The Lady of Shalott.'"

"Did the Lady wear gloves?" said Rachel, with crushing sarcasm. Honesty impelled her to add, "What I don't understand is why Lady Olivia would have any interest in befriending an . . . an utter unknown."

She couldn't quite keep an edge of bitterness from leaching into her voice. What did Lady Olivia need with her? She had a mother, father, brother, cousins. She was at the center of a world that Rachel could only view from the fringes, like a beggar child pressed against a bakery window.

Simon smiled crookedly. "Who wouldn't want to bask in the reflected notoriety of the glamorous Miss Vera Merton?"

That wasn't an answer. Rachel scowled at Simon. "I'm hardly notorious."

"Aren't you?" There was a decidedly cat-and-canary gleam to Simon's curved lips. "You might want to acquire a copy of today's *Daily Yell*." He pushed away from the wall, the urbane mask once more in place. "Ah! Cece, darling. I'd begun to fear you'd fallen prey to the blandishments of Dr. Radlett. . . ."

ELEVEN

There was a newsstand at the corner of South Audley Street, the day's headlines emblazoned on white pasteboard.

Rachel passed by the murders, the communist plots, the rising prices, and flipped, instead, straight to the society column. "The Man About Town," the byline read. She supposed it wasn't entirely surprising that Simon wouldn't use his own name. It was hardly an exalted profession, gossip columnist.

The first few paragraphs were what one would have expected. Peers' daughters making their curtsies and dancing on tables; flower shows and bottle parties. Elizabeth Ponsonby's name featured prominently throughout, along with Brian Howard, Stephen Tennant, the Lygon sisters, and, in the thick of it, Cece Heatherington-Vaughn. Rachel's cousin.

Rachel brushed that thought away and plunged resolutely on, heedless of the effect of newsprint on the pale leather of her gloves.

It was three paragraphs down before she spotted her assumed name. She nearly missed it at first. The piece began innocuously enough: *It was a lively crowd at Dean Street on Wednesday night.* The usual names came into play. Bons mots from Brian Howard. Ennui and diamond bracelets hanging off the incomparable Cecelia Heatherington-Vaughn. Evelyn Waugh had been sacked from the *Express*, leaving him free to devote himself to Miss Evelyn Gardner: would they wed and raise a brood of little Evelyns?

And there it was, halfway down the page.

The party was enlivened by the addition of the elusive heiress Miss Vera Merton. Usually found yachting off the South of France or riding one of her many horses at her stepfather's hacienda in Argentina, Miss Merton blazed onto the scene in flame-colored chiffon with gold accents, carrying an ebony-and-gold cigarette holder rumored to have been gifted to her by a certain very important personage whose name cannot, for obvious reasons, be repeated here. Although she would neither confirm nor deny the rumor, it is common knowledge that the gentleman in question is but one of her many conquests; she still wears, on occasion, the heirloom ruby gifted to her by none other than the Rana of Kildapur, who gave his congé to all his concubines in the hopes of enticing Miss Merton to take up sole occupancy in his harem.

When not flying her aeroplane over the plains of Kenya or breaking the hearts of minor rulers, Miss Merton delights her circle of acquaintances with her accomplished performances on the clavichord.

The edges of the paper crinkled beneath Rachel's gloved fingers. The clavichord? She wasn't even sure what a clavichord was. An instrument, presumably. Preferably a blunt one.

"Miss? Oy, miss!" Rachel was recalled to herself by the insolent call of the stallholder. "This ain't a lending library."

"Here." Rachel thrust a shilling into his hand and retreated with the paper firmly wedged beneath her arm.

She didn't feel particularly heartbreaking at the moment. Sweat dampened her hair beneath her close-fitting hat and made her frock cling to her back. No rana in his right mind would give her a second glance. And a certain very important personage? Rachel didn't know whether to laugh or swear.

It was absurd, all of it. How was she meant to pretend to anyone that she had been to or seen any of those places? Kildapur, Kenya—even the South of France. She knew Paris, or at least the bits of it one might visit on a half day, or with three sulky charges in tow, and she knew rather small patches of Normandy and Provence. Very small patches. As for horses, she had sat on the back of a rather sullen pony as a small child, but that was the last acquaintance she had had with the breed.

One couldn't even contemplate the clavichord.

If the porter thought anything of her choice of reading material, he didn't comment, although the ink from the paper was leaving dark smudges on the white bits of Rachel's dress. He sent her up in the lift with a smile and a nod, as though she had every right to be there, as though she had always been there.

And why shouldn't he? thought Rachel wildly. Compared to scaling the Himalayas or whatever else it was that Miss Merton was meant to have done, a flat in Mayfair was shockingly commonplace.

Letting herself into the flat, Rachel dropped the paper unceremoniously onto a table, stripped off her ink-stained gloves, and made straight for the telephone.

"The clavichord?" she said, without preamble, when Simon picked up the phone.

"And good afternoon to you, too, my pet. I presume you picked up a copy of the paper?"

He sounded so damnably pleased with himself. Rachel took a deep breath and counted to ten before saying, in what she hoped were reasonable tones, "You might have consulted me."

"Would you have preferred the virginals?" Without waiting for her to respond, Simon went on, "You're not likely to encounter a clavichord. If you do, all you have to do is disclaim modestly. Most people are only too delighted to be spared a recital. I doubt you'll be pressed upon to perform."

Rachel gritted her teeth. "That is not the point."

"Was there some other item to which you formed an objection?" asked Simon, sounding rather abstracted. There was a rustle of fabric in the background.

"Yes! To all of it. What am I meant to do when people ask me about the raj of—wherever it was?"

"Kildapur, my love. The Rana of Kildapur. You needn't worry about him. He's quite gaga, although he does have some quite lovely jewels. His hobby is toy railways."

"I see," said Rachel, in carefully controlled tones. "And my aeroplane?"

"You've given that up. What's the fun of flying over England when you've seen elephants stampede? Use a little imagination, darling."

Under other circumstances, Rachel might have been amused by the sheer effrontery of it. But this was her life Simon was playing with. What if someone thought to look into any of the details of that absurd story?

If she were discredited . . . the doors of Ardmore House would be well and truly closed to her. She could feel her father receding into the distance.

Her hand tightened around the receiver. "I wish you had used a little less."

"The point was to make you a sensation—and, after this, you shall be."

"Until someone decides to look into any of it," countered Rachel.

"By cabling to Kenya? Even if they did, no one likes to be left out of the know." Simon's voice was briefly muffled. He must, Rachel realized, be dressing. "There'll be half a dozen people to swear they saw the notorious Miss Merton doing high kicks on a billiard table at the Muthaiga Club—and no one will want to say them nay."

"You sound very sure."

"Fortune favors the bold." More rustling from the other end, then Simon's voice, clear again. "I'll call for you at nine. We have an engagement at the Cave of Harmony."

The last thing Rachel wanted was another night out and about. "I'll be at home—practicing the clavichord."

As if she hadn't spoken, Simon went on. "There's to be a treasure hunt of some sort. Bobbies' helmets and an olive from the Ritz. Bring a warm wrap."

As if she were an actress, on a stage of his devising. "I've already met my—" She caught on the word sister. "I've already met Lady Olivia. I don't see the point."

"How quickly they forget." Now that they were away from Heatherington House, Simon's voice was maddeningly cheerful. "The point, my sweet, is that we had a bargain. An entrée for you, copy for me."

Rachel kicked off her uncomfortable shoes, her abused toes sinking into the soft white carpet. "Can't you just make it up? Besides, I thought I was meant to be elusive."

"Not that elusive." There was a pause, the familiar snick of the lighter. "Nothing comes for free. Consider this the cost of your lodging."

It shouldn't have come as a shock. She'd known those were the terms of the bargain. But put that way . . . "That sounds like blackmail."

"I prefer to call it rent," said Simon. "Be ready at nine."

Slowly, carefully, Rachel replaced the receiver. The large drawing room was light and airy, sunlight streaming through the long windows, glinting off new chrome and old silver. Her hat sat discarded on the glass table, her keys in a bowl by the door.

There was no reason for it to feel, suddenly, like a cage.

All she had to do was walk away. Rent, he called it. She could leave at any time. Abandon the rich dresses, the golden fillets. She could find a reasonably priced bedsit in Holborn. No one would miss her. Simon was only sponsoring her because she had bullied him into it.

And she would be left where she had been before. Wondering.

Rachel dropped down onto the white sofa, facing the picture of the willowy woman cradling the little boy in the white smock, with his mischievous face and deceptively fair curls.

She hated the idea of being played like a puppet, but she couldn't walk out, not now.

These were, whether they knew it or not, her people, too. It was a strange thought. Rachel tested it, like a sore tooth. Her aunt, her cousin. Her sister. Simon had provided her the introduction—and, yes, if she were being just about it, the lodging and the means. For that, she would play his game. But only to a point.

It was time to start taking matters into her own hands. And she thought she might know how.

With new determination, Rachel crossed the room to the telephone. The operator knew the number; there was a slight delay while a maid chased down the corridors, time enough for Rachel to rehearse her opening line.

By the time a hand snatched the receiver and a voice said breathily, "Hullo?" Rachel was ready.

Rachel took a deep breath and plunged in. "Cece? Darling! It's Vera. Vera Merton. Might I persuade you to lunch with me?"

◈

Rachel was heavy-eyed when she left for lunch the next day.

From the Cave of Harmony, they had gate-crashed a party in Mayfair, although it hardly seemed to count as gate-crashing when most of their group appeared to have been on the guest list. Rachel had caught a brief glimpse of her sister, dancing neatly and properly with Mr. Trevannion, before Rachel's party had whisked away again, in an impromptu chase across London, piled into cars and taxis, everyone leaning out the windows, shrieking and laughing, before ending the night with strong black coffee and a bacon butty at the stands where the taxi men bought their breakfasts. By that time, it was dawn.

She had long since lost Simon somewhere in the scrum—hadn't seen him, in fact, since the beginning of that chase across London—but had, in the process, progressed to first-name terms with a sporting man with very pink cheeks, an earl's daughter named Mamie, and a very drunk young man just sacked from his job at a boys' school, who vomited copiously out the window somewhere past Trafalgar Square, but cheered up enormously at the sight of a bacon butty.

They had all, cheerfully and unquestioningly, accepted Rachel as what she claimed to be. She wasn't sure whether to be flattered or alarmed.

There was a small brown paper parcel just outside of Rachel's door. Moving very gingerly, she reached down to pick it up. Within was a stack of letters, all addressed to Rachel Woodley at Ivy Cottage, Netherwell.

Rachel hadn't arranged for her mail to be forwarded. She rather thought she knew who had.

Frowning, Rachel leafed through the pile. A letter from her mother's solicitors. An answer to a query about a bedsit. Notes of condolence from her mother's former pupils. Those, Rachel set aside to read and be answered properly. And, below them, four envelopes inscribed in Cousin David's familiar spidery hand.

"My dear..." began the first.

Rachel thrust it to the bottom of the pile. He could "my dear" her all he liked. It didn't change the fact that he had lied, and would have gone on lying if he'd had the chance.

Would she have been happier not knowing?

Rachel shoved that thought aside as immaterial. The three following letters grew more terse and more anxious. He had rung the post office to find that she had gone. The only forwarding address was a postbox in London. He was concerned for her. He felt responsible. He trusted she wouldn't do anything rash. There were matters she needed to know—

Rachel's lip twisted. *Now* she needed to know? That made a change.

The last note had clearly been written in haste. He was going down to London to view some documents at the British Library. He would be staying at his club. If she cared to call on him . . . any time . . . He would be at the Marlborough for the next fortnight.

Rachel's face softened. Dear Cousin David. She wondered who was taking his tutorials while he was away. He couldn't say right out that he had come to look for her. But he would be at his club if she needed him.

For a moment, she considered it. But what would he tell her? That it had been her mother's wish? That she should leave well enough alone?

No. Rachel drew on her gloves with unnecessary force. There was no one she could trust in this except herself.

And so it was that the fashionable Miss Vera Merton found her way to the Ritz, where Miss Cecelia Heatherington-Vaughn, the scandal of the season, was already waiting.

Cece lifted a hand in greeting as Rachel sailed into the dining room. "My dear, my head!" she said, without preamble.

She already had a cocktail in front of her, in a particularly noxious shade of green. It matched the bright hue of her dress.

"Mine, too." Rachel slid into the seat across from her, trying to look as though she lunched at the Ritz all the time. "What *was* in Tommy Digby's flask?"

"Petrol, I should think," said Cece with a shudder. "Mixed with crème de menthe."

Rachel nodded to Cece's glass. "Isn't that more of the same?"

"*Sans* petrol." Cece lifted her glass, shrugged, and downed it. "Hair of the dog, you know."

"In that case," said Rachel, suppressing a qualm at the thought of the cost, "I'll have one of the same."

"Make that two," Cece told the waiter, before saying, importantly, to Rachel, "We're both in today."

"In?"

"In *The Tatler*." Cece fumbled a folded magazine onto the table.

Rachel's own face stared back at her, her features bleached to fashionable blandness by the light of the flash, her hair falling in a perfect curve against her cheeks, her rouged mouth dark against her pale face.

Miss Cecelia Heatherington-Vaughn and Miss Vera Merton, read the caption.

"God, I look a fright! They never do get the most flattering angles, do they? It's too ghastly."

"Ghastly," Rachel echoed.

You have the cheekbones to be a Vera, Simon had told her, weeks ago. In that picture—she looked what she pretended to be. Not a nursery governess with work-worn hands. Not an earl's hidden by-blow. Someone rich, expensive, pampered.

What she might have been, had the world been otherwise.

"There's Aunt Violet," Cece was saying, "kowtowing like anything to the Prince of Wales. If she curtsied any lower, she'd go through the floor, don't you think?"

Rachel came back to earth with a thump. There, on the opposite page, was the Countess of Ardmore, her father's wife. She was broad and solid, an impression aided by a frock with too many flounces and a hat in the new romantic style, as broad around as its wearer. The Prince of Wales appeared as though he were about to be engulfed by several swags of tulle and a large stuffed cockatoo.

Rachel cleared her throat. "That's Lady Olivia behind her, isn't it?"

"Yes." Cece gratefully seized on her fresh cocktail. "Poor, dear Auntie Violet. She would so have loved to bag HRH for Livvy. They danced together once, and she all but had coronets embroidered on Olivia's underthings."

Rachel had seen the Prince of Wales. On newsreels. "Surely, there must be a suitably Germanic princess in his future?"

Cece smiled slyly across her broad-rimmed glass. "My dear, we live in modern times! If Elizabeth Bowes-Lyon could snag the Duke of York, why not a Prince of Wales for a Standish? At least," she added practically, "that's how Auntie Violet saw it. Never mind that she still reeks of pickles."

"Pickles?"

"Or was it tinned beans? Something of that sort. Too funny watching the airs she puts on when her father started out in one of his own factories."

Cece's cheerful snobbery stung like hail.

"Surely birth isn't everything." Rachel's cocktail tasted sour. She set it down. "As you say, these are modern times."

"Someone," said Cece languidly, "ought to tell that to Auntie Violet. Too laugh-making watching her coming over all grande dame." She stuffed the copy of *The Tatler* back beneath the table. "Will you have a chop? I'm not sure I can face one."

"After those bacon butties this morning, I'm not sure I ever want to eat again."

"Wasn't the taxi man a darling? Fancy sharing his breakfast with us." Cece scrutinized the menu, shrugged, and set it aside. "Besides, you oughtn't poke fun at family pride. The Montforts are rotten with it."

"I'm not a Montfort, I'm a Merton." Born of a chance moment's madness in a tea shop.

Briefly, Rachel wondered if there were real Mertons. There must be. Unless, like the de Veres, they had died out long since, another aristocratic dynasty risen and fallen to dust.

Cece waved a dismissive hand. "Simon's blood is so blue, it's a wonder he doesn't stain his shirts indigo when he cuts himself shaving. His mother's people are even worse than the Montforts. Not that it counted for much with Auntie Violet. We all thought she would have an apoplexy when—you know."

Rachel assumed a knowing air. "When Simon's mother bolted?"

"Which time?" Cece lounged back, glass in her hand. She appeared to be enjoying herself hugely. "My dear, don't tell me you didn't know! Everyone does."

"I've been so much abroad . . ." Rachel hedged.

Cece's pale curls caught the light. "They tried to keep it a great secret . . . but, of course, who could resist? It was all anyone could talk about for *months.*"

"What was?" Rachel didn't even pretend to have a clue.

"My dear!" Cece held her glass aloft. "Why, Olivia's engagement to Simon."

TWELVE

"They were engaged? As in . . . engaged to be married?"
"It was all terribly hush-hush." Pleased with the effect of her announcement, Cece sank back in her chair. "I probably oughtn't have said. It was all eons ago. Practically the Dark Ages."

"But Lady Olivia is all of . . . twenty-two?" As if Rachel didn't know her half-sister's age to the minute.

"Twenty-three," said Cece, her pale eyes alight with the joy of gossip. She rested her elbows on the table. "That was part of the scandal of it. Livvy was—sixteen? Seventeen? You wouldn't have thought she had it in her, would you?"

"No." Rachel's fingers tingled with nervous tension and crème de menthe. That odd familiarity. The tension between Simon and Mr. Trevannion. Simon's patronage, never entirely explicable as mere devotion to his newspaper column. She'd known there was more there than met the eye; she just hadn't imagined how much. "Whatever happened?"

"You mean after Auntie Violet went into hysterics and burst her corset? Uncle Edward nipped it in the bud, of course."

It took Rachel's fogged brain a moment to make the connection. "Uncle Edward . . . You mean the earl."

From far away, she could hear her mother's voice, chiding, "Edward . . ."

Seven years ago, Cece had said. Rachel had just begun working in France. But her father hadn't known that, had he? He had been too busy watching over his other little girl.

Rachel's throat felt as though she had swallowed a pack of pebbles. She managed to say, "He didn't approve?"

Drawing out a gold lighter, Cece lit one of her Egyptian cigarettes, waving it for emphasis. "Simon was so much older—and then there was all the scandal with his mother. She's not received—not by the sticklers. You can imagine which camp Auntie Violet falls into." Cece blew out a long plume of smoke. "She's quite wasted on the modern age, really. She ought to have been biblical. She'd have so enjoyed a good stoning. I can just see her scrabbling to get her fingers around the first stone."

Rather ironic, considering that her own husband's by-blow was currently sitting in the dining room of the Ritz. Or might men do as they pleased, while women were obliged to remain like Caesar's wife, above reproach?

"That doesn't seem quite fair." It was an effort to keep her voice light. Rachel forced herself to loosen her grip on the stem of her glass. "To visit the sins of the mother on the child."

"My dear! When has the world ever been fair?" Cece flicked ash into the air. "And one must admit that Simon did have the most eccentric upbringing—villas in Italy and cattle ranches in America and heaven only knows what else. Brian has *such* stories—most of them likely only half true. But then, there is that other half. . . ."

Rachel took a long swig of her cocktail. It was too sweet, cloying on her palate. "No wonder the match wouldn't do."

Not for Lady Olivia Standish.

One couldn't have the prized daughter of the house throwing herself away on a man of dubious repute.

Rachel could feel anger rising up in her. She drowned it in another wave of champagne and crème de menthe.

"Of course it wouldn't do—for Simon!" said Cece loyally. "Can you imagine being married to Olivia! Such a dear, but so deadly dull. And Aunt Violet! Fancy having her as a mother-in-law!" She shuddered dramatically. "Really, Simon should be lighting candles in gratitude. One can't imagine what they ever found to talk about."

Such touching concern for the masses, Simon had said of Mr. Trevannion, *for someone about to marry an earl's daughter.*

Rachel's frustration found a new target. "Perhaps it wasn't her conversation that interested him."

Cece gave a tinny laugh. "You *are* wicked. But, really—Olivia? She's hardly the type."

That wasn't what she'd meant at all. But if that was what Cece wanted to believe . . . Rachel shrugged. "Still waters."

Cece's pale eyes sparkled. "My dear, it would have to be a positive swamp. Aunt Violet watches Olivia like a . . ."

"Hawk?" provided Rachel.

"I was thinking more like a Victorian chaperone." Cece ground out her cigarette. "God, it's no wonder poor Jicksy spends half his time at the bottom of a bottle of gin. *Anything* must be better than an evening at home with Mayfair's answer to Lady Macbeth."

Listening to Cece was like sifting through a pile of diamonds, a glittering confusion of sharp edges. She sounded so entirely vapid that the incisive thrust beneath her words seemed to come out of nowhere, but by the time one had registered it, the topic had already shifted.

Rachel was reminded of Mr. Trevannion's complaint, of cleverness laid waste by idleness, a generation of leaders lost.

"I take it Lord Ardmore approves of Mr. Trevannion?"

"Oh, that was Auntie Violet's doing." Cece crossed one silken leg over the other. "Livvy didn't 'take,' you know. No SA. Or is it BA? Either way, she hasn't an ounce of it, poor darling. Not that you can entirely blame her when Auntie Violet chooses all her frocks."

Cece stretched her slender arms above her head, demonstrating to the appreciative waiter that she had both chosen her own frock and had no dearth of that elusive quality known as sex appeal.

"After three Seasons, they had utterly despaired of her."

Rachel tried not to be too pleased. "That sounds rather old-fashioned, doesn't it?" She fished a cigarette out of her own bag. "Parading around to catch a husband."

"Darling, Auntie Violet makes Queen Victoria seem progressive."

Rachel had often felt that way about her own mother. She missed her now, with a sudden, unexpected longing. They had clashed, certainly, but there had always been a leavening humor to her mother's strictures.

And, Rachel realized, her mother might have had more reason to be protective than she knew.

Her mother, more than any, knew the pitfalls that attended a fall from grace—what it was to be used and cast aside, left to a raise a child on one's own.

Cece was still talking. "Aunt Violet fancies herself a maker of men, and since poor Uncle Edward won't let her make anything of him . . ." Hunching her slender shoulders, Cece leaned forward confidingly. "That's how Aunt Violet caught John for Olivia. She's forever having *little political evenings*. They're deadly but no one has the guts to say no." She paused, cocking her head to one side. "Still. He's rather a darling, isn't he? If only one could stop him *caring* so."

It was the caring that Rachel found so attractive. Among all the whirl and confusion, the artifice and lies, there was something reassuringly solid about Mr. Trevannion, who said what he believed and believed what he said. Even when it opened him up to the mockery of exacting men about town.

Rachel held up her cigarette to be lit. "Does Mr. Trevannion know? About Simon?"

"He must do." A tiny blaze sprung up from Cece's gold lighter; her initials, Rachel saw, had been inset in emeralds in the center. "Unless he dislikes Simon on general principle. Simon does tend to have that effect on people."

Rachel held her cigarette gingerly between two fingers. "A rather deliberate effect."

Cece flicked the lid of the lighter shut. "Isn't he a lamb?"

If lambs had fangs. "Have you known Simon long?"

"Since the cradle. His mother bolted with the first of them—the Italian—oh, ages ago. He used to spend his school hols—" With an abrupt movement, Cece craned her neck, searching for the waiter. She flapped a hand to catch his eye. "Be a pet and bring me another of the same?" Leaning toward Rachel, she said, "You haven't said a word about your divine party! You simply must let me help you."

The sudden change of subject caught Rachel off guard. "I hadn't really thought much about it."

It had been a spur-of-the-moment idea, although whether she had done it to secure her sister's presence or to impress Mr. Trevannion, she wasn't quite sure.

Either way, it clearly didn't fall into Simon's master plan, whatever that plan might be.

Simon had lied to her. No surprise there. He had practically told her he would. But why? Why pretend he barely knew Lady Olivia?

Fear of showing a weakness, of baring an old scar? Like a magician, he preferred not to show how his tricks were performed; the magician stood imperturbable, garbed in his cape, while doves capered and cooed around him.

"—red scarves over the windows," Cece was saying. "Like a gypsy caravan."

Perhaps magician wasn't such a very bad analogy after all. Magicians were masters of misdirection. And so was Simon. All that, about needing material for his column . . . it might not be entirely untrue, but it couldn't be his main motive.

It all came back to her sister. To Lady Olivia. Lady Olivia, whom he had instructed her to befriend.

But on Simon's terms. In his way.

Was he, after all these years, still hoping to win Lady Olivia's hand? There was something less than convincing about the notion of Simon, prickly, polished, self-assured Simon, creeping hat in hand as suitor, especially to such a one as Lady Olivia. One might take Cece's opinions with a full shaker of salt, but there was no denying that Lady Olivia lacked presence.

She was like a whisper of breath in a still room, nothing more than a quiver in the air, as soft as chiffon, as insubstantial as the trail of smoke from a spent candle.

Doubt pricked Rachel. It would be convenient to think of her sister as a nonentity—but there had been those little flashes of something else. A look, a turn of phrase, a trick of inflection. Something that could catch and hold the affections of such disparate men as Simon Montfort and Mr. Trevannion.

Yes, said a cynical voice in her head. It was called being the daughter of an earl.

The legitimate daughter of an earl.

It wasn't fair to dislike Olivia merely because she was their father's daughter. No—she disliked her because she was cold and stilted, because she had looked through Rachel, because her very voice sang of snobbery. Not the honest, prattling snobbery of Cece, but a snobbery all the deeper for being so quiet; a complete lack of interest in anyone not of her world.

"I've told Stephen Tennant he must dress as a wizened old crone," Cece was saying. She had moved on from decoration to costume. "He's simply too pretty otherwise."

"Mmm," said Rachel, and nodded her thanks to the waiter as he set a second cocktail in front of her. Cece, not the least bit visibly impaired, was on her third, in what appeared to be an entirely liquid lunch.

Seven years seemed a very long time to carry a torch.

"—a month Tuesday, I think. We can't possibly have it any sooner. Late July. Or early August. But it would have to be before the twelfth or no one will be left in town. . . ."

But was it a very long time to wait for revenge? It was so obvious Rachel couldn't believe she hadn't seen it before. Pride, Cece had said. The Montforts were rotten with it. Simon might play at self-mockery, but Rachel would wager he was as proud as the rest.

Not love, but pride, quoth she . . .

"Do you think he was truly in love with her?" Rachel asked abruptly. "Simon, I mean. With Olivia."

Cece's plucked brows rose high on her forehead. "Simon? In love? My dear!"

Rachel forced a laugh. "I must be a romantic."

"How too sweet," said Cece, with withering scorn. "Next you'll be reading poetry like poor Livvy."

"*The Lady of Shalott,*" Simon had said. Rachel only vaguely remembered it from school, the Lady standing by her tower window, watching the world go by, until the curse came upon her and the web crack'd wide. *Singing in her song she died.*

All for love.

She wondered, abstractedly, what Simon's plans were. His real ones. The ones he hadn't confided to her. It would be romantic to think that she was meant to woo her half-sister on his behalf with Victorian poetry, an unlikely and unwitting Cyrano. Rachel doubted it was anything so sweet.

He wanted her in Olivia's confidence—but for what? To act as go-between? To draw her into a compromising situation?

It would not, Rachel imagined, look very good for her father if his daughter publicly broke off her engagement to run off with a gossip columnist, albeit one of unimpeachably blue blood.

If Simon wanted revenge on the Earl of Ardmore, wouldn't it just be simplest to sell Rachel's story to the papers? He didn't even need to sell it; he *was* the paper. All he had to do was plant little hints and innuendos, or, if he wanted his own hands clean, whisper hints into the ears of the right people.

Why hadn't he?

She wasn't sure to what extent her interest and Simon's were aligned. She didn't want revenge, not really. What she wanted was . . .

Well, she wasn't entirely sure. She wanted to know what happened all those years ago. Why her father had left them. If he had ever thought of them, missed them.

Did he love Lady Olivia as much as he had seemed, once, to love Rachel?

Did he sit across from Lady Ardmore at the breakfast table and imagine Rachel's mother into her seat?

"Do you know," said Rachel slowly, "I feel rather sorry for Lady Olivia. She does seem to live a bit of a cloistered life, doesn't she? Someone really ought to stage a rescue operation, draw her out a bit."

"Auntie Violet would have fits." Cece's pale-blue eyes glittered. She dropped her cigarette into her glass, where it fizzed out with a hiss. "And then again, Auntie Violet would have fits. It's just about that time, isn't it? Let's invite ourselves to tea."

Once Cece had made up to her mind to something, she was every bit as autocratic as her mother. Rachel found herself swept along in Cece's wake, through the Ritz, into a taxi, to Eaton Square, where, crane her head though she might, she couldn't see much of the facade other than stone, stone, stone, and more stone, and then up the stony stairs into a hall floored with marble and humid with potted palms.

The ground floor of Ardmore House possessed none of the arabesque grandeur of the great hall of Heatherington House. There was something very boxy about the hall. Admittedly, a very large box, but a box all the same, cold with marble and heavy with oak.

"Hullo, Hutton," said Cece, favoring the butler with her smile and her jacket, which she dropped into his outstretched hands. "Tea in the library? You needn't announce us. I know the way."

She flashed another smile over her shoulder, dragging Rachel behind her up the slippery oak stairs. "Darling Hutton," she murmured to Rachel. "I used to be half afraid of him as a child, but he's really just a paper tiger. All teeth and no bite."

The walls were thick with pictures, piled one on top of the other, but they were landscapes and flower studies.

What did she expect? Rachel mocked herself. Portraits of her ancestors? A lady in Elizabethan garb who was her spitting image?

Instead, the only portrait loomed at the head of the stairs, a self-satisfied woman in the costume of a quarter century ago, blazing with diamonds and triumph, from the tiara on her head to the large hoops of glittering stones on her fingers.

"Auntie Violet," murmured Cece. "Ghastly, isn't it?"

The Countess of Ardmore had certainly staked her claim. She had been slimmer then, but she still gave an impression of solidity. She was posed like a conquering general, feet planted firmly on the ground, chin up, her gaze seeming to dare the viewer to attempt to move her.

Had she known? It was a distinctly unsettling thought. Rachel hadn't spared much thought before for her father's wife. But now, she wondered. There was something so belligerent about that hard, blue stare.

The money came from the countess, Simon had said. Had that been the price her father had paid?

She was, Rachel realized, trying to find excuses for her father. It was a plot out of a fairy tale, the evil stepmother exiling the lost princess, sending her into the woods with a huntsman with an ax, or a poisoned apple, or whatever else it was that evil stepmothers were meant to do.

And what about the fathers in those stories? Where were they? Why had they never put their foot down?

The doors at the end of the gallery were half open. Through them, Rachel caught a glimpse of shelves heavy with books, leather bound, crimson, navy, green, brown, well worn and well read, the titles chased in gold worn almost away from the spines. The drapes were red velvet, tied with gold tassels.

There was something almost medieval about the large fireplace, with its broad stone cap. Before it, a tea tray had been set: a pot poised above a small spirit lamp, cake and sandwiches. Only one cup had been used. It sat on a small table beside a large winged chair.

Breezing gaily through the door, Cece sang out, "Livvy, darling! Prepare to be diverted!"

But it wasn't Lady Olivia sitting in the chair by the cold fire.

It was a man who rose from behind the chair. His fair hair had thinned; his gray eyes were obscured behind a pair of reading glasses. But even so, even across twenty-odd years, across the long room, there was no mistaking him.

"Uncle Edward!" Cece exclaimed. "Mummy never told me you'd come to town."

THIRTEEN

"Cece, child." Rachel's father set down the sheaf of papers he was holding and came around the chair to kiss his niece. "I didn't hear Hutton announce you."

Rachel stood in the shadow of the door, paralyzed, from her throat down to her toes, which stayed stubbornly planted on that one spot, like one of those nightmares where one couldn't speak and couldn't move; one could only stare and stare.

She would have known him anywhere, even with the spectacles, even with the gray that silvered his once fair hair. In her memories, he loomed large, tall next to her petite mother, a giant who could fling Rachel up in his arms and bring her safely to earth again; in the flesh, he seemed smaller, slighter than she remembered, his shoulders rounded from reading. Or maybe it was just the dusty grandeur of the library that made him seem small in comparison, in a way their tiny cottage never could.

But it wasn't the signs of time and change that made the words clog in her throat. It wasn't even that familiar shadow of a scar on his clean-shaven chin. It was the movement of his hand as he peeled off his spectacles, left to right, and tucked them into his pocket; a quirk of inflection; the lift of a brow. All of those tiny gestures that we see without ever seeing; the indefinable somethings that make up a character, so impossible to catch on film, so hard to translate into words, as unique and indelible as a fingerprint.

"Oh, Hutton," said Cece with a wave of her hand. "You know how he hates climbing stairs."

"You mean," said Rachel's father, with amused resignation, "that you didn't give him the opportunity."

The words washed over her, leaving only the familiar cadences in their wake, the same voice that used to read her bedtime stories and sing her silly songs. There was one, in particular, about a little warthog. How she had clamored for that warthog! And he had sung it, again and again and again, all through the long, cold nights.

Her mother had tried to sing it, later, but Rachel had turned her face away. It wasn't the same. She didn't sing it *right*.

It was dizzying, disorienting, seeing the man in front of her, overlaid with those images of long ago; that same smile, that same crinkle around the corners of the eyes, even if the crinkles were deeper, the eyes more tired than she remembered.

Papa.

The word resonated in her ears, so strongly that she feared she had blurted it out, that it was echoing around the wood paneling and crimson drapes, the ordered rows of books and the busts on their pedestals.

For a moment, she was a child again, and her father was going on a trip, just a short trip, not to worry, he would be back before she knew he was gone, and, oh, how she didn't want him to go, Papa, Papa, Papa . . .

And he had lifted her in his arms and held her close, just that one last time, his nose buried in her neck, blowing to make her giggle before setting her down again, smiling at her mother over her head.

As though everything were all right, as though everything would go on being just the way it was.

"You never told us you were coming to town," Cece was saying.

You never told us you were leaving forever.

Rachel felt like a leaf in a strong wind, shivering and trembling. Inside. In the hidden bit that was Rachel Woodley.

In the mirror, she could see Miss Vera Merton, her bobbed hair perfectly arranged, her crimson-lipped face as smooth as the priceless porcelain pieces on the mantel. There was something chilling about that image. Like looking into a lie.

It brought her forcibly back to the present. She wasn't a child anymore, braids flying, ready to run into her father's arms. She was here under false pretenses, to confront the father who had left her all those years ago.

"—just for a few days," her father was saying, and something about a debate in the Lords.

Rachel's fingers prickled with fear and anticipation. How to make her presence known, what to say? Did she blurt it right out? Or edge around it?

For now, it was enough to stand in the shadows, to catch her breath. She had thought, after seeing all the clippings, after speaking to Simon, that she was prepared for this, prepared to see her father. She would be, she had decided, contained and cool. She would hold out a gloved hand and say coolly, "Hello, Father. Remember me?"

But nothing had prepared her for this, for the aching familiarity that crashed and washed over her, turned her into a child again, with a child's love and a child's hurt, as if it had been only days since he had gone and everything might be made right by his flinging her up into the air and catching her close again.

"Heavens, I nearly forgot! Vera, darling, do forgive?" Cece wafted a hand in her direction, all fluid charm. "Uncle Edward, may I present my friend Miss Vera Merton?"

As in a dream, Rachel moved forward, her legs surprisingly steady, her feet, in their elegant heeled shoes, soundless on the timeworn Axminster rug.

Her father turned in her direction, held out a hand. "How do you do, Miss Merton."

"Lord Ardmore." Rachel's voice sounded strange to her ears, husky and foreign.

She lifted her eyes to his, the same eyes as his, Standish eyes, Simon had called them. Light-lashed on her father and Olivia, dark-lashed on her, but Standish eyes all the same. Her breath was tight in her chest as she waited, waited for some sign, some small flicker of recognition, of confusion.

But her father was already looking away, looking past her, to Cece, who was saying, "We'd thought to find Livvy. She isn't tucked away behind a curtain, is she?"

Her father half smiled, such an achingly familiar half smile. "I am afraid Olivia is out—as you would have known, had you allowed Hutton time to tell you."

Rachel felt like a ship becalmed in the middle of an uncharted sea. That was all? Not a second glance? Not a moment's hesitation?

From very far away, she could hear the discordant chime of Cece's laughter. "We won't stop, then. We had an idea of surprising her, hadn't we, Vera?"

"Oh, yes," said Rachel vaguely. Vera. She was Vera here. Not Rachel. Did a little paint on her lips make such a difference? Would he have known her if he had seen her on the streets of Netherwell, before—before her transformation into something plucked and tweaked and polished?

Her father was gathering up his papers, closely written in a clear, if somewhat cramped hand. "Hutton, I am sure, will be delighted to give you tea, should you choose to wait for her."

Cece made a face at Rachel, eloquent of horror. "I would never dream of putting Hutton out."

"An extra pot of tea is the least of Hutton's woes," said Rachel's father.

Cece's eyes lit up. "It's less than two months until Jicksy's twenty-first, isn't it? Mummy said—" She broke off, casting her uncle a look of arch penitence.

"Best you don't tell me, I imagine," he said drily, before adding, "I'll ring up your mother tomorrow."

Cece sparkled with mischief. "Then she can tell you herself. You needn't see us out. We'll horrify Hutton and make our own way to the hall."

This was it. Her opportunity. To turn and say—something. Anything.

Do you remember me?

Don't you know who I am?

Papa.

But her father was already settling himself in the winged chair, his spectacles again on his nose, his papers on his lap, and Cece was linking her arm through Rachel's, and Rachel's tongue was stuck fast, glued to the roof of her mouth.

"—the most tremendous fuss about Jicksy's twenty-first," Cece was saying. "Did you hear that they've shipped him off to Caffers to rusticate until the great event? Mummy says—"

Rachel hardly heard her. They were in the gallery now, steps away from the large portrait of the Countess of Ardmore and the flight of stairs that would lead them down to the hall, and out again into the world, her father receding with every step, away, away.

Rachel snatched her arm away from Cece's. "I-I lost a ring. In the library. I won't be a moment."

Without leaving time for Cece to protest, Rachel dashed back, her skirt swishing briskly around her legs, her heels drumming a warning against the polished floor of the landing.

She pushed back through the door, too hard. It banged against the lintel, making an unholy noise.

Her father glanced up, looking at her with an expression of polite inquiry which froze the tumult of words on her lips. "Miss . . . Merton?"

Nothing. Nothing and again nothing.

On either side of the mirror on the mantel, paired portraits looked down. She had been so focused on her father before that she hadn't noticed them. But she saw them now. One was Lady Olivia, painted into prettiness, wearing the feathers of court presentation. On the other was a boy Rachel didn't recognize, sulky in a sailor suit. Olivia and Jicksy. One to either side. The daughter and the heir, two fair-haired children for the house of Ardmore.

Rachel's dark head felt distinctly out of place, a blot on the family escutcheon. They'd hardly break out the fatted calf at seeing her, would they?

Rachel's tongue moved without conscious volition. "I'd thought I'd dropped a ring, but it must be somewhere else. I'm so sorry to have disturbed you."

"Not at all," said her father politely.

Rachel didn't wait to be dismissed. In a confusion of pleats, she backed her way out of the heavy oak-paneled door, all but crashing into Cece.

"You didn't find it?"

Rachel looked at her blankly.

"The ring," said Cece.

"Oh." Rachel gave a mirthless laugh. She lifted a ringless hand to push her hair out of her eyes. "I must have dropped it at the Ritz. It's no matter. It wasn't valuable."

There was nothing lost that she hadn't lost already.

But there was.

She'd lost the dream of him. The dream of the father who loved her and missed her, who had been separated from her only by some impossible mischance, who would see her and leap to his feet and throw his arms wide, and cry, "My own lost Rachel!" and she could fling herself against his bosom and weep for all the lost years and all the joy of being together again at last, of finding a berth and a harbor in a world where she had none.

"—in an airship! You will be there, won't you?"

Rachel had no idea what Cece was talking about. "I hadn't thought . . ."

"It sounds too frightfully misery-making, doesn't it? All of those vile ropes and really, what's the point of an airship if one never leaves the ground? But I couldn't tell Cecil no. We're all to dress as aviators." They were outside now, past a disapproving Hutton, into the bright glare of the June sun, and Cece looked at her, really looked at her, and exclaimed, "My dear! You look positively green. You can't be airsick already!"

Rachel grimaced. "Tommy Digby," she said succinctly, and Cece laughed.

"Whisky and soda. You'll feel worlds better." She brushed Rachel's cheek with hers, powder kissing powder. "Shall I drop you?"

"I'll walk." Rachel mustered a smile. "It's too nice a day to be indoors."

Cece gave a shrug over the vagaries of the human temperament. "If you like. Don't forget! Tonight."

"Tonight," Rachel echoed.

That was where she had stumbled, into a twilight world of night after night after night. Miss Vera Merton had her entrée now—but only into the demimonde of nightclubs and studio parties. She was relegated to the shadows. The daylight world of family portraits and great houses, that belonged to Cece and Olivia.

And why? What had she done that was so terrible that she was left to wander, homeless, rootless, while Olivia had her portrait on the wall?

Lady Ardmore had the money. That was what Simon had said.

Had her father divested himself of them that quickly and easily? Rachel remembered, in flashes, that nighttime flight from their cottage, the hasty packing, barely anything taken with them, just their personal effects, her own stuffed rabbit. Her father's chess set.

There had been one in the library, with pieces of ebony and ivory, on a board set with mother-of-pearl.

He'd replaced it just as he'd replaced them, with a more expensive, shinier version.

Rachel's calves ached with walking; there were blisters on her heels. She didn't pay any mind. She only walked faster, the sunshine burning through her cloche hat, making spots sparkle in front of her eyes. She'd left Mayfair now. She wasn't really quite sure where she was. It didn't matter, not really. There was no one to care where she was.

She found herself suddenly, painfully, missing that little cottage in Netherwell, where the water had to be pumped into the kitchen sink and the wind whistled around the warped pane that Mr. Norris had promised to fix but hadn't.

Where her mother had waited, faithfully, being father and mother both.

But she'd lost her mother and her home with her. In the ordinary course of things, she ought to have had something more. Siblings, cousins. Someone to condole with her. It was her father who had condemned them to this twilight existence, who had deprived her of not only the right to a name but of everything that came with it.

But had it made any difference to him? No. Not in the slightest. He had the grand house his wife's money had bought, old books and red velvet drapes, walnut and marble and potted palms. An heir. A daughter.

In fact, he seemed to have done rather well out of it all.

Rachel dodged an omnibus and ducked beneath the neck of a cart horse. The traffic was snarled at Piccadilly Circus, a policeman fruitlessly waving his arms about. The bustle of Piccadilly, the shouts and backfires and babble of voices, made a fitting backdrop to her disordered thoughts.

It didn't seem right that all the sins of the father should bypass him so entirely and be visited on the daughter.

A sensible voice in the back of her head interjected that she was really no worse off than most and better off than many. She had her wits and the skill of her hands, the little nest egg left her by her mother, a good and loyal friend in Alice. It would be a lie to say that her childhood had been blighted by her father's disappearance. Shadowed, yes, but certainly not poisoned by it.

Aside from the fact that it was all a lie, every moment of it. That if it had been known that her mother wasn't a widow, but an earl's mistress, they would have been shunned and whispered at. In fact, it was no thanks to her father that they hadn't. It was her mother's ingenuity that had saved them that. That and kept food on their table and coal in the scuttle.

Rachel caught sight of her own distorted reflection in the window of Fortnum & Mason, superimposed upon a display of candied fruit in a silver dish. What to do now? There was no point to continuing as Vera Merton. She'd done what she'd intended to do. She'd found her father. She had her answer, such as it was.

And wouldn't that be just what her father wanted? For her to meekly turn around and slink back—if not to the gutter, at least to the anonymous ranks of the working poor, just another typist in a sensible hat, clinging to a strap on the Tube.

While her father ordered hampers from Fortnum's and threw lavish parties to celebrate the coming of age of his other children.

The thought made Rachel want to spit.

She didn't let herself think of what she was doing; her legs felt strangely disconnected from the rest of her as they marched her to the call box. Rachel shoved her penny into the slot. She didn't need to look up the number; she knew it by heart.

"Are you at home?" she asked abruptly, once the operator had connected her.

"I must be," said Simon, lazily amused. "Or I wouldn't be answering."

Rachel felt a huge weight leave her at the sound of his voice. She hadn't realized just how much she was relying on his being there, the one person in whom she could confide.

"Are you receiving callers?" Without waiting for him to respond, she said, "I'm just down the street—near Fortnum's."

If he was surprised, he didn't show it. "Give me three seconds to drag on a dressing gown. I'd hate to shock you with my dishabille."

"I'm not that easily shocked," said Rachel, and rang off.

The flat was easy enough to find, up a short stair, one of two doors on the landing. It wasn't a modern box like his mother's flat; there was no lift, and no porter to inquire who she was or where she was going. The plain, dark door in the plain, dark hallway had an oddly monastic air.

Rachel rapped smartly with the brass knocker.

The door opened, revealing a small hall, and Simon, in a shirt but no jacket, the collar open at the neck. "My dear."

"No dressing gown?" Now that she was here, Rachel wasn't entirely sure what she'd meant to say. Her brain seemed to stutter and stop.

"I took you at your word." He stepped aside to allow her to enter. Behind him, Rachel could see a door open to a pleasant sitting room, sunlight slanting across a worn Persian carpet, a coffee cup on a tray, a newspaper strewn across a chair. "To what do I owe this unexpected pleasure?"

He looked down at her, head and throat bare, relaxed in his own hall, and Rachel realized, with a heavy feeling at the pit of her stomach, just what cheek it was, showing up like this, uninvited, to Simon's private sanctum.

"Invasion, you mean," said Rachel, wishing herself in Hades. She'd turned blindly to Simon, the only port in the storm, but he wasn't a friend, not really. Just an ally, and a rather unreliable one. "You needn't worry. I won't stay long."

Simon looked at her with veiled eyes. "I wasn't. Worried. I was in the midst of a coffee. Would you like to come through, or would you prefer to stand here?"

Rachel pressed her eyes briefly shut, hating herself and all the world. "I'll come through." She added quickly, "I'd hate for your coffee to grow cold."

"It's cold already. But come through all the same."

Rachel followed Simon into a small but well-appointed sitting room.

It wasn't at all what Rachel would have expected. There was no chrome, no distempered paint. One wall was lined entirely by bookshelves; the other was painted a deep hunter green. The books hadn't been arranged for show; the spines were cracked, the lettering worn.

Recesses on either side of the fireplace held old porcelain, black and red and white. A bowl of chrysanthemums sat on a low table, while another held a half-drunk cup of coffee and a plate of biscuits.

It was a room designed to be lived in, made for warmth and comfort rather than show. Rachel felt, acutely, just how much she was intruding.

"You're being surprisingly decent." Rachel hovered awkwardly in the doorway as Simon made several rapid repairs, shifting the table with the coffee tray, scooping a pile of papers off a chintz-covered sofa.

Simon paused, the pile of papers in his hand. "Damning with faint praise?" he said ironically.

"I didn't mean—"

Only, she had meant. And he knew it. Rachel felt the color rise in her cheeks.

"Never mind," said Simon curtly. He drew forward one of the leather chairs, creating a cozy little sitting area before the unlit fire. "What do you want, Rachel? I take it you do want something of me?"

She'd made a muddle of this. She'd made a muddle of everything. As to what she wanted . . .

Simon's voice softened, with a concern that was more jarring than any amount of scorn. "What is it, Rachel?"

Rachel drew in a deep breath, her hands clasping and unclasping at her waist. "You asked me—you asked me once if I wanted revenge."

Slowly, Simon set the pile of papers in his hand on a narrow Georgian table. His voice was carefully neutral. "As I recall, you said no."

Rachel looked him defiantly in the eye. "I've changed my mind."

FOURTEEN

Well?" Why didn't he say anything? "Aren't you going to ask why?"

"I imagine I can guess." Simon's voice was curiously gentle. "You've seen Lord Ardmore."

"He didn't know me." Rachel just managed to keep her voice from breaking. "I might have been anyone. A stranger."

Behind Simon, the flowers bloomed in their silver bowl, like something out of a William Morris print, impossible loveliness, frozen in place. "It has been some time."

Was that meant to make her feel better?

"Do you think I don't know that?" Rachel drew in a deep breath, hating herself for the way it shuddered against her chest, for the slight tremor of her hands. She clasped them together to stop them shaking. "I'm not sure why I thought—Never mind. It doesn't matter now."

"But it does." With a hand beneath her arm, Simon guided her toward the chair by the empty fire. She could smell his soap, sandalwood and musk. "Or you wouldn't be here."

"All those years." Rachel sank into the chair, the cushions molded by the imprint of Simon's body. She gave a brusque, bitter laugh. "Remembering him . . . missing him . . . And he was here all this time. With his new family. When I learned that he was alive . . . I wondered if he ever thought of us. Now I know."

Simon knelt by her chair. "You said you wanted to see him." Outside, Rachel could hear the backfire of an engine, an irate voice, but within, all was still. Simon's voice was soft, carefully neutral. "You've seen him. You could pack up now. Go home."

"What home?" Such home as she had had was gone, back to Mr. Norris. It had only been leased, not owned. As, apparently, had her father, and her name, and everything else she had believed to be hers. A feeling of raw panic subsumed her. Shaking back her hair, Rachel looked fiercely at Simon. "And what of our bargain?"

Simon rested a hand against the arm of the chair. "I'm not going to hold you to a pound of flesh."

His kindness was worse than his scorn. At least when he was being awful, it gave her something against which to pit herself.

Rachel resisted a mad urge to lean her cheek against that hand, to sob out all her frustration and disappointment. This was Simon, she reminded herself. Simon, who had an agenda and secrets of his own.

"That's the danger of a pound of flesh," Rachel said raggedly. "One can't take flesh without drawing blood."

Simon smiled at her, his lips quirking slightly around the edges. Softly, he said, "A Daniel come to judgment, yea, a Daniel!"

"Judgment, yes, but hardly a Daniel." Rachel pushed up out of the chair, away from that smile, half mockery and half caress. Abruptly, she said, "You never told me you were engaged to Lady Olivia."

Simon's face seemed to close in on itself.

"Ah," he said. And then, "Does it matter?"

Rachel gave a choked laugh. "It must, mustn't it? Why help me, otherwise?"

Slowly, he rose to his feet, using the arm of the chair as a lever. "If you put it that way . . . it's a nice little exercise in logic. If A, then B."

"An exercise in illogic, you mean." Even in her heels, he was a fair bit taller than she. She had to tilt her head to look up at him. "If it didn't matter, why conceal the fact?"

"Did it never occur to you that it might be of insufficient importance to relate?"

"You forget," said Rachel shortly. "I saw you yesterday at Heatherington House." There had been something there still, although just what it was, she couldn't say. And it was none of her affair. For the most part. "All I mean to say is that our interests appear to be aligned."

Simon crossed to the coffee tray. Silver tinkled against porcelain. "Hell hath no fury and all that?" He handed Rachel a cup of coffee, stone cold, thick with cream. "You do realize, if you want revenge, you don't need me. You can affect it easily enough, just by going to the papers."

"No!" The denial was instinctive and vehement.

Simon raised a brow.

Flushing, Rachel said, "That would be cheap."

"And blackmail isn't?"

Rachel set her coffee cup down carefully on a folded piece of yesterday's *Times*. "It's only blackmail if you want something in return."

Simon lifted his coffee cup in one graceful, long-fingered hand, pausing with it just beneath his lips. "But you do, don't you? You want payment—just not in coin."

Rachel folded her arms across her chest. "As do you."

"Two rogues together." Simon toasted her with his china cup. Draining the dregs, he said briskly, "All right, then. What *do* you want?"

That was the question, wasn't it? Rachel wasn't sure she knew.

A mélange of memories swirled through her mind. That last morning in the garden. Her parents' picture in her mother's drawer. A chess set, reverently handled, because it had been *his*. Sitting at dinner at the vicarage, imagining what it would be like to have a family, a sister.

No, hardly memories. Daydreams. Those daydreams she had held on to for so many years. But no more.

Turning, so Simon couldn't see her face, Rachel paced toward the mantel, moving in short, restless bursts.

"I want him to . . . remember. I want him to wonder. As I did."

"As revenge goes," said Simon conversationally, "that's rather milk and water, isn't it? Thumbscrews aren't in it."

"There are worse tortures than the physical." Rachel wondered what it must have been like for her mother all those years. How had she felt, cutting out those clippings? Had she hated him? Or had she, as she claimed for Rachel, loved him still?

I am married. And I shall be until I die.

Yes, and so was her father. To Violet, Countess of Ardmore.

"He must have thought he was well rid of us." The memory of her father's embrace was a physical ache. "Or, at least, easily rid of us. It would be rather nervous-making, don't you think, to suddenly be faced with the prospect of exposure?"

"There are greater men who have weathered worse scandals."

"Yes, but Cece says that Lady Ardmore is a great stickler." Rachel scarcely noticed the familiarity with which Cece's name rolled off her tongue. "And my father has a reputation for probity. It would matter to them."

"And," put in Simon blandly, "to Mr. Trevannion. A rising Tory MP cannot be too careful about with whom he allies himself."

Rachel paused in her pacing to look narrowly at her host.

"As you say," said Simon quietly, "our interests are aligned."

It was the admission Rachel had been angling for, but instead of feeling vindicated, she felt strangely disappointed. "Are you hoping to clear the field for yourself?" she asked. "Or merely to sow salt?"

"Does it matter?" he asked.

Are you still in love with my sister?

Rachel bit back the question. Simon was right; there was no practical reason it should matter. All that mattered was the help he was offering her in their shared enterprise. If he was using her to get to Lady Olivia— well, she was using him, too, wasn't she? At least they both knew where they stood.

"No," she said slowly. "I suppose it doesn't."

"Well, then." Simon set his coffee cup down on the tray, the fabric of his shirt stretching across his back. When he turned back to her, his manner was brisk, businesslike. "What are your plans?"

Hesitantly, Rachel said, "I have pictures. One of my parents together."

That one picture, previously so precious, sole relic of the lost years. She hated the idea of parting with it. But what was it, really? Testament to something that had never been.

Rachel swallowed hard and blundered on. "Also some of my mother with me. Some from before. And some . . . after." After her father had left them. Rapidly, she said, "If I were to put something in the post, would the earl open it himself, or a secretary?"

"Himself," said Simon, without hesitation. "The countess employs a social secretary—or, rather, a relay of them—but not the earl. His letters are brought to him at breakfast."

"Are you sure? It has been some time . . ."

"Since Lady Olivia jilted me? The habits of a lifetime don't change in six years. You intend to send the snaps one at a time, I imagine?"

Rachel nodded, the plan mapping itself out in her mind. "At irregular intervals."

"To keep him guessing?" Simon's expression was carefully bland. "You terrify me. The earl, I am sure, shall be found like something out of an Edgar Allan Poe story, the letters clasped in his hands and a silent scream on his cold lips."

"That," Rachel said acidly, "would defeat the purpose."

"Ah, yes, alive and remorseful. Tearing his hair and beating his breast and crying, ai, me!"

Rachel gathered up her bag in her gloved hands. "If you're going to mock, I'm going home. I mean—back to the flat."

There was something reassuring about being back in the familiar pattern of blow and counterblow.

Simon followed her through the door of the drawing room. "Is that my cue? Shall I implore you to stay? Would you like some coffee? A handkerchief? A shoulder on which to wallow?"

"I don't wallow."

"No, you plot. Admirable woman." Simon rested his palms on her shoulders, looking down into her face. In a voice devoid of its usual mockery, he said, "Are you sure this is what you want? Once you begin . . . there's no going back."

He was right, she knew. The masquerade as Vera Merton had been one thing; it might have been brushed off as a lark, a frolic. This was different. Darker. Blackmail, Simon had called it, and he wasn't far wrong.

But what was the alternative? To walk away, leave her father to his other life. Pretend that she and her mother had never existed—as, to him, they hadn't. She couldn't do that, any more than she could go back to two months ago.

Wearily, Rachel shook her head. "I can't just leave it."

"All right." Simon gave her shoulders a brief squeeze, then let go. "Do you want the countess to see the pictures?"

The move back to business was dizzying. "This is between me and my father."

She couldn't quite articulate why she felt it should be so, but she did, strongly.

Simon paused, one hand on the doorknob. "You do realize that there's little point to it unless you're inside the household. How will you gauge his reaction if you're not there to see it?"

Rachel was instantly wary. "Don't tell me to befriend Lady Olivia. That will take years. And I don't have years."

"No," Simon agreed, "you don't. I've been offered a job in New York."

For a moment, Rachel thought she must have misheard. "A what?"

"A job. Surely you've heard of them? Or have you become so nice in your tastes in your week of the high life?"

"Don't be horrid." The air in the little hall felt suddenly very close, hot and stuffy. Rachel frowned up at Simon. "Will you take it?"

"I haven't decided yet. You're welcome to stay on at the flat for as long as you like; I shan't evict you."

"Yes, but your mother might." If Simon left, she would retreat to the bedsit in Holborn, to the humble life of Rachel Woodley.

In fact, she could do so now. Letter writing didn't require a Mayfair address, or frocks made of chiffon and spangles.

But . . .

"New York?" Rachel echoed.

"It's the *New York Sketch*. Haven't heard of it? There's a reason for that. They want an Englishman as editor. Beverley Nichols chucked it, so . . ." Simon shrugged.

"You sound as though you might like it," Rachel said accusingly.

"Abandon my brilliant career as sycophant to the champagne-swilling set?" Simon flecked an invisible piece of lint from his sleeve. In profile, the stark lines of his face were even more pronounced, as were the hollows beneath his cheekbones. He was too thin, Rachel realized. Like someone burning with fever, consumed from the inside out. "I haven't given them an answer. There are . . . considerations."

"Considerations?"

Glibly, Simon said, "The plumbing, for one. It would be terribly tedious to have hot water whenever one wanted it. And those teeth! So terrifyingly white." Changing the subject, he said, "There is a way to expedite the exercise—getting you into Ardmore House. Do you remember that story Waugh was telling the other night?"

"Which one was Waugh?" She had met so many people, a blur of faces and names.

"The male half of the canoodling Evelyns," said Simon. And, more prosaically, "He was sacked by the *Daily Express*."

Ah, that one. The auburn-haired imp who wanted his name spelled correctly in the gossip columns.

"I wasn't paying much attention. My mind was on other things."

"Mr. Trevannion, for one?" Before Rachel could retort, Simon went on, with exaggerated patience, "Let me refresh your memory. The Lygon sisters forgot their latchkeys . . ."

"And had to knock up the prime minister." Rachel frowned at him. "I don't happen to be acquainted with Mr. Baldwin."

"I'm not suggesting you billet yourself on the prime minister. But if you were to contrive to leave your Crystal Ball and Bottle party at the same time as Olivia, you might share a taxi. And if it just so happened that you'd left your latchkey . . ."

"I don't know. . . ." The idea of pushing herself off on someone like that was contrary to everything she had been taught. "I wouldn't want to impose."

Simon's eyebrows soared toward his hairline. "Revenge, blackmail, impersonation . . . and you wouldn't want to *impose?*"

Despite herself, Rachel's lips twisted. "Old habits," she said apologetically.

"Break them," said Simon bluntly. "Cece's set takes delight in crashing in when they're not wanted; it's all but a religion with them."

"Yes, but Cece is the niece of an earl."

Simon arched a brow. "And you are the cousin of a Montfort. You're not Rachel Woodley here; you're Vera Merton."

But only for a few more weeks. Rachel set a hand on the doorknob. "When do you need to tell them about New York?"

"Soon."

She had always known the masquerade was meant to be a short-lived affair. She just hadn't realized quite how short.

Or how accustomed she might become to it.

Rachel pasted on a brave face. "Well, then. I'd better act quickly, hadn't I?"

❧

She sent out the first of the pictures that night.

FIFTEEN

"Those scarves! My dear, how too divine! And those earrings—!"

If a party were to be judged by the volume of conversation, the Crystal Ball and Bottle party was a smashing success. The air was shrill with the parrot twitter of a hundred excited voices, as the same people who had seen one another at last night's Hawaiian party greeted one another again, with as much surprised delight as a stranded traveler greeting a fellow castaway.

"However did you manage—"

"That shawl! Oh, the bliss of it!"

"And then Tommy said—"

"But, really, one could never—"

"My dear, how we *roared*."

"Vera, my sweetie-bo! Those earrings! I die for them!" Elizabeth Ponsonby enveloped Rachel in a cloud of scent and silk fringe. Elizabeth was one of Cece's dearest friends, a leader of the smart set, and permanently sloshed.

"Oh, do you like them?" Rachel extricated herself, by dint of several weeks' practice keeping her cocktail glass aloft in one hand, her cigarette in its long ebony holder in the other. "Maison Woolworth, my dear."

"You *are* clever," said Elizabeth admiringly. Beneath her shawl, she wore an abbreviated dress that sparkled as she moved. She pirouetted, sending the tiny crystals chiming. "What do you think of mine?"

"Darling!" Dropping Tommy Digby's arm, Lady Pansy Pakenham rushed over, splashing her gimlet over Rachel's shoes. "You haven't come as a crystal ball. *Do* tell me you haven't. It's too . . ."

"Too?" supplied Rachel, with an arched brow.

Tommy Digby leered in the general direction of Elizabeth's hem. "I can read someone's future in that."

Elizabeth tossed her head, the light catching the facets of the diamante fillet binding her brow. "Don't be vile, Tommy."

"Behave," said Rachel, tapping him with her cigarette holder. "Or it won't be your future."

Tommy guffawed appreciatively. "Read that in the cards, what?"

"No, just in Elizabeth's face."

"That's good, that is." Tommy gave Rachel a friendly elbow to the ribs. "In her face."

He wandered off in the direction of the bar, still chuckling to himself. Rachel had no doubt it would be even funnier after another drink.

In the past few weeks, Rachel had, somehow, acquired a reputation as a wit. Or, rather, Vera Merton had. Rachel couldn't see that it had taken terribly much. All she had done was speak her mind. Within limits. But coupled with an ebony cigarette holder and a Paris frock, what Rachel considered plain common sense was transmuted by the curious alchemy of champagne and ill lighting into cutting witticisms that were repeated and embroidered upon with a titter and, "Oh, *Vera!*"

It baffled Rachel sometimes, how quickly she had become the fashion, how rapidly she had moved from Miss Merton, an unknown, to "Oh, *Vera!*"

No one seemed to think it the least bit odd that she was staying in Simon's mother's flat. "How lucky to be you!" was the general chorus, with complaints about the pickiness of parents or the pokiness of shared flats. Perhaps it was as Simon said; perhaps her instincts were too bourgeois.

No one appeared to think anything of taking up residence with a relative, or even an acquaintance. It was applauded as a clever savings; more to spend on the all-important pursuit of amusement.

As the summer meandered on, Vera Merton had careened from party to party. Pirate parties and circus parties and Mozart parties where everyone came attired in white wigs and period garb, hastily hired out from costumers and theatrical outfitters. There seemed to be no end to the scrabble for costume, the endless parade of masks that did nothing to mask.

Rent, Rachel told herself. Fodder for Simon's column. If she was the rage, it was largely because her activities were dwelt and embroidered upon with loving detail by the Man About Town, who added luster to her fake gems and exploits to her earlier evenings. It was all part of the bargain.

There was something dangerously seductive about the endless whirl that deprived her of the necessity of thought: the constant round of parties, the cocktails, the telephoning. The phone upon the bed-stand was no longer an oddity; it was a constant feature of her life.

Rachel, who had always risen early, now spent the hours before noon lolling in her borrowed bed, the receiver of the phone in one hand, dissecting such important matters as whether it was really quite wise to wear silver shoes with a gold dress, "Like a goldsmith's shop, darling! All her wares on display!" or if there ought to be gypsy minstrels or a jazz band hired for the Crystal Ball and Bottle party.

It was all part of the masquerade, she assured herself. People would think it odd if she didn't, and, given the flimsiness of her credentials, she couldn't risk a crack in the facade, anything that might mark her out, in the laughing term of one of Cece's friends, as "non-U."

At least, that was what she told herself. When it came down to it, it was far easier to gossip about whether He-Evelyn would propose to She-Evelyn than to wonder whether her father was receiving an envelope . . . opening it . . . extracting the picture inside.

Since that awful day at Ardmore House, she had sent three pictures to her father, each enclosed in a sheet of blank paper, each with a brief message on the back.

The first had been the hardest.

Rachel had sat, cross-legged, on the bed, with the frame in her hands. It was real silver, that frame—pukka, her new friends would call it—but her mother would never have considered selling it. Rachel had never really noticed the frame before. Her eye had always been drawn to the picture within, her parents together, so very young. Her mother's eyes looked out at the viewer, but her father's eyes, by accident or design, were on her mother's dark head, and filled with an expression of such reverence that it had, in her romantic youth, made Rachel's heart clench.

It did now, too, but for very different reasons.

Ruthlessly, she had detached the photograph from the frame, and written, in as near a facsimile of her mother's hand as she could manage, *Pray, love, remember.*

Ophelia's line to Hamlet, after he had rejected and abandoned her. Just before she flung herself into the river.

Let him open that at the breakfast table, Rachel had thought vengefully. Let him be sitting smugly over his kipper and coffee and see *that*, hear that still, small voice from the past. Let him see that and squirm on his padded seat.

And wonder.

Four days later, Rachel sent another. Her mother was a shadowy presence behind her at the church fete, her broad-brimmed hat casting a shadow over her face, nearly obscuring the familiar brooch she wore on her breast, with its entwined *E* and *K*. Rachel was seven or eight, in braids and buttoned boots, and a too-short white frock with a wide sash at the waist. She could remember that frock, her mother fretting over there being no more material to let out.

"Growing like a weed," she had said, surveying her daughter with fond resignation. "You'll be tall, like your father's people."

How much had it cost her mother, to speak of her father without hurt or rancor? If she resented what he had done, leaving them, she never let it show.

It was harder than Rachel had thought to find a third picture without landmarks or identifying features, a picture old enough that her father wouldn't be able to see her childhood self in Vera Merton's painted face. Most of her childhood pictures had been taken by the vicar, who, for all his unworldliness, had a child's enthusiasm for new gadgets, some of which worked and most of which didn't. Alice was in nearly all of them, her fair head next to Rachel's dark one, their arms about each other's waists.

Rachel couldn't bring herself to take the scissors and snip them apart; as if in doing so, she would be cutting the last link that anchored her to her old life, the life where she was simply and confidently Rachel Woodley.

She found herself missing Alice with a fierce longing. Her fingers had twitched toward the phone—and then fallen away again.

In the end, Rachel had chosen a picture taken two years after her father had died—two years after he had left them, she corrected herself. Cousin David had snapped her on the pier at the seaside, grinning unrepentantly at the camera, proudly displaying the gap where one of her upper teeth had been.

No Shakespeare this time. Instead, Rachel wrote, *Do you know where your daughter is?*

It was only after she had sent it off that she became aware that it might be construed more than one way.

And where was her father's other daughter?

Rachel glanced unobtrusively toward the entrance, where gypsies mingled with witches, swamis, and the inevitable harlequins, the costume of least resistance. It was past midnight, and there was still no sign of Lady Olivia and Mr. Trevannion.

What if they had decided not to attend?

It had been maddening sending those letters off into the world, never knowing whether her father had received them. She knew he was still at Ardmore House; the Court Circular had been her friend in this. He had lingered in London, speaking at the Lords, escorting his wife to flower shows and garden parties, debutante dances and private concerts, events well above Rachel's touch, even as Vera Merton. There were Londons within London, a protected circle to which Rachel had no hope of entrée.

The earl's pictures in *The Tatler* told nothing; the flash could make even the healthy look ill, the resolute look alarmed.

Cece was no use; she was persona non grata with Lady Ardmore, and knew little of what went on inside the household. When Rachel had mentioned, delicately, that it seemed her uncle was lingering in London, Cece had only shrugged, and said that it must be Jicksy's twenty-first, heaven only knew they had done everything but hire elephants, and had she told Vera that she had acquired the most smashing dress—the cleverest little woman, my dear—and wasn't it just like Aunt Violet to be too mean to put them up at Caffers before the dance but was making them stay with the Grandisons, too deadly, darling; nothing but hunting talk, endless hunting talk, and with whom was Vera staying?

Rachel had hastily changed the subject. At the moment, she wasn't staying with anyone at all. She assumed that she could crash the dance—with so many invited, surely one more would occasion no comment—but finding someone to house her was a trickier task.

Rather ridiculous to hope she might wrangle an invitation to Caffers when she couldn't even get herself back through the door of Ardmore House.

Blast it all, where was Olivia? Rachel's fingers fumbled on the clasp of her bag as she drew out a fresh cigarette to place in her holder, masking her anxiety in the familiar ritual of clicking the flame of her lighter.

"I hope that frown doesn't mean that you've read something nasty in the cards."

Rachel looked up to find Mr. Trevannion standing just beside her, his hair wind-tousled, a half smile on his lips.

"Mr. Trevannion!" The lighter gave a cough and a sputter, and the small flame died. "I thought you didn't believe in such things."

"Not in the general way, no. But I hope I am open to conviction." Mr. Trevannion extracted his own lighter from his pocket, clicked the top open. Unlike Simon's, it wasn't a minor work of art; it was the cheap sort that could be picked up at any tobacconist's. "May I?"

"Thanks, awfully." Rachel put the cigarette holder between her lips, leaning in to the flame. "And that was a very politic answer, Mr. Trevannion."

"But true," he said. He slipped the lighter back into his pocket, where it jangled against a handful of coins. "And hadn't you better call me John? One doesn't stand on ceremony at events such as this."

Rachel gestured with her cigarette holder, which might not be proper gypsy attire, but was nonetheless de rigueur for her other masquerade. Costumes layered upon costumes. "And yet you're so terribly formal."

There was no costume for Mr. Trevannion. Her sister's fiancé was impeccably turned out in tails, a white silk scarf around his neck, a high-crowned black hat in his hands.

John turned his high-crowned hat over in his hands, as though unsure what to do with it. "I've just come from the Massinghams'. They had rather more in the way of imperial orders and somewhat fewer gypsies."

"One imagines they would." Rachel glanced casually over her shoulder. "Did Lady Olivia accompany you?"

"Properly speaking, I accompanied Lady Olivia," said John, with that wry little half smile that brought out the dimple in his cheek. "Although there don't seem to be such firm rules about such things these days."

"None at all," Rachel agreed, giddy with relief. Her mad plan might have a chance after all. Taking Mr. Trevannion's hat from his hands, she led him over to the side of the room. "There's not really a hatstand, I'm afraid, but if you stash your hat over there, below that ottoman, you might save it from being squashed."

Mr. Trevannion—John—stepped back as Rachel suited action to words, stowing the high-crowned hat beneath a rather dilapidated red velvet footstool. "You're very good."

"Call it practical, rather." Rachel straightened, dusting off her hands on the red chiffon skirts, which, by dint of the addition of several fringed shawls, had been converted to a gypsy costume. "A good hat is a terrible thing to waste."

John shook his head slightly. "I stand by my earlier opinion." The expression of frank admiration on his face made the compliment seem more than just words. Jokingly, he said, "Are you quite sure you're Montfort's cousin?"

The words were spoken in jest, of course. They had to be. There was no reason for the little shiver of alarm to run down Rachel's spine.

Rachel scooped her cocktail up off the ottoman, wrapping her fingers around the stem of the glass. "What *do* you have against Simon? Not that he can't be perfectly infuriating on general principle."

"I don't—" John began, and then broke off, laughing uncomfortably. "Oh, why not? He wrote a rather scathing article about a piece I wrote, on disarmament."

Rachel raised her perfectly plucked brows. "I hadn't thought the Man About Town involved himself much in politics."

"This one, he put under his own name."

"What did he have to say?" asked Rachel, genuinely curious. It was hard to imagine Simon serious about anything.

But he had been, a bit, that day at Heatherington House, and again when she had descended on him in his flat, that miserable, desperate afternoon. Beneath the barbs and the wit for wit's sake, there had been a thread of something, something real and dark and serious.

John shrugged. "Oh, the usual blather about the perfidy of our allies and another war being just around the corner. You know the sort."

"He's certainly not the only one to think so," said Rachel cautiously. The headlines of the papers screamed similar warnings every day.

"And what better way to create another war than to wave guns in the face of our allies?" said John vehemently. "It's men like Montfort who set us back decades. If we want to see peace in our time, we need more cooperation, not less. Naturally, the crusty old army sorts all took up his call. I nearly lost my seat."

Rachel looked up sharply. "Did you?"

Her mind churned with possibilities. Lady Ardmore had been willing to settle for a rising politician for Olivia. But what if the rising politician ceased to rise? What then? Would the match be retracted with a polite notice in *The Morning Post*?

John scrubbed his eyes with the heels of his hands. "It was a close-run thing. Mine is a fairly conservative constituency."

A pocket borough, Simon had called it. Were there even such things anymore? Mere nastiness, Rachel decided.

"But you prevailed in the end," she said lightly. "When do you and the Lady Olivia marry?"

"Oh, not until after Jicksy's twenty-first." As if he realized how vague that sounded, John added hastily, "They make rather a thing of the coming of age of the heir, the Standishes. And we're in no hurry, Olivia and I. We do have the rest of our lives, after all."

He didn't sound quite so pleased by it as he could.

"I'm sure Lady Olivia will be a brilliant hostess." Rachel took a deep drag on her cigarette. After three weeks, she had mastered the art of doing so without coughing. "Such an asset to you. I understand Lady Ardmore is very active in Conservative circles?"

John discovered a certain interest in the heavy silk folds of his scarf. "Yes. Lady Ardmore is quite . . . forceful." His eyes met Rachel's, ruefully amused. "I appreciate her dedication—even if we don't always see eye to eye on matters of policy."

On an impulse, Rachel said, "Whatever are you doing with the Tories?" Trying to soften her words, she said, "Your ideas sound . . . well, a bit progressive for that lot."

John grinned at her. "Mr. Churchill said somewhat the same thing to me last week. In a far less attractive guise."

"Yes, yes," said Rachel. "Compliment taken. But why, then?"

John thought for a moment. "I believe in Mr. Baldwin. He's a good man. A thoughtful man. As long as he remains at the helm . . ."

"And if he doesn't? What then?"

"That's the question, isn't it?" John's lips quirked in a smile. "Has anyone told you that you're really quite perceptive?"

Rachel could feel her cheeks warm beneath the layers of powder and rouge. She shrugged, saying, in her best Madame Zelda voice, "It is all in the cards, you know. Merely cross the palm with silver and hear the secrets of the ages! Or something like."

"You don't have to spout that nonsense," John said indulgently. "Not for me."

Rachel drew her fringed shawl more firmly around her. "You don't like my Madame Zelda?"

"It's not that." He was looking at her, looking through the silk fringe, the face paint, the gaudy trappings. "You pretend to be like the rest of them. But you're not, are you?"

He didn't know the half of it.

For a mad moment, Rachel wondered what it would be if she told him the truth, then and there. That she wasn't an international heiress with a taste for the clavichord. That she was, in fact, nothing more than a nursery governess in fancy feathers and a borrowed flat. *My name is Rachel Woodley* . . .

But she couldn't. Not now, and particularly not with him.

"You can't think what a relief it is," John was saying, "to have someone sensible to talk to at these things."

"That's one way of putting it. My cousin"—Rachel looked automatically over her shoulder—"tells me I'm hopelessly bourgeois in my outlook."

John was touchingly indignant on her behalf. "I should call that a compliment." He cast a disparaging look around the room. "Especially among this lot."

Pat on her cue, Cece swirled in upon them, resplendent in a gold lamé and crimson feathers. "*There* you are! We've been looking everywhere for you, you naughty, naughty things."

Behind her stood Lady Olivia Standish, the opposite of resplendent in dull pink chiffon, unbecoming flounces, and drooping roses.

"Cece! Lady Olivia!" Rachel covered her confusion with an excess of enthusiasm, slopping her drink in the process, all too aware of John's presence beside her, as though she'd been caught with her finger in someone else's pie.

One was allowed to chat about politics without feeling as though there were anything sordid about it. That was what one did at cocktail parties. Chat. And drink. She oughtn't to be feeling so flustered.

It was Simon, standing behind them, watching her with a decidedly ironical eye, who had put the idea in her head. Simon and his ridiculous notion that she had an eye on her sister's fiancé.

Rachel gathered up her drink and her draperies. "Darlings!" she exclaimed. "You've been an age!"

"We've been an age?" Cece wagged a finger at her. "We ought to be very cross with you, oughtn't we? I've been looking *everywhere*. Livvy wants her fortune told, don't you, Livvy?"

Lady Olivia looked as though she wanted nothing of the kind. And why should she? Her future was assured. Marriage to John and a cozy mansion in Eaton Square.

"Surely you don't need a crystal ball for that?" Rachel moved away from John with a swish of silk fringe. "I see orange blossoms and white tulle . . ."

"And a voyage over the water?" drawled Simon.

He'd dressed as a sort of swami, in a purple turban, puffy pants, and a pasteboard scimitar at his waist. He ought to have looked ridiculous.

He didn't.

Rachel flicked ash from her cigarette, striking a provocative pose. "Does the Thames count?"

Simon folded his arms across his chest, every inch the pasha. "Better make it the Seine, at least. Far more romantic."

Rachel wasn't going to allow him the last word. "If filled with frogs?"

"A geographical hazard."

"Oh, do stop being ridiculous." Cece gave Simon a little push. The force of the movement made her stumble on her high-heeled slippers. Swaying toward Rachel, she said imperiously, "You do have your cards?"

"They're about somewhere." Rachel had made sure to practice before leaving the flat, although she had hoped that, in the general scrum, she wouldn't be called upon to perform. Cunningly, she said, "But wouldn't you rather another drink first?"

She kept one eye on Lady Olivia, who was looking distinctly uncomfortable. And no wonder in that dress.

She couldn't let Lady Olivia leave. Not yet. Rachel's latchkey had been left at home, for verisimilitude—and so she couldn't get cold feet.

"Your glass is decidedly empty," said Simon to Cece. "Allow me to escort you to the bar."

He raised a brow at Rachel over Cece's head. Giving Rachel a chance to beg off the card reading? Reminding her to take the opportunity to further her acquaintance with her sister? Rachel wasn't sure. With Simon, one never was. One simply had to seize the main chance as it was offered.

"No need." With an arch smile, Cece held aloft a battered silver flask. "I nicked this off Tommy Digby."

"Darling, not Tommy!" The role came so easily by now. "After what happened last time . . ."

"Any port in a storm," said Simon blandly.

"It's gin, actually," said Rachel, just to see Simon raise a brow in exaggerated disgust. Since Cece seemed determined to stay for the show, Rachel said dutifully to Lady Olivia, "*Shall* we have a go with the cards?"

"That won't be necessary." Lady Olivia spoke in her soft, slightly husky voice. "I shouldn't want to put you out."

Was there a subtle dig in that?

"No trouble," said Rachel, with a smile that felt as though it had been painted on. She swept a corner of her shawl over her head, adopting a mystic voice. "Nothing is hidden from the all-knowing eye of Madame Zelda! In these cards, I hold the secrets of the future—and the past."

Cece was lit like a Roman candle, fizzing with excitement. "See?" she said triumphantly, swaying a little on her heels. "Didn't I tell you?"

Lady Olivia looked at Cece and didn't seem to like what she saw. Putting a hand on John's arm, she murmured, "We really ought to go. . . ."

"Oh, come," said John indulgently, giving her hand a perfunctory pat. "We came all this way, don't you want to see what Madame Zelda will reveal?"

He smiled, showing that he thought it all a great joke.

Lady Olivia attempted to mimic the smile, but she looked . . . uneasy. Rachel's eyes flicked from one to the other. To Cece, exultant with anticipation; John, determinedly amused; and Olivia, who looked distinctly uncomfortable.

And then there was Simon.

He slid a casual arm around Cece's shoulders. "You do know that it's all rubbish, don't you?" The words were light, but Rachel sensed something genuine beneath them. "The cards are only bits of paper."

"Don't be such a bore." Cece shrugged off Simon's arm, tugging at Rachel's hand. "There's a table over there. Let's sit, shall we?"

In the end, Rachel and Olivia sat. The others stood around them.

The table had been draped in red velvet, a crystal ball in the middle. John, Simon, and Cece all wavered in the glass, a series of carnival images, distorted and unnerving. Rachel ignored the ball and concentrated on the cards.

Rachel fanned the deck in front of Olivia. "I need you to draw seven cards. They must," she added in her best Madame Zelda voice, "be chosen with your own hand."

Lady Olivia's hand hesitated over the deck.

"Choose wisely," said Simon sarcastically.

Cece swatted him on the arm. "Hush. You'll destroy the vibrations."

"It will be what it will be," said Rachel soothingly. Particularly since she would be assigning the meaning. The silk fringe fell in her face. She brushed it back again. "Have you made your choice, Lady Olivia?"

The other woman started to reach toward the cards, and Rachel raised a hand to stop her.

"No gloves. Your bare fingers must touch the cards."

"For the psychic powers to be transmitted?" said Simon.

"Yes," said Rachel firmly.

There was an awkward silence as Lady Olivia tugged at the engagement ring that was lodged so snugly over the kid of her gloves.

"Do get on with it," said Cece impatiently.

Lady Olivia didn't grab at the cards, or take them all in a clump. Delicately, she drew the cards at intervals, picking each one as though it were a flower.

Her pale lashes flickered up, revealing those gray eyes that were so familiar and yet so different. Tentatively, she offered the cards to Rachel. "Here."

"Mmm," said Rachel, and wondered just what it was that Lady Olivia was so afraid she might see. The old scandal about her elopement with Simon? Or something more recent, more damning? She tapped the cards together into a little pile, then set the first one down, faceup. "Four . . . a change in your life. And not just a four, but the four of hearts. Marriage?"

Olivia glanced up at John, just the smallest movement, before looking down again, at her bare hands.

Rachel turned another card. "The eight of diamonds. There are festivities in your future, a celebration of some kind."

"A wedding?" suggested Simon, in dulcet tones.

"Or Jicksy's twenty-first," said Cece, leaning so far over Rachel's shoulder that she was practically nose-first into the crystal ball.

"You forgot the journey over water and the dark-haired man," said John, with a smile at Rachel.

"Madame Zelda needs quiet to work. All doubters and skeptics to the back of the line." Rachel turned another card.

She meant it jokingly, but there was no doubting that there was something charged in the atmosphere. In the background, the violins wailed a lament. Somewhere behind them, a glass shattered. With the press of bodies, the room was stiflingly close, the roar of voices muting to a blur. The entire room seemed to have narrowed to the glimmering surface of the crystal ball, the brightly painted figures on the cards.

Rachel frowned at the card in her hand. She was, she realized, just a little bit drunk. Not drunk like Cece, but enough to be just a little dizzy.

"What is it?" demanded Cece.

"Seven. The seven of spades." If ever she had been tempted to believe in the cards—which she hadn't—it would be now. This one was straight out of the pamphlet she had studied. And it couldn't describe their father more accurately. "There is an unfaithful or dishonest person in your life. I see broken promises."

Simon raised a brow. "Trevannion?"

In the crystal ball, Rachel could see John's lips tighten. "Not all politicians are dishonest, Montfort." He looked down at Olivia's bowed head. "And not all of us break our promises."

Olivia pushed back from the table. "Is that the time? I wouldn't want—"

Hastily, Rachel slapped down another card from the four left in her hand. "Secrets," she said loudly. "I see secrets."

According to her pamphlets, the jack of clubs was really a well-meaning but immature young man. But it was time to move this along.

Another card. The joker.

Fresh starts and new opportunities, according to the pamphlet.

That would never do.

Raising both hands, Rachel intoned, "A voice from the past is calling out to you, someone forgotten, someone wronged." Her bangles clanked and jangled on her wrists in the sudden silence. "A voice from the past is crying to be heard."

She raised her eyes to Lady Olivia's pale face.

But it wasn't Olivia who spoke. It was Cece, her voice high-pitched and excited. "Whose? Whose voice?"

SIXTEEN

"Whose voice?" Cece's long nails were like talons, digging into Rachel's arm, her voice high and shrill. "Whose?"

Simon slung a casual arm around Cece's shoulders. "You're tight, my dear. Don't you know better than to drink from someone else's flask?"

His pose was relaxed, but Rachel could see the pressure he was exerting to draw Cece away. Something, something was happening, and Rachel had no idea what. All that was sure was the cheap cardboard of the cards beneath her fingertips.

"Go to the devil." Cece pulled her arm away, stumbling into the small table with such force that the crystal ball—best Woolworth—rocked on its base. "Tell me. Tell me what you see."

"It's just a game." Simon's voice was harder now. "Isn't it, Vera?"

"Of course," said Rachel. She swept up the cards, shuffling them together. "It's all nonsense, really."

Cece grabbed the edge of the table, her knuckles white beneath her rings. "But what about Jean-Luc? And Leonie? And that horse . . . coming back to the stable. . . ."

"Leonie? Oh." With horror, Rachel recognized her own fictions.

"But, darling—all chance. And that was France. Things work differently there."

Cece grabbed Rachel's arm, clinging with the tenacity of the extremely drunk. "Do it again. Do it for me."

The cards fell and scattered. The joker winked at Rachel from the top of the pack.

"The forces grow weak. . . ." said Rachel in her best Madame Zelda voice. Only it wasn't a joke anymore. The urgency in Cece's face was both pathetic and terrifying. She made a lurch at normalcy. "The spirits need more gin. Won't you come with me to the bar, darling?"

"It's Simon, isn't it?" The black kohl stood out in stark lines around Cece's eyes, her rouge was too red on her pale cheeks. "He's got to you." She gave a vaguely hysterical laugh. "He won't even say his name. Will you, Simon? All I have to do is say—"

Simon's voice was sharped, clipped. "I think we've had enough fortune-telling, don't you?"

Cece grabbed at the flowing folds of his white shirt. "Don't you want to know? Or are you afraid of what he might say?" Her voice was rising, higher and higher, audible even over the rusty scraping of the motley minstrels. "You don't listen. You never listen. If you had listened, he might have—"

"Cece." Tentatively, Lady Olivia reached out a hand.

Cece knocked it away. "Don't you Cece me!" Her mouth was a scarlet O; the words rushed out like lava, tinged with flame. "What do you know about any of it? You don't care; you never cared. If you hadn't been so busy exchanging sweet nothings with Simon he might have seen—he might have heard—Oh, Lord, what a joke! What a sick-making, ridiculous joke."

Cece was laughing now, horrible, high peals of laughter that made her double over, clutching at her stomach with the force of it, tears making the eye-black run down her cheeks.

"*How* we roared. Peter said—Peter said—"

A horrible choking sound emerged from Cece's throat. It took Rachel a moment to realize that she was crying. Not prettily. Not crystalline tears, but great ugly, gulping sobs.

"Cece . . ." It was Simon who reached for her this time, but he was too late.

Cece whirled away, her fingers like claws, clutching at Rachel's shoulders. "Tell me! You said you could. You said you could read the cards—"

Behind her, as in a dream, Rachel could see John Trevannion and Lady Olivia. Lady Olivia had taken a step back, gloved fingers pressed against her lips.

Cece shook Rachel until Rachel's tawdry hoop earrings clattered and her brain felt as though it were rattling between her ears. "Tell me. Tell me *why*—"

"Cece! Cece, I can't, really. I don't—" Rachel was grasping for Cece's wrists, trying to wriggle free of her grasp, but the other woman was strong, surprisingly strong.

"Tell me, tell me, tell me . . ." The words came out in a hysterical mantra, in time to the rattling of Rachel's teeth. "You said you could. . . . Tell me, tell me, tell me . . ."

Tears poured down Cece's cheeks in rivers of black kohl, dripping unheeded onto the precious stuff of her dress.

And then, suddenly, the pressure was gone. Gently, but firmly, Simon pulled her away. "That's enough, Cece."

"Enough?" Cece's lips drew back over her teeth. She was laughing again, high and hysterical. "Enough? You'd like that, wouldn't you? You'd like to make it all just go away. As if you didn't—as if he wouldn't—"

Behind her, Rachel could hear John Trevannion saying, "She's hysterical. The poor girl's hysterical." And then, in a louder voice, "Too many drinks. Brandy on top of gin . . ."

Wildly, Cece turned from Olivia to Simon, from Simon to Olivia. Her voice sliced through the room, over the faltering scrapings of the violin.

"It's your fault! It's your fault, do you hear!"

Simon took a step forward. Rachel was reminded of a tiger keeper at the zoo, speaking slowly and carefully. "Cece . . ."

"Don't touch me!" Cece backed away, her jeweled heel catching on the trailing velvet table cover.

Rachel grabbed for her, but it was too late, Cece was already falling, falling, landing on the wooden floor with a hard, unromantic thunk.

For a moment, all was silence. Horrible silence. Cece lay crumpled on the floor, her gold lamé skirts pooling around her like molten gold. Then, from beneath her splayed fingers came the breath of sound, a whimper, a name.

Belatedly, awkwardly, Rachel scrambled down beside her. The fringe of her shawl caught on the back of the chair. She shrugged it aside. "Cece! Darling? Are you hurt?"

Cece curled into a ball, her knees tucked to her chest. Her eyes were closed, tears leaking out of the sides. "Peter . . . Peter . . ."

Rachel felt as though she was being turned inside out, left vulnerable and raw. Gone was all the affectation, the bravado she had come to associate with Cece. There was something gut-wrenchingly sad about the noises coming from Cece's lips, like a child crying alone in the night.

"Is it your head?" Desperately, Rachel reached behind the other woman's head, feeling for a lump. Easier to focus on the physical, on the things that needed to be done. No blood, and no lump, not that she could feel. "If I hold up my fingers, can you tell me how many there are?"

Somewhere above her, she could hear John Trevannion's voice, saying with false heartiness, ". . . had a bit too much, you know how it is. Mixing punch with gin . . . quite a head in the morning."

And the shrill, starling chatter of the gossips as the word eddied and spread, transmuted into something new and fantastical with each iteration.

". . . darling, didn't you know!" Rachel could hear someone saying, behind her. "They say it's Elmley's."

"I thought he was"—whisper, whisper, giggle, giggle—"with Barbara."

"Not for centuries! Besides, just *look* at her—"

"Let me." Moving Rachel aside, Simon knelt by Cece.

"S-Simon?" Cece's voice broke on a sob.

"Right here." He held out his arms to her, and Cece burrowed her face into his chest, eye-black smearing across the white of his shirt. Simon's eyes met Rachel's above Cece's head. In a low voice, he said, "I'm taking her home."

Carefully, he stood. The others had backed away, disassociating themselves from the spectacle. John Trevannion had escorted Lady Olivia a discreet distance away. Cece was still weeping, but softly now, the sound muffled by Simon's chest, her slippered feet dangling over his arm, the jeweled heels somehow absurd now, strangely out of place in the face of her dejection.

Their costumes suddenly seemed like the tawdry things they were, nothing but cheap glitter and paste.

Rachel rose creakily to her feet. She felt a hundred years old. "I'll help."

"There's no need." Simon's voice was abrupt, clipped. "You've done enough."

Rachel took a step back, the color high in her cheeks. That wasn't fair. If she'd known—She kept her voice low to keep the others from hearing. In a furious whisper, she said, "You might have warned me!"

Simon pressed his eyes shut. Beneath the gaily colored turban, his skin looked sallow; there were dark circles beneath his eyes. "Look, that was— I'm sorry."

She had never expected an apology. Rachel stared at him, caught off guard.

Cradling Cece in his arms, Simon mustered an unconvincing smile. "You have your own cats to flay. Remember?"

She couldn't leave them there like that. Rachel smoothed a bit of fair hair, fine as a child's, away from Cece's brow, her eyes on Simon's. "Are you sure? I—"

"She has her mother." And then, as Rachel stood there, in an agony of indecision. "It's all right."

The gossiping strangers parted, watching, as Simon moved toward the stair, his limp burden in his arms.

"Simon!" He turned back, just for a moment. "Who is Peter?"

"No one," he said, and turned and walked away, the crowd parting as he passed, the jewels on Cece's heels winking and glittering.

And Rachel was left standing there, beside the trailing velvet of the scrying table, with a sick taste at the back of her throat that had nothing to do with the contents of Tommy Digby's flask.

Peter, Cece had cried. *Peter.*

There were Peters in their set, Peters Rachel had met, but none for whom she could imagine Cece, polished, laughing, brittle Cece, reduced to a hysterical, biting, clawing, mass of misery.

Tell me . . . Tell me . . . Tell me why . . .

The touch of a hand on Rachel's bare shoulder made her jump.

She whirled, her fist pressed against her lips, to find only John Trevannion. "That was . . . unfortunate," he said.

Rachel reached for her shawl, but it had been dropped somewhere during the fray, undoubtedly sopping up the dregs of Cece's fallen drink. She wrapped her arms around herself, shoulders hunched.

"If I had known . . . I hadn't imagined. Oh, God." She looked down at her own red chiffon skirts, the cards scattered across the floor. "It was meant to be a game."

A game with a sting in it. But the sting had never been intended for Cece.

Ought she have known? Ought she have noticed that there was something abnormal about the force of Cece's interest?

Simon had known. And so had Lady Olivia. Both of them, watching Cece, worried.

John gave her bare shoulder a brief, reassuring squeeze. "It wasn't your fault."

Cece's voice, hysterical. *It's your fault. It's your fault.*

There was a small diadem in Lady Olivia's dark blond hair, a tasteful thing, without sparkle. Beneath it, Lady Olivia's face was pale and still.

"We—we really ought to be going," she said. She held out a hand to Rachel. "It was very kind of you to invite us."

The amenities must be observed. The *Titanic* was sinking but the band was still playing. An earl's daughter was bred to such behavior. Were there lessons on how to comport oneself after a fortune-telling fit of hysteria?

"It was Cece's party as much as mine." Rachel felt numb, numb and frozen, as though she were moving slowly through a wasteland.

Cece draped over Simon's arm. *It's your fault. Peter* . . . The horrible, guttural sounds coming from Cece's throat, pain and loss too terrible to contemplate. *Tell me* . . .

Stooping, Rachel retrieved her sodden shawl. "I—I think I ought to go, too. I couldn't stay. Not after—" Oh, Lord, she didn't want to do this, not now. But if not, what was the point of it all? "Would you mind terribly if I share your taxi?"

"Not at all." It was John Trevannion who spoke, holding out an arm to her. "Can we drop you at your flat?"

"Please," said Rachel. She managed a ghost of a smile. "One doesn't feel much like dancing . . . now."

Lady Olivia said nothing.

She never did, thought Rachel, with a flare of anger. But she must have once. *It's your fault*, Cece had said, and she hadn't been looking at Rachel. She had been looking at Lady Olivia, sweet-faced, silent Lady Olivia, who said nothing and admitted nothing, and left them all to dance and caper around her, like so many fools.

Abruptly, Rachel asked, "Who is Peter?"

"Peter was Cece's brother," said John.

Lady Olivia's eyes slanted toward him as he helped her into a taxi.

Rachel remembered the silver-framed pictures in Lady Fanny's sitting room: the girl and the boy in their white frocks and long curls, the young man in khaki.

Rachel followed her sister inside. "Was?"

Olivia busied herself with the clasp of her bag, seeming not to hear her.

Selective deafness, Rachel was learning, was very much the province of the aristocracy.

Mercifully, it wasn't the forte of rising politicians. John dropped heavily into the seat next to Rachel. "Poor old Peter. I'm surprised you didn't hear of it. But you were away, weren't you?"

"In France," said Rachel. That much was true. "Hear of what?"

"John . . ." said Olivia, but John didn't seem to hear her.

"I didn't know him, really. Not to speak to. He was a fair way ahead of me at school. And then there was the war. . . ." Oblivious to Olivia's warning glance, John rubbed a knuckle over his mouth. "He put a bullet through his brain."

SEVENTEEN

Somewhere, an engine backfired, with a sound like a shot. Rachel could feel the reverberations of it right down her spine.

A bullet. "He shot himself?"

"In '20—or was it '21?" John looked to Olivia for confirmation. "Cece found him. Horrible way to go."

"Horrible," Rachel echoed. A horrible way to go and a horrible thing to see. She couldn't begin to picture it. "Good heavens—why?"

"He'd been gassed during the war. His nerves were gone. And this," John said emphatically, "is why it is so crucial that we preserve peace at any cost. They say we were too young to understand what they went through in the trenches. But we have seen the cost of it, the toll in life and health, in industry and ambition."

It sounded like a portion of a speech. Perhaps it was.

"If even small measures might be taken to prevent such a tragedy occurring again—"

"Shots to the glands?" said Lady Olivia, and there was an edge to her voice that Rachel hadn't heard before.

John cast her a quick, reproachful look. "Among other measures." To

Rachel he said, "I've been told that Cece worshipped her brother. After he died . . . she went a little potty."

Rachel felt the weight of it pressing down on her. She had never imagined that Cece, silly, flighty, Cece, might be dogged by tragedy. She seemed to live in a perpetual Noël Coward production, in which more serious matters had no place.

"I hadn't known," she said numbly.

"I'm surprised Montfort didn't say anything," said John. "He and Peter were thick as thieves."

Olivia said nothing. She merely turned her head and looked out the window, at the irregular flash and glare of the lamps of passing cars, the dim rectangles of lighted windows, drapes drawn to shield them from the eyes of curious passersby.

John was still talking. "You never saw one without the other. I was only a fresher, but . . . if there was trouble afoot, it was invariably Montfort and Heatherington-Vaughn. They joined up at the same time, too, didn't they?"

"Yes," said Olivia distantly, and something about her tone was a distinct bar to further discussion.

Pas devant les domestiques, that was the timeworn phrase. Never discuss personal matters in front of the servants. Or strangers.

Rachel could feel the doors slamming around her, like shutters closing, window after window, turning a blank face to the stranger. They all just *knew*, didn't they? They knew one another, their histories, their pedigrees. They had played together in childhood, shared the same nurseries, attended the same schools; their parents knew one another.

It didn't matter how much Rachel looked the part, how much Standish blood might run in her veins, she was blundering in blind, the proverbial bull in the china shop. What was she doing? she thought desperately. This was all wrong. She wasn't meant to be here, stirring up old memories and old wounds. Her father, yes, he deserved it, but Cece—what had Cece done? She'd never meant to hurt her, had never known she might hurt her.

She could hear her own voice, painfully naive, demanding of Simon whether he was afraid she might use the wrong fork.

He'd warned her, hadn't he? That these were deep waters. And she'd ignored him and gone on.

He might have warned her tonight, Rachel thought furiously. He might have warned her before Cece crumpled in a heap on the floor.

They were in Mayfair now. The streets had become familiar to Rachel over the past month; she knew their twisting and turning. In only a moment, the taxi would turn down South Audley Street, draw up in front of the block of flats.

With a sinking feeling, Rachel remembered the latchkey, deliberately left behind. It would, in the words of Cece, be too *frightfully bogus* if she were to root through her bag, only to be betrayed by the clink of the supposedly missing keys.

Rachel suppressed the thought of Cece. She would visit her tomorrow. Make sure she was recovered. For now, as Simon had said, she had other cats to flay.

Rachel leaned forward to address the taxi driver through the partition. "My flat is only down the next street to the right. I'll just—oh!"

John rose easily to the bait. "Is something the matter?"

"My latchkey." Rachel made a show of scrabbling through her bag. "I know it was here. I'm sure I dropped it in after I locked the door this evening. . . ."

Her powder compact clanked against her lighter as she raked through the contents, her fingers shaking with nervous energy.

"It *must* be here. . . ." Unceremoniously, Rachel dumped the lot in her lap. Lipstick, compact, lighter, a crumpled tissue. "I can't think—oh!" Her hand flew to her mouth. "Someone bumped into me on the street as I was getting out of the taxi. The clasp on the bag is loose—I'd meant to fix it, but . . . I'd thought I'd got everything up again . . ."

She looked from John to Olivia with eyes wide with feigned distress.

"Might someone have found them?" suggested Olivia doubtfully.

"On the street? Oh, bother. I *knew* I should have fixed that clasp. . . . There's no night porter, you see, and the morning man doesn't come until six." Rachel sucked on her lower lip, a picture of polite indecision. "I know this is a bit of cheek, but . . . you wouldn't mind terribly if I imposed upon your hospitality, would you? I'll just curl up on the hearthrug; you'll hardly know I'm there." Before Olivia could say anything, she hastily added, "Oh, dear. Forget I said anything. It's not that long until dawn. Are there tea shops open, do you think?"

"Don't be foolish." John rapped on the partition, saying curtly to the driver, "There's been a change of plan. We'll go straight on to Ardmore House. Eaton Square." He looked over Rachel's head at Olivia. "There are—how many bedrooms at Ardmore House?"

"Twelve," said Olivia reluctantly. She drew in a deep breath, as though steeling herself for unpleasantness. "Of course you must come home with me."

"Thanks awfully." Rachel bared her teeth in a smile. "I can't think what I would have done. . . ."

"Not at all," murmured Olivia.

"Oh, good, that's settled, then." Oblivious, John smiled from one to the other as the taxi pulled up in front of the great pillared portico of Ardmore House. "I'll say good night to you both, then."

He handed them both out. There was, Rachel noticed, nothing lover-like about the kiss that he pressed to Olivia's cheek.

It might, she supposed, be ascribed to the inhibiting presence of a stranger, but Rachel doubted it.

"Good night," Rachel said, and, in a fit of perverseness, pressed her lac-quered lips to John's cheek, leaving a bright smear of red like a brand. "You *are* kind."

At the top of the steps, a door opened, held by an unobtrusive person in dark livery.

"'Night, Vera. Olivia." With a nod to each, John strolled away, his hands in his pockets, whistling as he walked.

Rachel gathered her draggled draperies around her, tucked her crystal ball under her arm, and followed Olivia up the stairs, past the waiting footman. This wasn't the fearsome butler of Rachel's first visit, but a much younger man, struggling to stifle a yawn as he pulled himself into the requisite stiff-backed stance.

"Thank you, William," murmured Olivia.

Did Olivia ever raise her voice? Rachel wondered. Ever stub her toe and shout, or laugh high and loud? It was as though she were wrapped in cotton wool, everything about her muted.

"Thank you," Rachel echoed. The sound of her own voice, too loud, too brash, sounded like an affront in the quiet hall.

From the crest of the stairs, the portrait of Violet, Lady Ardmore, glowered down at her.

"The Blue Room might be made up," Olivia said, as they passed up the same stairs Rachel had climbed with Cece. She didn't, Rachel noticed, trail her fingers along the rail, as Cece had, but walked with her arms pressed tightly to her sides, as though to keep from leaving marks on the shining surface. "Or there's Jicksy's room. It's kept ready for him, for when he comes down to London."

"Any old corner will do." Rachel flashed Olivia her best Vera Merton smile. "I just need a bolt to burrow in until dawn, and then I'll be on my way. I feel *such* a fool!"

Olivia looked at her uncertainly. "I'm sure it might have happened to anyone. They are such small things, keys, aren't they?"

Very small things, but terribly useful for keeping people in—or out.

They passed the landing with the library. The great doors were closed, the hall quiet and still. Rachel wondered where her father was, whether he had received her last picture. He had no idea that his discarded daughter had invaded the midnight fastness of his home, was creeping down his corridors and climbing his stairs.

"Yes, and with a will of their own," Rachel said gaily. "I'm constantly misplacing them."

The stairs narrowed as they ascended to the second floor, up past the grand public rooms. The paintings on the walls were smaller, the frames relatively dingy.

It was, Rachel thought, very different from Heatherington House, where the family rooms were quite as luxurious as the reception rooms below, old masters mixed with new artists, and priceless porcelain with odd bits of pottery crafted by one of Cece's artistically minded—if not artistically gifted—friends.

At Ardmore House, the upper corridors had a forgotten feel, like the backstage of a theater.

Rachel jangled her bracelets at Olivia. "I'm not going to disturb your parents, am I? Creeping through the corridors?"

"Oh, no," said Olivia earnestly. "My mother's rooms are on the first floor, quite on the other side. And my father's gone up to Oxfordshire. So, you see, we're quite alone on this floor."

Rachel's stomach twisted. "Has he been away long?"

So much for cunning plans. Her pictures, her precious pictures, with their subtle messages, were probably lying unread on a heap of correspondence.

"No." Olivia's pace quickened, her footfalls muted against the worn rug that ran the length of the corridor. "Just yesterday. There was a letter . . ."

"A letter?" Rachel hurried behind her. "How very mysterious!"

Olivia cast Rachel a quick, uncertain look over her shoulder. "Not really. It's most likely something to do with Jicksy's twenty-first. It usually is." She tried the handle of a door, letting out a quick breath of relief as it opened. "Here we are. The Blue Room."

The room was, indeed, quite blue. The walls were blue and the drapes were blue, and the chintz-covered furniture was patterned in blue flowers. The pictures on the wall were all reproductions of old masters, interspersed with uninspired watercolors of yet more flowers, most of them blue.

Olivia tentatively lifted the coverlet. "The bed does seem to be made up. . . . I can ring for someone if you need anything?"

"Oh, no, don't do that," said Rachel quickly. It was all too recently she had been one of those for whom she might have rung. "Just point the way to the lavatory, and I'm sure there's nothing more I could require."

She entertained the thought of creeping back downstairs, and just as quickly dismissed it. What did she expect to find? Her own letter, flung down on her father's desk, with a note next to it saying, *Horrors, horrors . . .*?

"The lavatory is three doors down to your left." Olivia twisted her hands together at her waist. "I could offer you a nightdress . . ."

Was she worried that Miss Vera Merton might disgrace her by parading down the corridors of Ardmore House in the altogether?

To be fair, it was the sort of stunt Cece would pull, just for the effect of it.

Rachel could imagine the sort of nightdress Olivia wore, impossibly sweet, with voluminous white skirts and embroidered flowers around the hem. The sort of thing that Major-General's daughters wore in regional productions of *The Pirates of Penzance.*

"My dear!" Rachel said, in her best Vera voice. "Do you still wear a nightdress? How too sweet!"

Olivia's cheeks colored, but she said doggedly, "I'm afraid I haven't any pajamas. My mother thinks they're fast."

"Are they?" said Rachel languidly. "Mine tend to stay where I put them. Most of the time."

"Um, well, yes." Lady Olivia backed toward the door. "If there is anything you need, do let me know. Or you might ring . . ." She paused in the doorway, her expensive evening bag still clutched between her hands. "I'm sure this isn't at all what you're used to."

She didn't know the half of it. There was a bellpull on the wall by the bed. Heavy cream writing paper on the table, embossed in gold. A far cry from Netherwell.

Rachel reached up to unscrew the French back of one of her earrings. "No. It's not."

Lady Olivia hovered in the doorway, one hand on the knob. "After all the exotic places you've been . . . this must seem very provincial."

Her voice was as stiff, as stilted as ever, but there was a hint of something else beneath it. Something a little wistful.

Head tilted as she struggled with the back of the other earring, Rachel looked curiously at her half-sister. "I hadn't thought you would read the *Daily Yell.*"

There was a long pause, and then . . .

"Cook takes it." Lady Olivia fidgeted with the pearl hanging from her ear. "I know it's silly—but it is rather exciting, reading about your adventures."

Lady Olivia looked like a child on the wrong side of a toy shop window.

Rachel's fingers stilled on the back of her earring. "But you have your picture in *The Tatler* all the time!"

"Yes, going to other houses in Mayfair." Olivia glanced down at her hands. "I was to have gone to Paris to be finished, but . . . my mother didn't want me to fall prey to unfortunate influences."

"You haven't been to Paris?" Rachel wasn't sure why, she had just assumed that the daughter of an earl would have traveled, would have stayed in the great rooms of the houses where Rachel had been governess.

"When I'm married. I'll be able to go then—" Olivia broke off, a small furrow appearing between her eyes. "If John says it's all right."

Slowly, Rachel set her earring down on the coverlet. "I'm certain he will." She didn't know what else to say. "Who could possibly object to Paris?"

Olivia shook her head slightly. "Well, there is the constituency to think about . . . and . . . Never mind." She gathered herself together. "If you need anything, you will ring?"

She turned, the flounce of her long skirt brushing the floor.

On an impulse, Rachel said, "It's all rubbish, you know. I've never even been to India. And I certainly don't play the clavichord!"

Lady Olivia paused, her hand on the knob. "But the paper—"

"That," said Rachel succinctly, "was all my dear cousin Simon's doing. I'm sure he did it just to irk me."

"That does sound like Si—Mr. Montfort. He does enjoy tweaking peoples' noses."

"Just their noses?" said Rachel drily.

She was rewarded with a small smile, but more than that, Lady Olivia refused to be drawn. "Breakfast is served at eight in the dining room. If you go to the foot of the stairs, past the statue of Niobe, it's the door to the right of the Canaletto."

Rachel dragged her dress up over her head. "Fear not. I'll drop trails of breadcrumbs."

Lady Olivia smiled uncertainly. "If you ask the footman in the hall in the morning, he'll show you the way."

And she was gone, before Rachel could explain that she was joking.

❧

Rachel came down to breakfast in the full splendor of her gypsy regalia.

The footman in the hall was too well bred to comment, but she could tell that he was bursting to run down and spread the news in the servants' hall. For his benefit, Rachel jangled and clattered her way into the dining room, a dark room toward the back of the house, made darker by heavy red paper and large oil paintings of various biblical personages being tortured in inventive ways.

Rachel's half-sister sat alone at one end of a table that might easily have seated forty. Spirit lamps flickered beneath a rank of silver chafing dishes on the sideboard, but her sister's plate held only a half slice of toast and a lonely kipper.

"Oh, good," said Lady Olivia. "You found your way."

"With a little help." Rachel wafted her way into a seat across from Olivia and tried not to blink when dishes and silver magically appeared before her. It was odd to imagine a world in which one never had to do anything at all. Odd and a little disconcerting. "I'm afraid I nearly gave your footman an apoplexy when I came downstairs in this."

"Perhaps he was afraid of what his future might hold." Lady Olivia lifted the coffeepot. "Would you prefer coffee or tea?"

Had her sister just made a joke? Rachel wasn't quite sure. It had sounded like one, or a tentative attempt in that direction. "Coffee, please."

"Oh, good." Rachel extended her cup as Lady Olivia poured. "The tea's gone quite cold, but the coffee is still drinkable."

"Why not add more hot water?"

"I don't like to bother Cook," said Lady Olivia vaguely.

Rachel busied herself in reaching for a piece of toast, a variety of comments unspoken on her lips. It was, she realized, like trying to speak a foreign language, one where the grammar was entirely different and the concepts didn't quite translate.

Falling back on safer territory, Rachel nodded at the paper next to Lady Olivia's place. "Not the *Daily Yell*?"

"My mother would expire of shock." Lady Olivia glanced quickly over her shoulder. "No. It's *The Times*. My father usually reads it, but as he's not here . . ." She extended the paper to Rachel. "Would you like it?"

The paper was warm to the touch. It must have been ironed, Rachel realized, so that unsightly newsprint wouldn't transfer itself to aristocratic fingers.

Rachel shoved it back. "But you were reading it. I wouldn't want—"

"My mother doesn't approve of my reading the paper at the table," Olivia confessed. "There's an article about Dr. Radlett's experiments."

Dr. Radlett? It took Rachel a moment to remember. That afternoon at Heatherington House felt like a lifetime ago.

She had thought her half-sister cold, cold and stiff. There was no denying the stiffness, but Rachel wondered if she might have been mistaken about the cold.

Rachel leaned her elbows on the white cloth. "What *did* you think of Dr. Radlett's lecture? You never said."

Lady Olivia poked at her kipper. "It is a noble project. . . ."

"But?"

"It really is rot." Glancing up, Lady Olivia favored Rachel with one of her fleeting smiles. "I don't think Dr. Radlett realizes that, though. He seems genuinely devoted to his project."

Not to mention John Trevannion.

"Why didn't you say, that day?" Rachel dipped her knife into the butter. "When Simon asked?"

Lady Olivia struggled with her kipper. "He does mean so well," she said apologetically. "Dr. Radlett, I mean."

If that was the real reason, Rachel would eat that kipper.

Rachel's knife made a scraping noise as she dragged the butter over her toast. "Is it better, do you think, to be an unwitting charlatan than a witting one?"

Olivia wrinkled her nose at her kipper. "It's more honest, at least. That does have to count for something."

There was a time when Rachel had considered herself honest. Before her world had turned on its head.

She took a vicious bite of her toast. "I'm not sure intentions make much of a difference in the end. I hear the road to hell is paved with them."

She'd meant it frivolously, but Olivia answered seriously. "Yes, but one does have to live with oneself."

"Not necessarily." Rachel abandoned her toast. She wasn't feeling terribly hungry anymore. "There are any number of ways to avoid living with oneself. Gin, for example."

"Yes, but you're still there at the base of it, aren't you? Only with a terrible head in the morning." At Rachel's look of surprise, Lady Olivia looked quickly down at her teacup. "At least, that's what Si—what someone once said."

"Mmm." Rachel took a quick sip of her coffee. She ought, she knew, to be scrounging for information about their father, but she couldn't help but wonder just what the true nature of the relationship between her sister and Simon had been. "If it's the same someone I know, then he doesn't seem to have taken his own advice."

"Would you like more coffee?" Olivia busied herself with the coffee-pot, giving Rachel a good view of the side parting in her gently waved blond hair.

"No, I've had quite enough." What would she do if Rachel were to ask her about Simon right out?

Ring for more coffee, most likely. Or discover a pressing need for fresh toast.

Her half-sister reminded Rachel of a puzzle box Mr. Treadwell had given her for her birthday one year. If one pressed on the right combination, the box sprang open. It was no use trying to shake it or prod it; that only jammed the delicate mechanism.

Rachel had detested that puzzle box.

There was the sound of a voice in the hall. "—tell Anna to bring it to my sitting room. *Not* the morning room. And I want the car for two. *Not* ten past."

The voice became louder as the door opened and a woman sailed through, still speaking rapidly and loudly, the slap of her solid heels against the floor punctuating her more decided utterances.

Fashions had changed since John Singer Sargent had immortalized Lady Ardmore in the painting on the stairs. Years had passed. Her hair had dimmed from brown to gray, corseting no longer cinched in her middle to the then-fashionable hourglass, and the large diamonds that adorned her in the painting were undoubtedly stashed away in a safe.

The woman in the doorway wore a skirt and crepe blouse; her graying hair was carefully marcelled; and her jewels, while large, were what one might pardonably wear during the day, pea-sized sapphires in the ears, a brooch at her collar, and old-fashioned hoop diamonds on her fingers.

But it was unmistakably the woman in the portrait.

The woman for whom Rachel's father had left them.

Lady Ardmore's chest puffed out like a pigeon as she stared at Rachel. Her voice dripped frost.

"And *who* is this?"

EIGHTEEN

L ady Olivia scrambled to her feet.

"This is—" She started to say something and checked herself. "This is Miss Vera Merton, Mama. She is a friend of Cece."

Slowly, Rachel stood, taking the measure of the woman who had usurped her mother's position, the woman who had barged in with her money, with that smug, pug-like face, and snatched her father away from them.

Maybe it was an illusion. Maybe he would have left them anyway. But Rachel wasn't in the mood to be rational about it.

"Lady Ardmore." She deliberately let her fringed shawl drape down around her shoulders, her bangles clattering on her arms. "Good morning."

"One of Cecelia's friends?" Lady Ardmore's nose pinched as though she smelled something nasty. To Olivia, she said, "Well, see that she leaves by the servants' entrance. We don't want people to talk."

And that was all.

Rachel was left standing at the dining room table, her hands braced against the white cloth, as Lady Ardmore firmly and pointedly turned her back.

Olivia's eyes darted toward Rachel. "Mama . . ."

"And you!" The sapphires on Lady Ardmore's breast glittered meanly as her blouse expanded. She stumped toward the chafing dishes. "Out until all hours, I hear. Never mind that the household is in utter disarray. Never mind that your father runs off to Oxford without so much as a by-your-leave. I am sure we have nothing better to do than to serve as a hostel for each and every one of Cecelia's dubious acquaintances."

With each word, Lady Olivia's face went a little more blank.

"I am sorry, Mama," she murmured, in that quiet voice. "We did not mean to inconvenience you."

Lady Ardmore gave an unpleasant laugh. "Oh, I'm sure you never mean it. You just gad on, with never a thought to anyone but yourself. Never mind the sacrifices I've made for you, the trouble I've gone to to put you forward—"

Sacrifices? Lady Ardmore hadn't the faintest notion.

Rachel was still standing. She heard her own voice saying, loudly, deliberately, "If anyone is to blame, it is I, Lady Ardmore. I forgot my latchkey. Lady Olivia very generously saved me from wandering the streets until dawn. It was an act of pure kindness."

Olivia gave a quick, anxious shake of her head.

Lady Ardmore's eyes narrowed. "Our home is not a boardinghouse, Olivia. I do not know what Fanny allows, but you, my girl, have a position to maintain. You won't be able to play these little tricks when you're a politician's wife."

"No, Mama," murmured Olivia.

It was, thought Rachel, the most incredible act of self-effacement. Olivia seemed to blend back into the richly figured walls, just a shadow among the shadows.

Slowly, Rachel sank down into her own seat. Her piece of toast was cold on her plate, the edges curling slightly.

Lady Olivia sent her a grateful look.

Lady Ardmore carried on, her voice rising with her grievances. "As if I hadn't enough to worry about! Your brother's twenty-first in four days— and that wretched Miss Lane has twisted her wrist. Or says she did," she added darkly. "One can never tell with these people. Malingering in her room, taking up good space in a bed. I am sure she did it on purpose to inconvenience me. And who, I ask you, who is to write up the cards?"

Lady Ardmore dropped her plate at her place at the head of the table with enough force that a sausage rolled off the edge.

She seemed hardly to notice when the footman pulled back her chair for her; she took it for granted that the chair would be beneath her when she sat, heavily, with the air of Hecuba contemplating the fall of Troy in all its gory misery.

"Miss Lane is Mama's secretary," explained Olivia, and then cast a guilty glance at her mother, as though she expected to be reprimanded for speaking out of turn.

"If I might be of any assistance . . . I've been told that I write a fair hand."

It was purely strategy, Rachel told herself. And not at all because Olivia looked ready to crawl beneath the lid of one of the chafing dishes on the sideboard.

What better way to secure a temporary position in the household?

In full Vera mode, she rattled on, "Consider it repayment for last night's room and this morning's board. It would be rather a lark, really, playing at secretary. So many of one's friends do seem to have jobs these days."

"We are not sunk so low as that, Miss . . ."

"Merton," Rachel supplied, smiling with bared teeth. "Merton."

What would Lady Ardmore say if Rachel rose, and said, oh so casually, "And, by the way, I just happen to be your husband's by-blow"?

"I shall have to call the agency," said Lady Ardmore, in the tones of one making a great sacrifice.

If Rachel hadn't curled up on her mother's bed that day . . . if she hadn't gone to Cousin David . . . if she hadn't met Simon . . . she might be the one answering that call to the agency.

It was a deeply distasteful thought.

"I can help, Mama," Olivia said tentatively. "If Miss Lane will tell me what is wanted . . ."

Lady Ardmore looked at her daughter coldly. "You would be better served setting a date for your wedding. You mustn't shilly-shally. There aren't many more fish in the sea. Not for you. Not after That Episode."

That Episode?

Olivia's eyes had dropped to her plate.

That only seemed to annoy Lady Ardmore more.

"But, then, you wouldn't mind, would you?" The acid in Lady Ardmore's voice was enough to strip the gold rim off the Spode. "You'd be just as happy to cloister yourself away with a horde of bluestockings, wasting your life on dusty old books. Never mind the bother of giving you a Season, the trouble of finding you partners—you haven't a particle of gratitude, have you?"

It was painful to listen to, painful to watch, all the more so because Lady Ardmore didn't seem to care in the least that she had an audience.

Perhaps, in her view, she didn't. The footman wasn't people to Lady Ardmore, and neither was Rachel. They might have been one of the elephants at the base of the silver epergne in the center of the table, or one of the plaster roundels on the ceiling above.

Olivia seemed to get smaller and smaller with each lash of her mother's voice. But all she said was, "I would be happy to help Miss Lane with the cards, Mama."

With an inarticulate noise of annoyance, Lady Ardmore stood, sending the footman scrabbling to pull back her chair. "Don't forget that you have a dress fitting at three. Your father was meant to be speaking in the Lords today. Heaven only knows if he'll be back in time. Oxford, indeed! What can there be in Oxford more important than in London?" The question was evidently rhetorical. Lady Ardmore paused in the doorway long enough to fire one last sally at her daughter. "*Don't* forget your fitting."

"No, Mama."

"And don't let her alter the pattern. I want it just so."

"Yes, Mama."

Lady Ardmore cast a narrow-eyed look at Rachel. "We can't have you looking *cheap*."

And with that, she sailed out, having consumed no fewer than six sausages and left havoc in her wake.

In the shell-shocked silence, Rachel and Olivia regarded each other across the table, like survivors of a military action after the all clear.

"Would you like to borrow this?" Rachel said wryly, indicating her gypsy-embellished evening dress. "You really might do with a bit of looking cheap. And just think how everyone would stare at your brother's twenty-first!"

"It wouldn't suit me." Olivia's eyes slid toward the door, where the footman stood silent sentinel.

Would this, Rachel wondered, make the rounds of the servants' hall later? Or were Lady Ardmore's diatribes to her daughter a daily course, served up with the kippers and the kedgeree?

"I do apologize, most awfully. It's the fancy dress. . . . Mother doesn't approve of parties. Not those sorts of parties."

Yes, and Rachel was Queen Mary. "I should be the one apologizing, invading like this. I don't wonder that your mother was cross! And her secretary's wrist and your father away . . . It's enough to make anyone fuss."

Olivia looked down at her plate. "Poor Miss Lane. It's not malingering, you know. She broke her wrist tripping on the steps of the Tube. And she would try to keep working despite it."

Rachel lifted her coffee cup. "She must be devoted to your mother."

"Miss Lane has an ailing mother in Ipswich," said Olivia seriously. "She's terrified of losing her position."

Feeling shamed, Rachel set the cup down. "I feel as though I really ought to write those cards for her. Just because."

"You're very kind, but, really, I couldn't ask you to."

"Why not? It's not as though I have terribly much else to do with my time."

Other than penning ominous messages to her father, who wasn't there to receive them. Instead, he had received a letter and gone haring off to Oxford, missing a speech in the Lords, risking his wife's ire.

Somehow, Rachel doubted it was in search of a manuscript at the Bodleian.

Rachel thought back on all of those years of visits to Oxford, of Cousin David slipping her pocket money behind her mother's back, solemnly inquiring about school, treating her to walnut cake in his rooms. He had always acted as a sort of honorary uncle.

What if Cousin David had been as much watchdog as guardian?

She had assumed, all these weeks, that her father had left and never looked back, that he hadn't known where she was or what she was doing. Rachel's stomach turned uneasily. But what if he had? A brief moment of warmth, at the thought that her father might, from afar, have been watching over her, was succeeded rapidly by something darker. What if it wasn't love, but policy? Now, of all times, with his heir's twenty-first birthday on the horizon, a scandal was the last thing her father needed.

There was a certain bitter amusement to the notion of her father dashing to Oxford to interrogate Cousin David as to how she had slipped her leash; Cousin David with his ineffectual attempts to keep her away from her father, away from London.

No. Rachel caught herself. None of that followed. If her father knew her, knew who she was, he would have made some sign of recognition in the library that day. Wouldn't he?

"Coffee?" Olivia said, and Rachel realized her half-sister was holding the coffeepot, and probably had been for some time.

"Forgive me. I was away with the fairies." Rachel's bangles jangled as she lifted her hands to rub her temples. "I ought to go home and change." A stray thought struck her. "What did your mother mean about your cloistering yourself away?"

"Oh . . . I had an idea about going to university." In a barely audible voice, Olivia added, "I won a scholarship to Somerville."

"A scholarship!" Rachel had spent enough time in and around Oxford to know just how much those meant. "Good on you!"

"Si—" Olivia caught herself. "A friend helped arrange it."

"Yes, but they don't take people just for arranging." Those examinations were stiff. Her mother had suggested that Rachel try for a scholarship, but, at the time, Rachel had been more concerned with adding to the family coffers. Besides, she knew herself well enough to know that she had no passion for study. She preferred to be out in the world, doing something. "Why ever didn't you go?"

Olivia tucked a strand of dark blond hair behind her ear, saying with painful restraint, "My mother . . . reminded me that I had a position to maintain. Earls' daughters don't turn bluestocking."

"I'm sure some do. In fact, I imagine a great many have." Rachel remembered what Simon had said about poetry. "Did you mean to read Greats?"

"No." Olivia cast Rachel a small, rueful smile. "Economics."

✑

Rachel garnered more than a few sideways glances as she took herself and her crystal ball back to the flat. The clothes that had looked so dashing by night were limp and tawdry by day, and her evening slippers pinched abominably.

The porter did a credible job of concealing his smirk as she passed his glass box on the way to the lift; Simon must tip well.

The porter also, obligingly, provided her with the spare key. Rachel fitted it into the lock, wishing she could make everything else fit quite so neatly.

It had been so satisfying despising her half-sister.

But the half-sister she had despised, the woman in the *Tatler* photos, was, it seemed, as much of a fiction as Miss Vera Merton. The real Lady Olivia Standish had won a scholarship to Somerville. To study economics.

And Simon had helped her.

Curiouser and curiouser, as Alice would say. Rachel plunked her crystal ball down in the bowl on the hall table and gratefully stepped out of her shoes. He might have assisted her during the tenure of their engagement. But that made no sense, either. She didn't think they accepted married women into college.

And if it had been after their engagement had ended . . .

If he was so furious about being shown the door, why help Olivia escape to Somerville?

That it was an escape, Rachel had no doubt. Rachel grimaced at her own reflection in the hall mirror as she padded, barefoot, down the corridor to the bedroom. If she had to spend breakfasts with Lady Ardmore, she would discover a sudden passion for academe, too.

Poor Olivia.

The thought took her by surprise. A month ago, the notion that she could feel sorry for her half-sister was laughable. Olivia had it all, didn't she? The name, the houses, the family connections. Their father.

And a mother who made her shrink into herself, who bullied her into speaking in a murmur.

Rachel found herself, suddenly, fiercely, missing her own mother, her mother who had never stopped her from climbing the highest tree or jumping into the deepest pond, who might scold her for tearing her frocks, but always sewed them up again, who taught her to play chess and sang to her when she was sick.

The bright room seemed darker; Rachel's own image swam before her eyes in the dressing-table mirror, the hoops still dangling from her ears. Madame Zelda tells all. . . . If only she could.

She understood it now, the urge that drove the credulous to spiritualists and fortune-tellers, the dangerous promise that she might see the shadow of her mother's face in the curved reflection of the crystal ball or hear her voice, once more, in the whisper of the cards, murmuring, as she had, not so very long ago, "I love you."

Closing her eyes, Rachel pressed her fingers to her temples, breathing in deeply through her nose. She wouldn't go hysterical like Cece. Poor Cece . . .

She should see her, make sure she was all right.

Or as all right as she could be. Rachel sobered at the memory of the story John had told in the taxi.

A quick scrub with cold water and a brush through her tousled hair made Rachel feel more like herself. She stopped at the newsagent's on the corner to pick up a copy of the latest *Tatler*. Cece did so love to see who was in and out.

With the magazine beneath her arm, cool and fashionable in her blue suit and cloche hat, Rachel presented herself at the house on Park Lane. She was a regular caller by now, and she smiled confidently at Sneller as the butler opened the door.

"Is Miss Heatherington-Vaughn at home?"

It was a pro forma question. At this hour of the morning, Cece was always at home, lounging in her boudoir in her silk pajamas, her eyes still ringed with paint from the night before.

But Sneller didn't send her through. His eyes didn't meet hers as he said formally, "A moment, miss."

"All right." Puzzled, Rachel followed him into the great Moorish Hall, with its potted palms and pointed pilasters.

"This way, miss." To Rachel's surprise, instead of taking her to the family wing, he led her up the stairs and into the sitting room on the first floor, which Rachel had visited once before with Simon.

Rachel bit her lip at the sight of the pictures in their silver frames; the boy beside Cece, the man in the uniform: they had to be Peter.

What must it feel like to walk past his image every day? Did Cece remember him as he had been then—or as she had last seen him?

Rachel could see a blond head over the back of the sofa by the cold fireplace. "Cece, darling!" she said with relief. She waved her *Tatler* in greeting. "Do you have the most frightful—Oh."

It wasn't Cece who rose from behind the sofa. In the light from the long windows, Rachel could see the silver in the blond hair. While skillfully applied makeup might provide an illusion of youth, it couldn't hide the years entirely.

Rachel checked her progress. "Lady Frances. Good morning."

"Miss Merton." Lady Frances was smiling, but there was something about that smile that made Rachel nervous. It didn't reach her eyes, those pale-blue eyes that were so like Cece's.

"I am sorry," Rachel said, taking a quick step back. "I didn't mean to disturb you. Sneller must have—I came to see Cece."

"No mistake." Lady Frances wasn't smiling anymore. She indicated a deep chair upholstered in chintz, set kitty-corner to the sofa. "I asked Sneller to bring you to me if you called. Do sit down, Miss Merton."

Rachel perched gingerly on the edge of the chair, her legs crossed at the ankle, her hands folded in her lap.

Lady Frances seated herself gracefully on the sofa. Her brows were plucked, her fingers manicured, and she had the strenuous thinness of one who watches her figure. Her movements were as carefully controlled as her appearance.

It all made Rachel exceedingly nervous.

"Yes, Lady Frances?" she said, feeling as though she were ten again, and being asked to account to the headmistress for the presence of a frog in the science tutor's desk.

Lady Frances regarded her rings. "I understand," she said, "that you had a little party last night."

"Yes. Cece and I—we planned it together." What would Vera Merton say? "We wanted something new—something special."

"Special. Yes, I understand it was that." Lady Fanny looked away to the side, putting her face in sharp profile. Stripped down to bone, her face was very like Rachel's father's. "Now, let me recall—are you one of Callista's girls? Or one of Penelope's?"

There was a copy of *Debrett's Peerage* on the side table, open to the M's. Rachel was reasonably certain that Lady Fanny knew that she was neither.

"Neither." Rachel's throat felt very dry. "I'm Katherine's daughter."

K and *E*, entwined forever in intricate engraving on her mother's brooch. She couldn't image Lady Frances would have known her mother; it seemed unlikely that her father would have let his sister and his mistress meet.

Lady Frances lifted her manicured brows. "I don't recall a Katherine among the Montforts."

Rachel lifted her chin. "It is a very distant connection." The width of a bar sinister. Glibly, she reverted to their prepared story. "My mother's health wasn't all it could be . . . so I have spent most of the past decade on the Continent."

"So I have been told." Lady Frances's voice was politely dismissive. Smoothly, swiftly, she went on the attack. "I did not realize that fortune-telling was among your talents, Miss Merton."

Was that what this was all about? If so, she couldn't blame Rachel any more than Rachel blamed herself.

"I am so very sorry about what happened last night. I had no idea that

Cece—" Under that cool, blue gaze, Rachel found herself scrambling for poise. "It was just a bit of silliness—a bit of fun. We were just playing at card reading. I'd found a pamphlet, you see—"

Rachel might not have spoken. Lady Fanny made a show of examining her perfectly groomed nails, before saying meditatively, "My Cecelia is a very sensitive girl—and a very trusting one. I should hate to see her taken advantage of." She smiled pleasantly at Rachel. "I trust we understand each other?"

Rachel stared at her aunt. "Oh, but of course! That is—"

"I am so glad we had this little chat." Lady Fanny rose, smoothing her smart skirt down over her knees. "I am afraid Cecelia won't be able to see you. The doctor was forced to give her a rather strong sedative."

It wasn't a pretty image. Rachel could see Cece as she had been last night, half wild with years of suppressed grief.

Clumsily, she rose from the chair. "Please, do give her my best wishes. I hope she feels better soon."

"She will." There was steel beneath Lady Fanny's polished facade. "As soon as she is well enough to travel, Cecelia will be visiting friends in Switzerland."

"I see." Rachel felt all at sea, not sure what to say.

"The Alpine air is so very good for her." There was no mistaking Lady Frances's meaning as she added smoothly, "Will you be staying long in London, Miss Merton?"

"No," said Rachel. She wanted to defend herself, but she wasn't sure how. Lady Frances was right; she was a fraud. She just wasn't that sort of fraud. "I'm to join my mother—in Latin America—in a fortnight."

"Latin America?" Her point made, Lady Frances could afford to be generous. She regarded Rachel with an air of faint amusement. "How very . . . exotic. I trust you will leave Cecelia your forwarding address. She will be so interested to hear of your adventures abroad."

With that parting shot, Lady Frances turned to go, leaving Rachel standing by the sofa, her face frozen, feeling like a charlatan in her fashionable clothes.

It's not like that, Rachel wanted to say. She had never wanted money. She hadn't meant to use Cece. . . .

Except she had.

She hadn't thought of Cece as a person. She was a convenience, a means to an end, a faintly comical character. She had never stopped to think that Cece might have feelings of her own.

Rachel bit down hard on her lower lip, so hard that she could taste the tang of blood in her mouth.

"Lady Frances?" Her aunt paused in the doorway. Rachel took a half step forward, her hands clasped at her waist. "You will tell Cece I hope she feels more the thing?"

This time, Lady Frances's smile reached her eyes. "I shall." Casually, too casually for it to be an afterthought, she added, "Sneller will show you out. Good-bye, Miss Merton."

"Good-bye," Rachel echoed.

The door clicked quietly shut behind her aunt. Rachel breathed in deeply, the blood pounding in her temples.

Words from *Hamlet* echoed through her memory. *What's Hecuba to him, or he to Hecuba?* She was nothing to Lady Frances, nothing but an imposter. Blood didn't call to blood; it didn't even whisper. To Lady Frances, she was nothing but a nuisance. Worse than a nuisance, a threat to Cece's health and happiness.

A bottom-crawling feeder off the weak and wealthy.

And what was she, really? Following Sneller for the final time down the staircase, through the Moorish Hall, and down the front steps of Heatherington House, Rachel forced herself to take stock. In the name of justice, she was living in Simon's mother's flat, wearing Simon's sister's clothes, dining out on Cece's tab at the Ritz, drinking Tommy Digby's champagne—or whoever else happened to be paying.

She might not have meant it, but that was what she had become: an expensive freeloader.

What had happened to the Rachel who had always prided herself on paying her own way?

She didn't know herself anymore, and she wasn't sure she liked the self she had become.

It was time to end it.

She would do what she ought to have done from the beginning; she would go straight to the source, to her father, in the one place she was sure he could be found.

NINETEEN

S imon didn't pick up the phone at his flat.

He had a club, Rachel knew, but she had never bothered to ascertain which or where it was. Not that it mattered. No self-respecting club would allow her through the doors, and not because of her birth or her choice of hat. Unless it was ladies' day, she could knock until she was red in the fist and it would do no good.

Rachel tried the flat again. Nothing.

The receptionist at the *Daily Yell* was extremely irate at being interrupted in the midst of varnishing her nails. Did Miss Merton expect her to be Mr. Montfort's social secretary? Didn't she have enough to do with getting Mr. Allerton's tea, and typing Mr. O'Connell's copy, and—Oh, all right. He was meant to be covering three parties that night. The receptionist rattled off a series of names and addresses. Rachel decided to start with Colonel McEachran's house in Brook Street; it was the closest to her flat, and the names on the invitation were ones she recognized.

It took her little time to dress; she had it down to an art by now. On with the cocktail frock, slick on the lipstick, slide into the heels, grab up her bag, and dash for a taxi. Strange how quickly one's routines changed, how rapidly the exotic became mundane.

There was no one to answer when Rachel rang the bell. She was hardly surprised. A gramophone was playing, the high blare warring with the chatter of a hundred excited voices. Letting herself in, she threaded through the throng, past an overturned hatstand and a spilled drink.

Gratefully, she spotted Brian Howard. It was always easy to find Brian; he held his pack of cigarettes in one hand so as not to ruin the cut of his suit, gesturing with them as he spoke.

Rachel tapped him on the shoulder. "Brian, have you seen—"

But it wasn't Brian at all. The quirk in the brow had been drawn on by eye-black rather than nature, and the broad grin was nothing like Brian's usual supercilious smirk.

"Like it? It's the eyebrows that do it," said Tom Driberg's voice from Brian's mouth. "If you're looking for Brian, you'll find him dressed as a German painter. Who are you meant to be?"

"Who am—" Belatedly, a memory of the receptionist's nasal voice, reeling off the details from the invitation, penetrated her brain. The Brook Street affair was an Impersonation Party, come as anyone you like. At random, Rachel said, "Oh, I've come as my last week's self. You haven't seen Simon Montfort, have you?"

"*Daily Yell?* Last I saw, he was dancing with Tallulah Bankhead."

"The real one, or someone pretending to be Tallulah?" Rachel demanded, but Driberg didn't answer.

He was too busy greeting an acquaintance with an approximation of Brian's distinctive drawl. "M-m-my d-d-dear!"

Giving up, Rachel turned with a tinkle of beads, weaving her way through the dizzying crowd, searching for Simon. It was like being in the midst of a kaleidoscope, everything turned on its head, nothing quite as it seemed. Elizabeth Ponsonby's whinnying laugh issued forth from under the sleek, red head of Iris Tree; Brenda Dean Paul, dancing past, turned out not to be Brenda at all, but a very sulky Olivia Plunkett-Greene, already several sheets to the wind and spoiling for a fight. The air was thick with perfume and spilled cocktails, adding to the general miasma of confusion.

"Simon!" He was there, dancing with Tallulah Bankhead, the real Tallulah, dressed like a French tennis star in jersey and beret, but still, unmistakably, Tallulah.

As for Simon, in defiance of the invitation, he hadn't bothered to come as anyone else. Instead, he wore the black-and-white garb of the harlequin, his face painted white, his mask dangling from one hand.

Rachel gestured at him over Tallulah's beret. Simon leaned forward to whisper something in the actress's ear, and she gave him a playful push, followed by a long kiss on the lips.

Queen Marie of Romania, Stephen Tennant under white face paint and pearls, applauded languidly.

Rachel narrowed her eyes.

Unconcerned, Simon sauntered toward her, dodging George Sitwell in a false nose and one of Cece's friends in a bathing costume and very little else.

"You're meant to be in costume," he said.

"I am," said Rachel impatiently. "I'm impersonating Miss Vera Merton. Lady Frances is sending Cece to Switzerland."

In a leisurely fashion, Simon inspected the back of his mask. Now that Rachel was closer, she could see why he wasn't wearing it. The string had broken.

He shrugged. "It won't be the first time."

Rachel stared at him. "She had a breakdown. They had to give her a sedative."

Simon tossed the useless mask aside. "I know. I was there. It wasn't pleasant. It never is."

Rachel could see, beneath his makeup, the faint trace of hollows beneath Simon's eyes, but there was no other sign of feeling in his face.

"Did you know—you knew that she had had these incidents before? You knew and yet you let me go through with that—that performance?"

"It was a Crystal Ball and Bottle party," said Simon sarcastically. "It was not unforeseeable that someone would contrive to tell fortunes."

Rachel wanted to shake him. "You might have told me about Peter."

"Did you imagine that yours was the only family tragedy in Britain?"

he said tightly. "Ah, thank you." Simon accepted a cup off the tray of a passing waiter and drained it without bothering to examine the contents.

Rachel waved the waiter aside. "That's not fair. I'm not a mind reader. I'm not even a card reader. You might—you *ought*—to have told me." How could he stand so still, look so supercilious? Rachel's voice broke. "If you cared at all—But, then, you don't, do you? It's all just a game, all of it, and all of us your pawns, there to make good copy. What does it matter if Cece has a breakdown? It's nothing to you—not so long as it makes for a paragraph in the *Daily Yell. Society Girl's Breakdown, the exclusive on page five.*"

She turned to go, but Simon's hand clamped down, hard, over her wrist.

In a clipped, toneless voice, he said, "From the time I was seven years old, I spent holidays with Peter. My mother had bolted; my father didn't want anything of my mother's get. Peter's home was my home, his sister was my sister." There was something in his eyes, something dark and dangerous. Rachel could feel his fingers digging into her wrist before he suddenly, abruptly, let go. He took a step back, his eyes dark in his white face. "Tell me again that I don't care."

Rachel's hand closed reflexively over her wrist, her mind muddled. There was such depth of emotion there. It made her feel small. Small and defensive.

"If you care," she blustered, "why don't you do anything?"

"If someone wants to go to the devil," said Simon shortly, "he will. There's nothing one can do about it."

"You mean like Peter Heatherington-Vaughn?"

In the midst of all the noise and motion, there was a horrible stillness. Simon's black and white stood out starkly against the gaily garbed throng.

"You know nothing about it." Simon's words might have been chiseled from ice.

No, she didn't, because no one had bloody told her anything.

Rachel fumbled to remember what John had said in the cab last night. "I know that the war did horrible things to people. I know that Peter"— she hesitated over the name, this man she had never known, but was so closely connected to her—"that Peter was one of those men. It's not surprising that he should bear the scars of what he had seen. Which is why it's so terribly important that we keep such things from happening again."

Simon fumbled at his sleeve, rooting around in the cuff for cigarette and lighter. The lighter stuck. Simon wrenched it free; Rachel could hear fabric tear. "Now you sound like Trevannion. All you need is a temperance band playing behind you and someone putting around a cup for donations."

"At least he has the guts to speak out for something."

Simon gave an unpleasant laugh. "Ignorance redeemed by vehemence? Now there's a pretty picture."

"If he's ignorant, maybe that's because those who know won't tell him."

"What do you want me to tell you? Would you like to hear about the rats that grew fat on human flesh? Or the men who would be speaking to you one minute and have a gaping hole where their heads had been the next? That was what Peter saw. That was what killed him, as surely as any shell." His hand shook on his lighter, making the flame sway and dance. Briskly, he shut it again and shoved it up his sleeve. "What did you want, Vera?"

The use of her assumed name felt like a blow. She had forgot, for a moment, that she was Vera.

Rachel pressed her eyes closed before opening them. Rapidly, she said, "Lady Frances knows I'm not who we said. She told me as much this afternoon. She warned me to stay away from Cece."

There was a lump in her throat. Just the stale air, she was sure. Nothing more.

"Well?" Rachel itched for action, for a plan. "What do we do?"

Simon took a long pull on his cigarette. "Nothing."

"Nothing?" She felt as though the ground had been pulled out from beneath her.

"My dear"—Simon flicked ash in her general direction, his voice a deliberately offensive drawl—"what you say is not exactly surprising. Your— how shall we call it?—your nom de guerre was not designed to withstand strict scrutiny. There are no Mertons on either side of my family tree. Don't you think that half the people in this room know that?"

There was a ringing in Rachel's ears. She shook her head slightly. "But then, how—"

Simon gave a sharp bark of a laugh. "We haven't precisely been frequenting the ballrooms of the good and great. Anyone with the right dress can get into Dean Street. Brian Howard doesn't care whether you're Vera Merton or Eliza Doolittle so long as you genuflect before his genius. Look at Inez Holden." Simon waved a hand toward a laughing group posing for a picture. "She was working as a receptionist at the *Daily Express* when Waugh picked her up. God only knows where she comes from—or how she pays her rent."

Rachel gaped at Simon. "They don't think—"

"That you're my mistress? Possibly." There was a bite to his voice, anger just beneath the civilized surface. "You needn't look so appalled. I'm sure most of them don't think of it at all."

So much for masquerading as a young lady of quality. Rachel had felt so smugly secure that she had pulled it off, that her father's people, her own cousins, accepted her as one of themselves. When all this while, they had known her for a fraud.

Rachel hardened her voice. "It doesn't matter. They won't be tainted with my presence much longer." She lifted her chin, looking Simon straight in the eye. "I need an invitation to Jicksy's coming of age."

Simon choked on a mouthful of smoke. "Would you also like a phoenix feather and the pearly tears of a unicorn? Those would be far easier to obtain."

Rachel felt like one of the mortals in old stories, who woke to find that the fairy gold for which they had sold themselves so dearly was nothing but dust.

"But . . ."

"It's not a studio party in Chelsea, my sweet. The guest list was determined months ago."

Rachel stared at him, feeling as though she'd never seen him before. "But—you promised. You said you could get me an invitation to Caffers."

"I said Olivia could get you an invitation to Caffers." The silk of his costume hugged his form as he turned away. "I made your introductions for you. If you botched it, it's down to you."

"Oh, no." Rachel followed doggedly behind him, through the nightmare throng of well-known faces distorted by wigs and makeup, one man's face on another man's body, everyone familiar and foreign all at once. "That's not what you said when we started."

Simon's voice was clipped. "I said you needed an invitation to Jicksy's twenty-first. I never promised to provide one."

Rachel felt as though the world were crumbling around her. She was abandoned, alone, in this room full of people, none of whom would notice if Miss Vera Merton were to disappear permanently from view. "And you never meant to, did you? That wasn't what this was about. Not for you."

Make friends with Olivia, get close to Olivia, Olivia, Olivia, Olivia. Simon couldn't have given a damn about Rachel's personal vendetta; he'd seen his chance and seized it. The veneer of sympathy, of interest, had been just that, a veneer.

He'd warned her not to trust him, hadn't he? *One foot on sea and one on shore, to one thing constant never.*

"Be logical, Vera." The very name was a barb. Simon looked at her sideways, through a haze of drifting smoke. "You can't really mean to confront your father in front of all five hundred of his guests."

"Why not?" All her frustration found its way into Rachel's voice. "It would certainly make copy for your column. That *was* what you wanted."

"Was it? I forget." He took a long drag on his cigarette. "You could probably find a party into which to insert yourself, convince them you've been invited."

"But not you." When she'd imagined going to Caffers to confront her father, she had assumed that Simon would be with her. She'd assumed rather too much. Rachel turned away, hoping Simon couldn't see her face. "Never mind. I won't ask you to soil your lily-white hands."

She felt his hand on her shoulder, a fleeting touch, quickly gone. "It's not that. It's—"

"You don't owe me any explanations." He'd made that much plain. "Don't bother yourself. I'll find someone else to take me."

Simon threw up his hands. "Oh, the hell with it. Why not? One last hurrah. For both of us. Nothing like burning one's last bridge." He dropped the butt of his cigarette and crushed it beneath the sole of his shoe. "I've taken the job in New York."

Rachel's emotions zigzagged crazily through relief, fear, and a strange, unaccountable sense of loss. "Should I congratulate you?"

Simon was watching her closely. "Or commiserate. Take your pick."

Rachel squared her shoulders. "You will still take me to Caffers?"

"For my sins." Gently, Simon's fingers touched her chin, tilting her face toward his. "Are you sure you want to do this?"

Rachel had never been less sure what she wanted. But she nodded anyway. Because there was nothing else she could think to do.

With false bravado, Rachel said, "What's the worst that can happen? We both knew this charade couldn't go on forever. Why not go out in style?"

Simon smiled crookedly. "If you must go to the devil . . . far be it from me to stop you."

TWENTY

R achel first saw Carrisford Court by sunset.

The setting sun turned the stones to gold and set the mullioned windows glittering with iridescent fire. In the shadow of the walls, swans swam lazily on a moat limned with gold, framed gently by the fronds of weeping willows.

"A fairy-tale castle come to life." Simon opened the door of the car, his long frame, elegant in evening attire, blocking the view. "I quote from the guide book, of course."

Rachel lifted her long skirt out of the way, stepping carefully out onto the turf. "If I remember my fairy tales, most of them were fairly gruesome."

It had been three hours from London. Rachel's legs were wobbly with disuse. Simon caught her before she stumbled, bracing her with a hand beneath her elbow, where her long kid leather glove ended.

"Nervous?"

"Numb," said Rachel succinctly. Her legs, at least. The rest of her tingled with nervous anticipation. "My leg has been asleep since Slough."

After that dreadful fight at the Impersonation Party, they had treated each other with gingerly politeness, like someone avoiding a sore tooth. Rachel missed their comfortable sniping.

"You might have said something."

"So you could rub it for me? Thank you, but no." Rachel picked her way carefully over the turf. Up in front of them, cars were circling beneath the portico. They had left the car some way from the house, in a field.

"You prefer to take your chances with the pins and needles?"

"I know, it's all the result of an inhibited bourgeois upbringing," said Rachel raggedly. Now that she was here, she wasn't entirely sure she wanted to go through with it. Confronting her father on his own ground had seemed like a grand idea—until she had seen that ground. "I'm sure Dr. Radlett can sort that for you with an infusion of pigs' glands."

"Rabbits, I should think," said Simon, "in that context."

Rachel gave a choked laugh. "An animal for every occasion?"

But she was grateful for him in that moment, grateful for the irreverent sense of humor and the warm hand so unobtrusively beneath her elbow.

Ahead of them, car after car disgorged its jeweled cargo: elderly gentlemen bristling with orders, ladies with tiaras still dusty from the vault, in evening capes that smelled mildly of mold. There wasn't a face that Rachel recognized.

The fairy-tale castle, the resplendent guests all made Rachel feel particularly out of place. She had thought she had been in society these past two months, but seeing the ranks of polished cars, the impassive chauffeurs, the elderly ladies with their fox stoles and old-fashioned diamonds, it became clear to Rachel just how far from it she had been, dancing on the fringes in her borrowed finery.

There had been only one long evening dress in Simon's sister's wardrobe. It was sea-foam green, and fitted. At least, it had been fitted to Simon's sister. It didn't fit Rachel at all, and a quick alteration had made it wearable, but not becoming.

She might, she supposed, have taken it to a dressmaker, but now, with her tenure in society winding to a close, she was reluctant to dip into her own closely held funds. Rachel wasn't a Paris couturier, but necessity had taught her how to sew a seam, competently if not elegantly. Real life was crowding back around her. The enchanted bubble had burst. Cece was in Switzerland; Simon was leaving for New York. And Rachel, like Cinderella, would see her finery turned to ashes at the stroke of midnight.

Or, if not to ashes, then to a typewriting machine, a stenographic pad, and a bedsit in Holborn.

But first, she needed to see her father. One last time.

Rachel's fingers closed around the brooch she had fastened to a ribbon around her neck. *E* and *K*, entwined in perpetuity.

Until they weren't.

"Pardon?" Simon had said something, had been saying something, but the words had buzzed around her ears without penetrating her consciousness.

"Are you feeling stirrings of ancestral consciousness?" inquired Simon. The words were facetious, but there was an edginess about him that Rachel knew was echoed in the tenseness of her own shoulders.

Rachel looked up at the manor house looming before her. Her father might live here, but she never could. It was the sort of house one saw in newsreels and magazines, the stately home of X, Y, or Z, for shopgirls to sigh over and Communists to deplore.

"I feel as though I ought to be paying two shillings for the guided tour," she said bitterly.

"As I recall, it's three and six. And it's well worth the ticket price. Caffers is a beautiful artifact."

Rachel glanced sharply at him. "Yet people live here still."

"Live is a relative term. Your father works here. It's a pursuit for him, not a home. Lady Ardmore performs here on Saturdays to Mondays. She uses it as a stage set. Jicksy is jailed here in between excesses. It's a prison for him. And Olivia . . ."

"Yes?" Rachel's gloved fingers were slippery on the sea-green flounces of her borrowed dress.

"Olivia truly loves Caffers." Simon spoke in the same detached, dispassionate voice. "If there were no such thing as entail, she might have done a brilliant job of running it someday. As it is, she'll have to content herself with murmuring bland nothings to Trevannion's constituency."

In front of them, the swans sailed blithely on the gold-spangled moat, trailing weeds like emerald ribbons. "Could you have done better for her?"

"It depends," said Simon, "on whether you prefer the devil or the deep blue sea."

"That's no answer at all."

"If you want answers, go to Trevannion. He has plenty and to spare."

"All right," said Rachel, goaded. "Perhaps I will. He's sure to be here tonight, isn't he? I imagine he'll be kind enough to spare me a dance."

Simon looked down at her, a sardonic expression on his face. "Kindness? Is that what you call it?"

"Would you prefer basic courtesy? You shouldn't snipe about him so, you know. Just because—"

"Because what?"

Because you're too much of a coward to reclaim the woman you love, she had been going to say. Something in Simon's expression made her rapidly improvise, "Because he has the courage of his convictions."

Belatedly, she remembered John's complaint at the Crystal Ball and Bottle party, about the article Simon had published under his own name. But it was too late to take it back.

"I had convictions once. Or thought I had." Simon stared up at the twin flambeaux on either side of the door, hissing and spitting in the waning light, flanked footmen in matching livery, white-wigged, decked out in knee breeches and silk stockings, a relic of an earlier age. "I was going to write the definitive history of the Norman conquest, did you know that?"

He was staring at the doorway, the flickering light of the torches casting an odd orange glow across his face.

"I had opinions on all sorts of things. I was so sure of myself. . . ."

Ahead of them, an elderly couple decked in orders moved, but Simon was frozen on the stair.

"Well, why didn't you?" Rachel said, hoisting her skirt so she wouldn't trip on her flounces. "Write your history, I mean."

Simon looked at her as though he'd forgotten she was there. "Why waste time praising the achievements of great men when I could spend my time scribbling the meaningless for the sake of the unmemorable?" The sarcasm in his voice bit like cheap gin, but it wasn't directed at her. He rubbed his gloved hands against his arms, as though he were suddenly cold. "To beguile the times, look like the times."

The great door loomed above them. Rachel looked sharply at Simon. The August night was cool, but there was sweat beading on his forehead. "Are you all right?"

With an effort, he mustered up a smile that was all teeth and no cheer. "Why wouldn't I be?"

Because he was as nervy as a horse scenting thin ice. It seemed rather an extreme reaction to crashing a party, even such a party as this.

Rachel gave up. "What happens next?"

"What happens," said Simon, making a good show of pulling himself together, "is that I give our names to that charming personage over there, who will boom them out at the top of his lungs. And then Lord and Lady Ardmore will either shake our hands or boot us out of the party."

Her father hadn't known her last time. But now, after the pictures . . . Rachel's fingers lightly touched the brooch at her neck. "What odds would you give us?"

"Aren't you the one with a crystal ball?"

A man in elaborate livery, a long staff in his hand, was leaning forward, inquiring their names. The pins and needles weren't just in Rachel's legs, they were in her hands, too, making her fingers itch and tingle.

"I've retired," said Rachel shakily.

"Have it your own way," said Simon. With an arrogant slouch and a pronounced Oxbridge drawl, he gave their names to the man at the door, who banged the ground with his staff, once, twice.

"Mr. Simon Montfort and Miss Vera Merton!"

There was no puff of smoke, no whiff of brimstone, no rush of angry footmen ready to throw them out on their ear.

No one paid the slightest attention.

Behind them, the staff clunked again. "Mr. Harold Conway and Her Most Serene Highness, Princess Sobiesky!"

Rachel glanced uncertainly at Simon. "We're through?"

"The first gate." The procession twined in front of them, up a great double stair.

It was daunting and mind-boggling, the cream of London society, tottering marquesses and beribboned generals, all queuing for the privilege of wishing Rachel's brother felicitations on the anniversary of his birth. Not that it was really about Jicksy, Rachel realized that. It was about tradition and ceremony and clinging to the old ways.

At the landing, below a vast baroque painting featuring various fleshy, mythological personages, Lord and Lady Ardmore received their guests. Rachel couldn't see much of them, just the glitter of Lady Ardmore's tiara, the glint of her father's glasses, and, between them, a dark head which had to belong to her brother, Jicksy.

"If you'd like," said Simon quietly, "we can break off now. There's no need to go through the receiving line."

"Less chance of being discovered?" Simon seemed to have control of himself now. And it was a logical suggestion. But when else might Rachel be sure of coming face-to-face with her father? The filigree border of her brooch rasped against her chin. She lifted her head high. "I wouldn't think of being so rude."

"When you make up your mind to something, you don't do it by halves, do you?" The look Simon gave her was half rueful, half admiring. "All right. It's your game. Lead on, Macduff."

Rachel gave a shaky laugh. "You might have chosen a less ill-omened play."

"Would you have preferred *Hamlet*?" It was a relief to be speaking nonsense again, something to draw her attention away from the reckoning awaiting her at the top of the stairs.

"Isn't there anything that doesn't end with the stage littered with dead bodies? *A Midsummer Night's Dream*," Rachel picked at random.

Simon raised a brow. "How I am translated?"

Trust Simon to think of that. "Do you really need me to make an ass of you?"

Simon looked down at her, and there was something in his face that made Rachel ache. "No. I do that very well on my own, don't I?"

"I didn't mean——"

"I know." They were only three couples from the top now. Simon said rapidly, "I don't know if I've done right or wrong in bringing you here, but whatever happens—Oh, bother it."

Whatever happens. They were two couples from the top now, Lady Ardmore's tiara bobbing above a man's turbaned head as he bowed over her hand. "It was my own choice. All of it. I was the one who twisted your arm, remember?"

The man in the turban and his wife, gorgeously gowned in a silk sari, moved off, leaving only one couple between Rachel and her father.

"Yes, but——" Simon's voice seemed to come from very far away.

Rachel could see her father now. His lips were smiling as he greeted his guests, but the expression failed to convey much in the way of joy. His face looked thinner than when she had last seen him; there were lines beside his eyes. He looked, she thought, like a man convalescing from fever, whittled to a husk, still caught somewhere between sleep and waking.

The people in front of Rachel were moving on, moving away. Her father turned toward them, the set smile of welcome on his lips.

And then his eyes, so distant, so vague, fell on Rachel's brooch and came, for the first time, fully open.

TWENTY-ONE

Rachel's chest was tight; she scarcely dared to breathe. There was no one else there; no one else mattered.

Simon's hand was firm on her arm. "Go on," he murmured.

Rachel went on. She didn't trip on her dress or fall up the stairs. Afterward, she would wonder at that. At the moment, her entire being was focused on her father.

Why couldn't she hate him? Rachel's ears were ringing, the world a dizzying kaleidoscope as her feet tripped blindly forward. She so wanted to hate him. It had been easy to revile him in the abstract, to plot and scheme and ascribe all sorts of dastardly motives, to call him venal and selfish and cruel.

But when she saw him, all of that fell away, as though it had never been, and all she wanted to do was lock her arms around his neck and bury her face in his shoulder, as she had done, so contentedly, so many years ago.

A discreet personage in black leaned forward to murmur something in Lady Ardmore's ear. Their names, Rachel realized.

Lady Ardmore's eyes narrowed on Simon. "Mr. Montfort," she said, tight-lipped. "I hadn't expected to see you at Carrisford."

"In the face of such beauty, how could I stay away?" drawled Simon, deliberately outrageous. He bent down low over her hand, giving Rachel time to pull herself together, to put the mask of Vera Merton once more in place.

Feeling raw, exposed, Rachel murmured a conventional word of greeting to Lady Ardmore, who summed her up and dismissed her, all in one unblinking stare.

Jicksy, frankly bored, lounged between his parents. His *Tatler* photos had flattered him. He showed to better advantage in riding kit. In the heat of the hall, his face was florid, his collar tight on a too-thick neck.

Rachel must, she assumed, have spoken to him, too, but she had no recollection later of having done so. He didn't interest her. Her attention was all for her father.

"Lord Ardmore," said Rachel's lips. What she really meant was *Papa*. "Felicitations on this happy occasion."

Do you know me? Do you know me now? Do you remember?

So foolish to hope, but she couldn't help it, not now, with the familiar voice in her ears, all the memories flooding back. In her mind's eye, the gray was gone, and the formal costume; he was two feet taller, and the world came alive whenever he came home.

Her father's eyes moved from the brooch to her face, back and forth between the two, a thin line between his brows.

Hesitantly, he said, "Miss . . ."

"Merton," Rachel supplied. Would it have been better to have said Woodley? Or was that not a name her father would know?

His eyes flickered between her brooch and her face, like a mathematician struggling to reconcile a recondite equation. "Might I ask——"

"Yes?" Rachel's fingers were digging into Simon's arm, but she hardly noticed.

"Ardmore!" Lady Ardmore deliberately recalled her husband's attention. "You do remember Princess Sobiesky?"

"Yes, most certainly." Lord Ardmore blinked, and the moment was lost. "Good evening, Miss . . . Merton."

No. No, no, no. Rachel balked, stubbornly lingering where she was, but there was Simon's hand on the small of her back, and the press of the crowd driving them forward, inexorably, down the other side of the stairs and through an archway, into a hall where tapestries gave the wood-paneled walls a suitably antiquated air, lacking only a few suits of armor. Rachel followed, blindly, resisting the urge to fall back, to crane her neck to look back over her shoulder.

Might I ask . . .

What?

"We're through," said Simon, his voice seeming to come from very far away.

"Yes," Rachel echoed, but her thoughts were still back up the other side of the stair, on the balcony where her father and his wife held court. She forced her attention back to the present. "I thought Lady Ardmore was going to throw you out on your ear."

"She didn't want to make a scene. Not in front of Princess Sobiesky." Simon fumbled for his cigarette case, clicking it open and closed, his long fingers restless. "Are you all right?"

Her hands were damp, her pulse racing. She felt unsettled, unsatisfied. "What do we do next?"

"Dance?" said Simon, gesturing toward the broad floor that had been cleared for that purpose.

They were in a vast hall with a mellow beauty that came of long use; it felt as though it had grown rather than been made. No decorator had chosen those pennants that hung from the beamed ceiling or selected the painting of Charles I on horseback that gazed benignly from above the chimneypiece.

The musicians had set up not on a manufactured stage, but in a genuine minstrels' gallery, suspended above them. In the vast space, cleared for dancing, couples looped and twirled to the vibrant strains of a Viennese waltz.

Rachel shook her head. "You can't be serious."

"Why not? There's nothing else to do until your father finishes receiving." For all his bold words, Simon seemed edgy, shifting from one foot to the other, his eyes darting around the hall.

It seemed frivolous, somehow. She wasn't here to enjoy the party. And what if her father emerged from his perch? "I don't know. . . ."

"If nothing else," Simon said persuasively, "it provides a useful camouflage."

The violinists lifted their bows. There was an eddy of activity around the dance floor as people searched for their parties, encountered acquaintances, tried to find their partners for the next dance.

"Come." Simon held out a hand to her, elegant and saturnine in his dark evening clothes, moonstones glimmering on his wrists. "Dance your demons away."

Rachel tried to tame her nerves, to speak as Vera Merton might. "Is that the proper protocol for dealing with demons?"

"I don't know." Simon's dark gaze was disarmingly direct. "But I'm willing to try it if you are."

Why not? Rachel thought defiantly. It would be something to beguile the time.

To beguile the times, look like the times. . . . Simon's words echoed through her mind. But that was the danger, wasn't it? Getting pulled into the charade, living the charade, believing the charade.

It was just a dance.

Rachel put her gloved hand into Simon's and let him draw her forward onto the dance floor, into the firm frame of his arms as the first strains of the waltz ebbed around them. Around and around they went, moving in perfect time, in the strange limbo of the dance floor, faces a blur around them, nothing real except Simon's dark shoulders, the curve of his chin, the sandalwood and musk scent of his aftershave.

A familiar voice broke in. "Simon! Miss Merton. I hadn't thought—"

It was Olivia, her cheeks flushed from dancing, a diamond diadem in her blond curls, much smaller than her mother's and a great deal less regal.

Simon swung them to a stop, Rachel's skirts swirling dramatically around her legs. All around them, other couples were bowing, parting. The song had ended, and she had never known.

"Miss Merton! Mr. Montfort!"

Olivia looked almost pretty, her fair hair waved, her cheeks pink, at home at Carrisford as she had never been in London.

Oh, be fair, Rachel told herself. There was no almost about it. Olivia would never be a stunner, but she had her own quiet charm.

Yes, like Little Bo Beep, all pink and white and ruffled.

A momentary hesitation crossed Olivia's face. "I hadn't expected to see you."

"We crashed," Simon said baldly.

"Hush." Rachel poked him in the ribs. "Don't say that so loudly."

Simon tugged at his tie. "What's the worst that could happen?"

"We might be asked to leave." And she wasn't ready to go. Not yet.

"What, with the daughter of the house here to vouch for us?" Simon bared his teeth in a smile. Before Rachel could respond, he turned to Olivia. "Where is your *prieux chevalier?*"

"John? Speaking with Mr. Baldwin, I believe." Olivia lifted concerned eyes toward Simon. Large, gray Standish eyes. "Are you quite certain you ought to be here? After—"

Simon made an impatient gesture. "Who do you have for this set?"

Olivia consulted her dance card. "Gerald Hamby."

"Good. I have no compunction in cutting him out. I knew him at school," he added as an aside, to Rachel. "Nasty little prat. I trust you can amuse yourself?"

For a moment, Rachel hesitated. Then she told herself not to be absurd. She couldn't cling to Simon forever. He had done what he had promised and more. One couldn't waltz the world away forever.

"I shall contrive not to be a wallflower," she said brightly.

"Never that," said Simon, and all but dragged Olivia to the dance floor, moving with a rapid gait nothing like his usual elegant slouch.

Rachel watched them for a moment, Olivia's white-gloved hand resting on Simon's arm, her head barely reaching his shoulder. If Simon wished to keep a low profile, dancing with the daughter of the house was not the way to go about it.

He didn't look like a man in love. He danced with a grim determination, his face set, looking out over Olivia's head.

For her? Nothing of the sort, Rachel told herself stoutly. A business venture, he had told her, all those weeks ago.

If Olivia jilted John, would Simon still take the job in New York?

She wasn't meant to be thinking about Simon and Olivia. Grimly, Rachel turned away from the dance floor. It was pure avoidance, that was what it was, a way to distract herself from the reality of being here, in her father's home.

Had her mother ever seen Carrisford? Rachel edged along the verge of the dance floor, past the paintings of long-nosed monarchs, weaving through eminences in knee breeches and the orders of half a dozen nations. There was so much she wanted, needed, to know.

If she could find her father, get him alone . . .

The receiving line had disintegrated; Lady Ardmore's tiara could be seen bobbing along, here and there, but of her father there was no sign.

Rachel hesitated below the minstrels' gallery, unsure of what to do with herself. There was no one she knew here, or, rather, no one who knew Vera Merton, or who would acknowledge her if they did. She thought she saw Lady Frances across the dance floor, but it seemed wiser not to inquire too closely.

She might, at least, take a good look around. It was the only time she was likely to see her ancestral home. Not without paying three and six, that was.

"Pardon me, miss." One of the footmen stepped forward, his white powdered wig oddly jarring with his youthful face and sun-reddened complexion. "Are you Miss Merton?"

Rachel threw a glance over her shoulder at Simon, but he was still revolving around the dance floor, his dark head bent to Olivia, who appeared to be murmuring something rather earnestly into his ear.

She might deny it, but to what purpose? Lady Ardmore would only send someone else.

"Yes," said Rachel defensively. "I am she."

She rehearsed her excuses. *There must be some mistake. . . . Couldn't imagine . . . Invitation lost in the post . . .*

"If you would be so good as to accompany me—that is—" Giving up the attempt to sound elegant, the footman said, "If you would, miss, his lordship was wondering if you might be willing to have a word."

❦

Rachel followed her guide down a passage and up a flight of stairs, over age-worn carpets, past priceless paintings. Another passage and another stair, and she began wondering if she ought to have brought breadcrumbs after all.

Her fingers were tingling again. Rachel wrapped them in her skirt and concentrated on following the footman. It was darker here. The windows were older, the panes smaller. The walls were heavily paneled.

"This is part of the original building, miss," he said.

"Yes, I gathered that." The doorways were lower, built for smaller people, for women in ruffs and farthingales, and courtiers in shoes that turned up at the toes. The sound of music from below was barely perceptible, just the faintest strain. "Are we almost there?"

"Just through here, miss." With obvious relief, the footman gestured her toward another flight of stairs, a short flight this time, only four steps in all.

Rachel ducked beneath the doorway and found herself staring down a long, narrow room with a soaring ceiling, decorated with elaborate plaster roundels and rosettes. Where there would once have been torches, now electric sconces lit the room, glinting off the painted eyes of the portraits that lined the walls.

All along the walls, generations of Standishes looked down their noses at her from within their gilded frames: Elizabethan Standishes in ruff and doublet; Georgian Standishes in white wigs, posing beside their horses; military Standishes with gold-buckled red coats and swords by their sides.

At the end of the long line of Standishes stood her father.

He looked like something from another century himself, in his knee breeches and silk stockings, with the Order of the Garter on its ribbon across his breast, but for his spectacles, which were mundane and modern and didn't at all fit the general effect.

They didn't suit the earl, but they did belong to the father Rachel remembered. He had worn spectacles even then. She had snatched them off his nose, smearing her small fingerprints across the lenses.

Now that the moment was here, Rachel found her legs surprisingly steady. She walked down the narrow aisle, between the portraits of her ancestors. "Lord Ardmore."

A strange elation buoyed her up. Her father had summoned her, he had brought her here, away from the crowd below. Surely, that must mean something.

The earl cleared his throat. "You may go, James." Rachel had forgotten the footman was there. Any more of this, she thought giddily, and she would be like Olivia or Simon, oblivious of the help around them. "Thank you, Miss Merton. It is Miss Merton, isn't it?"

Rachel found her voice. "For the present."

"Hmm, yes." Her father removed his spectacles, inspected them, and then returned them to their wonted place on his nose. "If you will forgive my curiosity . . . may I ask where you acquired that brooch?"

Why were they playing this game? Why not get right to it? But Rachel couldn't find the words.

"My mother gave it to me." Her fingers fumbled on the knot at the back of her neck. She held the brooch out to her father, trailing black velvet. "Would you like to see it?"

"Yes—thank you." He cradled it in the palm of his white-gloved hand, peering at it closely, holding it away, turning it this way and that. After several minutes, he said, "It is . . . a very unusual piece."

"Yes. It is." Rachel clasped her hands at her waist, her fingers twining tightly together. "My mother was never without it. It meant—it meant the world to her."

The earl turned it over in his hands, tracing the engraving. He pressed something, and the brooch dissolved in two. Involuntarily, Rachel started forward, but it wasn't broken. It was open, revealing a compartment she had never known was inside.

Inside were two twists of hair. One a dark blond, the other a deep brown, like Rachel's.

Edward and Katherine, forever, in perpetuity.

"I—I never knew that was there." Rachel's voice sounded strange in the vast room.

Rapidly, the earl snapped it shut again. His fingers closed around the locket. "Thank you," he said, and then, reluctantly, extended it to Rachel. His voice was hoarse as he said, "Do you—might you happen to know—where your mother acquired it?"

Was this a test?

"It was given to her by my father. Her name was Katherine, you see, and his was Edward." Her eyes met her father's, willing him to understand, to respond. "I always thought that was terribly romantic, that he had it made for her."

Her father didn't say anything. He just looked at her, and what Rachel saw in his face wasn't pleasant. Suspicion. Mistrust.

Rachel held tighter to the brooch. Rapidly, she said, "My father was a botanist. At least, that was what I was told. He wasn't terribly grand, but we were rather fond of him, my mother and I." Her voice was shaking. She made an attempt to control it. "I was told that he had died. I was told a number of things, many of which were untrue."

The earl's face was the color of old parchment; his face looked stripped down to the bones, all dents and hollows. "I don't know who gave this to you, or where you acquired it—"

Did he really not know? Or was it just that he didn't want to know?

"Have I changed so very much?" Rachel winced at how plaintive she sounded, how foolish. It had been twenty-three years. Of course she had changed. Fighting a sinking sense of events running away from her, Rachel said hopefully, "You haven't."

But that wasn't true, was it? In feature he was the same, but the father she had loved had never looked so stern, so pinched.

Her father turned away, staring fiercely at the intricate paneling of the wall, where gargoyle faces stuck out their tongues at elaborate Tudor roses.

When he spoke, it was in a carefully controlled voice, every syllable enunciated, every word pronounced evenly. "Would I be mistaken in thinking that you are responsible for the arrival of . . . certain pictures?"

He made them sound as though they were something of which to be ashamed. Not a little girl and her mother at a church fete, but something dirty, something unclean.

"No," said Rachel, her hands clasped tightly in front of her. "You would not be mistaken. I sent them. I wanted to remind you—that you had a daughter."

Her father's words cut through her like a knife. "I have a daughter. She is currently downstairs, dancing with her fiancé."

"I—" Rachel fought for composure. "I cannot blame you for being suspicious. But, surely, in the face of all the evidence . . ."

She was trying so very hard to remain logical, but every word tore at her like thorns; she felt as though she were crawling through a bramble thicket, losing a little more of herself with every desperate movement.

Her father's face was as set and still as the portraits on the wall. "Miss Merton, I do not know where you acquired these . . . items, but if you have come here tonight with the intent to blackmail me—"

"Blackmail!" Rachel's head came up sharply. "You can't think—"

But he did think. She could see it in his face, in the utter disdain that managed to convey itself despite his very stillness.

"What do you want, Miss Merton?" Her father's voice was clipped, remote.

He looked at her as though she were something foul.

I want my father back, Rachel thought wildly But he didn't exist any-more, had never existed. He had been an illusion, compounded of memory and—what? Boredom? Had he dallied with them for a while, playing at domesticity, until he found something better?

"I was right at the start." Her mother's brooch clutched in her hand, Rachel took a shaky step back. "I ought to have left well enough alone. I ought to have had the sense—the sense to realize that people who disap-pear generally don't want to be found."

He hadn't so much disappeared as made them disappear. But that was immaterial.

"I ought not to have come." Now, when she thought of him, she would always remember this, she would remember him pinched and sour, pretending not to know her. Rachel flung the words like a sword. "I was much happier when I thought you were dead."

Her father stood there, among the shades of his ancestors, the gargoyles and the roses, writing her out of his history as effectively as he knew how.

"How do I know you are who you claim to be?" he demanded.

"You can't even say my name, can you?" Rachel couldn't hide the hurt in her voice. She tried to make up for it with a show of bravado. "Or have you forgotten it?"

That, at least, got some reaction. Her father's nostrils flared. "Forgive me, Miss . . . whatever your name is. Your methods do not inspire one to trust you."

"Trust?" Rachel stared at her father in disbelief. It didn't matter what she said now. Her father was lost to her. This man, this man in front of her, was nothing. "You kissed me good-bye. You lifted me in your arms and told me you loved me and that you would be back soon. Trust you? I waited for you. I waited for you to come home, and you never did."

Once started, she couldn't seem to stop speaking, her voice rising higher and higher with every word. "I used to imagine that you weren't dead at all, that you'd been kidnapped by pirates, or dropped in an oubliette, or were employed by His Majesty's government on a secret mission. And one day you would come home to us and everything would be as it was. There was no body—so it was easy to imagine it was all a mistake."

"No body," her father echoed. For the first time, he looked directly at her, as though he were really seeing her. "Where is—your mother?"

"You needn't look over my shoulder for her. She's dead." The words came out, bald and ugly. Rachel had the satisfaction of seeing the earl flinch. "She died in April. Influenza."

"April," the earl repeated.

"I suppose it must be a relief, to know that she's finally out of the way. One less loose end."

Her father didn't seem to hear. He was half turned away, his face in shadow, his shoulders hunched. He seemed to have folded in on himself.

Hoarsely, he said, "If you need money . . ."

"I don't want your money. I don't need your money. I am perfectly capable of getting my own living. I have done for years. That wasn't why I came. I had a crazy idea that it—that it might mean something to see you again." Rachel's eyes stung. Blinking the tears away, she said fiercely, "I loved you once, you see. More fool me."

Slowly, her father straightened. The Order of the Garter was bright on his breast.

Rachel backed toward the door, her heels catching on her long skirt. "Isn't that what they say? Fool me once, shame on you. Fool me twice, shame on me." Her voice was Vera Merton's, high and sophisticated. If she kept talking she might keep from crying, and, at all costs, she wasn't going to let her father see her cry. Not for him. "You needn't worry that I'll trouble you again. I've seen all I need to see."

She had seen the portraits and the carpets, the porcelain and the tapestries. Hundreds of years' worth of items that were beautiful and rare, and an heiress with the money to maintain them.

She meant to sweep out, to leave with her head high and her dignity intact, or as intact as it could be, but there must have been just a little bit of that four-year-old Rachel left inside her, because she came to a stop on the threshold, her gloved hand catching against the intricately carved wooden arch.

She looked back at her father, so small at the end of the long room, and said, in the voice of that four-year-old she had been, "Did you love us at all? Even a little?"

Her father might have been one of the busts on their pedestals.

His silence was answer enough.

"Right." The jagged edge of a Tudor rose was digging into Rachel's palm. "That's all, then. Good-bye."

The stairs were worn, curving in the middle. She took them so quickly that only sheer momentum kept her from falling. Rachel stumbled into the corridor at something like a run, her skirts tangled against her legs.

Through the unshed tears, through the roaring in her ears, she thought she heard her own name, whispering down the corridor behind her.

TWENTY-TWO

S he was soon hopelessly lost.

It didn't matter. She didn't care where she went. All she wanted was away. One corridor and then another, down stairs that were too narrow for public use. She had stumbled into the servants' quarters.

How terribly appropriate, thought Rachel, with a laugh that turned into a sob. Just where she belonged. Tossed out by the back stairs.

She swiped the back of her hand clumsily against her eyes. Her father wasn't worth crying for, none of this was. What did she need with linen-fold paneling and six swans a-swimming? And her father . . . Well, she didn't need him, either. She hadn't for a very long time. It was the idea of him she had cherished. The idea of someone who would love her, absolutely, unconditionally, as her mother had, as he had seemed to do all those years ago.

Now she knew.

That was what she had wanted, wasn't it? To know. And now she did. There had been no mistake in his leaving them, he had meant to leave them, to trade them for all this.

She might have her revenge. She could go to the papers—Simon's paper, some other paper—but what use would it be? A six-minute sensation and then over. And she didn't want revenge, not really. She had never wanted revenge.

Rachel wanted her mother.

She wanted her mother with a raw longing that made her throat sting. She wanted her arms around her, her firm common sense, the smell of old lavender and fresh baking and washing soap. She didn't belong here, at Carrisford, or in London, with the smartly sophisticated set who found Vera Merton such a gas, darling, really too too.

She didn't belong anywhere.

Rachel shoved at the outlines of a door and found herself suddenly outdoors, in the chill of the August evening. It was full dark now, but there were lights twinkling in the gardens, and the sound of a jazz band playing on a terrace strung with Chinese lanterns.

The voices here were higher, brighter, the figures on the dance floor moving in less formal patterns than the ones in the ballroom inside. This was where the bright young people had got to, away from the stifling presence of their elders.

A footman was circling with a silver tray laden with glasses. Rachel snagged a glass of champagne and stepped forward, her long hem dragging against the dew-damp gravel of the path.

There was a fountain in the center of the terrace, Triton blowing his horn, flanked by a pair of adoring water nymphs and a quartet of very sloshed young men, ties askew, faces flushed, as they jostled and dared one another to scale the fountain.

"Bet you can't get"—word garbled—"on Triton's spear!"

More jostling and splashing.

"I'd like to spear—"

What idiots, thought Rachel angrily. What fools, the lot of them. This is the great and the good? It seemed such a waste, those vast edifices, all the wealth and education and culture, all come to this.

"One of them is going straight into the water," said a familiar voice by Rachel's shoulder.

"John!" Rachel hastily composed herself. Not John, not now. She didn't have it in her to make polite conversation, to be the person he thought her to be.

Different from the others, he had said. He didn't know the half of it.

"Are you cold?" John lifted the heavy white silk scarf from around his neck.

"A goose walked over my grave," Rachel said shakily. She could only hope that her eye-black hadn't run, or, if it had, that it was too dark for John to see it. "Shouldn't you be doing your duty indoors?"

"I have done." John's cheeks were flushed with excitement and champagne. "I had the most splendid conversation with Mr. Baldwin."

"Mmm?" Rachel plunked her empty glass on a tray, trying to think of a polite out. She had to find Simon, find a way to get back to London, pack up her things. . . .

But Simon was with Olivia.

"Mr. Baldwin agrees with me entirely on disarmament," John was saying triumphantly.

"How wonderful," said Rachel tonelessly.

Simon wouldn't thank her for intruding, not now. The chill breeze cut through Rachel's meager wrap, making her feel small and insignificant and miserably alone.

Oh, bother it. Rachel plucked another glass of champagne off a tray. She had never drunk to drink before, but if there was ever a time, it was now. One last hurrah, one last binge before Vera Merton packed up and disappeared forever.

She turned a bright smile on John. "Be a darling and find me a bottle?"

John gestured obligingly to one of the ubiquitous footmen, talking all the while. ". . . no greater spur to war than the accumulation of arms. Dash it all, it's common sense. If the weapons are there, someone's bound to be tempted to use them."

"Toys for grown-up boys?" said Rachel, holding the stem of her glass between two fingers, watching the way the crystal sparkled in the lantern light.

If Simon wouldn't take her, maybe she could find someone else to bring her to the station. A train back to London, and then she could just disappear, melt away as though she never was.

And she wasn't really. If Vera Merton was a sham, then Rachel Woodley was, too, just one of longer duration.

"You always have the *mot juste*," said John warmly, and Rachel mutely shook her head.

La vie n'est pas juste, the cook at Brillac used to say, with a shrug of her massive shoulders, and it wasn't, not at all. If it were—

Rachel cut off that line of thought. What use was it? What use would it be to wonder what life would be like if this had all been hers? If she were the one dancing with Simon in the ballroom, instead of lurking in the gardens, shaken and miserable, keeping to the shadows.

John went on, excited and oblivious. "That's just it, don't you see? And that's why I suggested to Mr. Baldwin that we extend the vote for women. Get rid of the property qualifications, bring the age limit down to eighteen—"

Would Simon wonder what had become of her? Perhaps. In the way one wondered about the ending of a book left unfinished on the train. A curiosity, nothing more.

"... gentler sex ..." said John.

Olivia was gentle. Olivia spoke in a soft, muted voice. But, then, she could afford to be gentle, couldn't she? She had a father who acknowledged her. Pain twisted like a knife. Her father, his face a cold mask. *I have a daughter. . . .* Olivia didn't have to battle her way through the world, earning her own bread. She had chevaliers falling over themselves for her: John, Simon ...

No, that wasn't fair, either. There was no point in being unkind about Olivia. The champagne might be the Frenchest of the French, but it still tasted sour to Rachel. She didn't want to be that person: petty, vengeful. She might have nothing else, but she had her integrity, such as it was. What was left of it.

Gate-crasher. Fraud. And what had it been for, after all? Her father didn't want her. Rachel pressed her lips tightly together, against a sudden, betraying rush of tears.

"... would never play with arms as though war were a game. Ah, thank you." The footman had reappeared, face impassive, with a bottle, which he presented, bottom first, to John. John paused, a hand on the cork. "Shall we toast to a world at peace?"

"Why not?" said Rachel. She lifted her empty glass to John. "And a Trevannion in the Cabinet."

She was only half serious, but John took her very much at her word. "It's not a done thing, of course. I'm far too junior. But—" Out came the cork with a pop. "In a year or two . . ."

They had moved a little bit away from the crowd, in the lee of a Roman temple—or perhaps Greek; Rachel's architectural background was sketchy at best—on a small rise.

"Good on you," said Rachel. She plunked down on the ground, which wasn't quite so dry as it looked. She felt the wet seeping through the seat of her dress. She hoped Simon's sister wasn't too fond of it. "You can bring government back to what it ought to be."

John had been pouring their champagne. He paused, the bottle on an angle. "Dash it all, I wish—" He jumped as cold liquid splashed on his hand. He shook it off. "Never mind."

"If wishes were horses, beggars would ride." Her mother used to say that, when Rachel had sighed for this or that. Reaching up, Rachel took the bottle from him and topped up her own glass. "They can be dangerous things, wishes."

She'd spent all those years wishing her father were still alive. She ought to have known better. Fate had a way of giving you what you wanted, but with a twist.

"It's just—you understand a chap, don't you?" Carefully, John spread out his jacket on the ground and sat down on top of it, next to Rachel. "Olivia—she doesn't care. It doesn't interest her."

"I'm not sure I would say that." Rachel's brain felt fuzzy with champagne. "It's hard to tell what Olivia is thinking."

She didn't want to think of Olivia, Olivia dancing with Simon, Olivia who she so dearly would have liked to hate.

Oh, let them all have each other, Rachel thought drearily, taking another swig of champagne, which tasted to her like nothing at all. It's nothing to do with me.

John scuffed his heels against the carefully planted turf. "I thought she would be more like her mother. Oh, not like that—not as pushing—but that she'd care about things. That she'd take an interest."

Why had she come out here with John? Because it was that or go back in the house. Go away, Rachel thought. Go away and leave me alone.

"I'm sure she has other strengths," said Rachel vaguely.

"Oh, yes, she can balance books," said John bitterly. "She told me. But what use is that?"

A great deal of use, Rachel could have told him. Especially when one was living quarter to quarter, payment to payment. "Well, what do you need, then?"

"Someone with—oh, I don't know." John leaned back on his elbows, staring gloomily out at the curves of an ornamental bridge that seemed to be missing its river. "Someone with energy, with ideals. Someone who can *manage* things. Someone more like—well, more like you."

Recklessly, Rachel said, "Then don't marry her."

John sat up abruptly. "It's hardly as simple as that."

"Why not?" Rachel's head was fizzing with champagne and defiance. Bother her father's world and its rules. "If it makes you feel better, I don't think Olivia is all that keen to marry you either."

John choked on his drink. "Did she tell you that?"

"Call it female intu—intu—instinct." Her tongue didn't seem to be working properly. Rachel solved the problem with another swig of champagne. "You haven't set a date."

"If I cry off, Lady Ardmore will kill me."

Rachel gestured expansively with her empty glass. "Marry Lady Ardmore, then."

John didn't appear to see the humor in this. "Worse than kill me, she'll kill my chances in the party."

Rachel braced a hand against the ground. "Then join a different party," she said with energy. "Go to the Liberals. Go to Labour. Strike a blow for Whiggery."

John gaped. "There haven't been Whigs for fifty years. Longer."

"Then refound them," said Rachel imperiously. "Take a chance. Be bold."

A reluctant smile touched John's lips. His fingertips brushed hers. "You're so brave." He leaned closer, his fingers inching up her glove to the bare skin above the elbow. He traced the path of the gold armlet she had clasped around her upper arm. "So bold. So . . . uninhibited."

Rachel could have told him that she wasn't uninhibited at all, that most of her youth had been spent at the vicarage, that her hair had, until April, fallen past her waist, and her skirts to a point well below the knee, but he didn't give her time. He leaned forward and kissed her.

"But—" Rachel began, but John only pressed forward, throwing her off balance, and it was easier to just wrap her arms around his neck and kiss him back, to lean into that illusion of intimacy, and feel, for that fleeting moment, as though someone, someone in this vast, lonely world, cared about her just a little.

John thought she was special; he had said so. And Olivia didn't want him, not really, so it wasn't as though they were betraying her. No, don't think of Olivia, looking up at Simon. Think of John, good, kind, earnest, conscientious John, whose tongue was wetting her ear and whose knee was bearing rather heavily on one of the flounces of her skirt.

"Vera," John murmured, his breath heavy in her ear.

Rachel pulled back just enough to say, "My—my mother called me Rachel."

"Rachel?" John's tie was askew, his breath came fast. "No. It's too workaday."

Rachel let out a helpless laugh. "I am workaday." A nursery governess in heiress's clothing.

"You haven't any idea, have you?" said John huskily. He touched his fingers to her smudged lipstick. "You haven't any notion how glamorous you are."

"Yes, but that's not me." Just a veneer, put on for the occasion. It seemed, suddenly, very important that John should know that. Rachel tried to sit up, but the world was wobbly. Her champagne glass tumbled over, rocking on its side.

John only smiled patiently and looped an arm around her waist. "All right . . . whatever you like."

"But it's not what I like. . . ." Rachel pressed her eyelids together, trying to remember what she'd been thinking, what she meant to say. John took advantage of the moment to lean forward again, his body mashing her backward. "Wait. What about Olivia?"

John leaned obligingly back. "What about her?"

Rachel looked at him blankly. "You're engaged."

"Does that really matter?" Rachel could feel John's champagne-sweet breath against her neck, her ear. "Olivia doesn't need to know about— well, about this."

For a moment, she thought she had misheard him.

"This," Rachel echoed.

As from a distance, she could see it, the whole sordid picture. Her own crumpled dress and smudged lipstick, the diamante clip in her hair askew. John, jacket undone, tie crooked.

"Get away from me." Staggering to her feet, Rachel scrubbed the back of her hand against her mouth.

"Don't be like that," John said plaintively.

"Like what? With morals? With values? With a basic sense of self-respect?" Rachel was shaking, but not with cold. The ground was still wobbly beneath her feet, but her head was clearing rapidly. She almost wished it wouldn't.

"I hadn't thought you'd mind." John assumed a wounded expression. "You're so sophisticated. So . . . modern."

Apples didn't fall far, Mrs. Spicer said. "Not that modern."

Was that how her father had justified it? That sort never minds anyway; she couldn't possibly have expected anything more. A modern version of the droit du seigneur, without the chivalric trappings.

Rachel pulled her wrap tightly around her. "And what about Olivia? Did you stop to think of her while you were pawing me?"

John saw his advantage. "It's not like that with Olivia," he said persuasively. "It's an arrangement. She knows that." Before Rachel could question that, John added, "And I am very fond of her."

"Fond," Rachel repeated flatly. Fond enough to kiss other women. "That's a curious sort of fondness."

John didn't let himself be distracted. "It's different with you," he said earnestly. "Olivia is so ordinary, so conventional, but you—you're something special."

"Did you know that Olivia wanted to study economics?" Rachel wasn't quite sure where the words came from; they just popped out. "Did you know that she won a scholarship at Somerville?"

"No," said John, giving Rachel a confused look. "Lady Ardmore never mentioned it."

Of course she hadn't. And John had never bothered to find out for himself.

She had thought she had known him, that he was something solid and good, when, instead, all he was was a pasteboard character of her own inventing. Just like her father.

"What a toad you are," said Rachel, and, gathering the scraps of her dignity around her, she turned on her heel.

"You won't—" John hurried along behind her, real alarm in his voice. "You won't tell Olivia?"

Rachel gave John a long, level look. "That," she said, as distinctly as she could, "is the least of your worries. Go away, John. Go to your fiancée. Because if you don't, someone else will."

He didn't make any effort to follow her. Well, that was hardly surprising, was it? Too busy scurrying off to secure his interest with Olivia and his safe seat.

Rachel blundered into a yew bush, the prickly shrubbery scraping her bare arms. In her eagerness to get away, she had gone too far, into a formal garden of dramatic scope, well away from the lights and music from the terraces above. These bushes could grow and grow around her and no one would ever know.

Don't be silly, she told herself, and wrenched her skirt free from a trailing rosebush. There must be gardeners. They would fish her out before she began to smell.

And wasn't that a cheerful thought?

"There you are." Gravel crunched behind her. Simon's voice came out of the darkness, smooth and sophisticated. "I was wondering if I ought to dredge the moat."

She should answer in kind, Rachel knew, make some light response, but there was no lightness left. She felt raw and bare, just a collection of bones with nothing left on them.

She pressed her balled fists to her eyes. "You were right," she said, without turning. "You were right all along. I ought never to have come. It was a mistake, all of it."

"Rachel." Simon was behind her, his hands on her shoulders, so different from John's hands, the smell of musk and sandalwood cutting through the sickly sweet smell of late-season flowers. "Rachel, are you all right?"

Mutely, Rachel shook her bowed head. "It was a horrible idea, from the start. You should have stopped me." Twisting, she faced him, breast to breast, nose to chin. "Why didn't you stop me?"

There was little light in this part of the garden. Her own face had to be as shadowed as Simon's. But whatever he saw in it made him draw her roughly into his arms, resting his cheek against the top of her head. "Oh, Rachel. I'm so sorry."

For a moment, she allowed herself the luxury of leaning against him, blinking bitter tears against the smooth wool of his jacket. Her head fit comfortably into the hollow beneath his ear; his arms just the right length to go around her waist. Around them, the garden was dark and still, the sounds of revelry very far away.

If she had been Olivia and Olivia Rachel . . .

Rachel pushed back, saying with a rough attempt at a laugh, "Well, at least you needn't go to New York anymore. You can stay here and marry Olivia."

Simon looked at her as though she'd grown a second head.

"She doesn't want to marry John. It's you she loves." Even as she said it, Rachel wasn't entirely sure of it. But shouldn't someone be happy? "You can live happily ever after together." The more Simon stared, the faster she spoke, her voice rising to fill the empty space. "That's why you took me on. Wasn't it? To get close to her. I don't know why she jilted you—"

"Olivia didn't jilt me." That was all he said.

Did it matter? "All right. My father made you break it off. There's nothing so romantic as star-crossed lovers." Rachel rubbed her gloved palms against her eyes. "What a wonderful revenge on him, throwing his by-blow in his face. Although I can't say it was an enjoyable experience, being a human cannonball. Quite unpleasant, really."

"Rachel. *Rachel.*" Simon caught her shoulders, giving her a brisk shake that left her teeth chattering but stopped the spate of words, the words she couldn't control, that poured out of her mouth without volition. "You have it all wrong."

TWENTY-THREE

Y ou mean I'm all wrong." Drunk, sloppy. A drag on him. Rachel
flapped a hand. "Go on. Go back to Olivia. I'll be all right."

As if on cue, one of her heels twisted under her.

"I'm not going anywhere." Gently but firmly, Simon led her to a bench,
so hidden by trailing vines that Rachel would never have found it on her
own. "As for Olivia . . ."

He had seated Rachel, but didn't sit himself. He stood over her, looking down, twin furrows between his brows.

Abruptly, Simon said, "I couldn't stick it—the engagement. I ran
out on her. Jilted her." Before Rachel could do more than make a small
sound of surprise, he added brusquely, "Do you know why I was here, at
Caffers?"

Why did anyone go anywhere? "For a Saturday to Monday?"

"How quickly you pick up the lingo." Simon's lips twisted in a grin,
but the moment of amusement was fleeting. He jammed his hands into
his pockets, spoiling the line of his suit, looking out somewhere over
Rachel's head, his eyes blank. "During the war, they turned Caffers into a
mental institution. Officers only, of course. Lady Ardmore wouldn't have

settled for anything less. It was no concern of hers if an enlisted man wanted to put a bullet into his brain. Let them shiver it out beneath the bridges, in the pub, in a cardboard box on the green. What was one more serf more or less?"

"Oh, Simon." The mockery in his voice was terrible to hear, but Rachel knew now that it was a front, and what she heard beneath it made her heart ache. How had she not guessed? How had she not known? "Did you try to kill yourself?"

"Not like Peter." Simon's hand shook as he drew a cigarette from its case. "Nothing quite so direct. Gasper?"

Without a word, Rachel took one, holding it out to Simon to be lit.

It took Simon several tries before he managed to touch the tip to the flame. Rachel didn't try to help, just let him get on with it. "It seemed quite ungentlemanly of Death to have taken so many and overlooked me. I used to fantasize about being hit by a lorry or falling down a well. Enough booze, a misstep on the street . . . and farewell, mortal coil."

Rachel struggled to keep her voice matter-of-fact. Pity was the last thing Simon wanted. "Why not just fall on your sword?"

Simon gave a twisted smile. "Because I'm not an antique Roman. Or a Dane. I couldn't do that to my mother. Or Ginny."

"Ginny?" Rachel felt a small, ugly spark of jealousy at the name, spoken with such affection.

"My sister. She was only ten. It would have been rotten for her."

Rotten. That was one way of putting it. Rachel thought of Cece, sobbing on the floor, what she had seen, and knew Simon was thinking of it, too.

"Since then, I've tried to stay away from them as much as I can." For a moment, Simon's eyes met Rachel's. "Easier for them not to get too attached."

With difficulty, Rachel found her voice. "You idiot. Of course they're attached." Not all the years she had been in France could do anything to lessen her mother's love for her, or her for her mother. Her tongue felt thick. "It's not the seeing that counts."

"I thought it might be rather easier on them if . . . It was all rather touch and go for a while." Simon took another deep drag on his cigarette. "I was meant to be working on a book about King Harold, but my hand shook too badly to form the words. Every time a car backfired, I thought it was a shell." He looked around, taking in the boxwood, the roses, the carefully plotted paths. "We were only allowed out here with a keeper. Too much chance of our doing damage to ourselves, as they so politely put it."

His voice was measured, precise, but something about that very lack of emotion sent a chill down Rachel's spine. "They?"

"The doctors. We had our exercise in the great hall, round and round and round about, double time. The chapel was for solitary confinement. You could hear the chaps screaming, sometimes. God. I can hear them still."

Did you think yours was the only family tragedy in Britain?

"Why didn't you tell me?"

"That I was mad? It's not something that generally comes up in conversation."

But it had, north by northwest. Rachel had thought it all a joke, nothing more than Simon's banter.

A kaleidoscope of images shifted and turned, clicking horribly and finally into place. Rachel's stomach twisted, sour with champagne and self-loathing. "That was why you didn't want to come with me? Because of . . . before?"

The men screaming. The keepers.

Simon chucked his cigarette butt away, grinding it beneath his heel. With the air of one determined to make a clean breast, he said, "Olivia was the only sane thing in this terrible place. Her mother wouldn't let her nurse, but she used to smuggle me poetry. Keats, Tennyson. When my hands shook too hard to turn the pages, she would read aloud to me. She brought me flowers from the hothouses and books on old masters, with glossy illustrations." For a moment, Simon stood lost in memory. "It was like living inside a beautiful box of stained glass."

Rachel could picture it all too well: Olivia, young and idealistic, her golden hair worn long, in curls, kneeling by Simon's bedside in a bower of flowers, reading poetry in that husky, hesitant voice, the two of them tucked away from the world.

Rachel shifted restlessly on the hard stone bench. "And you fell in love with her. I know."

"I fell in love with the idea of her." The moonlight silvered Simon's dark hair, lent an antique cast to the long lines of his face. "She stood for everything that was true and pure, everything that I had cared about before the war. And then Peter killed himself. And I realized it all for the sham it was. Lord Ardmore didn't break it off—although his wife would have liked to see him try. I . . . left. I ran away."

"You found Olivia a scholarship, at Somerville." It wasn't a question.

Simon made a quick, nervous gesture. "It was the least I could do. I'd dropped her in it, hadn't I? Her mother was bad enough before. After . . ." There was no need to explain after what. "She made Olivia's life a hell. And her father—he looked through her as though she wasn't there."

He didn't need to say more. Rachel knew that look. Those gray eyes, those Standish eyes, looking over and through her, dismissing her with chilling indifference. *I have a daughter*, her father had said, but he'd been no better to Olivia than to Rachel. He might provide her the protection of his name, but there was no warmth, no love.

So much for the father of her memory, a figment of imagination and wishful thinking. Had he ever been kind? Or had she made it all up out of whole cloth?

Rachel found she was shivering and couldn't stop. "He's a rather awful man, isn't he?"

She felt something settle around her shoulders. Simon's jacket, warmed by his body, smelling of tobacco and Simon.

"Won't you"—hunched inside its comforting warmth, Rachel made an effort to be noble—"won't you be cold?"

"That would sound more convincing," said Simon, "if your teeth weren't chattering." He didn't point out that it wasn't that cold outside. Her cold came from within. He knelt down beside her, one hand on the side of the bench. "Rachel—what happened?"

"Oh, what one would expect." Clutching the lapels of Simon's jacket in her shaking hands, Rachel made an unconvincing jab at lightness. "He accused me of being a fraud, trying to blackmail him. He told me he . . . he already had a daughter." Rachel looked up at Simon, feeling all the remembered pain of it, her father's coldness, his scorn. "It wasn't just that he didn't know me. He didn't want to know me."

She was shivering again, shivering even in the warmth of Simon's jacket.

Rachel made an effort to get hold of herself. "Stupid, I know, all of it. After this many years . . . I ought to have realized, oughtn't I?"

Simon's hand moved gently to cover hers. "What do you mean to do?"

Rachel pressed her eyes shut. Practicalities. Best to focus on practicalities. "What I always meant to do. A typing course. A bedsit."

Not in London, not now. She would meet the shadow of her old life everywhere. York, perhaps, or Edinburgh.

"And Ardmore?"

He didn't need to explain what he meant. Rachel shook her head, crowded with bittersweet memories of a humid café on a rainy day, Simon sitting across from her, a walnut-dotted slice of cake.

"I'm out of the revenge business." In the distance, Rachel could see the shadowy bulk of Carrisford, windows sparkling golden, the doors forever closed to her. "There's nothing for me here."

Simon's eyes were on her face, grave, inscrutable. "My ship leaves for New York in two days. The *Aquitania* out of Southampton."

So this was the end. Rachel swallowed hard against a burning sense of loss. "You're not staying, then."

Not that it made a difference. Their paths would never cross in the normal course of things. Not unless Simon needed a secretary.

Simon ducked his head. "My mother and Ginny are settled in New York now. I've been away from them too long."

"That's . . . wonderful. Really." Horrible to feel so sad for herself when she should be happy for him. Rachel pushed up from the bench, making an effort to speak lightly. "You needn't worry. I'll clean my bits and pieces out of the flat. You'll hardly know I was there."

Simon followed her to his feet. He raised a dark brow. "Won't I?"

"A bit of Jeyes Fluid. You said it yourself. It can clean away anything."

Rachel struggled out of his coat, dumping it unceremoniously over his arm. "If you like, I'll see you to the docks and wave my hankie at you."

She was speaking nonsense, she knew, but it was the only way to keep the dark, sinking misery from engulfing her. Sound and fury signifying nothing. Simon should understand. He was the expert.

Simon reached out, grasped her hand. His coat slipped unheeded to the ground beneath their feet. "Come with me."

Rachel looked down at their joined hands, back to his face. "To the flat?"

"To New York. That is where the ship is bound." The same old delicate note of irony, but there was something else beneath it, something uncertain, diffident. Simon's hands tightened on hers. "Well? Will you come with me?"

It was the champagne talking. Only she was the one who had been scarfing down the bubbly, not Simon.

Rachel shook her head blankly. "You don't really want me there."

"Don't I?" But then Simon ruined it by adding, "Did you think I would just leave you here?"

Rachel twitched her hands away. "Wouldn't it be easier just to find me a scholarship at Somerville?"

The words hung in the air between them.

Clumsily, earnestly, Rachel said, "Don't you see? I can't have you burdening yourself with me out of . . . out of guilt." She was twisting her hands together, drowning in her own words. "I thrust myself on you, remember? I pushed you into this. You don't owe me anything."

Mad schemes, a lifetime ago. The purr of the engine of his car. The reflection of the headlamps off the planes of his face, then so strange to her, now so vital.

A faint smile twisted Simon's lips. "Didn't I tell you before? My actions are invariably self-serving."

She didn't believe that, not anymore. "You don't have to rescue me." Rachel kicked at gravel with her toe, feeling the bite of it through her thin evening slipper. No point in allowing herself to dream of New York, New York with Simon. "We had a business arrangement. Which is now concluded."

"Is it?" Simon's voice was a lazy drawl, but there was something in it that made Rachel look up sharply. Gently, he ran a knuckle across her cheekbone, his eyes still on hers, with a single-minded intensity that took her breath away. "Let's put that to the test, shall we?"

Everything moved with tantalizing slowness. Simon's fingers, stroking the hair away from her face. His hand, cupping her chin. Slowly, so slowly, giving her time to object, to pull away.

She ought to pull away, Rachel knew, but her hands were already on his shoulders, feeling the flex of them, the taut muscles beneath her fingers, the tension he kept so carefully in check.

Rachel's eyes drifted shut and she lifted her face to the warm brush of Simon's lips, teasingly light.

"A business arrangement?" he murmured, and he sounded so amused, so ... Simon, that there was nothing for Rachel to do but go up on her tiptoes and kiss him, with a vague thought that it was a good thing her lipstick had long since worn off, since otherwise Simon would be bearing the imprint of it quite firmly on his lips just now.

And then Simon's arms came around her and his lips slanted to meet hers and that was the last thing Rachel was capable of thinking for quite some time. There was nothing but the feel of Simon's lips against hers, his arms around her, the dark gardens around them, the music from the party faint in the distance, and the dizzying smell of sandalwood, tobacco, and the flower in Simon's lapel, crushed to sweetness.

She had no idea how much time elapsed, only that, when they parted, the wind felt colder without Simon's arms around her, and her legs were embarrassingly unsteady.

"I thought—" So much for sangfroid. Rachel's voice was breathless, as much of a betrayal as the trembling in her hands. She took a deep breath and tried again. "You said that you didn't want a pound of flesh."

"The pound of flesh is optional," said Simon raggedly. He braced a hand against the back of the bench to steady himself. "Come with me to New York. You can share my cabin or not, as you please. If you'd rather not ... It's your decision."

Not entirely. At least, not if that kiss was any indication. She would like to think she was made of sterner stuff than that, but Rachel wasn't sure she could weather a transatlantic voyage with Simon a cabin away.

Paying for her passage, for her clothes . . . No. No matter how badly she might want to be with Simon, every feeling rebelled against such an arrangement.

It would gnaw at her, she knew. And what if he grew bored with her? He wouldn't toss her aside, she knew him better than that, but it would wear on them both, eating away at them, bit by bit, until all affection was gone.

Is that what had happened to her parents?

"As flattering an offer as that is . . ." Rachel bit down hard on her lip. What was the point of beating around the bush? "I can't, Simon. I won't be your mistress."

Looking down at Rachel, Simon said ruefully, "I had something more in the line of orange blossoms in mind. I'm making a pig's ear of this, aren't I? I'm out of the habit of proposing. Shall I go down on one knee? Or is that too much of a cliché?"

The shrubbery, the bench, the folly on the rise all suddenly seemed curiously insubstantial. The world dipped and swayed. "You were already there," Rachel said hoarsely. "You've the gravel on your trousers to prove it."

"So I have." Simon made no move to brush it off. "I've got it all backward, haven't I? But the sentiments remain the same It's not much of an offer, I know. One broken-down journalist, without much in the way of prospects, slightly mad about the edges. And then there's America to consider. A country full of people who've never quite learned to speak the language. My stepfather isn't a bad sort, though. And I rather think you'll enjoy my mother."

What would it be to be part of Simon's family circle? To sit across a dining room table from the dark, clever-looking woman in the portrait in Simon's mother's flat, go shopping with his sister? But, most of all, Simon. Arriving with him, arm in arm, leaving with him at the end of the evening, going to bed with him every night.

Wondering, always, if he had proposed out of pity.

"Stop, please." Rachel wrapped her arms tightly around her chest to keep herself from reaching for him. "Simon, I can't. I just . . . can't."

"There is the plumbing." Simon's voice was bland, but his eyes were watchful. "I hear the Americans do that rather well."

She had thought she hurt before, but this was a new ache. Rachel forced herself to say, "It's not that."

Simon abandoned all pretense at humor. "Would it make a difference if I said I love you?"

Rachel pressed her eyes shut, lips quivering on an unhappy laugh. "You can't even say it straight out." If ever she'd needed proof, there it was. If he really loved her—Rapidly, Rachel said, "I'll find someone to take me to the train. There's no sense in your leaving, too."

Simon made a quick, impatient movement. "Don't be ridiculous. Of course I'll run you home." He stilled, like a rabbit in a field. "Unless you'd rather be shot of me."

Rachel made an abortive move toward him. "Simon, no. The last thing I want is to be shot of you. I—"

I love you.

Rachel broke off, horrified at herself, at what she had so nearly said.

"Appreciate my assistance, I know," Simon said, with an approximation of the old drawl. "Don't worry. I'll spare you further importunities. One proposal a night is my limit."

She had hurt him. Numbly, Rachel followed along behind his lean form, striding through the gardens, toward a gate that let out into the field where he had parked the car, so many hours ago. She wanted to reach out to him, say something to put it right, but the words *I love you* were frozen on her lips, stilling all other speech.

Would it make a difference if I said I love you?

Not like that. And what did she know of love? Rachel stumbled miserably along in her heels, not sure if the problem lay with the shoes or with the turf, which seemed to be undulating alarmingly. She'd believed her parents loved each other; they had been the model by which she judged all others. Not the brief spark of infatuation, but real, enduring love, love that outlasted separation and death.

She tripped and would have fallen, but Simon was there, bracing her, his hand on her elbow.

"How much have you had?" he said, not unkindly.

"Too much." Rachel's tongue didn't want to move properly.

Did she love him? She didn't know. All she knew was that she wanted to go to New York with him, more than she had ever wanted anything, to explore new places with him, laugh over the eccentricities of the natives with him, spar with him, argue with him.

Desperately, Rachel tugged at Simon's arm. "You're better off without me. Really, you are. I'd be a liability to you." Foolish tears prickled at the backs of her eyes. "I'm not Vera Merton. I'm not even Rachel Woodley. I'm not anyone."

They stopped beside the car, Simon's arm around her, bracing her. "You're yourself. Isn't that enough?" His hand brushed her cheek, so fleetingly that she thought she might have imagined it. "You are," he said quietly, "the strongest person I know."

Rachel looked at him in confusion, listing to one side, one heel half off, not feeling strong at all, feeling, in fact, like a sodden mass of yesterday's wet washing.

"Although somewhat green about the gills just now," Simon added smoothly. With a practiced hand, he heaved her through the door of the Daimler. "Get in, lean back, and try not to be sick until we get to London."

✎

She wasn't sick, but she did fall into a sodden and restless sleep.

When she woke, she was on the vast bed in Simon's sister's room, chastely covered with a blanket, still in her green gown, and there was a jug of water and a bottle of aspirin on the bedside table.

There was a folded note propped against the water jug.

Rachel crawled her way across the coverlet with small, painful movements that didn't jar her aching head. The blinding whiteness of the pillows made her eyes hurt. The sunlight casting a striped pattern across the carpet made her stomach heave.

She had only the vaguest recollections of Simon helping her inside, of the porter's joking comments, and her own stumbling steps, and a brief, blurry recollection of fumbling for the latchkey.

Disjointed images of the evening bombarded her: her father in his vast gallery, John's self-satisfied puffery, and, above all, Simon. Had she dreamed his proposal? Rachel wanted to crawl back under the covers, pull them over her head, and stay there until day faded to night.

But there was Simon's note on the bedside table.

He had folded the paper into a tent. Rachel knocked it off the nightstand, catching it just before it fell to the floor. With clumsy fingers, she opened the note.

Stay at the flat as long as you need.——S

A wave of pure misery swept over her. Stop being an idiot, Rachel told herself. Simon was being kind. Kinder than she deserved.

She forced her wobbly legs out of bed, forced herself to fold the note and set it down flat on the nightstand, instead of reading it again and again and again in the vain hope that some other message or nuance might appear to temper the brusque finality of it.

What did she expect? She had turned him down. He was hardly going to be leaving her sonnets.

The idea of Simon leaving anyone sonnets brought a rueful smile to her lips. Although, once, with Olivia . . .

No. She wasn't going to be jealous of Olivia.

And, besides, what did it matter? Simon would be away in New York in a day, well rid of both Standish daughters. Drearily, Rachel dragged on a skirt and jumper, ruthlessly applying cold cream to last night's makeup.

Simon would have regretted it if she had said yes, she told herself belligerently, as she splashed cold water on her face in the bathroom. She might have delivered a blow to his ego last night, but she had saved him the much greater blow of finding himself saddled with a wife who couldn't mix in his world, a bastard without antecedents or connections, a sham and a fraud.

The strongest person I know.

For a moment, Rachel let herself bask in the memory. Tempting to think that all the rest could be pushed aside, that for him she could just be Rachel and valuable in herself, whatever her parents might have been or done. She had never, in all her life, felt so much herself with anyone as she had with Simon. Even with Alice, she had had to mute bits of herself, make allowances. But not for Simon. He met her head on.

And that was quite enough of that. Rachel dried her face roughly with a towel, not sparing the area behind the ears. People believed in the meeting of minds, but who really ever knew anyone else? Her own instincts had, for the most part, been spectacularly poor.

A shrill buzz drilled into Rachel's aching head. The doorbell, particularly strident after a long night out.

After one frozen moment, Rachel shoved the towel roughly onto the rack and bolted toward the door.

It wasn't Simon.

The porter was half hidden behind a large bouquet of hothouse flowers, tied at the bottom with a ribbon bearing the insignia of a fashionable florist. "These came for you, miss."

"Thank you, Suggs." Rachel managed to refrain from pouncing on the card until the door was already closed, her eyes going first to the signature.

In appreciation of your friendship, J. Trevannion.

Lovely. Flowers sent to buy her silence. Just what she wanted. As for friendship . . . If you can't say anything nice, her mother had always said.

Closing her eyes, Rachel leaned forward until the silky petals brushed her forehead. Once it would have filled her with unspeakable, guilty joy to have received flowers from her sister's fiancé. Now, it just made her feel vaguely irritated.

Well, they were pretty flowers. They added a touch of color to the flat. Prosaically, Rachel rummaged in the cupboards until she found a vase, then set the vase on the glass table in the drawing room, nearly knocking it over as the bell rang again.

It couldn't be flowers from John this time, unless he'd mistakenly sent a second bouquet. Which meant . . .

Breathlessly, Rachel flung open the door, Simon's name on her lips.

"Hello, Rachel," said her father.

TWENTY-FOUR

When Rachel didn't say anything, her father said hesitantly, "May I come in?"

No, Rachel wanted to say, but her tongue and her mind didn't seem to be working in concert. Instead, she mutely stepped aside, allowing him entry.

Her father took a gingerly step inside. He had seemed far more formidable last night, in his knee breeches and silk stockings. Away from the grandeur of Caffers, he seemed somehow diminished, uncertain.

Rachel could see him taking in the shaded walls of the drawing room, the angular statuary, the white, white rug.

"This is a . . . pleasant place."

"I'm moving out," said Rachel bluntly. "Did you want something?"

She ought to offer him something, she knew. Tea, a cocktail. But she couldn't force herself to perform the amenities, to pretend that he was just another visitor.

Go away, go away, go away, she thought. Hadn't he hurt her enough already? Did he need to come back for another go?

Her father turned his hat around and around in his hands, as though unsure what to do with it. "I'm meant to be in Oxfordshire. We have a house party. But I needed to speak to you—to apologize."

"If this is another offer to pay me off, you needn't bother." She had left magazines on the glass cocktail table, copies of *The Tatler*. *We're both in this week*, said Cece. Mechanically, Rachel began stacking the magazines. "I meant what I said last night."

Her father followed, hovering a careful distance away. "But I . . . When I received those pictures . . . Please, mayn't we sit down?"

Last night, he had deliberately received her in a room without chairs.

Rachel dropped the magazines into the wastepaper basket. "I am quite comfortable as I am."

Her father didn't argue. "You sound so like her." He looked at her, with something unguarded in his eyes, something painful to see. "Like Katherine. You don't look like her. There is little of her in your face. But your voice, the way you speak—"

"Is hardly unique." She didn't trust this sudden change of heart. "And, as you say, I don't look like either of you."

Except the eyes, but she didn't point that out.

"No," her father agreed. "You have the look of my mother. I never saw her—she died before I was old enough to know her—but there were portraits. . . ." He stared down at the hat in his hands as though surprised to find it there. "Forgive me. I seem to have forgotten myself."

"But you remember me. Now." Rachel folded her arms across her chest. It was all a little too convenient. Rather like John's flowers. An offering with strings attached. "To what may I attribute this sudden outpouring of paternal affection?"

Her father took a moment before answering. "When the pictures arrived," he said quietly, "I was quite certain that it was a swindle, of the basest kind, attempting to play on my emotions as a prelude to blackmail. The pictures were very cleverly done—but they can do incredible things in darkrooms these days." His eyes lifted to hers. "But I knew they couldn't be real."

Rachel's nails bit into her palms. "Why not?"

The earl drew in a deep breath. "Because my daughter—my Rachel—was dead."

Dead.

The word shivered through the bright, modern room, as out of place as a dirge at a nightclub.

"That's absurd," said Rachel flatly.

"It is," said her father quietly, "what I was told."

Rachel hardly knew what to say. She felt as though she had been presented with her own tombstone. There was something deeply disquieting about being told one was dead, even when one knew very well that one wasn't.

"So you see," he said, "when you appeared . . . what was I to think?" Gingerly, he set his hat down on the glass table. "Please, may we sit down?"

Wordlessly, Rachel gestured toward the white sofa. Her father waited until she had seated herself on one of the neighboring chairs before he awkwardly lowered himself onto the sofa, sitting on the very edge as though he mistrusted it.

"Even if you had been told—" It was curiously hard to say the words. "Why on earth would you believe it?"

Her father stared at the glass surface of the cocktail table. "I knew that she—that you—were dead because I saw the house. There was very little left of it. Just the charred walls. Some of the chimney. I saw"—his voice almost broke, but, with effort, he composed himself—"I saw one of your dolls. Her hair was all singed away. The porcelain had cracked and charred. . . ."

"Amelia." From far away, Rachel remembered that doll, a smirking, porcelain-headed doll with a frilly frock. "I hated that doll."

They had left Amelia behind, along with almost everything else.

But . . . a fire?

Her father leaned forward, saying urgently, "How did you do it? How did you escape? I had nightmares, for years, of you, in your room, in the fire—"

His face twisted, contorted. He rocked forward, his hands over his face, his shoulders shaking. A horrible choking sound emerged from between his splayed fingers.

Her father was crying, great, shuddering, terrible sobs.

Rachel didn't know what to do. She dropped to her knees in front of him, chafing his wrists, trying to get his attention.

"Please, would you like some tea? A cocktail?" It sounded so painfully inadequate.

"I—" Her father fought for control. "All these years—I thought—"

He didn't need to voice the words. Rachel could read the horror of it in the grooves in his cheeks.

"No," she said, and felt her father's fingers fleetingly brush her hair, before she pushed herself to her feet. Forcefully, she said, "There was no fire. At least, not while we were there. Please—I was never in any danger."

Her father shook his head, looking dazed.

"I saw the house. Your doll . . ."

"We left her behind. Mother said I could only bring one trunk." It was as though they were speaking separate languages. Rachel felt a slightly hysterical laugh welling up. "You see, we were told you were dead. That was why we left."

Her father stared at her as though she were speaking in tongues. "Dead?"

"Yes," said Rachel, "that's rather how I felt, too. Mother had a letter. She said it was from abroad, that you had died on a collecting trip. There couldn't be a funeral because there was no body."

Rachel, four years old, had never questioned it, any of it. The world was full of strange shifts, of grown-up decisions for which she was offered no explanation.

"I don't know why we had to go. But we did. All we took were our clothes—and your chess set. We kept your chess set. I have it still."

"Dead," her father repeated. He looked dazed, as dazed as Rachel felt. "It was my brother who had died. Katherine knew that. It was why I had to go home. I never—I cannot imagine—"

"I've spent my life believing that you were dead." Speaking as evenly as she could, Rachel said, "When I learned you were alive—I thought you must have left us."

"I did, but only for a month." Her father looked as though someone had put him through a wringer and hung him out on a line in a high wind. "I was gone for longer than I had intended. I'd meant to be away a fortnight; it took a month. I wrote your mother, telling her—"

"Telling her what?"

Her father picked at the upholstery of the chair. "Did your mother ever tell you—anything of our situation?"

"Yes. All of it untrue. I was led to believe that you were a botanist—and an orphan."

Her father's lips tightened. "It would have been easier if I were. I was fortunate. I was the younger son—and a disappointment from the moment I was born. My father didn't pay much attention to me." His expression softened, his eyes looking at images Rachel couldn't see. "We grew up together, your mother and I. She was the estate agent's daughter—did she tell you that?"

Rachel shook her head.

"She was always in and out of the house. Her mother had died, so there was no one to watch over her. And I . . . I had been meant to go to school, but I was a sickly child, so it was simpler to keep me at home with a tutor. We were company for each other."

His words painted a more vivid picture than he knew, of two lonely souls finding each other.

"We always knew we wanted to be married. I had thought, as a second son . . . but my father didn't consider your mother a fitting match for a Standish."

"Why didn't you just marry and damn the consequences?"

"Because he would have cut off my allowance," her father said simply. "We had nothing else on which to live. And then there was you." Awkwardly, he said, "Whatever else, I want you to know—we loved you so. You were our own private wonder."

Rachel's eyes stung; her throat was too tight to speak.

We loved you so.

Her father was still speaking. "We thought that all we had to do was wait it out. When my father died, I would inherit, not much, but enough to keep us modestly. My brother Marcus was nothing like my father; he wouldn't cut up stiff about it. But then Marcus died."

Dimly, Rachel recalled Cousin David telling her something of the kind, about her father inheriting unexpectedly. It all seemed a million years ago, that initial interview with Cousin David, a yellowed clipping clutched in her hand.

Hurriedly, her father said, "That was why I went home, for Marcus's funeral. My father announced to me that he had an heiress for me. The estate—it was all but bankrupt. I hadn't realized—"

That letter. Rachel could see that letter, sitting on the kitchen table. "So you told my mother you were leaving us?"

"No!" Her father was genuinely horrified. "I needed more time. There had to be some way, something my father hadn't considered. An asset he hadn't yet dissipated. That was what I told your mother—that I needed more time."

"I see."

And Rachel had blithely been grubbing in the dirt, playing in mud puddles in the garden, while all of this had been going on around her. Life, at four, had been a sea of knees and ankles, chair legs and the undersides of tables.

She wished, desperately, that she had paid more attention, that she had lifted her head and looked up.

"It has haunted me since—if I had only come home when I intended—if I hadn't stayed that extra fortnight." Her father's face was haggard, trapped in the same nightmare he had revisited year after year after year. "David sent me a telegram. I came as quickly as I could, but there was nothing there. Just the charred wreckage. And your doll—"

"We were in Norfolk." Rachel's head came up. "David?"

"My cousin." Her father was slumped in his seat. There was nothing of the earl about him now; just a tired, aging man with loss stamped in the lines of his face. "He was the only one who knew—about your mother. We were inseparable as children, Katherine, David, and I. I tried to see him last week, but he wasn't in college."

No. He wouldn't be.

David knew. David knew that they weren't dead. He should know; he had bought Rachel enough ices over the years. He'd sent her presents on her birthday, listened to her childish stories, read her books.

And, yet, it appeared that he had told Rachel's father that she had perished in a fire twenty-three years ago.

Her father's voice broke through the nasty suspicions gathering in Rachel's mind. "You said—last night. You said your mother was dead."

Rachel gathered her scattered thoughts together. "Yes, this past April. It was the Spanish influenza."

"It seems impossible to think that all this while, she was alive, and I never knew. I never imagined . . ." Her father removed his glasses, rubbing them on his sleeve, his thoughts somewhere far away. "I wasn't quite in my right mind. Not after seeing—" He shook his head as though shaking off the memories.

The fire. The doll.

How could Cousin David have been so unspeakably cruel?

Rachel leaned forward, her hand almost touching her father's. "But it wasn't real, any of it."

"No," said her father, and, tentatively, took her hand in his. For a moment, he held it very, very tightly, before letting go. "It might have been my father's doing. I hadn't thought he knew; we thought we had been so very careful. But he might have found out. . . . Not that it matters now."

If Cousin David had lied to her father, what might he have told her mother? Had her mother spent all of those years convinced that Rachel's father had abandoned them? She would have been too proud to write, too proud to beg for explanations.

There was too much to think about; she would have to mull it through later, after her father was gone.

"She never forgot you." Rachel wasn't sure what prompted her to say it. Perhaps the desolation on her father's face. That fleeting pressure of his hand. "She would never hear of marrying."

"No," said her father, half to himself, "she wouldn't." He looked up at Rachel. "Please—there is so much I missed. Will you tell me what you can? Where you lived? What your lives were?"

"There isn't much to tell," said Rachel. "We lived in a village in Nor-folk called Netherwell. . . ."

Haltingly, Rachel began to sketch in the details of their lives, the village fetes, the piano lessons, her mother's weekly chess match with the vicar, her adventures with Alice, the pronouncements of Mrs. Spicer.

The sun slanted across the drawing room floor before slinking back below the roofs of the buildings across the way. The sky was dusted with twilight and Rachel was still talking, stories upon stories: her mother's clever managing of Mrs. Spicer, so that Mrs. Spicer thought she was man-aging them; the matter of piano lessons; their battles over the question of typing lessons; Rachel's departure for Paris. So many memories, good and bad and in between.

Through them, Rachel could feel her mother taking shape again, but with a difference. There were missing pieces that made sense now. Her father's picture in the drawer. Her mother's reserve. The care she took of their reputations.

Rachel could even understand, reluctantly, why her mother might not have wanted to tell her, might have wanted her to keep her illusions. The life her mother had built for them had been harder won than Rachel knew.

What must it have cost her, night after night, knowing that the man she had loved was married to another woman? Believing that he had left her?

As Rachel's stories tailed off, her father shifted in his chair. "You were happy."

It wasn't quite a question, but Rachel thought about it anyway.

"Yes," she said. "I suppose we were."

It had been quite romantic to imagine her life blighted by the absence of a father, but the truth of it was that the day to day of her life had been quite content.

"And you?" Rachel asked hesitantly.

It felt odd to be thinking about her father's happiness, when she had spent the past few months hating him so. It also felt odd to think of one's parents as people, independent of oneself, people who might be happy or unhappy.

Her father looked as though it hadn't quite occurred to him, either. "They have been good years for Carrisford. There was so much that had been left to fall into disrepair. The first few years, I did what I could to stem the damage. But, after that—"

He talked about pig breeding and haymaking and new machinery and old feuds among the tenantry, and Rachel smiled and nodded and wondered where, in the midst of it, his wife and children belonged.

They didn't, it seemed.

"You sit in the Lords?" Rachel ventured. The intimacy of their earlier discussion was gone. It was rather like sitting next to a stranger at a dinner party.

"When I must. I prefer to be at Carrisford, when I can. I don't like to trust it to an agent." That was what Simon had told her, half a lifetime ago. Her father glanced at the clock on the mantel. "Is that the time? I should have been back an hour ago."

Automatically, Rachel stood. There was so much more that she needed to ask, so much more that had to be said, but he was the earl again, and she found herself feeling oddly shy with him, this father she didn't know at all.

"Thank you for stopping by," she said, her hand clasped at her waist like a schoolgirl. "It—makes rather a difference."

Her father retrieved his hat from the table. "Yes," he said. "Yes, it does."

They looked at each other across the dusky drawing room. "There's no going back," said Rachel. "Is there?"

"When I lost you," said her father, "you were only four. I am still coming to terms with . . . this."

"And you have another family." There it was, the elephant in the room.

"Yes," said her father, but he spoke as though the thought of it brought him little pleasure.

They were at the door now. Rachel paused, with her hand on the knob.

"I know this isn't my place, but . . . why didn't you let Olivia go to Somerville?" Rachel's father looked at her with an air of vague puzzlement. "She told me she was awarded a scholarship."

"Was she? I wasn't told. I suppose her mother . . ." Her father made an apologetic gesture. "I am afraid I don't have very much to do with Olivia."

Strange to think she had been so jealous of Olivia once, had seen the picture of her being escorted by her father and assumed that Olivia had everything Rachel had lost.

Haltingly, Rachel said, "It isn't my affair, but . . . her mother seems to bully her, rather. I would think, having lost one daughter . . . Never mind." She opened the door, stepping aside so her father could go. "It really isn't any of my affair."

Her father settled his hat on his head, casting his face into shadow. "It was necessary," he said, with difficulty, "that I have an heir. I understood that. But . . . it was a duty. They were a duty. And when that first child was a girl . . ."

He stopped in the doorway, looking back over his shoulder at Rachel, his face a picture of regret.

"Olivia committed one unpardonable crime. She wasn't you."

TWENTY-FIVE

Her father could be lying. But Rachel didn't think so. That sorrow had been too raw, too real to be feigned.

All these years, her father had believed her dead. Rachel couldn't quite get her mind around it. The more she learned, the less made sense, all of her easy assumptions and judgments scoured away.

She stood with her hand on the doorknob, long after her father's footsteps had retreated down the hall and the sound of the lift had faded away. Rachel leaned her forehead against the cool white panels of the door. She wanted, so very badly, to be angry, but she couldn't quite seem to manage it. All she could feel was a vast and all-encompassing bewilderment.

Why would someone have gone to such effort, such hideous and decisive effort, to keep her parents apart? There was something particularly chilling about the thought of that fire, despised Amelia lying scorched and blackened on the singed turf. Arson wasn't a business undertaken lightly.

His father, her father had said. Slowly, Rachel retreated to the sitting room, where the white sofa still bore the imprint of her father's body. Yes, she could see how Violet Palmer's money might have been a powerful inducement to her grandfather. But there it was—the sticking point. Why would David help him?

Turning on the lamps, drawing the curtains against the dusk, she couldn't wrap her mind around it; no matter how she turned it around and around, the pieces wouldn't quite fit. But then, Rachel reminded herself, all she knew of this version of events, the fire itself, came from her father. He had seemed genuinely shaken—but what did she really know of him, after all this time?

The fire could be easily enough checked. There must be records in the local papers if she could only recall the name of the village. And—with the memory of her father's stricken face—she really didn't think he was lying. Not about the fire, at any event.

But what if there had been other considerations? Her father had said he meant to come back to them. Had he really? What had been in that letter? Had Cousin David whisked them away to prevent her mother having to see the man she loved marry another woman?

A nice, altruistic motive, that, Rachel mocked herself, but it was hard to imagine Cousin David acting quite so positively, quite so aggressively.

Cousin David had always been a pale second to her mother's energy, a follower rather than a leader. His small acts of initiative consisted of slipping Rachel the odd shilling and hesitant suggestions of expeditions to places he thought might be of interest to small girls, some of which were, and many of which weren't. The Bodleian was all very well, Rachel was sure, but it had bored her silly, especially when Cousin David became absorbed in a manuscript and forgot about her entirely.

Impossible to imagine Cousin David as either villain or henchman.

Unless he was an unwilling henchman? Rachel paused, her hand on the drapes. It was absurd, a plot out of a serial in a magazine, but what if the old Earl of Ardmore—impossible to think of him as Grandfather— had found out about them, had intended, summarily, to put an end to his son's other family? The thought made Rachel feel more than a little ill. They hadn't been people to him, merely encumbrances.

If David had somehow heard of the earl's intentions, surely that, then, would be in character. He wouldn't have had the nerve to prevent it, just enough to shuffle them out in time, making sure the house was empty when the earl's minions did their worst, hurrying them away to a new life lest the earl try again.

Yes, and if she believed that, there were some pigs' glands waiting for injection.

Why not? Her life had certainly been fantastical enough recently. If she went on in that vein, there were all sorts of other plots she might pursue. Perhaps her mother was secretly the crown princess of a minor European principality and they had been burned out by angry anarchists.

Rachel smiled sourly. She had descended so far down into absurdity, she wasn't sure how to sort out the plausible from the impossible.

What she needed was Simon, Simon stretching his long length out on the white sofa, anchoring her thoughts, cutting through her more ridiculous notions with biting wit.

Rachel's hand twitched toward the phone, and then fell away again.

Stay at the flat as long as you need.

No, she couldn't ring Simon. Rachel felt a flush of shame at her own selfishness. She had taken his help for granted, ascribing him all sorts of ignoble motives so that she wouldn't have to be grateful, wouldn't have to acknowledge the extent of her own dependence on him.

When she thought what it must have cost him to take her to Carrisford last night—and then—in the garden—

Was it weakness in her that she wished she had given Simon another answer?

What she needed, Rachel decided vigorously, was to go to Oxford and ask Cousin David right out. No nonsense about ringing; he never answered his phone anyway. But it was gone eight; there would be no trains to Oxford at this hour, and, even if there were, she could hardly knock Cousin David up at midnight. Suggs would be appalled.

A crazy laugh bubbled up in Rachel's throat. After all this, one still wouldn't want to shock the Merton porter.

Bourgeois, murmured Simon's voice in her ear, but it sounded like an endearment.

Stupid to hope Simon might be up at Oxford tomorrow, too, saying farewell to his old tutor before he left for New York, brushing past her on that narrow stair as he had once before. That rainy day in April felt like a lifetime ago, a story about a different person entirely.

Rachel caught the earliest possible train out to Oxford the next morning, clanking with milk jugs and bleary-eyed travelers.

Cousin David's door was sporting the oak, but Rachel decided there were times when tradition could be honored in the breach. She didn't think she could bear to wait another day, or even another hour, endless speculation buzzing around her brain like a swarm without a hive.

She rapped neatly on the door, and, without waiting for an answer, let herself in.

"Rachel!" Cousin David was in his favorite chair, a book on his lap. If he was shocked at her landing in his lap before lunch, he didn't say so. He jumped to his feet, the spectacles he wore for reading sliding down on his nose. "Did my letters reach you? I stayed in town as long as I could."

Nothing could have been more disarming. One thing to speculate about Cousin David's motives from a distance, quite another here in the familiarity of his old rooms, his spectacles slipping with concern.

Concern for her? Or concern that his actions of twenty-three years ago had finally come to light?

Rachel shut the door firmly behind her. "Why did you tell my father we were dead?"

Cousin David removed the spectacles from his nose and put them carefully away in his pocket. "You've spoken to him."

Rachel looked uncertainly at her cousin, not sure what to make of that. "He cried."

"Poor Edward." Cousin David shook his head, saddened, but not surprised. "What a comedy of errors."

"I don't find anything particularly comic about it," said Rachel sharply.

"The words were ill chosen. Sit down, please." When she hesitated, he gestured toward her usual chair. "It hurts my neck looking up at you."

Rachel sat. She had sat here so many times, as a child, as an adolescent, as a woman about to go off into the world. It was Cousin David who had made the arrangements for her to go to Paris, as he had arranged so many other things.

"I want the truth this time." The specter of her mother made her add, "Please."

Cousin David didn't ring for his scout. He poured her a cup of coffee out of his own pot, stone cold and bitter. "I never wanted to lie to Edward—or to you."

Rachel fought a deep sense of disillusionment. If he had offered an excuse—she had been so willing to believe the best of him. "I suppose the devil made you do it?"

"No. Your mother." Cousin David seated himself across from her, taking advantage of her confusion to say, "Your mother summoned me to Hatherleigh. That was the village where you were living then. She told me she'd made up her mind to leave and to take you with her."

It didn't make sense, any of it. "Why would she leave? She loved him."

And had gone on loving him, all those years, even when she must have believed he'd left them.

"She left because she loved him." Cousin David leaned both palms on the table, his round face earnest. "She'd had a letter from Edward—your father. The estate was on the verge of bankruptcy. His father was pressing him to marry an heiress. Violet Palmer."

Rachel watched her cousin warily. "Yes, my father told me."

"Did he tell you that your mother was the former estate agent's daughter?" When Rachel looked at him in confusion, he elaborated, "She knew, more than anyone, what it would do to the estate if your father didn't marry quickly and well."

"I imagine it would be sold." The carved wooden arm of the chair was digging into her side. What had that to do with anything? "You can't think my mother cared about my father's inheritance."

"She did. Just not in the way you mean." Cousin David held up his hands, saying, "It wasn't just the house that would be sold. It was hundreds of acres of land, land that had been farmed by the same families for generations. What do you think would have happened to them? To their families?"

"I—" Rachel didn't know what to say. "They would have to find work elsewhere, I suppose."

"Yes, but where? How? Then there was the staff: gardeners, footmen, housemaids, laundresses . . . The list goes on and on. There were hundreds of people who owed their livelihood to Carrisford. Your mother knew that. She knew them." Cousin David pressed his palms flat against the blackened oak of the table. "Your mother came to me and told me that she wouldn't have that on her conscience. She needed to—to disappear."

"All for a bit of land," Rachel said skeptically.

"Not just a bit of land."

Rachel thought of the great hall at Carrisford, of the gallery where her father had received her. "Paintings, then, and sculptures, and porcelain figurines?" she said sarcastically.

Cousin David gave her the sort of look he gave undergraduates who came unprepared to tutorial. "Because of the choice your mother made, two hundred families retained their livelihood. Your mother knew them. She knew their families, their concerns. They were the ones your mother sacrificed herself to save, not a set of porcelain figurines."

The way he said it made Rachel feel very small. Defensively, she said, "Wasn't there anything that could have been sold?"

"Not enough. Many of the paintings are reproductions—or they were, before Violet's money replaced them. Your grandfather had been milking the estate of its valuables for years. Your father had the misfortune of being conscientious. He wasn't one to let Rome into Tiber melt. Nor, for that matter, was your mother." Cousin David drew in a deep breath. "You could say that that was their tragedy, that they were both people of principle."

He was silent, contemplating.

Rachel felt a surge of impatience. "Yes, but what happened?" It wasn't a Greek play they were talking about, it was her parents.

Oh, David, her mother would have said, with that tone of fond tolerance she reserved particularly for him. But Rachel wasn't feeling tolerant right now. She felt keyed up, on edge, reluctant to accept this new version of events. She wanted to stick her fingers in her ears, to drum her heels against the chair, to protest that this couldn't be true, it couldn't be her mother's own doing, it made no sense, none at all, none, none, none.

David roused himself from his reverie. "Your mother told me that her mind was made up. She was taking the decision out of your father's hands. And she would do it with my help or without it."

Rachel sat very straight in her chair. "You might have told her no."

Cousin David looked at her with resignation. "Did you ever try to say no to Katherine? When she was truly set on something?"

A little quiver of doubt pierced Rachel's resistance. On small things, her mother was infinitely reasonable. But when it truly mattered, she was as immovable as the Alps, and just as icy. They had argued for months over that ridiculous typing course in London. Or, rather, Rachel had argued. Again and again, month after month.

And, in the end, her mother had had her own way.

"When you think of it," said Cousin David hopefully, "it was really quite noble. She sacrificed her own happiness for the sake of your father's tenants and staff."

"Yes, very noble." If it were true. Rachel looked narrowly at Cousin David. "But it wasn't just her happiness."

Cousin David looked at her wistfully. "Were you really that unhappy?"

Yes, she wanted to say. She wanted to hurl the word at him like a stone, to hurt him as she had been hurt. But she couldn't. Because the truth was that she hadn't been unhappy, not at all.

Yes, she had mourned her father, but his loss had been a gentle shadow, not an all-enveloping darkness. When she thought of her childhood, all she could see was sunshine, sparkling on the surface of the pond, turning Alice's blond braids to gold, catching in the white net veil of her mother's best hat, bouncing like a skipping stone down the path to the village, dancing in the dust motes above the piano keys.

There must have been rainy days, days when she sulked, days when Alice had a sore throat and couldn't play, but they cast no shadow.

Rachel shifted uncomfortably in her chair. She felt as she had when she was eight and losing an argument with an adult. "That's not the point."

"It was for your mother." Something about the way Cousin David said it made Rachel feel small and petty. "She has—she had the strongest moral sense of anyone I have ever known."

We were inseparable as children, her father had said. *Your mother, David, and I.*

Moral sense, her foot. There was another possibility. Rachel seized on it with relief. Accusingly, she said, "You were in love with her."

David didn't bother to deny it. "Yes. From the time we were very small."

Rachel felt on firmer ground here. She leaned forward, prepared to do battle. "Did you think she would marry you if my father were out of the way?"

"It would be easier if there were a villain, wouldn't it?" Cousin David's look of understanding reduced Rachel once again to the nursery. "No. I was never that foolish. Your mother loved your father too much for that. And there were . . . other reasons."

"Other reasons?" Rachel said suspiciously.

"By then, your mother and I were too much like brother and sister. And I have enough self-love not to live my life in Edward's shadow. As much," he said gravely, "as I would have liked to be your father."

"You did enough," Rachel muttered. She wasn't entirely sure what she meant by it. Old loyalties warred with new resentments.

"No." Cousin David spoke with surprising firmness. Rachel looked up. "I was wrong in one thing. Once you came of age—you deserved to be told. You were right in that."

He stood abruptly, his chair scraping against the well-worn wood of the floor.

"Your mother had her say. I respected her wishes during her lifetime. But you're a woman grown now. You deserve to make your own choices." Cousin David seemed to be speaking as much to himself as to her as he crossed the room to the shelves to the right of the window. He gave a short, sharp nod. "No more secrets."

"It's a little late for that, isn't it?" Rachel stood, turning to watch him as he retrieved a box from the upper shelf.

It was a medieval objet d'art, a reliquary, intricately carved panels joined with strips of blackened gold. She hadn't been allowed to play with it when she was little; the carving was too delicate for small fingers. Or so she had been told.

Cousin David pressed a catch at the top, and the sides opened.

Rachel watched him narrowly. "Are you going to swear on St. Athanasius's knucklebones? There's really no need for that sort of thing."

She wasn't sure she believed him, but St. Athanasius wasn't going to make a difference one way or the other.

"It's Thomas à Becket," said Cousin David. Reaching inside, he drew out not a knucklebone, but a folded piece of paper. He held it out to Rachel. "Here. Take it."

It wasn't parchment. It was paper, a page torn from a book, folded, and then folded again.

Automatically, Rachel's hand closed over it. "This didn't belong to Thomas à Becket."

"No." David set the reliquary back on its shelf. "Your mother gave this to me twenty-three years ago."

Slowly, Rachel unfolded the paper. It was a sheet torn from a register, with ruled lines for names, dates, witnesses, some marked only with an X, where the signatories had made their marks rather than signing their names.

She had seen a dozen like it. She and Alice used to build forts out of the old parish registers. Or, at least, they had until Mrs. Spicer had caught them and scolded them for messing with the vicar's things. So many births, deaths . . . marriages.

Cousin David hovered over her, his body casting a shadow over the document. "Your mother asked me to destroy it. But I couldn't. I am," he said apologetically, "too much of a historian for that."

Rachel didn't say anything. She couldn't.

The ink had been cheap; it had faded with time. But two names seemed to burn out of the paper. Rachel couldn't have said afterward what else, or who else might have been there. All she saw were those two names:

Edward Arthur Standish and Katherine Newell.

TWENTY-SIX

Whoever the rector was, he wrote a clear hand. There was no mistaking the words.

> Married 2 May 1897 Katherine Newell, age 17, and Edward Arthur Standish, age 20.

The paper crinkled beneath Rachel's fingers. "This is—"

"Marriage lines," said Cousin David. "Your parents' marriage lines."

There was another name in the register. Rachel glanced up at her cousin. "You were witness."

Cousin David ducked his head. "We were all very young," he said apologetically.

She had never thought of her parents as being young. Parents were parents. But they had been young. So much younger than she was now. Seventeen. Impossible to think of her mother at seventeen or her father at twenty, marrying in secret, hoping everything would turn out for the best.

"Eighteen ninety-seven," Rachel said. She looked up at Cousin David in surprise. "That was two years before I was born."

"Did you believe—Oh, no." The tips of Cousin David's ears turned a delicate pink. "Your parents didn't marry because they, er, had to. They weren't like that. Either of them."

Rachel remembered the picture of her parents, the one that had lived in the drawer by her mother's bed. Not just any picture. A wedding picture.

Yesterday, when her father visited, he might have said something. But he hadn't. Had there been a little pause when he spoke of their plans to be married, a space where he might have told her? Rachel thought there might. But, in the end, for all his professions of affection, he had kept his secrets.

In a low voice, Rachel said, "He let me go on thinking that my mother was his mistress. My father."

"Are you surprised? Look at the date."

Two years before her birth. And six years before her father had married Violet Palmer. "Oh," said Rachel. And, again, "Oh."

"Oh," agreed Cousin David. He sat down heavily in his chair. "Poor Edward. It's none of it his fault, you know. He truly believed he was free to marry. Your mother *wanted* him to be free to marry."

"But he wasn't."

There was a word for that. Bigamy. It didn't matter that her father had intended it, hadn't known better; the existence of his first marriage made the second invalid.

Rachel stared down at the piece of paper in her hand. In one stroke, this little piece of paper could change everything. She was her father's legitimate daughter. His heiress.

And Olivia and Jicksy were illegitimate. Bastards.

"Poor Edward," said Cousin David again. "His will isn't entirely his own, you know. He owes a duty to the estate. He never wanted it, but since he has it—he isn't one to neglect his obligations."

Someone had had the foresight to remove the page from the parish register. It hadn't been destroyed, but it had been hidden.

Had her father—or mother—even then entertained the possibility that the marriage might be made to disappear?

Rachel glanced up at Cousin David, a furrow between her brows. The words came out with difficulty. "If my mother hadn't made the decision to go—would he have stood by us?"

Cousin David didn't pretend to misunderstand. He thought about it just a little too long before giving a slow nod. "Most likely, although he would have had to break up the estate to pay his father's debts. He would have hated himself for seeing his patrimony broken into pieces. It was an impossible situation."

"It is an even more impossible situation now." Rachel drew in a ragged breath. "If my father were to marry Lady Ardmore again, privately, would that legitimate Olivia and Jicksy?"

"No. Your father's existing marriage to your mother prevents him from legitimating any children by another woman born during the duration of that marriage. The law is very clear about that." Cousin David looked at her sympathetically. "Do you wonder that your father didn't tell you?"

Rachel folded the paper, carefully, once and then again. "If I were to assert my rights, what would happen to Carrisford?"

"It would go to a cousin, I believe. Not me," David said hastily. "The disposition of the unentailed property would depend on your father." As an afterthought, he added, "There would be money for Olivia and Jicksy—Lady Ardmore's father had it tied up in trusts."

In other words, they would be provided for. Financially, at least. "What would you do—if you were I?"

Cousin David looked helplessly up at the plaster of the ceiling. "As you say, it is an impossible situation. Perhaps I shouldn't have helped your mother take you away. I don't know." He hesitated a moment, and then said slowly, "I grew up in the shadow of Carrisford. When Katherine came to me—I thought we were sparing you."

"Sparing me a life of luxury?"

Cousin David looked troubled. "Carrisford was a cold place. It wasn't the life your mother wanted for you. If Marcus had lived, she and your father might have made their own life for themselves, but . . ." He made a helpless gesture. "I don't know. I don't know if we did right or wrong. But that's yours now. For good or for ill."

It was impossible to stay after that, to drink coffee and make polite conversation. They were both too lost in their own emotions, old betray-als creating a new reserve. Not forever, Rachel knew, as she kissed her cousin on the cheek, torn between love and resentment. But, for now, it was too hard to untangle her feelings, to treat Cousin David with the easy affection they had once enjoyed.

Last time, when she had stormed out of Cousin David's rooms, there had been Simon, provoking, distracting. This time, she had only her own thoughts to accompany her as she took the stairs down to the courtyard. Her thoughts and a folded piece of paper in her bag.

Instead of going straight to the train, Rachel went to Fuller's. Sunlight glared blindingly off the glass window with its bold legend scrolled in red. She caught sight of her own reflection as she opened the door: smart hair-cut, smart hat, smart suit. A world away from the rain-dampened nursery governess who had entered three months before.

Lady Rachel Standish.

She hadn't known her name then, but she knew it now. Lady Rachel Standish could take tea in any house in London. She could call Lady Fran-ces Heatherington-Vaughn "Aunt Fanny." She would be invited to all the dull dances from which Miss Vera Merton was excluded.

She would have ancestors, cousins. She could go to the Peeress's Gal-lery at the House of Lords, as Olivia did, and listen to her father speak.

A whole world would open up to her.

If her father didn't deny her. If the paper were proved legitimate. How did one even go about such things? A solicitor, she supposed.

If she were prepared to sacrifice Olivia and Jicksy.

Not Lady Ardmore. She didn't mind about Lady Ardmore. There would be a certain satisfaction in seeing her stripped of her title, twenty-three years a mistress. But her father's children . . .

Jicksy was a wastrel, everyone said so. Carrisford was most likely better off without him. Everything her mother had fought to save would be safer without Jicksy.

"Thank you," Rachel murmured to the waitress as the tea and walnut cake were set down before her.

But there was Olivia.

Rachel stuck her fork into the cake, a large piece, thick with icing, shedding nuts. And might it not be better for Olivia? She would finally be free of her mother's influence. John Trevannion wouldn't marry a bastard; it would be too dangerous for his political ambitions. Olivia could go to Somerville, study economics. Yes, there would be a scandal, but dons didn't care about that sort of thing, did they? And Olivia didn't seem to care much for society.

Possibly because she had never had to do without it.

The cake didn't taste nearly as good as Rachel had remembered. Or maybe it was just that she wasn't hungry.

She set the fork down and took a sip of tea instead, strong and bitter.

Her father had lied to her. Even in the midst of the emotion of their reunion, he had lied to her. Protecting—no, not Olivia and Jicksy, but Caffers.

Rachel stared down into the brick-red brew in her cup. Foolish to be hurt that her father didn't know her better, know her well enough to understand that she would have happily relinquished any claim on the estate in exchange for his own private acknowledgment. That was all she had needed, to hear it from his own lips that they had really been a family, that he had loved them, that he had always intended to stand by them, no matter the blandishments of a dozen Violet Palmers.

I thought we were sparing you, Cousin David had said. *It wasn't the life your mother wanted for you.*

What about what she might have wanted? What about growing up with a father, aunt, cousins? All that, about Carrisford being a cold place— perhaps it had been when Cousin David was there, perhaps her father hadn't been happy as a child, but that didn't mean they might not have lived differently.

Or would they have? Rachel had always taken for granted that if her father had lived, their lives would have gone on as they had before. But they wouldn't have. Her mother wouldn't have cooked dinner; her father wouldn't have sung her to sleep at night. There would have been servants and nannies, those white-aproned nannies she had seen wheeling their charges in the park. Her father would have had a myriad of other obligations—and her mother, too.

Two hundred families, Cousin David had said. Her mother wouldn't have shirked her obligations as countess. And then there were all those other obligations, the ones Rachel only dimly understood: committees, charity balls, dress fittings. Society, in other words. Would she have been left behind at Carrisford, while her parents went to London?

When her mother taught piano, it was only a few hours a day, in their own sitting room. She had been there for Rachel always, day in and day out.

And Rachel . . . Rachel had been free to splash in the pond, to roll a hoop down the lane, to climb trees and skip stones. There had been no nanny to reprimand her, no photographers to snap pictures of her. When she went to France, no one stood with flashbulbs at the pier, ready to make an article out of her departure, or describe, in detail, her dress and hat.

It was strange to think that, instead of being deprived, she might actually have been given a gift, a gift of time. And a measure of freedom.

She might have gone to France as Lady Rachel Standish, but she would have been chaperoned and supervised. Unless, like Olivia, she wasn't allowed to go at all.

No, her mother was no Lady Ardmore.

Except that she was. Or would have been, had she chosen to be. It wouldn't have changed her out of recognition, but it would have changed her. It would have changed them all.

There was no way of knowing. Now.

Last night, she had told her father that the fire was a lie, as much a lie as his being a botanist. But, thought Rachel, poking at her uneaten cake, it wasn't entirely, was it? Her father had believed it all this time. Stories took on their own truth. No matter how many times she sat across a tea table from her father, there would always be part of him that believed, deep down, that his Rachel had died in that fire, just as she couldn't quite reconcile the man she had met, the man who spoke so impersonally of crops and dry rot, with the father who had died all those years ago, in a faraway speck on the globe.

Too much time had elapsed. Those people might as well be dead. Fondly remembered, well loved, but truly gone.

Rachel tossed coins on the table, drew her gloves on, leaving her uneaten cake and half-drunk tea.

Unpardonable extravagance. Her mother hadn't approved of waste. Simon's training had rubbed off. She was, she realized, neither here nor there, caught between two worlds.

But did she need to be? Sunlight dazzled her eyes after the dimness of the shop. Rachel put up a hand, supplementing the inadequate brim of her too-smart hat. She could feel her spirits lifting, a dizzying wave of euphoria. Who said those were her only options?

You're yourself, Simon had said. *Isn't that enough?*

Rachel's pace picked up from a walk to something that was nearly a run. When her mother had been presented with impossible choices, she had made her own way through them. Not, perhaps, a way that Rachel would have chosen, but she hadn't let circumstances hedge her in. She'd been bold, struck out on her own.

And, in doing so, she might just have given Rachel an unexpected gift.

She didn't want to be Lady Rachel Standish, not really. Maybe if she'd been raised to it—but she hadn't. She'd been raised to independence.

The station platform was near empty; midday wasn't a popular time to travel. She'd bought a return ticket that morning, Oxford to London. Rachel chucked it in the bin, going quickly to the empty ticket counter.

"One to Southampton, please," she told the man at the counter.

The *Aquitania*, Simon had said. There was no difficulty in finding the ship, the smokestacks painted Cunard red, already belching smoke, the smell of burning coal warring with the salt tang of the sea, the sweat of the men heaving parcels and packages aboard, the varied perfumes of the travelers and guests, the sulfurous smell of flashbulbs popping.

Finding Simon was another matter. He wasn't part of the throng leaning against the rail. Rachel wove her way through the excitedly chattering groups, family members and well-wishers bringing bouquets of flowers, boxes of chocolates, weeping children being peeled from parental legs by white-capped nannies, women in fur coats with small dogs cradled in their arms, journalists darting everywhere, looking for a celebrity to snap. Rachel passed unnoticed among them.

She found Simon, at last, on the leeward side, leaning against the rail, a cigarette in one hand.

He looked terribly alone, standing there, away from the madding crowd, the ocean spreading along beyond him.

Now that she was here, Rachel wasn't quite sure what to say. She resisted the craven urge to slip away. "Simon?"

Simon's head came up with a jolt. He turned, so quickly that he bumped his elbow on the rail, letting out a grunt of pain.

"Hullo," said Rachel inadequately.

A series of emotions flashed across Simon's face, buried, quickly, beneath his old urbane mask. Meticulously, he ground his cigarette beneath his heel. "Have you come to wave your hankie?"

"I left my hankie at home, I'm afraid."

All around them, there was bustle and movement, but Rachel felt as though they were encased in their own private bubble. The silence grew and grew, and with it, Rachel's doubts. Had Simon changed his mind? Had that moment in the garden been nothing but a reaction to being back at Carrisford again, hastily said and just as hastily regretted?

"Why did you take me up, all those months ago?" She hadn't meant to say it; the words just came out. "Why didn't you just drop me at the station and send me on my way?"

"Your cousin . . ." he began slowly.

"Don't fob me off with that," said Rachel sharply.

"No." A glimmer of a smile crossed Simon's lips. He buried his hands in his pockets. "When you landed in my lap like that . . . I'd an idea I could use you to help make things right for Olivia. I owed her a debt, you see. It wasn't a very clear plan, but, then, you see, I hadn't planned on you."

Something about the way he said it made Rachel's head come up.

Simon's eyes met hers, reluctantly, ruefully. "And you were so . . . gallant. So bedraggled and spitting defiance. In that horrible hat."

Rachel, opening her mouth to retort, bit her lip. "It was a horrible hat, wasn't it?"

"But there was you," said Simon, and there was something in his face that made Rachel's chest tighten. He turned away, bracing a hand against the rail. "I'd spent so much time running away from things, and there you were, running into them, headlong."

"Pigheaded, you mean," said Rachel faintly.

"Brave." He turned back to her, his shoulders straightening. "I wouldn't have taken the New York job but for you. I'd meant to turn it down. Too much responsibility, too close to everything I'd tried so hard to avoid. But when you showed up at my flat that day—if you could face up to your demons like that, how could I do less?"

Considerations, he had said, and she, blinded by her own preoccupations, had assumed he meant Olivia.

"My demons—they're hardly on the same order as yours." Belatedly, Rachel remembered the paper in her bag. "There's something I wanted to show you."

Simon was quicker than she had been. After a rapid perusal, he glanced up from the single sheet of paper. "Shall I call you Lady Rachel?" Folding it carefully, he handed it back to her. "It's happy endings, then. You've everything you wanted."

No, no, no. This wasn't at all the way Rachel had meant this interview to go. They might have been polite strangers, standing at a careful arm's length at the rail. Where was all the easy banter of the past months?

Rachel clutched the paper in both hands, making new creases against the old folds. "But it's not what I want. I want to come to New York. With you." When Simon didn't speak, she added, "If you'll still have me?"

The breath was crushed out of her as Simon's arms clamped around her, lifting her off her feet, whirling her in a giddy circle.

"I thought you'd come to say good-bye," he was saying, between kisses, while Rachel said confusedly, "No! Would I come all this way for that?"

She could feel Simon laughing into her lips. "And that's why I love you. Why waste time on the amenities?"

"I can observe the amenities," Rachel protested breathlessly, and then, "Love me?"

"Didn't you know that by now?" There was a wicked glint in Simon's eye. "I'd profess it trippingly off the tongue, in limping rhyme, but you'd have me over the side of the ship."

"Yes, if all you could manage was limping rhyme. Don't I deserve a sonnet?" Rachel felt giddy with happiness, lightheaded in the salt air.

"A sequence of them," promised Simon extravagantly. "All written with a quill pen."

Rachel put a hand on his breast. "Spare the chicken, I beg you. A simple I love you will do."

Simon pulled back, looking down at her. "Will this do, then? I love you."

Not a question this time, but a statement, simple and unvarnished, with none of the usual protective smokescreen of verbiage.

"Very nicely," said Rachel softly. A vision of the future spiraled out before her, an unknown city with all its hustle and bustle, but Simon beside her. "Very nicely, indeed."

Simon's hands tightened briefly on her shoulders, his expression growing sober. "Are you sure? You'll peg your future to a broken-down wretch such as I? You could be the toast of London. You might have your pick."

His tone was light, but she could hear the uncertainty beneath it.

"You are my pick," said Rachel bluntly. "Can you see me sitting in a drawing room, pouring tea for Lady X and the Honorable Y? I'd die of boredom. I'd rather spar with you than murmur polite nonsense with anyone else."

"Bad dreams and all?"

"Bad dreams and all." A thought struck Rachel. "Will your mother be appalled?"

Simon's arm tightened around her. "She'll be delighted." His lips curved in a grin, making his face look very young, and very boyish. "She doesn't believe in polite nothings either. We will have to tell her the whole story, you know. She'll be frightfully disappointed that she missed your star turn as Vera."

"She won't think less of me?"

"She'll be sorry she didn't think of it herself." When Rachel still looked unconvinced, Simon said drily, "My mother has made a career of flouting society's conventions. She'll give you three cheers and throw you a dinner party."

Whistles sounded, unbearably shrill. The tempo of the deck had changed, the creaking of the winches stilled, the stevedores fading away, stewards moving busily through the crowd, chivying visitors away down the gangplank.

"That's me, I suppose." Reluctantly, Rachel pulled away. "I'd best book a cabin on the next ship over."

Simon snagged her around the waist. "Do you really want to go back to the flat and follow in a fortnight?"

"Of course not! But I've no cabin, no clothes—" Rachel darted a look up at him, struck by sudden suspicion. "You didn't book me a cabin, did you?"

"No, nor pack you a dressing case," said Simon mockingly. "I wasn't that sure of myself. But, by God, now that I have you, I'm not letting you slip out of my clutches. There's plenty of room in my cabin. I'm sure the captain would find the voyage much enlivened by a marriage at sea."

Rachel set her hands on her hips, trying to look indignant and failing utterly. "And the small matter of clothing?"

"I seem to recall having to outfit you once before. Albeit in somewhat different circumstances." He looked down at her, his expression tender. "Let's not ruin our record. Mad schemes are what we do best."

Rachel smiled mistily up at him. "Only north by northwest."

Simon's hand tightened on hers. His expression grew serious as he said, "Do you still wish you could go back, to before?"

Two nights ago, at Carrisford, she had longed for nothing more than to go back to the simplicity of being Rachel Woodley, secure in her history and her name. She thought of the Rachel who had bolted from the Château de Brillac only three months before, so sure of herself, seeing the future stretch on in familiar, recognizable paths. Another post as a nursery governess. Possibly, if she were bold, a typing course and a secretarial job. And maybe, someday, marriage to someone as steady and responsible as she.

It had been a safe life, but a narrow one. Her opinions, her judgments, all those had been narrow, too. Bourgeois, even, Rachel thought with a half smile.

Life with Simon might sometimes be rocky, but it would never be dull. Diamond cut diamond. They might occasionally feel the sting of sharp edges, but there was no one in the wide, wide world who suited her half so well.

She had fallen through the looking glass, and she found she rather liked it.

"You're a vast improvement on Amelie, Albertine, and Anne-Marie." And then, because she felt he deserved something more, she added honestly, "I wouldn't go back, even if I could. For all the pain, it was worth it in the end. It brought me to you."

She half expected Simon to mock, but he didn't. "And all say amen."

They stood together for a moment in peaceful silence, the bustle of departure ebbing around them. The final whistle sounded. Rachel could hear the creak of the gangplank being drawn up, people shouting their final good-byes. Ahead of them stretched the gray waters of the Atlantic, and New York on the other side of it.

Rachel leaned back against Simon, feeling a bone-deep sensation of satisfaction. She felt a crazy grin begin to spread across her face. No clothes, no baggage, no papers, even, but what did it matter? Mad schemes were their specialty.

Simon nodded to the paper she held. "What do you mean to do with that?"

"Oh, that." She'd nearly forgotten about it.

"Yes, *that.*" Fondness and amusement mingled in Simon's face. "Just your passport into the peerage."

On an impulse, Rachel tore the paper down the middle, then folded the pieces together and tore them again. Opening her hands, she let the wind take the scraps, scattering through the air, whirling and swirling like dust motes above the waters of the Atlantic.

She took a step closer to Simon, standing in the shelter of his body. "It doesn't matter anymore."

"No, it doesn't, does it?" Simon drew her closer, resting his cheek against her hat. "We can name our first daughter Vera."

"No." Rachel smiled up at him through a sparkle of tears. "Katherine."

ACKNOWLEDGMENTS

Writing this book with my right hand in a splint made for a new and challenging writing experience. Special thanks go to my husband, who took on the dull duties like dishwashing and diapering so I could save my wrist for writing; to my mother, who stepped in for extra babysitting; and to Lutchmie, who cuddled and cajoled the little one and kept everything running. Thanks also to the staff at my local Starbucks (Camille Robles, I'm looking at you!) for commiseration, encouragement, and endless lattes.

Thanks as always to my editor, Jennifer Weis, for pushing me to make this book as good as it could be, and to Sylvan Creekmore and the rest of the team at St. Martin's for all the creativity, patience, and hard work of taking *The Other Daughter* from manuscript to book. This book was something of an experiment—I had never written a single-narrative, single-viewpoint novel before—and I am so very grateful to my sister, Brooke Willig; my college roommate, Claudia Brittenham; and my two fellow W's, Beatriz Williams and Karen White, for endless hours of character analysis and plot advice. (Also, Irish coffees and proseccos.)

These acknowledgments wouldn't be complete without a moment of remembrance for the late great Mary Stewart, who passed away just as I was beginning work on this book. As I was working, I jokingly called this my Mary Stewart tribute book, and while, in the end, it turned into something rather different, I am so very grateful for the lessons her books taught me and the hours of pleasure they afforded me.

Read on for a sneak peek at Lauren Willig's next novel
Available Spring 2017

ONE

New York, 1899
January

Knickerbocker Murders Wife and Kills Himself!
Murder and Suicide on the Hudson!

It was impossible to ignore the headlines; they screamed out in bold black type from either side of the street, in the hands of newspapermen waving the latest editions.

"Miss Van Duyvil! Miss Van Duyvil! Did you see him? Did you see the body?"

"Miss Van Duyvil! Did you know he was going to kill her?"

Janie kept her head down and kept walking. She had never been one of those debutantes whose doings had been chronicled in the papers, except for that one brief flurry in *Town Topics* when the man whose name society had paired with hers had chosen to marry her cousin instead. *You see?* her mother had said austerely, as though the fault were somehow Janie's, for allowing herself to be spoken of, for allowing people to pair Teddy's name with hers. A Van Duyvil didn't court the press. That was for the new people, the people whose money was as shiny as their carriages, whose voices were too loud and whose dinners too elaborate. A Van Duyvil lived her life behind heavy velvet drapes and quickly closed carriage doors. Like a mouse, scuttling into her hole, Janie thought, but didn't say.

But now, suddenly, she was news, and the reporters flocked to the door of her carriage, scribbling down descriptions of her clothes, her demeanor, putting words into her mouth, spinning tales about what she was supposed to have seen.

Police had created cordons on either side of the front steps, keeping the press and sensation seekers at bay. But they couldn't contain the sound of them, the babble and rumble of the crowd, pushing and clawing for a better view, shouting out questions and opinions. They had managed to evade the reporters at Grand Central Depot, but the house was another matter. They had been waiting for them already when they arrived, reporters and curiosity seekers, masses of them, mobs of them, wanting to get a look at the sensation of the hour, a proud old family brought low.

It had been only a day and a half since they had found Bay, but since then, the story had whirled about them like a snowstorm, growing in force with every hour. All of the old nonsense had been dragged up: the whispers of Annabelle's affairs, Bay's jealousy, the adultery going on right beneath the marital roof.

Lies, all of it, but so much more compelling than truth.

And what was the truth? Janie had no more idea than they. She knew only that Bay could never have done what the papers claimed.

And yet, in a way, this story—this story that took shape and weight with each new embellishment—was her fault.

"Miss Van Duyvil! Miss Van Duyvil! Is it true that he bashed her head in?"

Janie kept her head down and kept moving. The Cold Spring constable hadn't believed her, not at first, when she said she'd seen a body in the water. He'd dismissed it as fancy. At least until they found a blue silk slipper on the bank.

They hadn't found Annabelle's body, not yet. The ice was too thick, the water too deep. It might never be recovered, they said.

It. It, that had once been a she.

Janie could feel the beginnings of a headache pinching her temples. How had it come to this? It wasn't real, any of it. The noise, the clamor, it was all the stuff of nightmare; the past two days were nothing but a bad dream. Bay and Annabelle were at Illyria, their estate on the Hudson, sitting by the fire, the twins curled between them as Annabelle sang them a lullaby, soft and low.

She tried to picture it, but all she could see was Bay, sprawled on the floor of the folly, his lips forming one last word as Annabelle's body drifted beneath the ice, like something out of a painting by Mr. Millais.

"Miss Van Duyvil! Did you see it? Did you see him stab her?"

Shoving Janie ahead of her, Anne addressed the crowd over her fur-trimmed shoulder, saying, in a carrying voice, "Surely there must be a brawl at a beer hall somewhere in the city. Go find it. Or, if not, I'm certain you'll have no trouble starting one."

The laughter from the crowd stung the journalist into retaliation. He jostled forward, pushing his way free from the crowd. "Mrs. Newland! Where's your husband?"

Only Janie felt the way Anne went still, like a hunted animal, every sense on alert. "Leave it," Janie whispered. "Just go inside."

But Anne didn't go. She turned, slowly and deliberately, letting all of the journalists and gawkers look their fill. The evening editions would be full of every detail of her dress, the cut and color provocatively Parisian against the frost-bleached New York street; the sketch artists were already at work, blowing on cold fingers to warm them.

Anne looked the journalist up and down, her very pose a provocation. In a bored drawl, she said, "Why don't you ask him?"

Janie tugged at her hand, but Anne didn't need tugging. She turned on her heel, sweeping into the house with one magnificent flounce of her skirt, leaving Janie to scurry along behind. The slam of the front door behind them didn't cut off the cries of the press, but it did dull them.

In the parlor, the drapes were drawn and the lamps were lit; night in the midst of day. Janie shivered in her furs. They weren't to have returned until Monday. The house still had the chill of emptiness about it. Or maybe it was a different sort of hollowness entirely.

Janie's mother looked up from the mirror by the side of the window, one of the innovations of their Dutch ancestors, glass cleverly angled so that one could spy on the street while seeming to look away.

"You shouldn't perform for them, Anne. It only encourages them." Janie's mother's features looked narrow and pinched; she seemed, in the lamplight, like a portrait of herself, flat and grim. She turned away from the window, letting her pale eyes rest full on her niece. "But, then, we do know how much you love theater."

The color rose in Anne's cheeks. Or maybe it was just the snap of the cold, cold and scandal.

Anne sank into a chair, a sinuous movement, even in her stays. "You have to give the vultures something. If they're talking about Teddy, they might not—" With a convulsive gesture, Anne's fingers closed around the slim gold case hanging from a chain at her waist. "Does anyone else need a cigarette? Janie?"

Janie ducked her head, an instinctive gesture of negation.

"Not in my house," said Mother coldly.

"Even Ruth Mills smokes them these days, Aunt Alva. And *she's* a Livingston." Anne's voice was its usual drawl, but her hands gave her away, shaking so badly she could hardly work the clasp on her cigarette case. "Isn't that so, cousin dear?"

"So I've heard," said Janie cautiously. She wouldn't know. She'd never been invited to any of Ruth Mills's house parties at Staatsburg. She was invited where her mother was, to select gatherings of the elect, parties that wouldn't be sullied by the new people of their conspicuous expenditure.

And, of course, to Illyria. A silly name for a house, her mother had sniffed, but it was what Annabelle and Bay had chosen to call it.

Better than Beaulieu or Bellomont, Bay had retorted without heat. What else were they to call it? Duyvil's Kill?

Bay. The lamplight dazzled Janie's eyes, refracting into the light of a thousand icicles. The snow had thickened after they found him, crusting his body with diamonds, turning him into a creature out of fancy, a sleeping prince waiting to be woken.

"Janie!" Her mother's voice was sharp.

"I'm sorry. I was—"

"Not attending. You never do. Go see what's keeping the girl. You'd think she was harvesting the tea herself."

Anne rose from her chair with something less than her usual grace. The cigarette was still clutched, unlit, between her fingers. Even she didn't quite have the gall to light it, not in the face of direct objection. "I'll go."

"No. It's all right." The parlor felt like the inside of a coffin, velvet-lined. Janie could feel herself smothering in it. "I won't be a moment."

She escaped before Anne could object. If there was one skill Janie had learned over the years, it was the art of absenting herself. One could be absent in the midst of a crowded drawing room if one really tried.

If the parlor was a coffin, the hall felt like a tomb, the marble floor cold and bleak, the frieze of urns that skirted the ceiling disappearing into the gloom. Janie escaped gratefully to the nether regions of the house, down the half-stair that led to the kitchen. She could feel the warmth even before she entered; warmth and coal smoke and the strong smells of food in various stages of preparation.

"Is something burning?" said Janie.

"The cakes—" Mrs. O'Malley started up from the table, grabbing for a towel and catching up a newssheet instead. She stared at it as though not sure how it had got there. "I was just—"

"Yes, I can see that."

Double Murder on the Hudson! shouted the headline.

Somewhere, they'd found pictures of Annabelle and Bay. Neither looked at all like themselves. Annabelle's was an artist's sketch, her hair piled high atop her head in a style she didn't favor, her chin pushed into an unnatural position by the strands of a pearl choker Janie couldn't recall her ever wearing. And then there was Bay. Janie recognized the picture; taken on the occasion of his graduation from the Harvard Law School six years before, his hair slicked down at the sides, high collar stiff around his throat. The same picture that sat in a silver frame on a table in the parlor.

Someone in the house must have provided the picture. Mrs. O'Malley? Or Katie, the downstairs maid? Katie was standing by the scullery, holding herself as though her very stillness would keep her from notice.

Janie nodded at the newssheet. "You'd best not let Mrs. Van Duyvil see you with that."

Mrs. O'Malley clutched the paper close to her thin chest. "Yes, miss. No, miss."

Janie had always wished she could be like a girl in a story, the sort of girl who was beloved by peers and servants alike. But she had never had the gift of commanding allegiance, either by love or by fear. The servants, she knew, took their cue from her mother's treatment of her: an extraneous female, but a Van Duyvil still, to be treated with nominal respect to her face and derision behind her back.

Janie held out a hand. "May I?"

Reluctantly, Mrs. O'Malley surrendered the newssheet. The print was grainy, smeared by the touch of eager fingers. How many had read it already? And this was only one of many. They were hawking them on the street corners. Not since the discovery of a dismembered body in the East River two summers ago had there been such a sensation.

Murder. Janie still couldn't quite make her mind close around the word. Murder was something that happened in the tenements of Hell's Kitchen, in the dark segments of the city through which a carriage passed with closed curtains, not in her family. Not in Illyria.

"I'll dispose of this," said Janie, and was aware of just how much she sounded like her mother. A movement by the door caught her eye. A man, behind Katie, in the narrow passage between the scullery and the street. Sharply, she said, "And who might this be?"

Katie cast an agitated glance at Mrs. O'Malley. "It's . . . my cousin. Jimmy."

The man unfolded himself from the wall, stepping into the light, the gas lamp casting a reddish glow against his black hair, casting shadows beneath his cheekbones. He moved with an actor's limber grace.

He held his cap in one hand; the other hand he extended to Janie. "My condolences for your loss, Miss Van Duyvil."

Janie kept her own hands pressed close to her sides. "This is not a time to be receiving callers—even cousins."

If he was one. The ink on his fingers said otherwise.

The byline on the article in Janie's hands read James. James Burke.

James Burke. The name sounded oddly familiar, as though she had heard it before. On the pages of a newssheet? The family didn't read those sorts of papers, but it was hard to ignore them entirely, plastered as they were across the city.

Janie pressed her eyes shut, seeing the glare of the gaslight against the inside of her lids. "It would be a great deal less painful if people would respect that loss."

The interloper in her mother's kitchen met her eyes, unabashed. "Surely, truth should be a consolation to the family, Miss Van Duyvil."

"Do you call this truth . . . Mr. Burke?"

He didn't deny the charge. Instead, he inclined his head in something that was almost, but not quite, a bow. "Truth comes in all sorts of forms, Miss Van Duyvil."

On his tongue, the use of her name sounded impossibly intimate. "But seldom in the *News of the World*. I take it that you are the person responsible for perpetrating this . . . nonsense?"

The man had the gall to widen his eyes innocently. "We prefer to call it investigative reporting, Miss Van Duyvil."

"I call it scandalmongering, pure and simple." Janie was too angry to be shy; all she could think of was Viola and Sebastian in their white nightclothes, crying for their mother. They were too young, now, to understand what was being said. But what of when they were older? It was easier to fling mud than to scour a reputation clean. "Making capital out of the suffering of innocent souls."

Mr. Burke leaned one hand familiarly against the back of a chair. "And isn't that the same way most of your friends on Fifth Avenue made their fortunes?"

"That's not—" That was what he wanted, to keep her talking. She'd find her own words, flung back at her in the press, twisted and distorted. Stiffly, Janie said, "This is a house of mourning. I would urge you and your colleagues to remember that." To Katie, she added, "Mrs. Van Duyvil is waiting for her tea."

Katie bobbed a curtsy. "Yes, ma'am."

Janie kept her attention fixed on Katie, her voice prim. "I trust you will, in future, restrict your family reunions to your half-day. They have no place in this kitchen."

She sounded like her mother. No. Worse. She sounded like a sour spinster, tyrannizing over the staff to mask her own powerlessness.

Mr. Burke stepped forward, a knight-errant in a shabby gray suit. "It's not Katie's fault."

"In which case, it must be yours." Janie turned her displeasure where it belonged, squarely on Mr. Burke. With as much dignity as she could muster, she said, "This discussion is over, Mr. Burke. You are disrupting the household and keeping Katie from her duties."

"And we mustn't have that." Mr. Burke's eyes met hers, the gray-green of moss over stone. "Good day, Miss Van Duyvil."

"Good-bye, Mr. Burke."

His only reply was a tilt of his cap as the door closed behind him, leaving Janie standing, thwarted and unsatisfied, at the kitchen door, wondering how he had managed, while so clearly in the wrong, to make her feel like the villain.

A hint of French perfume warred with the scent of burning crumpets. "Who was that?"

Janie turned hastily, blinking at Anne in the kitchen door. "No one. One of Katie's cousins."

Anne shrugged, already losing interest. She looked out of place in the domestic confines of the kitchen, her taffeta gown too rich, her blond hair too bright for workaday use. "Aunt Alva wants her tea sent to her rooms. Sometime this century."

Mrs. O'Malley sprang into action, assembling a tray with more force than grace.

"You're to go to her." Anne waved one long, white hand at Janie. "When you're done with your . . . reading."

Janie had forgotten that she was still holding the paper. Her fingers tightened around the page as she hurried after Anne, up the stairs. "I was simply disposing of it."

"Whatever you like." Anne's tone was derisory, but Janie didn't miss the glance she darted at the paper.

Janie would have laughed if it hadn't been so miserable, all of it. To be reduced to reading the scandal sheets for word of one's own family.

Somewhere in Putnam County, Bay's body lay on a slab in the morgue. Somewhere, along the sides of the frozen river, the search went on for Annabelle's body. Or so they presumed. Their sensibilities, it seemed, were too delicate to be imposed upon by the police. Whatever they knew of their own tragedy came at third hand. They were starved for news, all of them, as isolated as Robinson Crusoe on his island.

Anne, with all her tricks and her charm; Janie's mother, with her lineage and her money. All of their powers were reduced to nothing when it came to the workings of the masculine world of the law.

Janie looked anxiously at her cousin. "What happens next?"

Anne deliberately misunderstood her. "Supper, I should think."

Janie pressed her eyes shut, schooling herself to patience. Grieving came upon people in different ways, and if it made Anne even more prickly than usual. . . . Well, there could be no doubt that she was grieving, or that she had the right to grieve. If there had been one person in the world who Anne truly loved, it was Bay, had always been Bay, from the time they were children together. Janie's earliest memories were of the echo of their laughter, always a room away, always just out of reach.

There were times Janie had wondered if there might be something more between her brother and her cousin, if the rumors of Annabelle's affair with the architect were just a screen for—

No. Janie bit down hard on her lower lip. Now she was being as bad as Mr. Burke, as the scandalmongers howling at the gate. Bay had loved Annabelle. If Janie was sure of anything, she was sure of that. Not the fevered love the papers meant to convey, something harsh and jealous, but a comfort with their own company, the intimacy of a hand on a shoulder in passing, a message conveyed with a look.

Words might lie, but not that.

Janie paused at the foot of the stairs, stopping Anne with a fleeting touch to her arm, the most contact they had had in weeks. "What they're saying—Bay would never have done that. He would never have hurt Annabelle. Not Bay."

"Because you knew him so well."

Anne had always known just where to slide the knife. Janie forced herself to honesty, even if honesty felt raw and painful. "I wish I had."

Ever since she was little, all she had wanted was for her brother to notice her. It wasn't that Bay was particularly outgoing. His smile was a slow thing; his wit, quiet. But there had been something about that very reserve that had promised riches to those admitted to the inner circle.

But that would never happen now. Bay was gone, and all his subtle charm with him. Janie would never, now, be privy to his confidences; never have him turn to her as he had to Anne.

Except that once, at the last, when his lips had spoken a name she didn't know.

"Anne—" Janie stood at the bottom of the stairs, one hand on the newel post. She felt foolish asking, but if anyone would know, it would be Anne. "Who's George?"

Anne paused, halfway to the landing, her back to Janie.

When she turned, her blue eyes were as flat and hard as the tiles around the hearth. "You'd best go up to Aunt Alva. You know how she hates when anything makes her late for supper."

London, 1894
February

"Fancy a free supper?" Kitty popped into Georgie's dressing room without knocking, banging the door cheerfully behind her.

Georgie eyed her friend doubtfully in the streaked glass of her mirror. "What is it this time?"

Kitty adjusted her hat, frowned at the results, and tweaked it again, examining herself this way and that. "Not what, who. A Sir Something and his rich American friend."

Kitty had removed the wig she wore as Maria in the Ali Baba's musical evisceration of *Twelfth Night*, but her cheeks were still streaked with red, her face lavishly painted and powdered. Coupled with her feathered hat and new crimson brocade walking dress, it made her look, thought Georgie, like the more prosperous sort of streetwalker.

Picking up a cloth, Georgie scrubbed vigorously and ineffectually at the grease paint on her cheek. It was a bad job, she knew; no matter how much cream she used, how much soap, it never entirely came off. She went into each performance with the shadow of the last beneath it. "How can you tell the American is rich?"

Kitty winked at her in the mirror. "Aren't they all?"

The ones who showed up in London were, at any rate, and London was the entirety of Kitty's world. There must, Georgie was quite sure, be poor Americans, struggling Americans, ordinary humdrum Americans, but they weren't the ones who showed up at the stage door of the Ali Baba, eager for a little Old World decadence.

"I don't know. . . . We have a matinee tomorrow." Georgie certainly didn't fault Kitty for supplementing her income. Anyone who had lived as she had lived knew you did what you must to pay the rent. But it made her uncomfortable all the same.

"Here. Let me." Kitty obligingly yanked the tapes of Georgie's corset closed and began hooking up the back of her dress. Georgie's dresser was meant to do that, but she had sloughed off the previous week, complaining about the size of her pay packet. They'd been playing to half-empty houses for the past six months and it was beginning to show. They were already dressing themselves; they'd be making their own sets next. "I just need you to entertain the friend."

"What kind of entertainment?"

"Nothing like that, I promise. It's just a meal, that's all." Kitty hooked the last hook and stepped back, her eyes meeting Georgie's in the mirror. "A girl needs to fill her stomach somehow."

And the show wouldn't run much longer. Kitty didn't need to say it. It was there in the dusty dressing room, in the empty seats out front, in the desperation beneath Kitty's crooked smile.

"All right," said Georgie slowly. Champagne was better than stout any day, particularly if someone else was paying. A lady would say no, would blush at dining with strange men, would balk at the implied cheat of taking something for nothing. But she wasn't a lady, was she? She was an actress. She showed her legs for a living. "Where are they taking us?"

"The Criterion," said Kitty, with satisfaction.

Georgie narrowed her eyes at her as she slid off the stool. "Let's hope your American is as rich as you claim."

"Your American," Kitty retorted. "I have my eye on the toff."

Georgie grabbed her old coat off a hook on the wall. "Whatever you say, Lady Kitty."

"Go on!" said Kitty, but the way she preened at the words made Georgie wish she'd kept her mouth shut. Kitty held out a flask to her. "Just a nip?"

Kitty had had a nip already. Georgie could smell the gin on her breath, gin and cloves to hide it. Add a bit of orange peel and she'd smell like Christmas punch.

It wasn't an escape to which Georgie had resorted, not yet, but there were times when she understood the appeal of it, particularly now, with the chill of winter still permeating the drafty back areas of the theater, and wet and slush seeping through the thin soles of her boots.

But they didn't know these men.

"I'd rather keep my wits about me." Such as they were. But they'd got her this far, hadn't they? She'd survived. There was something to be said for surviving.

"Suit yourself." Kitty took her nip, and then another.

Reluctantly, Georgie said, "Had you ought to, Kit?"

Kitty shrugged. "The cold gets in your bones, doesn't it?"

She shoved the flask back in the hidden pocket of her coat before pushing open the side door and tumbling out into the cold, Georgie following more soberly behind.

Two men waited in the alley, tall hats pulled low over their brows, the points of their cigars glowing red in the gloom. Their heads were bent close together, their voices low. They appeared to be engaged in some sort of whispered dispute, all the more vehement for being so quiet.

Georgie fell back a step, the door handle hard and cold through the thin material of her gloves. The tall hat—the caped coat—if she moved quickly, she could be away, into the warren of corridors in the back of the theater, up into the machinery that skirted the stage.

Breathlessly, Kitty called, "I've brought her!" and the two men turned and Georgie's breath came out in a rush that created a cloud in front of her face.

It wasn't Giles. This man was taller, broader, the hair beneath his hat fairer. It was a stranger who stood there, as the other man, the shorter, slighter man, tossed away his cigar, ground it beneath his heel, and sauntered forward to take Kitty's hand.

The other man stayed behind, in the shadows. Not Giles. Georgie could feel the clammy sweat in the small of her back, under her arms. She struggled to control her breathing. Not Giles. It was the caped coat that had made her imagine him. The caped coat and the red glow of a cigar in the gloom.

In a Mayfair drawl, the man with the dark mustache pressed a kiss to the back of Kitty's hand. "Madama Katerina."

"That's Miss Frumley to you, my lord," said Kitty with mock severity.

Kitty's real name wasn't Frumley at all; it was, she had confided to Georgie, Potter. But Frumley sounded better on the bills in the front of the theater, more aristocratic, like those earls of what's-their-name, and Georgie hadn't the heart to tell Kitty that the family whose name she had borrowed spelled it Tholmondelay.

"And this is Miss Evans." Kitty displayed Georgie like a prize, dragging her unwillingly forward. "Georgie, this is Sir, um——"

"Hugo. Hugo Medmenham. You may call me . . . Sir Hugo." With a mocking bow, he gestured toward his companion, "Ladies, may I present to you Mr. Bayard Van Duyvil, of our former colonies."

"Ladies," murmured the man who wasn't Giles. Now that he had stepped into the uneven light of the lamp over the stage door, Georgie could see that they were nothing alike. Tall, yes, and broad in the shoulders, but there any resemblance ended. Giles had affected long chestnut sideburns that curled beneath his ears, and a cavalryman's mustache; this man was clean-shaven, the lamplight making the fair hair that curled beneath his color glow the color of old gold.

But Georgie hung back all the same; foolish as she knew it to be, the old fear still gripped her, tightening her chest, constricting her throat.

Not Giles, she told herself again. Not Giles.

Kitty lowered her lashes, speaking in tones of exaggerated refinement that made Georgie wince for her friend. "Charmed, I'm sure."

Sir Hugo possessed himself of Kitty's gloved fingers, drawing her to his side. "What are you waiting for, Van Duyvil? Do they not teach you manners in America? Miss Evans wants an escort."

Miss Evans did not, in fact, want anything of the kind. What Miss Evans wanted was to pull her hat down about her ears and walk as rapidly as she could to her boardinghouse. A free supper was one thing; Sir Hugo, another. She'd heard of him before, the sort who still believed in the *droit du seigneur.* Toss a few coins on the bed afterward and think the girl honored by his attentions. There'd never been charges brought—but there wouldn't be, would there? The juries of the world were made of men. A man could hold his honor dear in such masculine matters as gambling debts and never mind that he left a trail of ruined women behind him.

Men diced with coin; women diced with their lives.

Kitty was already walking off ahead, her arm twined cozily with Sir Hugo's, so Georgie had no choice but to follow, falling into step with Mr. Van Duyvil, who, reluctantly, extended his arm.

Georgie placed her fingers gingerly on his sleeve. "I am afraid I didn't quite catch your name, Mr. . . . . Vandeville?"

"Van Duyvil." When he spoke, his voice was warm and rich, the vowels strange to Georgie's ears. Strange, but not unpleasant. "It's Dutch."

"Devil's spawn," contributed Sir Hugo, with a grin. He leaned closer to Kitty, saying with mock solicitousness, "Don't be alarmed, my dear. He seldom swallows down more than one soul a night."

2